the SUMMER HOUSE PARTY

CARO FRASER

HEAD of ZEUS

First published in the UK in 2017 by Head of Zeus Ltd

9 7 5 3 1 2 4 6 8

A catalogue record for this book is available from the British Library.

ISBN (HB) 9781786691484
ISBN (XTPB) 9781786691491
ISBN (E) 9781786691477

Printed and bound by CPI Group (UK) Ltd, Croydon, CR0 4YY

Head of Zeus Ltd
First Floor East
5–8 Hardwick Street
London EC1R 4RG

WWW.HEADOFZEUS.COM

PART I

1936

1

IT WAS AN afternoon in late August, and Daniel Ranscombe was travelling on the 4.49 train from Waterloo to Surrey. The train drew to a creaking halt just outside the sleepy village of Staplow, and settled with a hiss of steam into the summer silence. Dan gazed out of the window at a field of mournful-eyed cows twitching their tails at flies. Half-remembered lines of poetry from school slipped into his mind, something about a train stopped at a country station... *No one left and no one came on the bare platform* – tee tum tee something *Adlestrop* ... and *willows, willow-herb and grass, and meadowsweet, and hay-cocks high...* He tried to string the verses together – he had known them by heart once – but his lazy mind wasn't up to it. He stretched his legs out, closed his eyes, and contemplated in his mind the coming house party, which was being hosted by his godmother, Sonia, and her husband Henry Haddon, the renowned artist. The prospect of spending ten days at the fag end of summer enjoying the comforts of a fine country house was more than agreeable, especially as there would be other young people there, in the shape of Sonia's niece, Meg, and Paul and Diana Latimer, to keep things lively. Meg he had yet to meet, though he had heard a few things about her from both Paul and Diana. The Latimers were the son and daughter of old friends of the Haddons, and Dan knew them well. Diana was a regular on the London social scene, and she and Dan flirted with one another whenever their paths crossed, though more as a matter of course than with any genuine conviction. Diana's older brother, Paul, had been Dan's senior by three years at Eton, and then at Cambridge, and Dan had certain misgivings – misgivings which he freely admitted were born out of envy and resentment – about meeting him again.

It seemed he was constantly being made aware of Paul's achievements, which markedly eclipsed Dan's so far unspectacular headway in the world. Paul had been a veritable hero to Dan at school – athletic, brainy, captain of the First XV and head of house, friendly and decent, full of charm and self-confidence. When Dan had encountered him again at Cambridge the schoolboy charm had begun to wear a trifle thin – the self-confidence was turning into self-importance, and the bluff affability had taken on a somewhat patronising quality – but there was no doubt that Paul's star continued to burn with undimmed lustre. He had a reputation as a fine oar, an excellent bat, and a debater of such formidable skill that a career in Parliament was confidently predicted. Not that Paul had much need of a career. His parents had died while he and Diana were still in their teens, and to come into that much money at so young an age – well, it just seemed damnably unfair to add wealth to such a store of talent. Dan was acutely resentful of Paul's ability to spend half the year climbing mountains and crossing deserts, and generally leading the life of the English gentleman adventurer, and the other half idling in his club and studying the stock market. Lucky blighter. He would probably arrive at Woodbourne House by car, with a ton of luggage and a manservant. Dan's own luggage consisted of one suitcase containing his dress suit, the few decent shirts and ties he possessed, flannels and a blazer, underwear, pyjamas, shaving kit and toothbrush. It was all he could afford, and it would have to do.

Dan himself had come down from Cambridge two years ago with a degree in modern languages and, unwilling to follow his father into the diplomatic service, had taken a job as a reporter on the *London Graphic*. Despite his innate laziness he had been surprised to discover that he was, even with the minimum of effort, quite a good journalist. Now, a year later, he had graduated to being the *Graphic*'s arts correspondent. It wasn't a job that brought him a great deal of money.

Dan contemplated the cows as they ripped up soft mouthfuls of cud, and wondered how much he would have to tip the Woodbourne House servants. That kind of thing could bleed a man dry. Not a consideration which would worry Paul Latimer – but then, nothing much worried Paul, favourite of the gods.

The train gave a creak and chugged slowly into life. Dan rummaged in his pocket for his cigarettes. As he pulled them out, the stout matron sitting opposite raised her eyes from her knitting and gave him a reproving glance. He returned them to his pocket and glanced at his wristwatch. Only ten more minutes till they reached Malton where, his godmother had informed him, her niece Margaret would meet him.

As the train slid into a tunnel, Dan contemplated his reflection in the carriage window. Aware of his own good looks since the age of twelve, he had yet to become bored by them. The face that looked back at him was handsome, the features nicely chiselled, the mouth sensitive and not too full, eyes blue and soulful. If the old bird hadn't been present, he might have practised his charming, crooked grin, but he made do instead with passing his fingers through the waves of his thick blond hair and giving his reflection a final admiring glance before the train slid back into sunlight. He hoped there would be a few decent girls at the house party.

Dan was the only passenger to alight at Malton. He saw a little two-seater Austin parked next to the fence by the road, a girl in a short-sleeved blouse and linen trousers leaning against its bonnet. She waved when she saw Dan, and he carried his case over to the car. So this was Meg. Neither Paul nor Diana had mentioned quite how attractive she was. She had long, curling chestnut hair and dark eyes flecked with green, delicately arched brows and lightly tanned skin, and a very pretty figure. His hopes had been fulfilled. At least one looker on the premises.

'You must be Daniel. I'm Meg Slater,' she said.

Dan smiled and shook her hand. 'Please, call me Dan. Good to meet you at last. I've heard a lot about you from Paul and Diana.'

'Nice things, I hope. Here, chuck your bag in the back.' She got into the car and settled herself behind the wheel. Dan guessed from the intentness of her gaze and the set of her body that she hadn't been driving for long.

With a grinding of gears they set off.

'Sorry!' said Meg. 'I only passed my test two months ago.' She glanced at Dan. He was nice-looking. She liked fair-haired men. 'I can't tell you how glad I am to see a house guest under fifty.'

'Am I the first to arrive?'

'The first non-geriatric.' She made a face. 'It's been rather grim at dinner the past few nights. Gerald Cunliffe – you know, the poet? He and his wife arrived three days ago. They're nice enough old people, but not terrifically exciting.'

'When do the Latimers arrive?' asked Dan.

'They should be here tomorrow. You and Paul were at school together, weren't you?'

'He was a few years ahead of me. Very much a hero of mine when I was in the lower fifth.'

'I can imagine.' She gave him another glance. 'Isn't it funny we've never met? I've known Paul and Diana for the longest time. Di's bringing one of her friends along, too – a girl called Eve Meyerson.'

'Really? I know her. She's a fellow journalist. Works on the *Daily Herald*.' Dan reflected that this might be a most interesting ten days. He and Eve had already had more than a couple of flirtatious encounters in London.

'And then there's some fellow called Charles Asher, one of Aunt Sonia's protégés. I've never met him.'

'So, when did you come down?'

'Three weeks ago.'

'Bit slow for you, I'd have thought.'

'I could be spending the summer on the Côte d'Azur with my mother, having a very glamorous time, but I decided I'd rather be here. I don't share my mother's social stamina. My debutante season last year was absolutely exhausting, thanks to her. She insisted I go to every single party. I'm quite glad of the rest this summer.' After a pause she remarked, 'So, Aunt Sonia's your godmother?'

'Yes. She's rather taken me under her wing since my mother died last year. This is my first visit to Woodbourne House. What's it like? Is everyone terribly proper?'

'I wouldn't say that, exactly. The house runs like clockwork, meals on time, all that kind of thing, but Aunt Sonia doesn't stand on ceremony' – Meg paused to concentrate as she rounded a bend a little on the fast side – 'though she does like everyone to dress for dinner. I think that's rather down to the Cunliffes. He's a dry old stick, and she's terribly strait-laced. But I imagine things will loosen up a little with more young people around. I hope so, at any rate.'

They drove through the village of Chidding, then after a quarter of a mile Meg tooted the horn and swung the car between a pair of stone pillars and up a curving driveway. Woodbourne House came into view. It was handsome, built of reddish stone, three storeys high, with roses and creepers surrounding the leaded windows on either side of a wide stone porch. Meg parked the car in a courtyard at the back of the house. As they got out she pointed down through a sloping apple orchard to a large barn.

'That's Uncle Henry's studio. He spends most of the day there. It's my job to trek back and forth with meals and mail and cups of tea, and clean his brushes when he's finished for the day. Sometimes he lets me sit and talk to him while he works – a great privilege, I assure you. Hardly anyone's allowed in there.'

Dan took his case from the boot and followed Meg to the

house. She pointed to a line of trees. 'Through there's the tennis court. Aunt Sonia had it put in only this year. The gardener's boy spends most of his time rolling it. Do you play?'

'Rather. I didn't think to bring a racquet, though.'

'Oh, Aunt Sonia's got several, all brand spanking new. We can have a game later, if you like. It's always nicer in the evening, when things have cooled down a bit. Perhaps we can get a set in before dinner.' The smile she gave him seemed full of promise.

Sonia Haddon emerged from the house to greet them, three small pekes pattering behind her. She was a tall, graceful woman, clad in a long dress of moss-coloured crêpe de Chine, and wore several bracelets and a long beaded necklace. She extended a hand to Dan.

'Dan, how lovely! Meg must be very glad of your arrival. I'm sure she's been bored to death with a house full of old people this past week.' Sonia was in her mid-forties, attractive, with a long, narrow face, a generous mouth, and grey, slanting eyes, and an authoritative and gently incisive manner. 'Meg, dearest, would you hunt down Avril and Madeleine? It's time Avril had her tea. Come with me, Dan, and I'll show you where I've put you. We'll all have drinks on the terrace before dinner, and you can meet everyone. We dine at seven thirty – I'm sure you think that's too early, but we old people aren't good at late nights, and Henry gets cross if he isn't fed punctually. Tell me, how is your father?' And with a trail of conversation she led Dan through the garden room and into the house.

Dan's unpacking was the work of a moment. When he had finished, he unfastened the window and leaned out to inspect the view. His room was at the back of the house, and below him lay the courtyard, and beyond it the kitchen garden, where a gardener in a straw hat was bent among the raspberry canes. To the left stretched lawns and flower gardens, and Dan could glimpse the stone balustrade of the terrace which curved around the side of the house, situated to catch the last of the sunlight. Far away lay the Downs, and in the near distance the Surrey countryside basked in summer serenity.

He could see figures coming through the orchard – Meg, with two girls following behind. One appeared to be a teenager, dressed in a button-fronted frock, her fair hair swinging in a long plait. The other could have been no more than five or six, with bobbed brown hair, and was clad in a pair of overalls. As they came closer Dan realised that the youngest girl was wailing – a screeching sound which grated on the ears. Meg and the other girl paid no attention. Dan watched them as they passed through the kitchen garden and crossed the courtyard, his gaze held by Meg's neat, pretty figure.

He closed the window, stowed away his case and inspected the delights of the room which was to be his for the next ten days. His thoughtful hostess had left a tin of biscuits and some light novels by his bedside, a Lalique vase of roses and jasmine stood on the bureau, and clean towels hung by the washstand. Dan checked his reflection in the looking-glass, and sauntered downstairs. On a polished table stood a large bowl of arum lilies, scenting the hallway with their fragrance. He paused on the threshold of the garden room. Meg appeared in the hallway, looking cross.

'Why the face?' asked Dan.

'That wretched child, Avril, my cousin. I had to fetch her in to tea in the nursery and she hacked me on the ankles, the little beast. Anyway, if you've finished your unpacking, how about that game of tennis?'

'I think Sonia said something about drinks before dinner.'

'Oh, that's not for ages. An hour at least. Come on – I'm dying to play.'

'I'll have to go and change my shoes,' said Dan. 'I'll see you out there.'

They started the game gently enough, but it wasn't long before a competitive element crept in. Although Dan regarded himself as a pretty good player, he had to work hard to beat Meg. They stopped after a set.

'You play tennis the same way you drive a car,' remarked Dan.

'How's that?'

'With beady ferocity.'

'Thanks!' replied Meg. 'I used to play for my school. It's nice to have a decent game for a change.'

'What about Sonia? I thought the tennis court was her idea.'

'Aunt Sonia's tennis is a somewhat stately affair, and Uncle Henry just strolls round the court smoking a cigar, hitting anything that comes his way, generally out. Madeleine doesn't play. Maybe we can have some doubles when the Latimers come down.'

'You're very keen.'

'I'm very bored!'

Dan pulled out his cigarette case and offered it to her. Meg hesitated. She didn't really smoke, but she didn't want to appear unworldly, so she took a cigarette. As he struck a match Meg found herself transfixed by the hand that cupped it, the strong, shapely fingers, the dusting of gold hairs on the wrist. She bent her head to let him light her cigarette, aware of his proximity and a strange sensation in the pit of her stomach. Her eyes followed the flexing of his fingers as he flung the match away. He grinned at her, and she grinned shyly back.

'By the way,' asked Dan, 'who's the blonde girl I saw you and Avril with earlier?'

'Oh, you mean Madeleine? She's one of Aunt Sonia's deeds of mercy. Her mother is an old friend of Sonia's who got in the family way when she was a girl. The chap did the decent thing and married her, but then he died and since then her family won't have anything to do with her. Now the poor woman has TB and is in some sanatorium in Suffolk. So Aunt Sonia has taken Madeleine in. She's meant to be looking after Avril, but she's next to useless. Has her head in a book most of the time. I'm always having to dig them both up and bring them in at mealtimes, and I generally get kicked on the ankles for my pains.' She glanced at her watch. 'We'd best go in and change.'

They strolled back up the path and across the lawn to the house.

Meg was much in Dan's thoughts as he dressed for dinner. A very pretty thing, though still something of a schoolgirl. Her determined efforts to beat him at tennis gave her a certain *garçonne* appeal, and he found himself wondering if she'd look as good in a cocktail dress as she did in tennis shorts.

He went downstairs and through the drawing room to the terrace, where he found Sonia sitting with Meg and Gerald Cunliffe. Sonia procured a whisky and soda for Dan and introduced him to the great poet. Cunliffe was a little deaf – Sonia murmured to Dan that he was awaiting the arrival of a new hearing-aid in the post – so Dan's initial attempts at conversation proved somewhat awkward. He persevered nonetheless and, having disposed of the subject of travel from London and Cunliffe's liking for the countryside thereabouts, ventured some vaguely topical remarks on the subject of modern poetry, in deference to the great man's standing. Cunliffe cupped his ear and asked him to speak up, and Dan repeated in a roar his enquiry as to whether the great poet had read and liked the works of the new young poet, Dylan Thomas.

'Thomas? Detestable! Rhymeless, pretentious meanderings!'

Meg caught Dan's eye and gave him a wink, and Dan returned it with a smile. She looked quite delightful in her evening dress of rose silk.

'Edith Sitwell thinks him a perfect genius,' remarked Sonia. 'She's quite taken him under her wing. He's very poor, of course, so she tells me she has been writing to any number of people trying to find work for him.' She glanced towards the French windows. 'Oh, Madeleine, there you are.'

Seeing Madeleine close to for the first time, Dan was struck by how lovely she was, with clear-cut, delicate features, pale, almost translucent skin, and blue eyes so dark as to be almost violet. She made her entrance hesitantly, darting shy glances at everyone. Dan guessed she could be no more than sixteen. Bustling in behind her came Gerald's wife, Elizabeth, a portly creature clad in bottle-green velvet. Sonia rose to usher her on to the terrace with tender concern.

'How are you, Elizabeth? Did you manage a little sleep?'

'I'm afraid not. The flies were buzzing at the window so, and with the state my nerves are in, it was all I could do to close my eyes for ten minutes. No, no – just plain soda water for me, thank you.'

Sonia had looked in on her guest twice in the past hour, and had found her on both occasions slumbering peacefully, and snoring lightly. When Elizabeth was settled in her chair with her soda water, Sonia introduced her and Madeleine to Dan, and half an hour or so drifted by in idle conversation, which Sonia deftly steered into mundane waters, knowing Gerald Cunliffe's tendency to irascibility on matters of the day, politics in particular.

Madeleine sat with a glass of untasted sherry in her hand, glancing from face to face, not daring to venture any remark, but with some strange kind of ardour shimmering within her. With her fair hair pinned up and in her pale blue evening dress, she looked curiously like a sophisticated child, excited to be among adults.

The shadows began to lengthen across the lawn, and Dan was just wondering whether he could help himself to another whisky and soda when Henry Haddon made his appearance. The hitherto languid atmosphere coalesced into attentiveness and expectation. Haddon was in his late fifties, tall and broad-shouldered, and strikingly handsome. He wore his thick, silver hair long over his collar, and his contrastingly dark brows gave him a somewhat menacing aspect, even when he smiled. He was an impressive, charismatic figure, conscious of his own powers of attraction to men and women alike. When he was in good spirits, his ebullience and enthusiasm could light a room; when in a rage, his cold fury could freeze and terrify those around him. Tonight, however, his temper was tranquil and mildly playful, and he greeted the company with smiles and a couple of dry remarks. Drinks were refreshed, and after a few more minutes of conversation on the terrace, dinner was announced.

Madeleine was seated on Dan's right, Elizabeth Cunliffe on his left. Elizabeth immediately began a testy little discourse with Sonia on the vagaries of servants, so Dan, searching for a topic on which to converse with Madeleine, remembered Meg's remarks earlier about how Madeleine always had her head in a book, and asked her what she was reading at the moment. Her eyes brightened, and she responded with an enthusiasm which was like dawn breaking over a still pool. They talked on and off about books and poetry for the entire meal, with occasional interruptions when etiquette demanded that Dan should turn to his left to converse with Elizabeth Cunliffe, which involved listening to her diatribe on the inadequacies of Harley Street specialists. During these intervals Dan was aware that Haddon, who was seated at the head of the table on Madeleine's left, paid not the slightest attention to the girl, preferring to continue with Cunliffe an apparently mutually agreeable grumble on the subject of the new King. Dan wondered if Haddon thought it infra dig that the nanny should be part of the company; even so, his behaviour to the girl seemed rude.

Madeleine was scarcely conscious of being slighted. Since her arrival at Woodbourne House she had become deeply infatuated with Henry Haddon; he seemed to her the epitome of manhood, a romantic and thrilling figure, but the idea of being made to converse with him terrified her. What could she possibly have to say that would interest him? She was happy to be seated near him, to be able to observe him at close quarters, to listen to his deep, confident voice, watch his expressive hands, and steal occasional glances at his face.

2

THE FOLLOWING MORNING Dan took himself off to the library to wile away a couple of hours until the Latimers arrived. He was deep in a leader on the Spanish Civil War when Sonia came in.

'Dan, may I ask you to do a small chore? I've had to send Meg into Chidding in the car to fetch the meat, because the butcher's van has broken down, and I have a million things that need to be done.'

'Yours to command,' said Dan, folding the paper and getting to his feet and putting out his cigarette.

'Henry likes to have some barley water and biscuits around eleven. Would you be a dear and take them down to him?'

'Of course.'

Dan followed Sonia to the kitchen, where a jug of barley water, a glass, and a plate of plain biscuits were laid out on a tray. 'There you are. I hope you find Henry in a good mood.'

Dan carried the tray down through the orchard to the studio. The large wooden door was ajar, but Dan knocked. Haddon's voice boomed for him to enter. The barn was spacious, with large windows set in the sloping roof, so that light spilled in. Half of the roof space was occupied by a loft area, from the days when the barn had been used to store hay, with a long ladder leaning against the upper storey. Against one wall of the barn stood two trestle tables, their paint-splashed surfaces littered with brushes, jars, tubes, rags and artist's debris. Canvases of all sizes lay stacked on the stone floor and against the walls. On a raised dais stood a red velvet divan. The air was filled with the reedy smell of oils and turps. Haddon himself was strolling about, dressed in loose, paint-spattered trousers and a disreputable old jumper, charred in patches from pipe-droppings. Even in this attire he managed to look majestic.

'Ah! Young Daniel comes to the lion's den. Welcome.'

'You have a marvellous space here,' said Dan, setting down the tray.

'I like it. A decent size, a good, mellow atmosphere – those beams are at least two hundred years old – and far enough from the house for me not to be troubled by women and servants.' He pulled up a chair for Dan and settled his own tall frame into a creaking cane armchair. 'So, how is the world of journalism? Sonia tells me you've been made arts correspondent.'

'I only got the job because I know a bit more about art than anyone else on the paper, which isn't saying much. Still, it's a job, and it will do till I write my great novel.'

'A man needs to live. I must have started off with some creative ideals, I suppose, but money gets in the way. This house, Sonia, and all the attendant expenses, have to be paid for somehow. Still life is what I like to paint best. That's what I was fiddling with back there. I've even been experimenting with some of the newer techniques. There's a veritable Rue de la Paix of movements out there. But it's not where the money is. Not for me, at any rate. I turned my hand to portraiture twenty years ago, not because I especially care for it, but because I found I could make a decent living out of it.' He ate a biscuit and drained a glass of barley water. 'I am but a humble servant of Whistler.'

'I hear you're painting Mrs Cunliffe at present?'

'Not one of my easier commissions. Blasted woman's a fidget. Can't sit still. But it's nearly finished.'

Dan took his cigarettes from his pocket and lit one, as Haddon filled and lit his pipe. They smoked in silence for a moment, then

Dan said, 'If I were an artist, I rather think I would want to paint that girl Madeleine.'

Haddon raised a dark eyebrow. 'What, the nanny?'

'She has... she has a sort of radiant quality, don't you think? As though she were lit from within.'

As Haddon was reflecting on this, there came a scratching tap at the door, as though from some invisible rodent. A face peeped round, that of Elizabeth Cunliffe. Dan and Haddon got to their feet, and Haddon knocked out his pipe, his face a mask of courtesy.

'My dear Elizabeth, have you come for a sitting?'

'Why, I thought I would just pop down, as Sonia said you were here. I'm sure you must be keen to get on. You artists, once you get the bit between your teeth!' She gave a little laugh and fanned herself with a lace handkerchief. 'Warm in here, as ever.'

'Don't let me delay a work in progress,' said Dan. 'I'll be getting back to the house.'

Haddon gave Dan a conspiratorial glance as Elizabeth scuttled to take up her pose on the divan, and said, 'Drop by again, my boy. We can continue our little discussion.'

As he crossed the flagged courtyard, Dan saw Avril crouching by the fountain, peering intently at the ground. Dan wondered what it was that so engrossed her. Then as he drew nearer he saw winged ants pouring out from the crevices between the flagstones, a trembling mass of tiny black insect bodies twitching in excitement, wings shimmering in the sunlight as they rose into the air; he looked down at his jacket and saw some clustered there, and brushed them hastily away, then lifted a hand to his hair, in case any were tangled there. Avril glanced up as he came near. Dan smiled and, feeling in an amiable, pedagogic mood, squatted down beside her.

'They're male ants, looking for the queen so that they can mate with her. But only one of them will manage it. The rest will die. When the sun goes down at the end of today, they'll all be dead.'

Avril looked at him with wide eyes. 'What about the one who finds the queen? Will he marry her?'

Dan straightened up. 'Queens never marry. They're too jealous of their power. Like Elizabeth the First. The one who mates with the queen will die, too, but at least he'll have achieved his purpose. He'll die in the knowledge that he has fathered the next race of flying ants.' Dan pointed to the ground. 'Perhaps it will be him – or him.'

Avril gazed speculatively at the ants for a moment, then suddenly brought her small sandalled foot down hard. 'No, it *won't* be him! *Or* him!' She mashed her foot down on the clustered ants. 'I'm going to kill as many as I can!'

Dan was both amused and somewhat appalled. 'I say, don't do that. It isn't kind, you know.'

'They're all boy ants! I don't like them!' She stamped on a few more. Then she glared at Dan. 'You're a boy! I'll kill you, too!' And to Dan's astonishment, she started to deliver kicks to his shin. Resisting the impulse to deliver a smart flat-hander to Avril's backside, Dan reached out and grasped her firmly by one small arm. Avril began to scream and wriggle. As he held her, uncertain what to do next, Sonia came hurrying from the house, her long jet beads bouncing up and down on the front of her smock.

'What on earth is the matter?'

'I'm not entirely sure. We were watching the ants, and she suddenly got into a bit of a state and began kicking me.'

'Oh, Avril!' Sonia knelt down in front of the child, who was still twisting in Dan's grasp. 'Avril, how could you? Mama has told you about kicking. It really will not do!'

'I hate him!' screeched Avril. 'And I hate *you*!'

'Darling! Darling!' Sonia tried to gather up her errant offspring, and got handsomely pummelled for her pains, but eventually managed to restrain her. 'I'll take her inside. Oh, where on earth can Madeleine have got to?' Winged ants clustered on Sonia's dress, and she brushed them violently away. 'Come inside, Avril. Quickly now!'

As Sonia and Avril disappeared indoors, Avril still screeching, Meg pulled up in the Austin on the far side of the courtyard. As she got out of the car with the parcel of meat she flicked at the air to ward off the drifts of flying ants.

'Lord, these ants are a pest!'

'Your cousin Avril had a shot at eradicating the entire species a moment ago.' Dan told Meg what had just happened.

'So now you know what it's like to receive a hack on the ankles from darling Avril. Isn't she a perfect poppet?'

'She's a little savage.'

'Don't let my aunt hear you say that. To be honest, I don't think she ever expected to have a child, not in her forties. Avril coming along was something of a surprise. One can't help feeling sorry for the kid. There are no children of her age hereabouts to play with. Uncle Henry takes scarcely any notice of her, and Sonia hasn't the first idea how to deal with her. As soon as Avril gets the slightest bit ratty or looks like throwing one of her famous tantrums, Sonia makes a smart exit, leaving her to Madeleine. And Madeleine's not the type to discipline anyone. Anyhow, I'd better deliver this lamb to Cook. I believe she needs it for lunch.'

Meg went inside, and Dan sat down on the edge of the fountain, contemplating the shimmering swarms of ants among the flagstones, and wondering about Avril, and what made her such a spectacularly obnoxious child. From the driveway came the purr of an engine, and a few seconds later a smart blue and black Wolseley pulled up in the courtyard, with Paul Latimer at the wheel, and three passengers. Dan crossed the courtyard to meet them.

Paul got out and shook Dan's hand. 'How are you, old chap? It's been an age.' He was tall and well-built, with light brown hair, blue eyes and handsome, even features, and had an air of bluff, somewhat self-conscious manliness designed at once to be assertive and reassuring. He seemed the epitome of English masculinity.

The passengers emerged from the car. Diana Latimer, tall and blue-eyed like her brother, was blonde and elegant, with a wide, amused mouth and a languid manner. She and Paul both carried themselves with the casual assurance of wealth and breeding. Diana's friend Eve, was petite, with pale, soft skin, shining black hair swept up in a neat chignon, and dark, shrewd eyes. She was wearing a blue dress with a matching jacket, and with her crimson lipstick and matching nails, was every inch the polished, sophisticated city girl.

Diana gave Dan a kiss. 'Darling Dan – so good to see you. I don't believe I need to introduce Eve, do I?'

'No, we're pretty well acquainted,' said Dan, exchanging a smile with Eve.

'And this is Charles Asher. Charles, Dan Ranscombe.'

A small, wiry man in his early twenties, somewhat shabbily dressed in a jacket and grey flannels, stepped forward and shook hands with Dan. He had a narrow, handsome face with large, dark eyes and a profusion of black hair. His manner was guarded, and he seemed shy and somewhat ill-at-ease.

'Well,' said Paul, 'let's go in and find our hostess.' Paul caught sight of William, Sonia's odd-job man, on the other side of the courtyard. 'I say,' he called out, 'would you mind fetching the luggage from the car and taking it in? There's a good chap.'

After lunch, while Eve took a stroll down to the village, Meg and Diana settled themselves in the summerhouse to gossip and catch up on news. The summerhouse was set at the top of a slope and looked out across the garden and the far-off Surrey Downs. Diana stretched herself out on the cushions, took the last cigarette from a small shagreen cigarette case, and lit it.

'I haven't been down to Woodbourne in an age. Not since the parents died.' She drew on her cigarette. 'Heaven to be in the countryside. London is so achingly dull at the moment, with everyone away. Mind you, I don't think I could spend the entire summer here. Aren't you frightfully bored?'

Diana was twenty-two, and nineteen-year-old Meg was rather in awe of her friend's superior wisdom and sophistication. She had to confess to her that so far the summer had been somewhat slow. 'But it'll be better now that you and Paul are here.'

'I think you'll like my friend, Eve, too,' said Diana. 'She's terribly clever, but lots of fun.' She cast a lazy eye at Meg. 'How do you like Dan?'

'I haven't really got to know him yet. He only arrived yesterday. He seems rather nice.'

Diana smiled and drew on her cigarette. 'Nice' was not necessarily a word she would have applied to Dan. 'Good-looking, don't you think? Such thrilling blue eyes.'

Meg smiled and shrugged, glancing away.

'And what of Uncle Henry and Aunt Sonia? All serene? Horrid old Henry not been chasing any more ladies' maids?'

'What on earth d'you mean?' Meg looked startled.

'Oh, darling, there was the most awful row last Christmas when Henry was caught in flagrante with one of the maids. Sonia tried to hush it up, but everyone knew.'

'Oh,' murmured Meg. 'I had no idea.'

'Not the first, and most probably not the last. He has quite a reputation, that old uncle of yours. Don't stare at me like a wide-eyed infant! Time you knew about such things.'

Meg made no reply to this. The child in her didn't in the least like having such dark secrets about her uncle revealed, and she sought to change the subject.

'Tell me more about this Charles Asher person. He didn't say much at lunch.'

Diana sighed as she blew out some smoke. 'He's another of those penniless intellectuals Sonia insists on collecting. Calls himself a writer, or a poet, or something. No doubt Sonia thinks it will help his career to meet Gerard Cunliffe. I don't mind him particularly, but he and Paul don't get on at all. They had an out-and-out row a few months ago, to do with politics and that man Oswald Mosley. There was something of an atmosphere between them in the car coming down. Not the most convivial of journeys.'

'Pity Aunt Sonia invited him, in that case. It's going to throw the numbers out for bridge.'

Diana put out her cigarette. 'Well, hurrah for that. I loathe blood sports. The rest of you can play bridge and I'll take myself off to the Gaumont in Malton. Have you seen any films there yet?'

'Sonia and I went to *The Petrified Forest* last week. I do so adore Bette Davis.'

And they sat talking of films and film stars until it was time for Meg to go and take tea to Henry's studio.

The atmosphere at dinner that evening was richer and rounder than hitherto, now that the gathering of guests was complete. Sonia was queenly and serene. Haddon was still in an affable temper, and was a jovial host. The younger guests, possibly in anticipation of escape and gaiety later on, behaved with charming deference to their elders, so that even Cunliffe, now equipped with his new hearing-aid, basked in their flattery and became expansive. Charles Asher did not share in the light-hearted chatter of the others, but seemed content to listen and observe. After dinner the Haddons and Cunliffes played a few rubbers of bridge while the younger guests took themselves off to the drawing room to talk and smoke and play gramophone records. Madeleine excused herself and went to bed.

Eve got Dan up to dance, and they glided around the room, talking and laughing in low voices. Meg watched them from the sofa, thinking how effortlessly elegant Eve looked, how slim and white her hand, with its crimson nails, was on Dan's shoulder.

Diana coaxed a reluctant Charles into dancing, too, and she sang along to the record in a thin, sweet voice as they moved in a slow foxtrot around the rug. She gave Charles a teasing smile, and glanced towards the others. 'I say, everyone, did you know that Charles is going off to Spain to fight the Fascists in a few weeks? He told me just before dinner.'

Charles looked faintly embarrassed at the attention this provoked.

'Why on earth would you want to go and fight in Spain?' asked Dan. 'It's not your war.'

The song came to an end, and they sat down on the sofa while Diana went to hunt for another record.

'The war against oppression, against Fascism, is everyone's war,' said Charles. His tone was mild, but the expression in his dark eyes was fierce. 'The International Brigade is a brotherhood. Every man of conscience should be engaged in the struggle to free the working classes from the oppression of totalitarianism.'

'That's sheer Communist cant,' observed Paul.

'I can't imagine you learn a great deal about Communism from the pages of the *Daily Telegraph*, sitting in the comfort of your club in St James's.'

Paul smiled. 'I take it that you think there's greater truth to be found in the *Daily Worker*? There's nothing constructive in that rag, just the irresponsible carping of people who never have been in power and are unlikely to be. Thank God.'

Paul's smile and his words seemed to infuriate Charles. 'Face up to it,' he retorted. 'The usefulness of the British ruling class is at an end. The moneyed classes are nothing more than parasites. Perhaps if you worked for a living you'd have a better idea of the social injustice that exists in this country. But I imagine you'd rather cling to your privileges than see improvement in the life of the ordinary man.'

'Ah, the voice from the third-class carriage! As it happens, I'd sooner see this country governed by people with some sense of duty and tradition, than by a load of Communists without an ounce of patriotic blood in their veins.'

'Frankly,' said Dan, 'I think going off to kill other people for political reasons is insane. Why does every European nation seem to be itching for another dogfight?'

'Well, I'm itching for another dance,' said Diana, 'and I don't want to hear any more of this stupid talk about wars. I'm going to put on another record.'

Paul, bored with the argument, turned to Dan and said, 'I say, I've just had a thought about those flying ants you were talking about earlier. You know what it means, don't you? The trout will be feasting tonight. If we go to the lake with a couple of rods, we'll catch any number.'

'Then why don't we?' said Dan.

The idea of a night-time fishing expedition enthused everyone. The political disagreement forgotten, they all went to the garden room to hunt up fishing tackle. Meg and Eve and Diana slipped on coats to ward off the evening chill, and the party set off, laughing and chattering, across the moonlit garden and through the fields to the trout pool.

3

SONIA'S GUESTS SPENT the next few days in pleasant relaxation. They had the gardens, the tennis court, the croquet lawn, the library and the billiard room to keep them entertained, to say nothing of one another, and the sun shone every day. Towards the end of the week Sonia decided they should take advantage of the settled spell of weather and venture out to picnic in the surrounding countryside.

Meg and Diana were summoned after breakfast to Sonia's small private sitting room to discuss the details. Sonia spent each morning here conducting the household business, discussing menus with Cook, paying tradesmen's bills, issuing invitations and answering letters. It was a charming room, dedicated to Sonia's sole use, the walls distempered in a *dégradé* style, pale rose at the top darkening to deep Venetian red at the bottom, and filled with tasteful items – a Sèvres bowl full of roses from the garden, a low divan scattered with silk cushions, a portrait of Sonia by Haddon on one wall, a pewter jug filled with poppies on a bleached wooden table by the long window. The individuality of the various items hinted at Bohemianism, but Sonia's sense of style lent a distinct and beautiful unity to all.

When she had announced the picnic project, Sonia explained the arrangements to Diana and Meg.

'I should like you two to give some thought to the kind of food we should bring along. I'm sure you can come up with something adventurous and delicious, more than mere sandwiches. Do you suppose quails' eggs are to be had in August? And we shall have to ask the men to sort out which cars to take. I thought of asking the Davenports to come along – you remember Constance Davenport, don't you, Diana?'

'That girl with the face like a pig that Paul and Meg and I always had to play with during the holidays?'

'She's quite a pretty girl now – well, after a fashion. I thought if we motored over to the woods just beyond Cutbush Farm on the other side of Malton – there's the loveliest clover field, with beautiful views over the Downs. Cook says the weather is set to hold for the week, and she's always right.'

After some further discussion, the girls left Sonia to her menus and letters and wandered out into the summer sunshine. They found Dan lounging in a chair on the terrace, smoking a cigarette.

'I hope you've come to relieve my tedium,' he said when he saw the girls.

'I'm all for tennis,' said Meg.

'Excellent idea.' Dan glanced at Diana. 'Can we persuade you and Paul to a game of doubles?'

'Oh, no thanks,' said Diana with a yawn. 'Too warm for all that.'

Meg smiled at Dan and squeezed his shoulder lightly. 'Just you and me, then.'

He returned the smile. 'I'll see you on court in ten minutes.'

As he went up to his room, he wondered whether Meg might not be as unattainable as he'd begun to think. Having set his sights on her at the beginning of the house party, he had lately abandoned any hope of bedding her, since in his experience the sweetly virginal ones required painstaking seduction, and time was not on his side. Besides, she seemed utterly enthralled by Paul, who behaved towards her with a cumbersome gallantry which Dan completely despised, to the point where he'd pretty much decided that if Paul was that keen, he was welcome. In the time left, it seemed easier to resume the promising dalliance that he and Eve had begun back in London. But the touch of Meg's hand on his shoulder a moment ago, the look in her eyes – perhaps he should reconsider. It would be amusing to put Paul's toffee nose out of joint by stealing his girl from under it, so to speak. And Meg was a more interesting challenge than Eve, who, he guessed, was there for the taking. With these noble thoughts coursing through his mind, he changed and strolled down to the tennis court.

Meanwhile, Madeleine had been despatched by Mrs Goodall to collect raspberries from the kitchen garden. As she wandered among the canes, her flaxen plait of hair swinging over one shoulder, methodically filling the large, white pudding basin that Cook had given her, Henry Haddon came across the courtyard, heading in the direction of his studio, and caught sight of her. Remembering what Dan had said the other day about what a wonderful subject she would make for a picture, he paused to observe her. After a moment he changed tack and headed towards the kitchen garden. Madeleine looked up, holding the basin with fruit-stained fingers as he approached, feeling her heart flare in the strange way it did every time she saw him.

'Raspberries for tea, eh?' Haddon inspected her for a moment, then said, 'Come with me.' He took the bowl from her and set it on the ground. 'Come along.' He strode through the orchard to his studio, Madeleine following.

Once there, Haddon roamed around, selecting and discarding various props. In the end, he settled on a simple wooden chair with a cane seat, which he placed a few feet from his easel.

'Now, sit yourself down here.'

'You want to paint me?'

'That is the general idea.'

Madeleine sat down awkwardly, not sure what was wanted of her.

'No, no,' said Haddon, 'not like that. Put your ankles together, your feet on one side. Lift your chin.' Madeleine made some ineffectual movements, failing to achieve what Haddon desired. 'Look, like this,' he said impatiently, rearranging her arms, moving her fingers and her feet until her pose was more graceful.

'Let's turn you to the light – so.' He moved her around, then stood back. 'A little further round – that's right. I want you looking back.' He moved her torso, his long fingers pushing her gently into position. 'Now' – he lifted her wrist – 'one arm on the back of the chair, so. As though you were glancing over your shoulder. As though you were waiting for someone. Do you understand?' Haddon continued to adjust her pose, all the while murmuring instructions in his deep voice. With the toe of his sandal he manoeuvred her feet so that one was tucked behind the other, then lifted Madeleine's forearm from the back of the chair.

'Put your hand beneath your chin. That's it – but still leaning back. That's excellent. Very good.' He stared intently. She was wearing a yellow button-through cotton sundress, with narrow shoulder straps, and he realised how much better the effect would be if one of the straps were to fall a little way from her shoulder.

'Unbutton the top two buttons of your dress,' he ordered.

Madeleine stared at him.

'Oh, for heaven's sake, don't look so alarmed.' He stepped forward and deftly unfastened the buttons, tweaking the straps back a little way from her pale shoulders. Although he was deeply struck by the translucence of her skin and the wonderful contours of her face and neck as she tilted her head towards the light, every touch and thought was entirely without sensuality. She was merely an object to be arranged.

How different the experience was for Madeleine. As his hands grasped her body, moving her gently into position, tugging and shifting the folds of her dress, she felt her skin and her senses begin to glow with the warmth of being handled and moved by him, each touch lighting a small, soft fire within her. She felt a delicious inertia as he casually arranged her limbs and body.

Haddon stood back to survey her. She was perfect. He had posed her so that she was sitting half-turned, as though listening for some sound, a note of music, or some approaching footfall, the expectancy of her attitude touched with a light despair. He gazed at her for a moment, then came forward and lifted the plait of blonde hair from her shoulder. 'How does this unfasten?'

Wordlessly, without losing her pose, Madeleine pulled off the ribbon, and let Haddon unplait her hair and spread it loosely over her shoulders. Her scalp prickled deliciously, and her skin felt silvery with sensation. She half-closed her eyes.

Haddon stepped back. 'No, open your eyes. Look away. That's right. Now, stay still.'

He sat on a stool, sketchpad on knee, and began to sketch with swift strokes. After ten minutes she felt her back begin to ache a little from the position she held, but each time she tried to shift to ease it, he would command her not to move. So she stayed as still as she could. She would steal a look at him from time to time, a warmth burning within the pit of her stomach. She felt an odd sense of power, posed as she was, while he drew busily, glancing up at her from time to time with an eagerness that seemed like hunger.

At last he put down his pad. 'There. Excellent. You may sit round.'

Madeleine moved her body out of its pose. 'Now,' said Haddon, 'I want you to come here each day and pose for me. I am going to paint you. Are you flattered?'

Madeleine hesitated. 'Shouldn't I ask Mrs Haddon first?'

'I shall speak to her.' Madeleine took her ribbon from the pocket of her dress and began to replait her hair. 'I want you here every day at half ten. Now, off you go. Go on. Oh,' he added, as Madeleine stood up, 'I want you in that same dress each day.'

*

Avril was playing by the fountain when she saw Madeleine walking through the orchard from the direction of the barn.

'Where have you been?' she demanded.

'Nowhere in particular,' replied Madeleine.

'Have you been in the place where Papa paints?' Avril, who was forbidden to go to the studio for fear of disturbing her father, seized jealously on the possibility that Madeleine had somehow received special favour. The more her father ignored her, the more Avril longed for his time and attention. 'Have you?'

Madeleine went over to the raspberry canes and retrieved the bowl of raspberries she had been picking.

'Come on,' she said to Avril. 'It'll soon be time for lunch.' She took Avril's hand and led her towards the house, while the child tugged at her hand, demanding to know what she had been doing in the studio and why. But Madeleine would not tell her, and eventually Avril gave up.

Distracted as he was by the pleasure of watching Meg's lithe figure as she darted round the tennis court, Dan beat her by four clear games, towards the end winning point after point with perhaps unnecessary decisiveness.

'Did you have to make such utter mincemeat of me?' she asked, as they strolled back through the trees to the house.

'What? Would you rather I'd let you win?'

'Paul does.'

'And don't you find that mildly irritating? Or is his tennis just not that good?'

They had stopped on the path.

'His tennis is wonderful,' said Meg spiritedly. 'He's a superb athlete. I don't think there's a thing he can't do well.'

'You don't have to defend your hero quite so ferociously. I'm aware of Paul's many virtues. I just thought you might find it a tad patronising, being allowed to win.'

'Oh, he doesn't do it in that way. He just believes in... well, treating women a certain way. And he's not my hero.'

'Fine, I'll let you win every game we play from now on, if you like.'

Meg swiped at a dandelion clock with her tennis racquet. 'I'm not sure there's much point in our playing any more.' If anything, she looked even more desirable in her mild sulk, her eyes dark and troubled, her mouth pouting slightly.

Dan reached out and broke off a spray of wild roses from a nearby bush. He handed it to her with a smile. 'A peace offering. Please don't stop playing tennis with me.'

She smiled and took the roses. Sensing his moment, Dan leaned forward and kissed her. She drew back at first, startled, but he persisted, and she gave in, melting into his arms with delightful enthusiasm.

In the long moment of their kiss, the first proper kiss Meg had ever known, it seemed to her that the world had shrunk to the little patch of dappled sunlight in which they stood, and all sound to the rustle of leaves and sleepy call of the wood pigeons. She felt as though she could happily stay with his mouth on hers for ever. A fire that felt like more than happiness flooded her body. Then from the house came the muffled clamour of the luncheon gong. Dan lifted his head. Meg remained motionless, her eyes still closed. Dan smiled and touched her nose lightly with his finger; her eyes opened.

'Come on,' he said, 'I'm ravenous. Let's go in.'

For the rest of the day, Dan could sense Meg hovering. She behaved entirely normally, not seeking him out, not letting her eyes stray too often in his direction – but he was aware that she was thinking about him, waiting and hoping for another moment of intimacy. What interesting fires he seemed to have lit within her.

Teatime was a fluid affair, with tables and chairs laid out in the shade of the big horse chestnut tree, and people coming and going, idling over tea and sandwiches and cake, pausing in groups of conversation, then fragmenting and drifting off to the next pleasurable activity. The day was hot and still, with barely a leaf stirring.

Diana, not feeling like teatime chatter, took herself off to a nearby hammock with a couple of cucumber sandwiches and her book, where she swayed in happy solitude in the dappled afternoon light.

After a while the Haddons and Cunliffes departed, and Dan, Charles, Eve and Meg remained together on the grass, chatting. Paul was nowhere to be seen. Eve left the group and crossed the lawn to sit down on the grass by Diana's hammock.

'Bored?' asked Diana.

'I came to escape the game-playing between Dan and your ingénue friend, Meg. It's getting a mite tedious.'

'You sound peeved.'

'I am, rather. I had hopes of him.'

Diana was aware that there had been something of a flirtation between Eve and Dan in London, so it was hardly surprising that Eve was put out to discover she had competition – particularly in the form of Meg. Diana brushed the crumbs from her book and closed it, and contemplated Dan, who was sitting cross-legged in his shirtsleeves, a plate of strawberries on his knees. The sun of the past few days had given his skin a light, golden tan. She had known Dan for over ten years, and she had to admit that from a scrawny, lanky schoolboy he had grown into the most astonishingly attractive man.

'You know, darling, Dan Ranscombe may be desirable,' she reflected, 'but he's quite unsuitable. Apart from what he earns, he's hardly got a bean. One needs someone who can afford dinner and the theatre and taxis, that kind of thing. And who has prospects, of course. Who wants a husband without money?'

'I'm not looking for a husband. The fact is, I'm absolutely sex-starved, and I hoped this house party might provide some light relief.' She gave Diana a knowing smile.

Diana returned the smile. One of the ties that bound her in friendship to Eve was that both of them were rather more worldly than most girls of their age, particularly in matters of sex. Two years ago Diana had been introduced to its pleasures by a charming Italian whom she had met while on a trip to Europe with an elderly aunt – who would have been scandalised if she'd known what Diana was up to in the warm, small hours of the Mediterranean night. Eve herself, now twenty-three, had already had a couple of older lovers, men in their forties, and she and Diana had spent enjoyable hours together comparing notes.

Diana yawned and swatted away an errant bee. Both women watched as Dan picked a particularly luscious strawberry from the plate, pretended to be about to put it in his mouth, then held it out to Meg, who ate it, laughing.

'Honestly,' said Eve, 'I could slap his face for him. After the way we were in London.'

'Let's give it a minute or two, then go and put a spoke in his wheel,' said Diana.

Meg sat alone with Dan, the plate between them empty of strawberries. The maids were clearing away the tea tables, Charles had gone for a walk, and Diana and Eve were talking together on the other side of the lawn. She had Dan all to herself. But now that she was alone with him, Meg could think of nothing to say. She stared at the grass, parting it with her fingers and pretending to scrutinise insects. Dan, lounging on one elbow, regarded her with lazy-eyed pleasure. She really was the least opaque creature he had ever met. No longer able to sustain her interest in beetles, Meg glanced up. She caught his amused expression.

'Why are you smiling like that?'

'Because you're a funny thing.'

'Am I?'

'You're adorable,' murmured Dan. 'I haven't been able to

think of anything for the past few hours except how much I want to kiss you again.'

Meg's inexperienced ear missed the casual yet practised manner in which this was delivered. She heard only the words, and her heart began to beat very hard.

Dan put out a hand and stroked the back of hers. 'What do you say we go for a walk somewhere?' Meg brushed a dark curl from her eyes and nodded. They rose from the grass, and at that moment Diana and Eve came strolling across the lawn.

'Come on, you two,' said Diana. 'The oldsters are frowsting indoors with books and newspapers, and everyone else seems to have disappeared. How about a game of croquet?'

Meg glanced at Dan. He didn't return her look, simply said, 'Wonderful. We were boring each other to death, anyway.'

Meg couldn't disguise her pique as she followed them to the croquet lawn. It took her a full round of croquet to emerge from her bad mood, and it was only later that night, when she was in bed, that she realised how naïve she had been.

She lay in bed, her book open and unread, going over it all, and realising that Dan could hardly have behaved otherwise. She blushed to think how easily Diana and Eve must have read her disappointment, and would now no doubt tease her remorselessly for the rest of her stay. She liked Eve well enough, but she could be quite sharp-tongued. Meg's intuition also told her that Eve had something of a thing for Dan herself, which didn't help matters.

The thought of it all made it impossible to concentrate on her book. The room suddenly seemed hot and airless, and she got up to open the window as wide as possible. She leaned out, hoping to drink in some refreshing coolness, but the air outside was heavy and lukewarm. A full moon silvered the silent gardens. She set the window open on its hasp, and as she passed her dressing table on the way back to bed, she saw lying there the spray of roses that Dan had given her after their game of tennis, the moment before he had kissed her. She had dropped it there before lunch, and now the petals and leaves were limp.

She broke off one of the blooms, and carried it back to bed. She inspected it for a while, marvelling at the blush-pink silkiness of the petals, then opened her book and placed it between the pages. She switched off her lamp, closing her eyes and trying to conjure up the memory of Dan's mouth on hers, before falling fast asleep.

She had no idea whether it was minutes or hours later when she heard a light tapping on her door. Who on earth would come to her room in the middle of the night? Perhaps Avril, having a bad dream? No – she would be far more likely to go to Sonia or Madeleine.

She swung herself out of bed, groping for the light switch. 'Just a minute,' she called.

Outside in the corridor, Dan winced at how clearly Meg's voice carried. He would have expected her to be more discreet. Although he hadn't been able to get her on her own in the interval between dinner and bed, he thought he'd pretty much made it understood that he'd be along to her room later, when everyone had turned in. He had left it until one o'clock to be on the safe side.

Meg opened the door, wearing nothing but a thin silk nightdress that left nothing to the imagination. It was all Dan could do not to let his eyes linger on the arousing curves of her breasts. With her hair loose about her shoulders, she looked utterly delectable.

Meg stared at him in astonishment. 'What is it?'

Dan swallowed a laugh and gave a quick glance along the corridor. 'Um – may I come in?'

Meg hesitated, then stepped back. Dan came inside and closed the door. It didn't matter that she hadn't understood and hadn't been expecting him. He was here now. He cupped her face in his hands and kissed her long and hard, his tongue seeking hers. Her response was tentative; beneath it he could feel uncertainty, and even slight fear. He moved his body closer to hers, his hand cupping her buttocks. After a few seconds she pushed him away.

'What's the matter?'

'I honestly don't think you should be here at this time of night.'

He laughed. 'When else am I supposed to get you alone? At least no one's likely to come along and suggest a game of croquet.' But when he tried to kiss her again, she backed away.

'Dan, it isn't right.'

'But going into the woods with me this afternoon would have been?'

She stared at him, the colour rising in her face. 'That was just for a walk. In the daytime.' She struggled, her voice breaking to a whisper. 'This afternoon I only wanted... I only wanted to be kissed again.'

The way in which she said this, her pitiful struggle between shame and dignity, had a peculiar effect on Dan, and regret instantly washed away desire.

'I'm sorry. I didn't mean to be beastly.' He gazed at her in bemusement. Clearly he wasn't going to make much headway tonight. 'I should go.'

Meg put a hand on his arm and smiled hesitantly. 'I would like to be kissed again. Nothing else.' She lifted her face with tender expectancy, as though she were offering something sacred. The gesture seemed to Dan both ridiculous and profound.

'By Jove, yes,' he murmured, and put his mouth to hers. Without any expectation of the fulfilment of desire behind it, the kiss was strangely potent. Something seemed to give way within him. He had kissed many women in his time, but never had the experience made him feel so vulnerable.

When it was over, he held her for a moment, running his hands lightly over the satin softness of her skin.

'I need to go to bed now,' said Meg.

He kissed her lightly on the forehead and left the room, aware of some disquieting emotion, which he attributed to unsatisfied lust. He would have to wait till they got back to London, but the signs were all very promising. And it would be a delightful piece of unfinished business to look forward to.

4

As SONIA HAD feared, quails' eggs were not to be had, but Diana and Meg prepared a list of other delicacies and prevailed upon Cook to stretch her talents to their limits in aid of the picnic. Mrs Goodall was an excellent cook and jealously guarded by Sonia, for good servants were at a premium in the neighbourhood, and often the object of treacherous bribes and seductions. She had provided a magnificent raised pork pie, with delicious pickles of her own bottling by way of accompaniment, some cold roast fowl, a large stone jar of potted Morecambe Bay shrimps, excellent cheeses and fruit, three plum tarts made with plums from the Woodbourne House orchard, and a pot of clotted cream. Bottles of lemonade and beer were packed as well, together with linen and cutlery, plates and glasses.

'And just to keep things lively,' said Diana with a wink to Eve, 'a couple of shakers of gin and French. There!' She closed the lid of the hamper and fastened the leather straps with satisfaction. 'We're all set. Let's find one of those big, strong men to take this to the car.'

It had been arranged that Sonia, Meg, Diana and Eve should ride in Daphne Davenport's Daimler, while Henry Haddon would take the Cunliffes, Madeleine and Avril in the big Bentley, and Dan, Paul and Charles would drive to the picnic in Paul's Wolseley.

'Such a bore, going with the Davenports,' said Diana, as she lounged on the window seat in the morning room with Eve and Meg, waiting for the arrival of the Daimler.

'Are they so dreadful?' asked Eve.

'Constance is – or was. When we came down in the holidays as children Paul and I were made to play with her, and she was perfectly useless, always afraid of falling over and getting dirty or spoiling her frock. Do you remember, Meg?'

'Oh, she's not so bad,' murmured Meg.

Henry Haddon, smartly attired in a green linen suit, strode downstairs to the hall with Sonia in his wake. He was not best pleased at having to go on a picnic, regarding such al fresco frivolities as a footling waste of time, and was irritated at the interruption to his new project, the portrait of Madeleine. The portrait itself had, two days ago, been the subject of a row between Haddon and Sonia, one in which Sonia's attempts to conduct the argument *sotto voce* had been utterly confounded by Haddon roaring at the top of his voice, so that the household guests, while politely feigning either indifference or deafness, had been able to listen with interest. Sonia's principal objection lay in the loss of Madeleine's services. Madeleine might be the daughter of an old friend, temporarily taken into the family as an act of benevolence, but her duties included looking after Avril and keeping her amused, together with sundry little domestic tasks, and Sonia didn't see that she should dispense with her just so that Henry might use her as an artist's model. Added to which, while it seemed to Sonia perfectly proper that Henry should undertake a portrait of Elizabeth Cunliffe, or any one of their guests for that matter, why should he choose to paint Madeleine, of all people?

The fatuity of these arguments met with the great artist's rage and scorn, and indeed Sonia might have spared herself the trouble of articulating them, for she knew that Haddon would have his way. The result was that poor Madeleine was caught in the middle, and Sonia vented her vexation by finding as many tasks as possible for her to do in the hours free of the studio.

Thus Madeleine endured a double penance, for it was no great pleasure to have to sit holding that back-aching pose for long stretches of time, which she beguiled by creating fanciful stories to tell to Avril later – the best way of keeping Avril docile, she had discovered. The part she still looked forward to, however, was the random touch of Haddon's hands upon her body as he set her in her pose each day.

Despite these tensions and Haddon's irascibility, spirits that Thursday were high – the weather was still pleasantly warm, and there was a general childish air of excitement at the prospect of an outing.

The purring of a heavy engine and the crunch of wheels on the gravel announced the arrival of the Davenports' Daimler. Diana glanced out and saw Sonia greeting Daphne and Constance as they emerged from the car.

'Oh, my Lord!' said Diana. 'Constance is wearing gloves, of all things – and on a picnic! Bad as a hat at a cocktail party.' She rose from the window seat. 'Come along, let's go and meet them.' Meg picked up her straw hat and followed Diana and Eve.

It was a distance of some ten miles to the picnic site. With Paul at the wheel of the Wolseley, the men roared along the country roads and arrived well ahead of the rest. They claimed to have found the perfect spot, a pleasant dip in the slopes of the clover field just at the point where it met the fringes of Hadley Wood, and by the time the others arrived they had already established themselves there with a travelling rug, the daily papers and bottles of beer.

The older members of the party were naturally not expected to lie around on rugs, and Mrs Davenport's driver produced from the boot of the Daimler a folding table and chairs, which he and the younger men carried to the picnic spot, together with the hamper and more rugs. The girls set out the picnic fare to exclamations of delight, and even Haddon, as he opened and handed round bottles of beer and lemonade, seemed to have decided to enjoy the day after all. Mrs Davenport's driver, once he had made his final journey across the field with the large basket of cream cakes which were Mrs Davenport's contribution to the feast, left in the Daimler to take his own lunch in a nearby pub, and the picnic began.

After three quarters of an hour, little was left of the feast except a few buttery shrimps, chicken bones, the dregs of ginger beer, and the remnants of a cream cake which Avril had rejected, and around which a couple of idle wasps buzzed.

The party sat or sprawled about, chatting and smoking. Daphne Davenport sat beneath an immense Chinese parasol and busied herself with her knitting, while Sonia and Elizabeth read. Henry Haddon took himself off with his sketchbook to the crest of the hill. Gerald Cunliffe fell asleep beneath his panama with his mouth open. Madeleine and Avril went to scout the field for four-leaf clovers and sufficient daisies to make a gigantic daisy chain.

Diana lay back and gazed up at the trees. 'The chestnuts are already beginning to fade,' she said. 'Summer will soon be over.'

'They're always the first to turn,' observed Sonia. 'What will you do this autumn, Diana?'

'Oh, I don't know.' Diana stretched her arms above her head. 'I might go to Italy. The Favershams moved there last year, you know. Edwina Faversham says one can live quite comfortably on three hundred a year. Perhaps I'll try it.'

Paul gave a dry laugh. 'I doubt if that would keep you in underwear, dearest sis.'

Sonia turned to Constance. 'What about you, Constance dear?'

Constance, who was a plump, pretty girl with intelligent, fearful eyes, blushed slightly. 'I'm going to university,' she replied, 'to study medicine. I got my place at the beginning of summer.'

There was a general murmur of interest from the rest of the party. 'How splendid,' said Meg. 'I wish I were clever enough to do something like that.'

'Really?' said Paul. 'I don't wish to denigrate Constance's ambitions in the slightest, but one has to ask what ultimate value there is in educating women to such a high degree.'

Constance, who sat hugging her knees, stared at the rug with downcast eyes and said nothing, though her cheeks burned even brighter.

Paul went on, 'Most women end up marrying and having children, after all, and their careers become defunct.'

'What rot,' said Eve. 'Women are just as capable of being good doctors as men. Why do you talk as though women have to be consigned to some sort of domestic dustbin?'

'I don't regard the duties of child-rearing and home-making in that light at all,' replied Paul. 'I believe women should take them very seriously indeed. Look at Sonia, a model wife and mother.'

'Oh, stop being such a pompous ass!' exclaimed Diana.

'Just because it absorbs one's energies doesn't mean it's sufficient,' said Sonia, her voice mild, her gaze wistful. 'I often wish there was more to my life. Women of my generation were mostly brought up to marry well, and that was the end of it. But what kind of life is that? Investing one's whole being in a husband and a family, sacrificing one's whole identity – for what?'

'Well, quite evidently, for the good of the next generation,' said Charles Asher, though it was hard to tell whether he was being ironical or not.

'Wasn't it George Eliot who said that women have to put up with the lives their husbands make for them, or something like that?' murmured Dan, lying on the grass with his jacket off, hands clasped behind his head.

'Every woman should be able to make her way in life without depending on some man,' remarked Eve.

'But the dependency is mutual, surely,' said Paul. He turned to Sonia. 'You bemoan your lot, dearest Sonia, but haven't you given thought to the fact that without you to run his home, and to see his meals are cooked and his clothes washed, Henry would hardly be able to function as the great artist he is?'

'Oh, I've given more thought to it than you imagine,' murmured Sonia.

'I often think you women belittle the contribution you make. Where would every great composer or writer or artist be without some woman in the background, making sure that his domestic life runs smoothly?'

'Perhaps *we'd* like to be the great composers or writers or artists,' said Meg.

'But you're not, are you? History has shown us that much.'

'That's because we're too busy darning socks and making beds,' yawned Diana.

'I don't ever see you doing very much of either,' replied her brother.

'True, and I don't intend to. I'm all for the rights of women, but quite frankly, I shall be content to marry someone with a great deal of money. A *very* great deal. Then the question of whether to work or not simply won't arise.'

'Quite right, my dear,' said Elizabeth Cunliffe. 'The best thing any sensible young woman can do is find some decent man to marry, and leave it at that.'

'There will come a time,' observed Charles Asher, 'when all women will be obliged to work, and the business of rearing children will be handed over to the state.'

'Poppycock! Only in your Marxist utopia,' said Diana scornfully. She sat up and shaded her eyes as she gazed across the field. 'Here's Madeleine – without Avril.'

'Madeleine, where's Avril?' asked Sonia in mild alarm, as Madeleine approached, her skirt held out before her, filled with daisies.

'She's with her father,' replied Madeleine. 'She saw him sketching at the top of the hill and went to see him. Then she wanted to stay with him.'

'And he didn't mind?'

'No.' Madeleine sank down on the grass and let her cargo of limp daisies spill out on to the grass. She looked like some beautiful, bewitching child, and was the unwitting focus of attention as she bent her lovely head over the flowers. Charles Asher watched her with something approaching fascination. Constance picked up a handful of the daisies and began to weave them together.

Diana, who had been dispensing gin and French from the cocktail shakers to those who wanted it, poured some into a tumbler and handed it to Madeleine. 'Refreshment for the daisy picker.' Madeleine, thirsty and bored from looking after Avril, drained the glass. 'I say, easy!' laughed Diana. She glanced at Paul, who frowned in reproof.

'My goodness,' said Daphne Davenport, laying down her knitting and fanning herself, 'the weather just seems to get warmer and warmer!'

'I think it may break soon,' said Meg, pointing to a darkening mass of cloud in the sky to the west. A distant rumble of thunder seemed to echo her words.

A hush fell upon the group. Constance and Madeleine wove their daisy chain. Eve lit another cigarette, and Diana sipped reflectively at the remnants of her gin. Elizabeth Cunliffe closed her Agatha Christie novel and dozed. Meg sat with her knees drawn up, her chin resting on them, staring thoughtfully at the grass. Charles pulled a small volume from his jacket pocket and lay on his stomach to read. Paul turned the pages of the newspaper and sucked on his pipe.

After a while Eve asked, 'Who fancies a walk in the woods?'

Charles Asher closed his book and returned it to his pocket. 'I'll come.'

'Me too,' said Diana. 'Come on, Meg.'

Meg hesitated. She had been hoping that there might be some way of going for a walk with Dan, just the two of them. But he hadn't made the slightest effort. Perhaps it was just too difficult, with so many people around. Dan was aware of Meg glancing at him, but some mischief made him turn to Madeleine.

'Madeleine?'

Madeleine looked up at Dan, and was about to shake her head, when Charles added, 'Please do.'

Surprised, Madeleine hesitated, then brushed the daisy chain from her lap and got up.

'Come on, Constance,' said Diana.

'No thanks,' replied Constance with a smile. 'It was bad enough trying to keep up with you and Paul when I was eleven. I'll stay here.'

'Please yourself,' replied Diana. 'We shan't be long.'

The group set off through the woods, Paul taking the lead and choosing the route, pointing out various species of bird in an authoritative fashion as he strode along. A brief argument sprang up between Paul and Charles as to the markings of what Paul maintained was a nuthatch. Dan took Charles's side in a light-hearted fashion, but Paul refused to be corrected. Indeed, his manner grew so dogmatic that Dan was relieved when Charles shrugged and let the matter drop.

After a while the dense woodland opened up to a clearing beneath some oak trees, with paths leading off in various directions. The girls were by now lagging behind the men, and Paul, who had already reached the clearing, called to them to get a move on. While Meg and Diana hurried to catch up, Madeleine stopped and took off her shoe. Charles Asher saw Madeleine kneeling down, examining her foot, and went back to help her.

'What's wrong?'

Madeleine pushed her hair back from her face. 'I've got a thorn in my foot. And I can't pull it out,' she gave a half-embarrassed laugh, 'because I bite my nails.'

'Let's have a look. Come on. Sit down here.' He led her to a fallen tree and knelt down to inspect her foot, thrilled at this chance of intimacy. Although he liked to present himself to the world as a cynical intellectual, Charles was in fact a romantic idealist with little experience of women. The easy forthrightness of girls like Meg and Diana made him shy, but from the first moment he had met Madeleine he had been enchanted not only by her beauty, but by her reserve. He was aware of her indeterminate place in the household, hovering somewhere between guest and servant, and his sense of his own inferiority made him feel there was a bond between them. The fact that she so rarely spoke gave her a depth and soulfulness. He felt that in her company he could be eloquent – as eloquent as in all his writings – but so far the chance to be alone with her had eluded him. Now he was sitting in the quiet woodland, cradling her foot.

'There.' He gripped the tiny spur of thorn between his fingernails. 'It's out.'

Madeleine pulled up her foot to examine it. Asher caught a tantalising glimpse of curving white thigh.

'How does it feel?'

Madeleine stood up and put on her sandal. 'Much better, thanks. My mother's always telling me not to bite my nails. She's right. I shouldn't.'

'I don't think of you as a nervous type,' said Charles awkwardly, with a sense that he was failing to capitalise on his moment.

'I'm not. It's just absent-mindedness. I don't even know I'm doing it. We should catch the others up.'

Asher looked round, trying to work out which was the most likely path for them to have taken. 'I think they probably went this way,' he said, and set off on the right-hand path, Madeleine following.

As they walked, Charles began to talk. At first he spoke about the woods, and about his own love of walking, then about a hiking holiday he had taken with some friends earlier that year. He expanded this to social and political themes, he told her of his work, how hard it was to make a living, of his ambitions and his beliefs. Madeleine only half-listened, a little bored, but the polite smiles and glances she gave warmed his heart. Some ten minutes after they had left the clearing, they still hadn't found the rest of the group, and Charles suggested that they stop and rest for a bit.

They sat down on the grassiest part of a small copse a few yards from the path. Charles watched as she gathered a handful of early acorns. She held one up.

'There's a superstition that if you carry an acorn, you'll never grow old.' She tipped open the breast pocket of his jacket with one finger, and dropped the acorn in. 'There,' she smiled, 'now maybe you'll live to be a hundred and see your dream of a socialist world come true.'

The diffidence of her movements, the casual way she accepted his proximity, letting her hair fall across her face and near to his hand, suggested desires and expectations which made Charles both nervous and excited. He picked up an acorn, felt for the pocket in the side of her skirt, feeling his fingers graze her thigh as he did so, and dropped it in. 'Now you'll never grow old, and you'll stay as beautiful as you are today.'

Madeleine smiled awkwardly and looked away, then glanced back at him. She liked his face, his soulful dark eyes, his unruly dark hair. He laid his hand upon hers, then put his other hand around her waist and drew her towards him. Madeleine resisted for a second, then let him kiss her. She had never been kissed in her life, and the experience was intensely delightful. His mouth was soft and full, and delicious sensations flooded her body. She let him lift the hair back from her face with clumsy fingers. He kissed her again. She found herself thinking of Henry Haddon, and pretended it was he who was kissing her. The thought was overwhelming. Charles slipped the strap of her sundress down from her shoulder and touched her breast, and although she pulled his fingers away, she let them wander back there a few seconds later. The sensation was too intensely pleasurable to resist, and her Haddon fantasy had taken intense hold. She lay back on the dusty, pine-needle softness of the forest floor. He kissed her breast, and then her mouth, harder this time, and pushed her skirt towards her thighs, giddy with lust.

It was at this moment that Paul came striding through the undergrowth some yards away. He stopped abruptly when he saw them. Startled, Charles pulled down Madeleine's dress and rolled away from her. He got awkwardly to his feet, Madeleine quickly adjusted the straps of her dress and brushed pine needles from her hair.

Paul said nothing, but his face was grim. 'We thought you two had got lost.'

One by one the others appeared, each taking in the scene in their own way. By now Madeleine was on her feet.

'Far from it,' said Charles coolly. 'We've been perfectly fine.'

There was a silence, one in which the embarrassment of all was palpable.

'Just as well we met up with you,' said Diana. 'Time we were all getting back.'

They headed back to the picnic place.

That night Madeleine lay in her bed. She pulled up the hem of her nightdress, feeling the cool sheets against her skin. She touched her breasts, she caressed her body with fingers which she pretended were not her own, her thoughts wandering to the studio in the barn, and her appointment for ten thirty the next morning.

5

'BLOODY LITTLE OIK!' muttered Paul.

Dan, stretched out on the window seat in the library, gave up trying to read the morning paper and let it flop across his chest.

Paul continued to pace the room. 'I've a good mind to have a word with him.'

Dan stared through the window at the mass of thunderclouds blackening the sky. The air was sultry, the light in the library strangely yellow. 'What business is it of yours?'

'Damn it, Dan, when a man takes advantage of someone who's scarcely more than a kid, we have to make it our business. In Sonia's house, too.'

'She's sixteen. Old enough to let someone kiss her if she wants to.'

'You saw what was going on! It was damn well indecent. She's Sonia's responsibility. Someone ought to tell her.'

Dan sighed and got up. 'You do what you like. Just leave me out of it.' He left the library, taking the paper with him.

Diana, Meg and Eve were seated under the chestnut tree in the garden, having a conversation on the same subject, though of a somewhat different nature.

'I can't think of a single attractive thing about him,' said Meg. 'I suppose he's intelligent, but not in a very nice way, if you ask me, and he hasn't got much else to recommend him.'

'Perhaps she was flattered by the attention,' said Eve. 'I mean, he's so evidently *épris*. Everyone can tell.'

'But still – to let him take that kind of liberty with her. I mean, her clothes were all over the place!'

Diana stretched her arms languorously above her head. 'Haven't you ever let anyone make love to you?' The air up till now had been very still, the light leaden, but a sudden breeze shivered the highest branches of the trees.

Meg thought of Dan. 'No, I haven't.'

'Ah, but you must have *wanted* to,' said Eve with a smile.

Meg said nothing, thinking of that night when Dan had come to her room. She didn't regret what she had said to him then. She still felt that whatever she might want – and he had opened up longings in her which she hadn't known existed – it wouldn't have been right just to let things happen. Her heart tightened every time she thought about that night. He had kissed her in a way that had made her think, well, that she mattered to him. Yet since then he hadn't come near her. She didn't know what any of it meant – if it meant anything at all. To add to the confusion of her heart, she had since her schoolgirl days – the precise day being the Eton and Harrow cricket match, when Paul had scored all those runs and taken the winning wicket – been rather in love with Paul. She was utterly bewildered by her feelings.

'Paul seems to think Charles is some kind of sex fiend, taking advantage of a juvenile,' observed Diana. 'He's very het up about it.'

Meg tore her thoughts away from Dan. 'Perhaps Madeleine's judgement isn't very good. Maybe Aunt Sonia should speak to her.'

'Darling Meg, can you imagine how *distrait* Sonia would be if she had to undertake anything of that kind? I think it would be a kindness *not* to tell her.'

Eve yawned. 'He was only kissing her, after all, and Paul's been going around giving poor Charles such savage glares that he must be feeling thoroughly intimidated.'

Fat drops of rain, slow at first and then thick and fast, began to splash upon the leaves of the chestnut tree.

'Come on,' said Diana, 'let's run before we get drenched!'

The girls sprang to their feet and hurried to the house.

Charles was doing his best to persuade himself that he wasn't bothered by the incident in the woods, or by Paul's disapproving looks. He disliked Paul intensely, loathed his easy arrogance and his patronising manner. He tried to find comfort in telling himself that Paul was a blind reactionary who neither felt nor thought deeply, and that the days of his kind would soon be numbered. Nonetheless, Paul's evident disdain galled him. He was aware, too, that the others thought it was rather common to be caught kissing the nanny, especially one not much more than a child, and he was savagely miserable.

Avril stood by the duck pond watching the soapflakes float down on to the surface of the water. They melted most satisfactorily. She picked up the box and emptied some more out, then looked at what was left in the box and decided to put the whole lot into the fountain. When she had finished with the soapflakes, Avril scampered off to the orchard to hide from Madeleine, who was no doubt looking for her right this minute. She saw her father in the orchard on his way to the barn, and watched as he picked up a couple of windfalls, munching on one and putting the other in his pocket. She thought of darting out from her hiding place to surprise him, but he would only hand her over to Madeleine, so she stayed where she was. She wished he would let her come to the studio while he worked. She would be quiet as a mouse, really she would, she wouldn't play with the paints and brushes, fun though that was. But he always sent her away, even though she simply wanted to be with him. As she watched her Papa making a tour of the orchard, inspecting the crop of fruit,

Avril had an idea. It was such a good idea that she put her hand over her mouth to stifle a giggle. Then she crept out from behind her tree and tiptoed to the barn, pushing open the heavy door and disappearing inside.

A few minutes later Haddon went into his studio. He prepared his materials, then went to the easel to look with fresh eyes at his work so far. The portrait was a full-length one of Madeleine seated on the wicker chair, half-turned towards the window, one arm resting on the chair back, her slim legs entwined. It pleased him as few things did these days. He studied the brushstrokes, examining his treatment of the light. The girl looked luminous. He had caught her turn of the head so exactly, that wistful pose somewhere between hope and disappointment, and the lovely curve of her body. He felt his heart tighten with a feeling of accomplishment, a sense that he had grasped something almost beyond his own powers. He had always thought of genius as something almost extraneous to the artist. This, he knew, was the nearest he had ever come to it. The marvel was that he had done so much in so short a time. Apart from some detail around her shoulders, the thing was nearly finished.

Madeleine was on her way through the orchard when the first drops of rain began to patter on the leaves of the apple trees. She broke into a run and reached the barn just before the worst of the deluge broke. Haddon was at the trestle table mixing paints as she came in. Both looked up at the sound of the sudden tumult of rain thrashing on the roof of the barn and on the big, sloping windows. The feeling of being in a safe haven made Madeleine smile. She pulled the ribbon from her hair and spread out the slightly damp tendrils on her shoulders, in anticipation of resuming her pose for the picture. She didn't mind the ache in her back any more. She liked being here in the turpentine and oil smell of the barn. All morning she had been looking forward to the sweet, strange moments when Haddon would set her body into the desired position, moving and touching and arranging her limbs.

Haddon was struck by the radiance of the girl as she tossed her hair and settled herself in the wicker chair. She was still slightly breathless from her run through the orchard, her breast rising and falling, her eyes limpid but expectant.

In that instant there came a frantic knocking on the barn door.

'What the devil!' exclaimed Haddon.

The face of Dilys the housemaid appeared round the door. Rain had plastered her hair to her brow below her cap. She was very wet indeed, her eyes anxious. 'If you please, sir, madam says she needs you to come at once, and Miss Madeleine. The fountain's full of bubbles – so's the duck pond!'

'Damn it!' roared Haddon. 'How dare you come down here? What the devil has the duck pond to do with me? Tell your mistress I will not be interrupted in this way! Tell her—' He broke off with an expletive and made for the door, brushing past the hapless maid. 'Stay here!' he commanded Madeleine.

Haddon strode up through the wet orchard and across the courtyard to the house, where he found Sonia in agitated conversation with the gardener.

'Damnation, Sonia, what d'you mean by sending maids down to my studio? I have expressly forbidden anyone to come there!'

'Henry, I simply cannot cope on my own with Avril! She's taken a whole box of soapflakes from the wash-house and emptied it into the fountain and the pond! It's made the most frightful mess! I tell you, it's too bad of you to take Madeleine away for hours on end when I need her here. I insist that you send her back up to the house. I need her!'

'*You insist?*' roared Haddon. 'I don't damn well care what you need or don't need! My work is more important than any damn duck pond or your inability to look after your own offspring! I am painting, woman! I am *working*! The girl stays there with me! Do you understand? And if you, or Dilys, or any other member of this benighted household so much as sets foot inside the door of my studio again today or any other day, then all hell will break loose! Is that clear?' And with that he turned and went out.

He went back through the rain to his studio, closed the big wooden door and paused for a moment to let his temper cool. He brushed the raindrops from his forehead, shook out the wet ends of his trouser legs, and strode around for a few moments, gathering his thoughts and some paint rags.

Madeleine was sitting waiting, holding her ribbon in her lap, watching the torrents of rain on the window. She moved roughly into position, but deliberately not quite correctly. Haddon moved forward to adjust the set of her shoulders, gently turning her torso into its pose. With his fingers he held her face, tilting her chin and arranging her hair over one shoulder. His touch was firm and delightful to Madeleine. She felt the familiar fire glowing in her loins, and spreading through all her limbs. She had a sudden, urgent longing for him to do more, touch her everywhere.

'Now, the dress – yes, let's see, the dress...'

Haddon tugged the bodice a little lower and, as he unfastened the buttons and adjusted the strap to its customary position on her shoulder, became aware of the girl's gaze fixed upon his face, inches away. Her lips were parted, and he felt the blood surge in his veins in sudden response. A moment passed, and he did nothing. Then, with his eyes still locked on hers, he traced his fingers experimentally downwards. Apart from a light shiver, she did not move, let alone resist. The rain drummed fiercely upon the roof of the barn. He slid his fingers inside the bodice of her dress and found the fullness of her breast. He was ready at any moment to be repulsed, but her gaze remained ardently fastened on his.

Suddenly, unexpectedly, she leaned forward and kissed him. He drew back, startled, but Madeleine, emboldened by what she had learned from Charles Asher yesterday, and filled with a new sense of her own power, found his mouth again. As they kissed, he cupped and fondled her breast, now fiercely aroused, and unfastened the remaining buttons of her dress with his other hand. His mind faltered at that moment – what if they were discovered? He thought of the scene which had just occurred at the house. No one would come down here now. They would not dare to. His conscience was too blurred by desire to feel any scruples. The girl was offering herself to him. He bent his head to kiss her breast.

Madeleine closed her eyes, a gasping moan escaping her, and grasped his shoulders. In that moment she had no idea whether she had meant to let things come this far. Instinct told her she should stop him, but the sensations flooding her body were too strong. The moment which had been interrupted in the woods the day before, the intense pleasure she knew awaited her, would be fulfilled now. It was what she wanted. Henry Haddon was what she wanted, the object of her love. She had never known that desire could be so powerful.

Haddon lifted her skirt, his mind ablaze, all thought or sense driven from it, and tugged her pants down. As he pushed himself into her, she gave a wincing cry, and her eyes flew open. For a moment he expected her to thrust him away and run screaming from the barn. But she merely paused for a moment, drew a deep breath, closed her eyes, and arched her back. He pushed into her further, over and over, with a deep, gentle rhythm. She let her head fall back, her hands still on his broad shoulders.

At last Haddon shuddered to his climax and withdrew. He bowed his head, panting. Madeleine didn't move. He picked up a paint rag to wipe himself, then pulled his trousers together. She put out a hand to him, but Haddon drew himself upright, suddenly aware, now that his lust was spent, of the folly of what he had just done. He felt a huge misgiving. He had seduced plenty of young women in his time, but this girl was under Sonia's nominal protection. She was not much more than a child.

Madeleine plucked her underpants from the floor and put them on. She glanced at Haddon, understanding a little of what he was feeling. She stood up and put a hand on his arm.

'Don't be angry with yourself. I wanted it. I wanted it more than anything.' Her voice was low and soft, and he turned to glance at her. God, she was lovely. She drew close to him, reached up and kissed him lightly. He closed his eyes briefly, then opened them to look at her, studying her expression, marvelling at the confidence, the trust of her smile as she added, 'I love you.'

He let out a ragged sigh. 'No, you don't love me.'

She kissed him again. 'I shall be here tomorrow. I shall be here as often as you want me.' With that, she left the studio.

In the hayloft, Avril kept very still. She had been still throughout it all. She had watched Papa undo Madeleine's buttons and kiss her, and then watched Papa crouching over her with his trousers unfastened, doing that pushing thing. She was completely puzzled by all she had seen, and scared, though she didn't know why. What she wanted most to do was to go down and cuddle Papa. He looked sad sitting in his chair. She wanted to sit on the ground next to him with her arm around his leg, the way she had at the picnic. But something told her Papa wouldn't want her there, not the way he had yesterday. Then it had been just her and Papa at the top of the hill, with all the fields and trees below them, Papa drawing and humming, and she sitting next to him, feeling safe and special. Why didn't he want her here? Why did he let Madeleine come here, and do those things with her? She didn't want Madeleine here in the barn. She didn't want Madeleine and Papa to be alone and playing games like the one she had just seen. Her throat went tight, and she wanted to cry, but she dared not make a sound.

After a few moments Haddon rose from his chair. He ranged around the studio, moving things in a distracted fashion, then gave up and went to the house. There he changed out of his wet clothes and went to his study, where he remained for the rest of the day.

Long after her father had left the studio Avril stayed crouched in the hayloft, the matted straw prickling her knees. She dared not go back to the house, too frightened by what she had just seen. She cried for a while, listening to the sound of her own whimpers and licking the salty snot from her upper lip. The rain was still coming down, drumming hard on the roof just above her head. She lay down on the straw and tried to think, but she didn't like the dark pictures in her head. She sat up, wondering what she should do. Then she realised that they would be looking for her, and they might come here and find her. And she knew, above all things, how angry Papa would be if he found out she had been hiding here all this time. So she got up, carefully brushing the little sticks of straw from her dress, and went down the ladder. She approached the canvas standing on the easel and stared at the portrait of Madeleine. It was so lovely, so sad and beautiful, that it made her want to touch it. In the painting Madeleine looked like she had a secret, like she had thoughts in her head which no one else could know, while she waited for the person she knew would never come.

Avril stood for a few moments, staring at the picture. Then she went to the barn door and peeped out to make sure there was no one about, and ran to the house, almost longing for the normality of people scolding her, hungry for her lunch.

By the end of the afternoon the storm had eased. The grey clouds began to drift away to reveal a blue, watery sky, and the earth was scented with rain. Only a few scummy bubbles now floated on the surface of the duck pond.

Avril and Madeleine had spent the rainy hours of the afternoon in the nursery playing board games and drawing. Madeleine's thoughts of what had happened in the barn ebbed and flowed, dwindling in the absorption of play, then suddenly flooding back to shock her with violent sensuality. She wanted to be on her own, to lie on her bed and close her eyes and replay it all, the gathering pleasure after the first shock of pain had subsided, the sweetness of being desired, the *fact* of Henry

Haddon making love to her. But Avril's chatter and demands kept her from herself. She longed for it to be night, when she could lie alone and relive the moment of possession.

The atmosphere in the house had a strangely fractured air. Sonia was conscious of it well before dinner. She went to her husband's study to speak to him about the leak in the summerhouse. Haddon was at his desk, bent over some books. After his failure to appear at lunch she was half afraid she might find him as ill-tempered as he had been that morning. Instead, he seemed distracted and inattentive.

'The rain has come through and quite soaked the chairs,' Sonia told him. 'I propose asking Lobb to move all the furniture until we can get the roof seen to, but that will mean storing it in the barn.'

'Roof? What roof?'

'The summerhouse,' said Sonia impatiently. 'It's leaking. We should have had it looked at months ago. I want to know if you'd mind having the furniture put in the studio to dry out. There really is nowhere else but I know how you hate having your workplace disturbed.'

He nodded. 'Very well. Put the furniture in the studio.'

Sonia, turning to go, hesitated. 'Are you quite well, Henry?'

'Yes, yes, I'm fine.'

'I think it's time you dressed for dinner. We'll be having drinks in half an hour.' She paused. 'By the way, I hope you won't need Madeleine for much longer – I'm finding Avril such a handful.'

'No,' said Haddon, after a moment. 'I don't need her now. The thing is finished.'

'That's a relief,' said Sonia, and left the room.

Haddon went to his dressing room. He meant what he'd just said. What had happened this morning was, even by his standards, beyond the pale. He had seduced parlourmaids in the past and thought little of it, but Madeleine – she might be a mere nanny, but she was in the house under his wife's protection, and wasn't much more than a girl. Yet such a girl! He recalled her face in those moments in the barn, the look in her eyes. The longer she remained, the greater the possibility that something further could occur. He didn't trust himself. Such temptation was more than he could stand. She would have to go, he decided, as he fastened his collar studs. He would speak to Sonia tonight.

The younger guests were moody and quiet as they assembled for drinks in the drawing room. Dan had spent much of the afternoon playing chess with Charles, which was regarded by Paul, in his determination to cast Charles in the role of blackguard, as a form of personal disloyalty. His manner this evening towards both men was chilly. The girls, too, were quiet, sitting in murmuring conversation by the window with their drinks, waiting for something – they knew not what – to happen.

Haddon, on coming in to the drawing room, was relieved to see that Madeleine wasn't there. He poured himself a whisky and soda, intending to conduct himself robustly and cheerfully, but almost immediately a mild enquiry by Dan as to the progress of his painting drew his nerves to the surface, and he made some sharp response which provoked an uneasy silence in the company.

Diana went to replenish her drink for the third time. She felt it might be an evening for getting a little tipsy, the atmosphere being so vile. That was the trouble with house parties; they so often went sour in the last couple of days.

As everyone took their seats at the dinner table, Sonia noticed that Madeleine's place was empty.

'I wonder where she can have got to?' she murmured. 'I'd best go and see. Please, everyone, do begin.'

'I wouldn't blame her if she didn't care for the company this evening,' remarked Paul, 'after all that's happened.' He glanced meaningfully at Charles.

A few moments later Sonia returned to the dining room. 'She doesn't want to come down to dinner.'

'Is she unwell?' asked Meg, who was thinking what all the

younger guests were thinking – that things might really have gone too far yesterday, further than anyone had realised.

'She's fine – she's playing snakes and ladders with Avril.'

Haddon, who a few seconds ago had had a ghastly vision of a regretful, distraught Madeleine making a weeping confession to his wife, relaxed.

Diana, who had drained a glass of wine directly on sitting down, decided she would not be bored this evening, and threw in a conversational squib.

'So, tell us, Charles, when do you plan to travel to Spain?'

'To Spain?' asked Sonia in surprise.

'To fight against the Republicans – it is the Republicans, isn't it, Charles?'

Paul laughed. 'I hardly think he's going to be fighting on the side of Franco. I hope he's got that much clear, at any rate.'

Diana shrugged. 'There's so much about it in the papers, how can I be expected to follow it all?'

'Spoken like a true female,' observed her brother. 'Nonetheless, you might trouble yourself to understand some of it, if you're going to talk about it at the dinner table. There's a wealth of information available that even you could understand.'

'So much is written about foreign affairs these days,' sighed Sonia, 'that one feels not so much enlightened as in a perpetual state of crisis.' She glanced at Charles. 'But now, tell me, Charles, is this true? Do you really propose to travel to Spain to fight? I can hardly believe it.'

Charles nodded. 'I regard it as my intellectual and moral responsibility.'

Paul gave a snort of derision, and Charles eyed him coldly.

'Responsibility!' exclaimed Elizabeth Cunliffe. 'What about responsibility to your poor mother?'

Sonia shook her head. 'I think all wars are very wrong. I agree with Mr Huxley on that.'

'Huxley may be a pacifist,' replied Charles, 'but he recognises the threat of totalitarianism. As do I. It's because I can identify very closely with the persecuted and oppressed that I want to do my part. The struggle belongs not just to Spain – it's worldwide.'

'You mean you'd like to see the Left gaining control of Spain – and of the whole world eventually. That's the Communist agenda, isn't it?' asked Paul. 'Overthrow the forces of law and order and impose the rule of the mob.'

'Naturally, Latimer, you're afraid of anything which might threaten your privileged way of life,' retorted Charles. 'Perhaps you haven't the humanity to see that the war in Spain is about more than mere politics. It's about morality and social justice. Possibly those are concepts you don't readily understand.'

Haddon intervened to deflect the growing hostility. 'A righteous war? Is that what you imagine it to be? If so, you're sadly mistaken, my young friend. All wars are wicked, and a righteous war is only one degree less wicked. Take my advice and stay at home.'

'If Charles wishes to go to Spain and get himself shot, then let him,' observed Paul calmly. 'The fewer Communists the better, I say.'

'Paul, don't be so foul!' said Diana. 'I think going off to fight is a noble and rather romantic thing to do.'

'You would.'

'Well, I don't,' said Meg. 'I think it's beastly. I can't think why anyone would want to be a soldier, whatever the cause. Not if they could be a writer.'

'Or a poet,' added Sonia who, in her position as hostess, felt that it might be diplomatic to switch to a more innocuous subject. She turned to Gerald Cunliffe. 'Did you read, Gerald, about that speech which Baldwin gave last month in Cambridge, calling on the universities to produce more poets?'

Cunliffe dabbed his mouth with his napkin. 'I did. Though why on earth anyone would want to be a poet nowadays, I can't think. It hardly pays enough to keep a man in tobacco.'

The conversation moved into calmer waters, but a certain

tension remained. A pity, thought Sonia, on everyone's last night, but probably the house party had gone on long enough. She had found the last few days, what with Madeleine spirited away to the studio for hours on end, extremely trying. It was a relief to know that wretched portrait was finished.

After a couple of rubbers of bridge the Haddons and the Cunliffes decided to go to bed, as the Cunliffes were catching an early train the next morning. They left the girls listening to the wireless, and Dan, Charles and Paul engaged in a somewhat moody game of cards, which Dan had suggested in a half-hearted attempt to cure the bad atmosphere.

As Sonia sat at her dressing table, her hair unpinned, taking off her jewellery, her husband came and stood behind her. She smiled at his reflection in the mirror, and he picked up one of Sonia's brushes and began to brush her hair with long, slow strokes. It was something he hadn't done in a long time.

'I want to talk to you about that girl,' said Haddon.

Sonia paused in the act of removing an earring. 'Which girl?'

'The Fenton girl. Madeleine.'

'Now, Henry, don't ask me for more of her time. I need her here at the house. Besides, you said you were finished with her.'

Haddon said nothing for a few seconds, continuing to brush her hair. 'I don't think she should go on living here.'

Sonia's eyes widened. 'What *can* you mean, Henry?'

Haddon laid down the brush and turned away. 'What I say. She should go.'

'Oh, don't be absurd. I promised Olive I would look after her.' She paused, then turned to gaze anxiously at her husband. 'Why? Has she done something? Is there something I should know?'

'Of course not. But I think it's about time Avril had a proper governess.'

'A governess? Henry, she's hardly—' Sonia broke off at the sound of a commotion and shouting in the garden below. 'Gracious heavens! What on earth is going on?'

Both of them went to the window and Haddon flung it open.

Below them, outlined by the light from the drawing room, two figures struggled on the grass. The girls stood nearby, shrieking at them to stop.

'My God,' said Haddon, 'it's Latimer and that Asher fellow – fighting!'

'Oh, good Lord, make them stop!' exclaimed Sonia. She hastily pulled on a robe and went downstairs. By the time she got there, Dan was endeavouring to separate the pair, who were grappling fiercely. Paul seemed to have landed a couple of telling blows, for Charles's nose was bloodied and one eye was closing up.

'Get off him, man!' shouted Dan. 'Paul, for God's sake – that's enough!'

Paul allowed himself to be dragged away from his opponent. Charles sat there on the dewy grass, his thick hair over his eyes, wiping the blood from his nose with the back of his hand.

Sonia stood in horror, her hands over her mouth. Haddon had by this time made his way down to the garden.

'What do you two mean by brawling like this?' he demanded.

Charles, breathing heavily, got to his feet. 'He accused me of cheating at cards – and he insulted me.'

'You're beneath insult!' Paul pushed his hair out of his eyes and straightened his jacket.

'That's enough!' said Haddon. 'I don't care to hear the reasons. I suggest you both come inside and have a brandy, and apologise.'

They trooped through the French windows and into the drawing room. Paul, eyes still blazing, accepted the brandy that Haddon poured for him, and swiftly knocked it back.

Charles declined the brandy. 'Thank you, I won't. I think it's best if I go and clean myself up and get to bed.' He turned to Sonia. 'I apologise for my behaviour, Mrs Haddon. I lost my temper and acted unforgivably. You didn't deserve this, after all your kindness.'

'My dear boy, I'm just concerned for your eye. It looks so painful. Can't we put something on it?'

'I'm sure I'll be fine.'

'No, I insist. Come with me.'

Charles turned to Haddon. 'I apologise to you, too, sir. Goodnight.' He left the room with Sonia.

There was a silence.

'I must say I'm surprised at you, Paul,' said Haddon. 'You and Mr Asher may not see eye to eye on many matters, but I don't take kindly to fighting in my house.'

'As I didn't strike the first blow...' Paul frowned and stopped. 'Naturally, I apologise. It's just the fellow has done things that I can't abide in any man.'

'Oh?'

The room was hushed. Dan, Meg, Eve and Diana were silently willing Paul to say nothing more, but he went on. 'That young woman – Madeleine. When we' – he glanced at the others – 'when we were in the woods, during the picnic the other day, we found her and Asher together in a somewhat compromising situation. It's evident that he was, to say the least of it, taking advantage of her. I've had a pretty low opinion of him since then, and I'm afraid tonight my feelings rather got the better of me. I'm sorry.'

Haddon's expression was inscrutable. After a moment he said, 'Whatever your feelings, I don't think it justifies the kind of behaviour you both exhibited this evening.'

At that moment Sonia returned to the room. 'Charles has gone to bed. I suggest we all forget this unpleasantness and do the same.'

People drifted out of the room, murmuring goodnight. Dan stayed behind to finish a cigarette. Meg began to gather up the scattered playing cards. After a moment she sat down on the sofa with a sigh.

'Are you OK?' asked Dan.

'Yes, I'm fine. It was just rather horrible. I hate to see people fighting like that.'

'They're a couple of damned fools,' said Dan. He took a last drag from his cigarette and put it out. He stood for a moment, his hands in his pockets, then crossed the room and sat down next to her.

Meg could feel her heart beating very hard as she shuffled the cards. Dan leaned back against the sofa cushions and watched as she dealt out a game of patience.

Meg felt she must break the silence. 'Not a very pleasant end to your stay.'

'Oh, I don't know,' said Dan. 'This is rather nice. Sitting here with you.' He put out a hand and stroked her hair. She gazed at the cards, mechanically turning them out in little bundles of three.

'Red five,' said Dan. He lifted her hair to one side and began to stroke her neck. Meg gave a little shiver of pleasure. She closed her eyes and sat very still, lips parted, concentrating on the sensation of his fingers on her skin. Dan wondered if perhaps he wasn't in with a chance after all, on this, the very last night of the house party. As he gazed at the sloping curve of her shoulders, the softness of her dark hair, the lashes of her closed eyes, a feeling suddenly swept over him that was more than mere desire, unlike anything he had ever experienced before. For reasons he couldn't define, he wanted the moment, the game of patience, the room, the fact of her, here with him, to go on for ever.

The door opened and Paul put his head round. Dan drew his hand away.

'How about a game of billiards before turning in?' Paul glanced at Meg. 'Care to come and keep score, Meg?'

Meg began to gather the playing cards together clumsily. 'No, thanks all the same. I'm off to bed.'

By the time Paul and Dan finished their game of billiards, it was almost half eleven. Paul went upstairs, and Dan wandered through the drawing room and on to the terrace to finish his brandy and smoke a last cigarette before turning in. The night sky was clear and the moon almost full. The garden was awash with shadow and silver, and Dan leaned on the stone balustrade, breathing in the night air and ruminating on the events of the last two weeks. A pity Paul had spoiled that promising moment between him and Meg an hour ago. Just as he was wondering whether it might not be worth going up to Meg's room and tapping on her door again, someone switched on a lamp in the drawing room behind him. Dan turned and saw Eve standing by the French windows, clad in a mauve silk kimono, her black hair loose about her shoulders, an unlit cigarette between her fingers.

'I see I'm not the only one who can't sleep,' she said.

'Can't say I've tried yet,' replied Dan. He left the terrace and came into the drawing room, and picked up a lighter from a side table and lit her cigarette for her.

Eve blew out a plume of smoke. 'Thanks.' She nodded at his brandy glass. 'I think I could do with one, too.'

Dan went to the drinks tray and poured her a small snifter of brandy. She sat down on the sofa and Dan sat down next to her, loosening his black tie.

'Quite a night.'

Eve sipped her brandy. 'Actually, I'm surprised nothing has happened before now. According to Diana Paul can't stand Charles Asher, and the business with the nanny was the last straw.'

'Well, that's rather the point. It wasn't his business.'

'I suppose one should be prepared for a positive barrage of sex hormones flying about during a house party. It does build up a peculiar kind of heat, wouldn't you say?'

'Can't say I've noticed,' replied Dan, thinking how right she was.

'Of course you have.' Eve smiled and leaned back against the cushions, the folds of her kimono parting slightly, revealing the pale curve of her breast. 'For instance, in a situation like this, wouldn't it be wonderful if two people who are mutually attracted could reach some kind of an arrangement and just...' she paused, 'make the most of it?'

Just as she was sliding her hand on to his thigh, the drawing-room door opened. Eve swiftly removed her hand, closed her robe and picked up her brandy glass.

It was one of the housemaids. She hesitated in the doorway. 'Beg pardon, sir, ma'am. Mr Haddon asked me to lock up. I need to close the windows.' She gestured towards the terrace.

'I'm sure we can attend to those,' said Eve.

Dan got to his feet. 'No, you go ahead, Dilys. Miss Meyerson and I are just off to bed.'

Eve put out her cigarette, drained her brandy, and rose. She and Dan left the drawing room together. They mounted the staircase in silence. When they reached the landing, Eve put out her hand. Her fingers felt cool and light in his. When he kissed her, it held none of the depth or tenderness of kissing Meg, but the sensuality and promise of pleasure were enough. He slipped his hands beneath her robe and found her naked body. He thought momentarily, regretfully, of Meg and her delightful innocence, and wished he could try, for her sake, to be a better person.

'Your room or mine?' he murmured.

Eve smiled. 'Mine's closer.'

He followed her along the corridor, slipped into her room behind her, and locked the door.

6

DAN WOKE LATE the following morning, and when he went downstairs he found only Sonia and Diana in the breakfast room.

'So sorry I'm late.'

'I'm sure we all needed a good sleep after last night's excitement,' said Sonia.

Dan helped himself to kedgeree from one of the silver chafing dishes and sat down.

'How's Paul this morning?' he asked Diana.

'Oh, fine. Not a mark on him. Poor Charles came off worst. He's already left, apparently.'

Sonia nodded over her teacup. 'He decided to catch the same train as the Cunliffes. Very diplomatic, in the circumstances.' She rose from her chair. 'Do excuse me. I have a few things to attend to. I hope I shall see you all before you go.'

Avril and Madeleine were in the nursery, tidying up the toys on Sonia's instructions. Madeleine was telling Avril a story as they did so. Avril squatted by the dolls' house, straightening the rooms, listening.

'But why did the princess let her father lock her up in a tower?'

'She had no choice. She was a king's daughter and she had to do as he said. Anyway, he thought he was protecting her.'

'I wouldn't have let him lock me in a tower. I'd have kicked and screamed. *And* I'd've bitten him. Very, very hard. Really, *really* hard. Right on the arm. Like this.' She sank her own small teeth into her forearm, then drew back to inspect the mark she had left. She showed it to Madeleine, who nodded, and then stood up.

Avril looked up at her. 'Where are you going?'

'I've just remembered something I have to do. You stay here. I shan't be long.'

'But you haven't finished the story.'

'I'll finish it later.'

Avril feigned absorption in the dolls' house until Madeleine had left the room. Then she went out and crept down the passage towards Madeleine's bedroom. The door stood a little ajar and, peeping in, Avril could see Madeleine. She was changing her dress. She was changing into that yellow sundress, the one she wore when she went to Papa's studio.

As quiet as a mouse in her plimsolls, Avril went downstairs and out of the house, and ran through the orchard to the studio. She was ready to be chased away by Papa if he was already there, but when she pushed open the big, creaking door, the barn was empty. She hurried to the ladder and climbed up to the hayloft. There in the fragrant dark she waited, excited and fearful.

Haddon fought against the idea of going to the studio. After his determination that Madeleine should leave the house – though that was still an unfinished conversation with Sonia – it would be beyond foolish to allow the events of yesterday to be repeated. Yet, as he had always known he would, he went. He passed through the orchard, noting the fullness of the fruit and the tinge of autumn in the air, pretending on some false, careless level that he had no other purpose in mind than to put the finishing touches to the painting. He pretended, too, that the question of whether she would come or not didn't even enter his mind. He felt like two people, one aware of the other's lies, unable to prevent them or their consequences.

In the studio he cleaned his brushes and tidied various props and artefacts. She wouldn't come. He let this certainty take shape with the passing minutes, and pretended he would be relieved if it were so. Then he heard the door open and looked up, dry-mouthed, to see Madeleine come in. She came straight to him, and with the frankness of desire put her arms around his neck and kissed him.

The softness of her mouth and the swell of her young breasts against his body caused his heart to jump, almost to lurch, and then he was aware of it beating thickly and painfully, with a sensation of fullness that was not entirely pleasant.

'I couldn't stop thinking about you,' she murmured. Taking his hand, she placed it beneath her skirt, between her legs, and he realised she was wearing no underwear. He fell against her, moving her back against the wall of the studio, and she gave a soft gasp of satisfaction and pleasure as he spread her legs and began to unfasten his trousers.

Above them, hidden in the darkness of the hayloft, Avril watched.

It struck Dan, after he had finished his packing, that it was a pity he hadn't taken up Haddon's invitation to visit him again in his studio. He had enjoyed the conversation that first day; he should go down now and say farewell and thank him for his hospitality. He sauntered across the courtyard and through the orchard.

When he reached the barn, Dan knocked as he had done on that first day. There was no reply, so Dan opened the door. The sight of Haddon and Madeleine together against the wall of the studio was the last thing he had expected. They turned and saw him, and immediately Haddon moved away, pulling up his trousers. Whatever might have been said or done by any one of them in that moment, all possibilities were swept aside by a sudden scraping sound; the three of them looked up and saw the ladder to the hayloft toppling sideways in a slow arc. It came crashing to the floor, catching the edge of one of the tables and sending pots and brushes flying. There at the edge of the loft crouched Avril, peering down. She began to cry. No one quite knew what to do.

Haddon shouted something at his daughter, and went to seize the ladder from the floor, trying to lift it. Dazed by the whole bizarre scenario, Dan went to help. Madeleine took the opportunity to hurry out of the barn. Between them, Haddon and Dan managed to prop the ladder against the edge of the hayloft, where Avril stood screaming and crying.

'There, I've got it,' said Dan, steadying the ladder. 'You can get down now,' he said to Avril. 'Come on.'

But Avril backed away from the edge, wailing.

Haddon stood panting in the middle of the floor. 'Get down!' he roared. 'Get down here now!'

'I say, steady on—' began Dan. He stopped, because Haddon suddenly winced and staggered, then keeled over on to the floor. 'Oh, dear God,' muttered Dan. He abandoned the ladder and knelt down, gazing anxiously at Haddon's prone figure, trying to remember what little first aid he knew.

Avril's crying faded to a whimper. She climbed down the ladder and stared at her father. He was groaning, making puffing noises, and his mouth was a strange colour. Dan turned to her. 'Run up to the house and get your mother! Get anyone! Tell them we need a doctor. Go on – run!'

Terrified, but obedient for once, Avril scampered out of the barn.

Dan tried to hoist Haddon into a sitting position, assuring him help was coming. Haddon sat breathing painfully for a while, then he reached up and grasped Dan's lapel with one shaking hand. His face was beaded with sweat, and he was trying to say something, but the words seemed to choke him. His grip on Dan's jacket slackened, his breath grew shallow, and his eyes dimmed. His body went slack and fell sideways on to the dusty studio floor.

'Christ and damnation!' muttered Dan. He put a hand to

Haddon's neck but could feel no pulse. He stood up, running his hands through his hair in desperation. He looked around and saw the broken easel and the fallen canvas. In a pathetic attempt at least to set something right, he picked up the canvas, which was lying face down, wiped away fragments of dirt and dust, and set it with its face to the wall. He gathered together the broken easel. Haddon lay on his back, his sightless, staring gaze fixed on the high beams of the barn. After a moment Dan knelt down, put out a hand and closed his eyelids.

After she had told everyone, and they had all run from the house to the barn, Avril didn't know what to do. She didn't want to go back down there. So she went up to the nursery. She crept behind the big, wooden rocking horse and sat huddled there. Images of all the things she had seen flapped in her mind like dark shadows, like the wings of a big black bird. She pictured the bird strutting and scratching across her brain, the way the crows did on the roof sometimes. She wanted to beat the bird away, make it fly off. She squeezed her eyes shut and told herself that if she tried to forget everything about Madeleine and Papa and the ladder and every other horrid thing, it would fly away. She would push out the thoughts, she would never again let them creep across the edge of her brain, the place where the rest of the world stopped and her own mind began. Never, ever. After a long moment she opened her eyes and let out a breath. There. The bird had lifted its wings and flapped away, and it would never come back. She sat listening to the commotion in the house far below, all the commotion about Papa, and it was some time before anyone thought to come and find her.

The shock of Henry Haddon's death spread quickly throughout the house. None of the guests knew the neighbourhood, or who to call, and it fell to Meg to pull together the disparate strands of the fractured household and weave some kind of order. She rang the doctor to attend to Sonia, who was too shocked and distraught to deal with anything, then called the undertaker, and attended to various necessary domestic rearrangements. The rest of them were mere bystanders, uncertain, in the face of this appalling tragedy, whether to stay or go.

After the undertaker's men had brought Haddon's body up to the house, Sonia retreated to her sitting room. In the moments when Dan caught glimpses of Madeleine, as members of the household moved around in a state of panic and uncertainty, she was careful not to meet his eye.

Charles's earlier departure meant there was a spare seat in the Wolseley, and having accepted Paul's offer of a lift back to London, Dan went upstairs to put his things together. When he had finished packing, he went to close the bedroom window and saw Madeleine and Avril sitting by the edge of the fountain in the courtyard below. He watched Madeleine pluck moss from between the stones and crumble it into the pond. Bubbles appeared on the surface of the water as fish gathered greedily, thinking the moss was food. Avril said something, and Madeleine nodded.

Questions crowded Dan's mind. Had Avril, hiding in the loft, seen what he had seen? And if so, what could she possibly have made of it, at her age? Was Madeleine swearing the child to silence? The idea seemed far-fetched. If Avril had seen her father and Madeleine together, it had probably made no sense to her. The sight of her father gasping his last breath would probably eclipse every other memory. But maybe Avril had said something to her mother about Madeleine being in the studio. What would be made of that, once the immediate tragedy of Henry Haddon's death subsided and surrounding events came into perspective? The events of the morning lay on his mind like a heavy weight, one he didn't know how to shift. That Haddon had been a lecherous old goat was a commonplace – but Madeleine was no more than a girl, the daughter of his wife's friend, and someone in his charge and care. Even to Dan's cynical turn of mind, it was a bit much. If others were to find out, it would mean misery all round. He would rather not have been the repository of such deadly knowledge.

As he took his case downstairs, a small figure emerged from the shadow of the staircase. It was Avril.

'Hello, Avril.'

She searched his face with her eyes for a few seconds. She really had a most uncomfortably penetrating gaze. He crouched down to bring himself to her level. She might be tiresome, but she was still only a little child, and had seen things that morning no child should. He asked gently, 'Shouldn't Madeleine be looking after you?'

'I don't want to be with her.'

'Why?'

'I just don't.' She kicked at the newel post with her plimsolled foot.

'Avril...' Dan hesitated, 'did you tell anyone about Madeleine being in the barn this morning?'

Avril stared at him, her mouth turning down as though she might cry, then shook her head. At that moment, Meg came out of Sonia's room, closing the door gently behind her. Dan stood up, and Avril made for the door. 'I want to see Mama.'

'Not now, darling,' said Meg gently, stopping the child. 'Go up to the nursery. I'm sure Madeleine must be looking for you. You can see Mama later.'

Avril looked darkly from Meg to Dan, then turned and ran upstairs.

'How's Sonia?' asked Dan.

'In a pretty dreadful way. I can't imagine what she's going through.'

There was a pause, then Dan asked, 'Will I see you in London?'

'I honestly don't know when I'll be back. I rather think Aunt Sonia will need me here for a while.'

He nodded, then reached into his jacket pocket to find paper and pen. He scribbled down his address and office telephone number. 'Here. Give me a ring when you get back. In the meantime, I might drop you a line, let you know how things are in the teeming metropolis.'

'I'd like that. I think things are going to be pretty miserable here for a while.'

'I can imagine.'

Meg glanced up as Paul, Diana and Eve came down the staircase with their luggage. 'Oh, here are the others. I'll tell Aunt Sonia.'

Sonia emerged from her sitting room to say goodbye, overwrought but dignified, determined to take a proper farewell of her guests. In saying his goodbyes, Paul offered a short, gracious tribute to their lately departed host, which Dan had to admit was nicely judged, if rather pompous. But when Paul took his leave of Meg, holding her hand for just a little too long, and then a moment later glancing back at her with a smile of affection, Dan felt an unpleasant and unaccustomed smart of jealousy. It was a pity he hadn't made greater headway with her, but in a way he didn't mind. Last night Eve had provided the perfect short-term distraction. Meg presented a more interesting long-term challenge.

The preparations for the funeral lent Woodbourne House a bleak vitality, keeping Sonia and Meg and the servants busy right up until the day itself – a day unfittingly bright and soft – but in the weeks that followed, after guests and friends had long departed and the great man himself lay stiff and cold in the ground, a deadness fell upon the house. Meg had hitherto assumed that Sonia, whose taste and influence spoke in every room, whose domestic authority directed very meal and social event, was the essence of Woodbourne. But now that her uncle was gone, she realised that it was he who had been its heart and restless soul. Without his existence, nothing mattered. All Sonia's efforts to make Woodbourne House a charming and restful place in which to live, and to keep it running smoothly, had been for the sole purpose of nourishing her husband's spirit, so that he could work without distraction or worry. After his death, she scarcely seemed to care what happened in the house from one day to the next.

'Grief takes some people that way,' observed Mrs Goodall to Meg, on one of Meg's frequent visits to the kitchen, where at least there was warmth and activity, as opposed the bleak inertia of the rest of the house. Sonia had already had dust sheets draped over the furniture in the guest bedrooms and some of the reception rooms, giving the house a chilly, deserted atmosphere.

'I would have thought she might take some comfort in spending time with Avril,' said Meg. 'But she hardly sees anything of her.' She watched Mrs Goodall chopping the leaves from a bunch of carrots, in preparation for peeling them. 'Oh, please let me do that. I like to be busy.'

'On you go, then.' Mrs Goodall handed her the knife. 'I know what you're saying, but Miss Avril's not the easiest of children.'

'Perhaps not, but she's Aunt Sonia's daughter, and she must love her. If my husband died, and I had a daughter, I would want to spend all my time with her.' Meg bit off a piece of carrot.

'Well, like I say, she'll come round.' Mrs Goodall began to weigh out flour and butter for pastry. She gave Meg a glance. 'I would have thought you'd have been back to London before now. Not much of a life for you here.'

That was certainly true. Although Meg was glad to have been of help to Sonia, the last few weeks had been stultifying. It was already mid-October, and the thought of watching autumn slide into winter in the depths of Surrey was far from appealing. The letters she received from friends in London made her feel almost as though she was living on another, distant planet.

'What I always say—'

But Mrs Goodall's next remark would remain forever unuttered, for at that moment Sonia appeared in the kitchen, telegram in hand, more animated than she had been in some time.

'Meg, I will need you to drive Madeleine to the station. The sanatorium have telegrammed to say that her mother is... well, I think she is very near the end. I have been so thoughtless. The poor girl has not been once to visit since Henry died, though she must have been longing to. But of course, she wouldn't ask, knowing I needed her here.'

Meg laid down the knife. 'Of course I'll take her. What time's the train?'

'There's one at eleven twenty. Then when she gets to London she'll have to get another train from – oh, I don't know which station. But she's made the journey before. I must give her money for her ticket. Should I go with her, do you suppose? I really don't think I can.' Sonia was flustered, gazing anxiously from Mrs Goodall to Meg.

'Madeleine can manage the journey perfectly well,' Meg reassured her. 'As you say, she's done it before.' She hesitated. 'Does she realise that her mother might be...?'

'The telegram was addressed to her, so, yes, she does. Poor thing.'

Sonia began to cry softly, her hand pressed to her brow. Mrs Goodall ushered her to a chair. 'You sit down, madam, and I'll make some tea.'

Meg went upstairs and found Madeleine in her room next to the nursery, packing the small suitcase with which she had arrived at Woodbourne House six months earlier. Meg could see from her red eyes that she had been crying, but she seemed calm now as she folded her clothes.

'Sonia told me about your mother,' said Meg. 'I'm awfully sorry. I'll run you to the station.'

'Thanks.'

There was an uncomfortable silence. Meg and Madeleine had never really been friends, not for want of trying on Meg's part, but because Madeleine had never known quite how to respond to Meg's overtures. She found the older girl's easy, confident demeanour attractive, yet at the same time intimidating.

Avril appeared in the doorway, and saw Madeleine packing. 'Where is Madeleine going?'

'She's going to visit her mummy,' said Meg gently. 'And I'm going to take you down to see *your* mummy. Come on.' She took Avril's hand, adding over her shoulder to Madeleine, 'I'll bring the car round.'

It would be no bad thing, Meg reflected as she took Avril downstairs, for Avril and her mother to spend time together over the next few days. Sonia's grief had been so self-centred that Meg suspected she had given scarcely any thought to Avril's own loss of her father.

'You must call me,' Sonia told Madeleine. 'And if for whatever reason things don't go well with your grandmother, remember I am always here.'

'Where will you stay?' asked Meg, as they drove to Malton station.

'With my grandmother, perhaps.' Madeleine's voice sounded remote, wistful. She glanced out at the passing fields and hedgerows. 'I've only met her once. She was there the last time I visited Mother. It was the first time she'd seen my mother since I was born.'

Meg wondered what it was like to know that you were the source of your own mother's shame, the reason why her family had cut off all contact. She could not imagine such isolation.

In the evening Meg and Sonia were sitting listening to the wireless, Meg with her sewing, Sonia toying with a jigsaw which she seemed to have been doing for ever, when the telephone rang.

Dilys put her head round the door. 'Telephone call for you, ma'am.'

Sonia rose and went to the hall. She reappeared a few moments later. 'That was Mrs Cole, Madeleine's grandmother. Madeleine's mother died an hour ago.' She sank into her chair. 'It was to be expected, but dreadful nonetheless. Poor Olive. She didn't have the happiest of lives.'

'What will happen to Madeleine?' asked Meg.

'Mrs Cole is taking her to live with her. If only she'd done more for her daughter while she was alive.' Sonia sighed. 'I've grown fond of Madeleine. I hope she will visit sometimes. Avril will miss her. And of course, I shall have to find a new nanny.'

'I don't mind staying on till you find someone.'

Although she was itching to get back to her family and friends in London, Meg reasoned that it couldn't take long to find a new nanny. A fortnight at the outside.

'Thank you, my dear,' said Sonia. 'I'll set about finding someone first thing tomorrow.' She glanced at her watch. 'Do turn the wireless up a little. There's a rather nice concert coming on in a few minutes.'

Meg turned up the volume. The fact that her aunt had been reading the *Radio Times* was a good sign. Perhaps Mrs Goodall was right. At any rate, she liked to think her aunt would cope perfectly well after she was gone, which could not, surely, be long from now.

7

FOLLOWING HENRY HADDON'S death, Paul made regular visits to Woodbourne House. He came ostensibly to see Sonia and to assist her with matters concerning her late husband's estate, but it was plain to Sonia that it was Meg he came to see. On his third visit, when he offered to take both Sonia and Meg out to lunch, Sonia declined, saying that she had correspondence to catch up on, but that Meg must go. Paul drove Meg to the pub in the village, where they lunched on steak pie and beer. Afterwards they took a walk through the woods that skirted the village. Meg was delighted to have Paul all to herself, but was acutely conscious of feeling like a child in his company – he seemed so much a man of the world.

'Lord,' said Paul, 'it's good to get away from London. The air is so much better, you know, and the people are friendlier.' He breathed in the autumn air with deep appreciation. 'As a matter of fact, I've been thinking for a while about getting a place in the country – Berkshire probably. Somewhere like Copley Hall.'

'That was a wonderful house,' said Meg, remembering countless childhood visits to Paul and Diana's home.

'It was an ideal place to grow up in. I was sorry when Father sold it after Mother died, though it was understandable. Berkshire is a first-rate county, and I'd like to live there again.'

'You sound as though you're thinking of settling down,' said Meg, her heart lurching a little at the thought of Paul marrying some society beauty and setting up house on a splendid estate.

'Well, I've led a pretty free and easy existence the past few years. About time I started taking life seriously.'

'What do you intend to do?'

'At the moment I'm setting up a racing car business. It's always been an enthusiasm of mine, and I'm hoping the investment will pay off. We're designing a prototype, and I'm trying to find a good driver. I need to get an understanding of business, something to stand me in good stead when I eventually enter Parliament.'

'It all sounds terribly grown-up,' said Meg. 'I can't say I feel remotely grown-up.'

'Well, you are. You have to start thinking about what you want from life.'

'Oh, I suppose I want the same things most girls do. A home, a husband, children. Just to be content.'

'You deserve all those things, and you deserve to be supremely happy,' said Paul, ruffling her hair lightly, then slipping his arm through hers in a brotherly fashion.

'I'm not sure I'm very deserving of anything. I'm just longing to get back to London. That's the only future I'm contemplating right now. As soon as Sonia finds a new nanny for Avril, I shall be back like a shot.' Suddenly a clump of wild mushrooms at the base of a tree caught her eye. 'Look!' She stooped to gather a handful. 'I say, Cook will be pleased with these. I've never seen so many in one place. I wish I had something to put them in.'

'I'd be careful if I were you. You can't be sure they're safe to eat.'

'Yes, I can,' replied Meg, pleased for a change to know more than Paul. 'These are wood mushrooms. Have a sniff.' She held one up to Paul, who smelt it dubiously.

'Smells of aniseed.'

'Exactly. And they're quite delicious. Now, hand me your cap. I want to gather as many as I can.'

*

While Meg and Paul were carrying their harvested mushrooms back to Mrs Goodall, Dan was making his way back to his office from a rather tame Cork Street exhibition of watercolour seascapes to write up his review. He felt mildly depressed. Was he really destined to spend the rest of his life earning a few measly quid a week writing up the work of 'safe' society artists? The smaller arts magazines were happy to publish his pieces on avant-garde artists and writers, but they paid next to nothing.

He glanced up at the heavy sky; spots of rain had begun to fall. Fingering the small change in the pocket of his raincoat, he decided to cheer himself up with a cup of coffee in one of his regular Covent Garden haunts before going back to the office.

He was sitting by the steamy café window with his coffee and a reflective cigarette, when a familiar figure came hurrying in out of the rain.

Dan raised a hand. 'Harry!'

Harry Denholm returned Dan's salute and came over. He shrugged off his tweed overcoat.

'Blasted thundercloud!' He sat down, running his fingers through his hair to shake off the raindrops, then raised a finger to a passing waiter. 'Coffee, please, Marco – black.'

He was a tall, barrel-chested man, a few years older than Dan, with coarse pudgy features, and thick hair worn long over his collar. Although not conventionally handsome, the playful intelligence of his eyes and his dark, drawling voice lent him surprising charm, and he wore his clothes with a style that more expensively dressed men could only envy.

'So, how's tricks?' asked Harry. 'Don't usually find you in here at this time of day.'

'I'm on my way back from a putrid exhibition of watercolours. I have to write a review for Tuesday's arts page. To be honest, I can't think of a single original thing to say.'

'I'm hardly surprised. Why don't you chuck that lousy job and come and work for me?'

Harry was the proprietor and editor of a liberal arts magazine called *Ire*, which brought to the attention of its limited circle of readers the work of experimental poets, writers, painters and sculptors, whose creations might never otherwise receive any critical consideration, and who were mainly friends of Harry's. It brought in little or no money, so it was as well that Harry had a small private income on which he managed to live precariously.

'Because I need to earn a living,' replied Dan. 'You still haven't paid me for the piece on Oskar Fischinger that I wrote for you last June.'

Harry rubbed his chin. 'Haven't I? I'll ask accounts to chase it up.'

Dan gave a wry smile. Harry ran the magazine from a room above a bookshop in Brewer Street and was its editor, features writer, art, theatre, film and book critic rolled into one. His frequent reference to 'accounts', when harried by unpaid contributors, was one of those happy little fictions by which he hoped to deceive people into believing the enterprise possessed greater substance than it did.

Harry's coffee arrived, and he plucked three sugar lumps from the bowl on the table and dropped them in one by one.

'How's Laurence?' asked Dan. Laurence, a twenty-four-year-old artist, was Harry's lover.

Harry's head drooped slightly; he stared into his coffee as he stirred it. 'He's gone off to fight in Spain. Never picked up a gun in his life, but thinks because he can speak Spanish he might be of some use.' His voice was bleak. 'Of course what's happening there is appalling, people being destroyed just for wanting a better way of life. But why does anyone here think they have to make it their fight? Fascism's a dirty thing, but in my view we should leave it to the Spaniards to sort their own mess out.'

'I know someone who was idiotic enough to go out, too,' said Dan, thinking of Charles Asher, and wondered how he was faring. 'I hope Laurence comes safe home. I hope they all do.'

Harry picked up Dan's cigarette from the ashtray and used it to light his own. He fished in the inside of his overcoat pocket and produced a rolled-up magazine. 'Have a look at this. French journalist friend gave it to me yesterday.' He unfurled the magazine, *Vu*, flicked to a page, and placed it before Dan. 'I look at that picture and think – that might be Laurence, if he's careless, or unlucky. Frankly, Dan, old boy, I'm terrified. Terrified.'

Dan gazed at the photo. It accompanied a piece in French about the Spanish Civil War, and was of a fighter clad in canvas trousers, braces over an open-necked, short-sleeve shirt, who had clearly been shot, caught in the awful moment of death, knees bent as he fell backwards on to a grassy slope, rifle flying from his grasp. It looked as though a small part of his head was exploding. Dan was appalled, yet fascinated. He scanned the article, then returned to the photograph.

'Truly terrible,' he murmured. 'I wonder who the photographer was.'

'Doesn't say,' said Harry, twisting the magazine round towards him. 'Who knows? He may be dead himself by now.'

Harry continued to stare morosely at the pictures, till Dan flipped the magazine shut. 'Stop tormenting yourself. It won't do any good.'

'I know.' Harry sighed, rolled up the magazine and slipped it back inside his coat.

Dan wiped clear a patch on the steamy window and peered out. 'Rain's eased off. I'd best be going.' He stood up, chucked a few coppers on the table, and put on his hat. He gazed down at Harry's gloomy face. 'How about dinner at Savarino's on Saturday? Cheer us both up.'

Harry's face brightened. 'Why not? Half seven?'

'See you there,' said Dan.

He wandered back to the office, thinking about the photograph Harry had shown him. To be a journalist out there – hell, it must be a damned sight more interesting than cobbling together pieces about St Ives' watercolourists.

*

When he had finished writing up his piece, he left the office and went back to his rooms to freshen up, then headed to a cocktail party being thrown by an old schoolfriend. Diana was among the guests. She spotted Dan and sauntered over.

'Hello, stranger. Where have you been hiding yourself? I haven't seen you in an age.'

'I keep myself in short supply, to excite demand.' This wasn't strictly true. He was out and about as much as possible, to the extent that funds allowed. He helped himself to another drink from the tray of a passing waiter and inspected Diana, who was wearing a cocktail dress of russet silk which seemed to cling to every part of her.

'You're looking very modish. I like the dress.'

'Thank you, darling. Vionnet. It's all in the cut.'

'How's Paul?'

Diana made a face. 'Boring everyone to death with his racing car business. I don't see much of him. He keeps sensible hours, whereas I, as you know, am more of a night girl.' She sipped her cocktail and glanced around the chattering crowd. 'Actually, he seems to be down at Woodbourne House a lot these days. Making a play for Meg, no doubt. She'll make the perfect wife, and it's about time he got married. At least I'll be blessed with a sister-in-law I can stand. Think how dreadful it would be if my only darling brother married someone I couldn't abide.'

'Frightful.' Dan's expression was distant.

'Are you coming along to Quaglino's later? Freddie says Hutch will be playing. Last time he arrived with his piano strapped to his limousine – too killing.'

'Yes, possibly.'

'Good. See you later, in that case.'

She moved away. Dan lit a cigarette and examined the unexpectedly disturbed state of his feelings. Why should he care whether or not Meg Slater married Paul Latimer? It would put her out of his reach, which would be a pity, but there was more to it than that – Paul was entirely the wrong man for her. He might be rich and good-looking, but he was also a stuffy reactionary. Meg had the potential to be a beautiful, exciting woman, but if she married Paul she would dry up like some sad, desiccated rosebud. Well, if that was the choice she wanted to make, there was nothing he could do about it, not while she was buried in the depths of Surrey. He helped himself to another cocktail and resolved to think no more about her.

The next morning Dan woke with a wretched hangover. He lay in bed and let the events of the night before come back to him in slow degrees. His mind worked its way backwards through recollected fragments of drunken hours at the jazz club, to the cocktail party, and the conversation with Diana. It was that which had started it off. Hearing about Paul and Meg had made him want to get drunk. He had to face the fact that he was a little infatuated with Meg. The reason for that, he decided, was that so far she had proved unattainable. Well, he would put that right. He hadn't bothered to write to her, as he'd said he would. He would do so now. It would be the start of an all-out campaign. If what Diana had said was true, he would be acting not only in his own interests, but hers – to save her from marrying a prig like Paul.

He got out of bed, pulled on the shirt and trousers which he had dropped on the floor the night before, and knelt to light the gas fire. Then he sat down at the table that served as his desk, found pen and paper, and sat for several minutes trying to assemble his bleary thoughts and find words to begin a letter to Meg. He struggled at first, screwing up and throwing aside several first attempts, until at last he found the right tone. He kept it light, and the content friendly and newsy. The important thing was to renew the link, to maintain contact. The rest would follow.

From time to time he cast a glance over his shoulder at the girl lying in his bed, hoping she wouldn't wake up for a while.

*

Paul came down to Woodbourne House again the following week, but since he spent much of the time discussing some business matter on which Sonia required his advice, Meg assumed that this was the sole purpose of his visit. She saw him only at lunchtime, and was glad to be able to bask in his company and listen to him expound on matters of the day, her admiration of him so familiar that she never questioned it.

That evening Sonia observed, 'Paul Latimer is being very attentive, don't you think?'

'I think it's perfectly natural,' responded Meg. 'I'm sure he's very concerned for your well-being since Uncle Henry's death.'

Sonia was amused by Meg's assumption that she was referring to herself, and not to Meg. It confirmed Sonia's suspicion that her niece had no idea that Paul had, as Sonia had divined during the August house party, set his sights on Meg.

She was about to say something along those lines but Meg forestalled her by asking, 'Have you made any headway finding a new nanny for Avril?'

'Why, yes, I think I may have found someone. She came to see me yesterday. She's been nanny for a family in London for the past twenty-five years, and now she is looking for employment in the country. Her name is – let me see...' Sonia laid down her sewing and cast around among the letters on her work-table to find the one she wanted. 'Irene Bissett. She's rather older than I had in mind, but she's very experienced and has quite a no-nonsense air about her. I think Avril needs someone with a firm hand.'

Amen to that, thought Meg. 'When will she start?'

'She's free to start in a week. It's just a matter of taking up her references.'

That meant, by Meg's calculation, that she would be back in London by the end of the month, and her heart rose at the thought.

'So you may tell your mother the glad news,' said Sonia,

smiling and folding up Miss Bissett's letter. 'I'm sure she'll be pleased to have you back, though I shall miss you.'

On the day that Meg was due to leave Woodbourne, Sonia found her consulting the railway timetable.

'Why is it that there are no fast trains on Thursdays?' asked Meg, frowning.

'You won't need to take a train,' said Sonia. 'Paul is coming down to pick up those manuscripts Henry left him – I daren't trust them to the post – and he's offered to drive you back.'

'Oh.' Meg gave her aunt a glance. 'Well, that's very convenient.'

'Isn't it? So much nicer than the stopping train. Now, I have a few letters to write, so I shall see you at luncheon.'

Meg spent the morning finishing her packing. When she came downstairs, she spied a bulky letter addressed to her among the post on the hall table. She didn't recognise the handwriting. She ripped open the envelope, and when she saw that it was from Dan, her heart lifted with surprise and pleasure. She had assumed he'd completely forgotten his promise to write.

She took the letter through to the morning room, where she knew there would be a fire, and curled up on the window seat to read it. It was long and breezy and full of news. He gave Meg accounts of exhibitions he had been to, and of a ghastly dinner party, and of an evening spent with some of Diana's friends in Soho, all of which Meg hugely enjoyed. He described for her his rooms in Bloomsbury, the view from his window, the comings and goings of fellow tenants, and painted a deft and funny portrait of his landlady. The letter was so good she read it twice. She was faintly disappointed that the tone was no more than friendly. But what had she expected? Clearly stolen kisses and bedroom visits in the middle of the night were to be expected at a house party. She shouldn't attach any particular significance to them. Dan evidently didn't. She couldn't help recalling with some wistfulness that kiss in the woods. But then, one's first proper kiss would always be unforgettable, she supposed.

As she folded up the letter, she glanced across at the writing desk and wondered if she should try to answer it now. No, such an excellent letter deserved a better reply than she could give in the short interval between now and Paul's arrival. She put it back in its envelope and tucked it into her bag, resolving to write when she got back to London.

'You must come and visit often,' Sonia said to Meg, as she got ready to go. 'The house is going to be very dull without you.'

'I shall, but you must come up to town as well, Aunt Sonia. It won't do you any good to stay here all alone.'

'You're right. I feel much stronger in myself now. And that's largely thanks to you, my dear.' She embraced Meg and kissed her. 'Give my fondest love to your mother, and tell her I will come up to London before Christmas.'

'That's the spirit!' said Paul. He slapped his driving gloves against his palm. 'Come on, we'd better get going if we want to get back to London before dark.'

It was like Paul to stick to the thirty mile an hour speed limit, thought Meg, as they made their way diligently along the country roads. Had it been Diana at the wheel, no doubt they would have been flying along. But Paul only ever channelled his adventurous spirit in legitimate ways. She liked that about him, his dependability, his reliable goodness, but she sometimes wished he could be a bit more unpredictable, reckless even. At twenty-seven, he seemed wise beyond his years. Even his attractiveness owed more to maturity than youthfulness. How refreshing it would be if Paul were to behave occasionally as though he hadn't a clue what he was doing. But that was hard to imagine. It was Paul's nature always to know exactly what he was doing, which was comfortable, if not exciting.

They chatted all the way back to London, Meg carefully steering Paul away from political and economic topics on which he might become too ponderous. They discussed the scandalous rumours of the King and Mrs Simpson, speculating on how it would all end, and by the time they reached London they had developed an intimacy which Meg had never felt with Paul before. For the first time, she felt on a level with him. All her life she had been accustomed to Paul treating her with brotherly condescension and amused tolerance, but now she felt he was treating her as properly grown-up. The realisation led her thoughts in unexpected directions.

Paul stopped the car outside the mansion block in Kensington where he and Diana shared a flat.

'Here we are,' he said, pulling on the handbrake. 'Why don't you come up to the flat and have a drink before I take you home? You might like to see the results of Di's interior decorating enthusiasms.'

The flat was on the second floor, and when Paul opened the door with his key he called out, 'Hello? Anyone home?' But he was met with silence.

'Di must be out with her friends,' he said, shrugging off his coat and then helping Meg out of hers. 'I'll just take these manuscripts through to my study. You go into the drawing room, and I'll be through in a tick to mix those drinks.'

Meg was impressed by Diana's redecoration of the flat. No expense seemed to have been spared. The drawing-room walls were painted a delicate shade of eau-de-nil, and a large art deco mirror set above the fireplace reflected the long windows opposite, which were swagged with curtains of dark green velvet to match the cushions on the sofas. Meg paced the room, admiring objects and furniture, musing on what fun it would be to have so much money you could furnish a home any way you liked, without worrying about the expense.

'The room is lovely,' she told Paul when he arrived. 'Di has such exquisite taste.'

'An exquisite taste for spending, you mean.' Paul went to the drinks trolley and unstoppered a decanter of Scotch. 'Whisky do? Or would you prefer something else? Gin and bitters, perhaps?'

'Gin is fine. Just a small one, thanks.'

'Of course, I haven't let her near my study,' went on Paul, as he poured their drinks. 'My private domain remains strictly masculine. No cushions or glass ornaments allowed.'

They settled themselves on a sofa, and Paul lifted his glass. 'Cheers. Here's to your long-awaited return to London.'

'Cheers. It's lovely to be back.' Meg rarely drank spirits, and the first sip sent a pleasant fire fizzing through her limbs.

'Seriously,' said Paul, gazing at her, 'I'm looking forward to being able to see more of you.' Meg couldn't look at him, aware of the atmosphere having shifted subtly. 'If you want to, that is.'

Meg realised with astonishment that Paul was nervous. She turned to him. 'Of course I do. It's always lovely, being with you.'

Paul took another hard swallow of his whisky, then set the glass down. 'The fact is, all these months since the house party, I've been missing you like hell.' He moved closer, his expression earnest, vulnerable. 'And having you here to myself is heaven. Ever since we took that walk in the woods a couple of weeks ago, I've been longing to tell you.' He put out a hand to touch her hair, then her face. 'Dearest Meg.' He leaned forward and kissed her.

When he drew away, Meg gave a light, trembling laugh. 'Oh, Paul—'

'Hush,' he said, and kissed her again. 'I know you've only ever thought of me as Diana's big brother, but I wonder if you can begin to think of me in another way. Because the fact is, I think I'm more than a little in love with you.'

'Paul… I don't know what to say. I didn't realise…' Meg was truly lost for words.

'Really? You didn't know? I should have thought it was rather obvious.' He caressed her face gently, and kissed her again. There was silence between them, then he said, 'Do you think you could learn to care for me, Meg? To love me?'

The question opened such a world of possibilities for Meg that she felt dazzled. Following her instincts, she said carefully, 'I don't know, Paul. This is very sudden.'

'You're right. The last thing I want to do is to rush you into anything.'

The conversation moved hesitantly to other things, and after a while Paul said, 'Come on, finish your drink and I'll take you home.'

'Thank you,' murmured Meg, and swallowed the remains of her gin, feeling it burn its way down her throat and into the pit of her stomach. 'Yes, I think perhaps I ought to go home.' She truly wanted to be able to think, to reflect, to examine this new and unexpected change in their relationship. It was too much to take in at this moment.

Paul dropped Meg off in Chelsea, and came in for a few moments to say hello to her mother. When he left he threw Meg a meaningful smile, and promised to telephone soon.

'Dear Paul, he doesn't change,' remarked Helen Slater, as she and Meg went through to the drawing room. 'His manners are so impeccable they positively wear one out. I've known him since he was a small boy, but he's still so formal with me. I wish he would call me Helen, and not Mrs Slater. It makes me feel quite geriatric.'

Helen was younger than Sonia by three years, and though not so tall, shared her sister's graceful, imperious manner and good looks. If Sonia, with her narrow face and flowing dresses, had something of a look of elongation, Helen was altogether more compact, her lightly made-up features neater and more vivid, her hair fashionably shingled and curled. At forty-three she still had a very good figure, of which she was justly proud, and she dressed expensively and well. She had been widowed for ten years, but showed no inclination to remarry, leading a busy London social life, and holidaying abroad on a regular basis.

'No one could accuse you of being that,' said Meg with a smile. Her mind was still a little dazed by the events of the past half-hour.

Helen gave the fire a brisk poke and said, 'I'm sure you'd like a drink after that long drive. A sherry, perhaps?'

'No, thanks. I had a drink at Paul's flat.'

'Oh, you stopped off?' Helen gave her daughter a glance.

'Yes.' Meg couldn't fight the blush which rose to her cheeks. 'He and Diana have had the place redecorated. He wanted to show me.'

'Well, I think *I'll* have one.' Helen tugged at the bell on the wall. 'I've had such a busy day.'

'Your days are always busy, Mother. I don't know where you get the energy. If you don't mind, I think I'll go straight upstairs to unpack, then get to bed.' She kissed her mother. 'It's lovely to be back. Aunt Sonia is a dear, but it's been somewhat dreary down in Surrey. Enjoy your sherry.'

On her way out she bumped into Dora, the maid, in the doorway.

'Hello, Dora. Here I am, back, like a bad penny.'

'Nice to see you, I'm sure, miss.'

'A sherry, please, Dora,' said Helen. 'Sleep well, darling,' she called after her daughter.

When Dora had brought the sherry, Helen sat by the fire, sipping it and mulling over the matter of Meg and Paul. She already knew from Sonia that he had been down to Woodbourne House several times in the past months, and both sisters had surmised that Meg must be the reason. Well, thought Helen, Meg might do a good deal worse. Paul was something of a stuffed shirt, but he was handsome, well bred, and possessed a nice lot of money. All in all, he would do very well.

Paul's courtship of Meg was careful and conventional. Two or three times a week he would pick her up from her mother's house in Cheyne Walk and take her out for the evening. They would go for dinner, perhaps to the theatre or cinema, once for a long, wrapped-up weekend walk in Green Park followed by supper at the flat. His physical approach to her was circumspect, never moving beyond kisses. He didn't kiss her the way

Dan had – that had been impulsive and delicious – but decorously and gently. Meg tested her heart constantly for feelings of love, but because she had never been in love, she didn't quite know what it was she was looking for. Sometimes, rather than feeling that she and Paul were building something together, she had a sense of simply being absorbed into Paul's existence, filling in a predetermined place in his life-plan. But the notion did not trouble her often.

Conviction came one sleety November Sunday, when they had driven to a pub in Kent for lunch. While Meg sat toasting her legs by the warmth of the pub fire, she looked across at Paul standing at the bar. The sight of his tall, broad-shouldered figure, his face in profile as he chatted to the barmaid, brought such a rush of feeling that she was convinced she must love him. All her life she had trusted and looked up to him; now all she had to do was to say the word, and she would have his love and protection for ever. What more could any woman want?

Diana, of course, was in favour of Paul and Meg's relationship. She knew there were any number of young women in London who would have given their eye teeth to land a catch like Paul, and had no wish to have some greedy, calculating beauty marry Paul for his money and then make him miserable. She was protective of her older brother, knowing only too well that the instincts that made him honourable and decent – and sometimes a little stuffy – tended to blind him to faults in people. Not that Paul, to the best of her knowledge, had ever had a relationship with any woman. He preferred the company of men. But Meg was sweet and kind, and Diana was convinced that if she loved Paul, then she would make him very happy. Whether or not Meg did truly love him was something Diana could not properly gauge. She knew that Meg had adored Paul since girlhood, seeing him as some kind of paragon, and wondered if this wasn't simply a continuation of that state of mind. Even if it was, she decided, it was a pretty good basis for love, and she approved of the prospect of having Meg as a sister-in-law.

One afternoon in early December, after an afternoon spent shopping in Bond Street, Diana and Meg went for tea at Fortnum's, just around the corner from Paul's club. Paul had arranged to meet them there. They found a table and sank into the seats in happy exhaustion, setting their purchases on the floor around them.

'Thank goodness to be out of that wind,' remarked Meg, removing her hat. She took her compact from her handbag and snapped it open, inspected her reflection and rearranged some stray curls.

Diana signalled to a waitress and ordered tea, then disappeared to the powder room.

It was as she was putting away her compact that Meg saw, with a pang, Dan's letter lying crumpled at the bottom of her bag. The bag itself was one she hadn't used since she had returned from Woodbourne House, so the letter had been there for over a month, she realised, and she had entirely forgotten to reply. She took the envelope out and smoothed it. He would think her horribly rude. She sat, letter in hand, feeling strangely bereft.

Diana came back and sat down. She saw Meg's face, and glanced at the letter, and at the dashing, distinctive handwriting. 'What's up?'

'Do you happen to have Dan Ranscombe's telephone number?'

'My dear, what on earth makes you ask that?'

'It's just that he wrote to me while I was at Woodbourne House, and I never replied. I've come across the letter now, in my bag. I feel so awful. He gave me his telephone number, too, but I can't for the life of me think where I put it. I feel I should at least get in touch with him. We got on so terribly well, and had such fun. I don't want him to think me rude. Do you happen to have it?'

'No, I don't believe I do,' said Diana, as tea arrived. The waitress set out the plates of sandwiches and cakes.

'Perhaps Paul does,' said Meg. 'I'll ask him.'

Diana gave Meg a glance. 'Is that wise?'

Meg met her gaze. 'I suppose not.' She put the letter back in her bag.

'Actually,' went on Diana, 'I saw Dan a while ago at a cocktail party. He was all on his lonesome, and then two hours later at Quaglino's he'd acquired some very pretty creature. With Dan it's a never-ending stream of girls. He doesn't change. Oh look, here's Paul.' She gave a smile and waved to her brother.

As Paul crossed the tea room, Meg hastily tucked the letter back in her bag.

At home that evening, she emptied the contents of the handbag on to her bed. She gathered up her lipstick, comb, powder compact and purse and put them on her dressing table. The letter lay on the eiderdown. She picked it up and thrust it back into the bag, which she threw into the bottom of her wardrobe. She needn't feel bad about it. Evidently Dan had enough to occupy him without being bothered about whether or not she answered his letter. No doubt he had forgotten all about her.

8

DAN HAD BEEN confident that Meg would reply to his letter, that they would then see one another in London, and that an extremely satisfying romance would then take its course – completely eclipsing Paul – and he felt quite galled when no reply came. He checked the post every morning and evening, but by the end of November he no longer expected anything. He tried to pretend that he wasn't in the least concerned – not every woman could be a conquest, after all – but Meg haunted his thoughts in a way that he found disconcerting.

In the first week of December Mr Hitchcock, Dan's editor, called him into his office. He held out a couple of theatre tickets.

'These any use to you? They're for that new hit play, *French Without Tears*, at the Criterion. Vera and I were going tonight, but our first grandchild has just made her entrance into the world, so we're obliged to motor to Oxford to pay homage. They're rather good seats in the stalls. I don't want any money. I just don't want to see them go to waste. Here – take them, and enjoy yourself.'

Dan rang Harry Denholm and offered him the other ticket. Harry would normally have affected to despise light theatrical comedy, but as he had nothing to conceal from Dan and as the prospect of seeing a smash West End hit for free was too tempting, he accepted with alacrity.

The play was a roaring success, as it had been every night since it opened, and the stalls seats were among the best in the house. At the end of the evening, as he and Harry emerged from the theatre with the rest of the crowd, Dan heard a shrill female voice calling his name. 'Mr Ranscombe! Dan!'

Dan turned and saw Elizabeth Cunliffe, swathed in furs, bobbing towards him through the crowd. They shook hands, and Dan introduced Harry, casually dropping in the fact that Harry was the proprietor of *Ire*. There was always the possibility that forging a connection with a poet as eminent as Gerald Cunliffe might be of some advantage to Harry.

'An arts magazine? How interesting,' breathed Elizabeth. 'I must ask my husband if he knows it.'

'Mrs Cunliffe's husband is the poet, Gerald Cunliffe,' Dan told Harry, who nodded and murmured appreciatively, though Dan could guess what Harry probably privately thought of Gerald Cunliffe's school of poetry.

'Have you been to the play?' Dan asked.

'Yes, and wasn't it just too wonderful? I do adore Kay Hammond, and that young man Rex Harrison is a perfect revelation! I loved every minute.'

'Is Gerald with you?'

'He's somewhere trying to find a taxi. Of course, he grumbled all the way here, saying that if James Agate didn't like the play, he was sure he wouldn't either. But he roared with laughter all the way through. I haven't enjoyed anything so much in years.' Her expression turned grave, and she laid a hand on Dan's arm. 'Of course, I haven't seen you since we were together at Woodbourne House. What a ghastly turn of events. I understand you were absolutely there when it happened?'

'Yes – it was ghastly, as you say.'

'Meg told me all about it. I had a little soirée a few weeks ago, and she came with Paul Latimer. Did you know that they're very much a couple these days?'

'I'd heard something,' replied Dan.

'I'm having a cocktail party at Christmas, and they will be there, so you must come, too. And do bring Mr Denholm.' She flashed Harry a smile. 'You know,' she added, 'after Henry died, dear Sonia was kind enough to send me my portrait, the one Henry painted of me. It was such a thoughtful thing to do, given that she had so many other things to think about. I have it hanging in the library, above the fireplace. You will see it when you come at Christmas. I suppose it must have been the last thing he painted. It makes it even more special, somehow.'

Inevitably Elizabeth moved on to the topic of the abdication – people had talked of little else for the past few days – until at last Gerald Cunliffe appeared, slightly out of breath, to announce to his wife that a taxi was waiting round the corner. Dan greeted him, and hastily introduced Harry, but it was evident Gerald was anxious to be getting home.

'I've invited Dan and his friend to our little Christmas gathering,' said Elizabeth, gathering her furs around her.

Gerald nodded. 'Yes, yes – of course you must come.'

Elizabeth twinkled her fingers at them. 'So delightful to see you again! Goodnight!'

The Cunliffes departed for their taxi, and Dan and Harry headed towards Soho.

A week later, when Paul and Meg were in a taxi en route to dinner, Paul mentioned that Elizabeth Cunliffe had been in touch, asking for Dan's address.

'You remember Dan? Fair chap from the house party? She wants to invite him to her Christmas cocktail party.'

'Yes, of course I remember him.'

'I thought at one point you were a bit sweet on him,' said Paul. 'I was mightily jealous, I can tell you.'

'What rot. We played tennis a few times, that's all.'

'Mm. I recall you preferred playing with him to me.'

'That's because you always let me beat you. Dan at least gave me a proper game. He didn't patronise me.'

'Ouch!' laughed Paul. He gave her a tender glance. 'Come here.'

He drew Meg towards him and kissed her. Meg returned the kiss reluctantly. She really wished Dan's name hadn't come up. She felt bad about not having replied to his letter, and the prospect of meeting him at the Cunliffes' made her uncomfortable.

The next day Meg went Christmas shopping, and came home in a state of some triumph.

'At last,' she told her mother, 'I've found the perfect present for Paul.'

'Oh?'

'It's a portable gramophone, in the nicest red leather case. I'm having it delivered.'

'Hard to imagine what Paul's musical tastes run to,' remarked Helen, who was sitting by the fire opening Christmas cards which had come in the afternoon post. 'Rather old-fashioned, one imagines. Gilbert and Sullivan and a bit of Elgar, possibly.'

It occurred to Meg that she didn't really know what Paul's taste in music was. Whenever they were out together at dinner, he didn't pay any attention to the band, and he didn't really care much for dancing – although he did it to please Meg. She would make a safe selection of popular songs.

'Oh, my goodness!' Helen laid down her letter knife. 'You simply won't believe...'

'What?'

'It's a letter from Sonia. That girl who was Avril's nanny, Madeleine. She's come back to Woodbourne House. She's pregnant.'

'No!'

Helen turned the page and read on. 'It seems that her grandmother turned her out, and she had nowhere else to go. Like mother, like daughter, I suppose.'

Meg's thoughts turned instantly to that moment last year at the picnic, when they had found Madeleine and Charles Asher together in the woods. It looked as though Paul had been right.

Clearly things had at some point gone further than anyone had guessed.

Helen handed the letter to Meg. 'Here, I think this last part is meant for you.'

Meg took the letter and read.

She will not say a word to me about who the father is. I think she might be more forthcoming with someone closer to her own age, and wondered if Meg might find time to pay a visit before Christmas? It is a great deal to ask, I know, but I am at my wits' end as to how to deal with this dilemma.

Meg looked at her mother. 'She wants me to go to Woodbourne. I will, of course, if she thinks it will help. I'll go and telephone her now.'

Two days later Meg took the train to Surrey. When she arrived at Woodbourne House Avril scampered to the door to greet her and announced, 'Madeleine's come back!'

Meg bent to kiss Avril. 'Has she? Well, how nice.'

'Miss Bissett doesn't like her.'

'That's quite enough, Avril,' said Sonia briskly. 'Upstairs with you now.'

When Meg had taken off her coat, she followed Sonia through to the little sitting room, where a cheerful fire burned in the grate and tea was laid out.

Meg sat down and Sonia poured tea. She handed Meg a cup. 'I can't thank you enough for coming. Such a crisis.'

'What's going to happen?'

'My dear, I haven't the faintest idea. She only arrived here four days ago, with her pathetic little suitcase, and not even a proper winter coat. She was chilled to the bone, and seemed to me to be running a temperature. So I called Dr Egan, and that's when I found out. And to think this Cole woman simply sent her packing. It's perfectly monstrous behaviour. How could she behave so callously? The girl seems more upset by her grandmother's treatment of her than her own predicament. I suppose the reality hasn't quite sunk in.'

'How many months?'

'Around four, according to Dr Egan. Give or take.' Sonia met Meg's eye. 'Exactly. It must have happened while she was here during summer, but she absolutely refuses point-blank to say who the father is. It's impossible to get a word out of her. Not that it was an easy subject to broach in the first place.'

'And you think she might be more willing to confide in someone closer to her own age?'

'That was my hope.'

'I'll speak to her after tea, if you like.'

'I'd be so grateful, my dear.'

There was silence for a moment, then Meg asked, 'Will she have the baby here?'

'I don't see a choice. Oh, I know there are homes for unmarried mothers, but I wouldn't countenance sending her to one of those. Olive was my dear friend, and Madeleine is her daughter.' Another silence ensued, then Sonia said, 'But a baby – I simply can't imagine...'

Neither could Meg. If Madeleine could be persuaded to admit that Charles Asher was the father, then it would be up to Charles to take responsibility. He was possibly in Spain – at least, that had been his plan a few months ago – but he would have to come back at some point.

'So,' said Sonia, refreshing their teacups, 'let's talk of happier things. Tell me all that's been happening to you in London.'

Meg told her aunt all about Paul, and Sonia received the confidence with the satisfaction of one who had predicted the whole affair months before.

'I can't tell you how happy that makes me. He'll be lucky to have you as a wife.'

Meg laughed in surprise. 'Well, things haven't got quite that far.'

'Trust me – men like Paul Latimer don't trifle in such matters. I knew in August he had his eye on you.'

Meg fell silent. The thought of surrendering her life to Paul, to building a home and a family with him, was both daunting and exciting. As though divining her thoughts, Sonia added, 'And you would be equally lucky to have him as a husband. You wouldn't have to face the struggles that so many young couples have when they're starting out.'

'I won't pretend I haven't thought about it. But I always imagined marriage as a partnership of equals, and Paul already has so much. He has a splendid life. If I were to marry him, I would simply be, well, grafting myself on to it. Nothing so romantic as struggling together. There would be none of that. He talks of buying some grand house in Berkshire, and if I were his wife I would be put in charge of it without having the first idea how to run it.'

'No woman has the faintest idea how to run a house until she has one of her own. It's all trial and error. My dear, when Henry and I set up our first home – oh, the disasters! But I have every confidence in you.'

'Well, I don't think we should be speculating on such things,' said Meg firmly. 'There hasn't been the faintest mention of marriage.'

'I have a sixth sense about these things. Let's see what Christmas brings,' said Sonia mysteriously, before moving on to talk of other affairs.

When tea was over, Meg went in search of Madeleine and found her sitting on the window seat in the morning room with a book.

Madeleine seemed thinner than in the summer; nothing of her pregnancy showed as yet. Her long fair hair hung over her shoulder in a thick plait, and the green frock she was wearing, with its white collar and cuffs, made her look like a beautiful child.

Her face wore its usual settled expression of expectant calm, but something in her eyes seemed haunted and anxious.

'It's nice to see you again,' said Meg. On impulse, she took one of Madeleine's hands in both her own. 'Aunt Sonia told me why you came back. And about your grandmother. I'm so sorry.'

Madeleine turned to gaze at the fire. She knew Meg meant to be kind, but how did she think she could possibly help?

'I thought she would help me. But she was just angry. So angry. I came here because I didn't have anywhere else to go. I wish my mother was still alive. I wish she was here…' Madeleine's voice broke, and tears spilled from her lashes and down her cheeks.

'I know how lonely you must feel. But you mustn't think you've been completely abandoned. My aunt will help you. We all will.' Madeleine continued to cry. 'But you know, there is a very important person in all of this, someone who can't be ignored. Here…' Meg fished in her cardigan pocket and produced a clean handkerchief, which she unfolded and handed to Madeleine. 'My aunt tells me you don't want to say who the father is, but I think it's important that you do. He has a responsibility. And perhaps if he knew, he might be happy to shoulder that responsibility.' Still Madeleine said nothing. At length Meg asked, 'Have you told him?'

Madeleine wiped her eyes and nose and met Meg's gaze. 'I can't,' she whispered.

Well, thought Meg, at least she was prepared to acknowledge his existence. She thought carefully for a moment, then said, 'Madeleine, you know that during the summer house party there was some talk – not very nice talk, I'm afraid – about you and Charles Asher?'

Madeleine looked at Meg with frank astonishment.

Meg said gently, 'If he is the father, you might as well come out and say so.'

Madeleine uncrumpled Meg's handkerchief and spread it out

on her knee. So that was what people believed. She'd had no idea. The incident in the wood had seemed so trivial. She let her mind wander back to the studio, the things she had let Henry Haddon do to her. It was as if the uncontrollable urges which had overwhelmed her had been felt by someone else entirely. She could not now recollect those feelings, only the fact of them. She had only a sketchy idea of the facts of life, and when changes in her body had begun to occur a few months ago, it had taken her some time to comprehend them, and to realise how they had been brought about. What she had done was wicked, unforgivable. Her grandmother had made that very clear. Now all consequences were in the nature of punishment for her wickedness.

Meg, feeling she was close to an admission, persisted. 'Don't be afraid. It can only help to tell the truth.'

Madeleine knew that if she were to tell the truth, then every hope would be gone. There would be no one to help her, no place of safety. But a lie would not help her either.

'It isn't Charles Asher.'

'Well, if he isn't the father, who is?' Although she still spoke gently, Madeleine could tell that Meg didn't quite believe her.

'It doesn't matter.' Madeleine's voice was almost a whisper.

'But it does,' said Meg. 'It matters very much.' There was a silence. 'Madeleine? Whoever the father is, he has to be told.'

Madeleine shook her head. Her voice grew firmer. 'There's no point in you asking me. I won't say.' Her gaze roamed about the room, her expression inscrutable.

'Madeleine, we have to know.'

'Why?'

'Because it isn't fair on my aunt. What is she supposed to do when you have the baby? What happens then?'

'I don't know. Babies can be adopted, can't they?'

'Yes,' said Meg, surprised. 'Yes, I suppose they can.'

'And then I can leave here and not be a bother any more.' Madeleine got up from the window seat. 'May I go now?'

'Yes, of course,' sighed Meg, realising there was no point in pursuing it further.

Meg relayed the conversation to Sonia that evening.

'I didn't get very far, I'm afraid. She stubbornly refuses to say who the father is. Though I have my suspicions.'

'Really? Who?'

Meg recounted to Sonia what had happened on the day of the picnic. 'I must admit it looked rather compromising at the time. Later on Paul accused Charles of taking advantage of Madeleine. That was partly what the fight between them was about that night.'

'Gracious – I had no idea.'

'But when I put it to Madeleine this morning, she denied it.'

'And do you think she's telling the truth?'

Meg shrugged. 'I don't know. If he's not, I can't think who is. Maybe someone should tell Charles, and see where that leads. But he's in Spain – at least I think he is.'

Sonia sighed. 'What a dreadful muddle.'

'Madeleine mentioned having the baby adopted.'

'Well, that is a relief, at any rate. It's bound to be the best solution in the long run.'

When Meg got home the following evening, she and her mother discussed the situation.

'My sister is far too forbearing,' said Helen firmly. 'There are homes for girls like that. Has she any idea the responsibility she is taking on? And what will people say?'

'I don't think Aunt Sonia cares about any of that. She simply wants to help her.'

'If my sister has a weakness, it's that she's too kind.' Helen sighed. 'How was everything else at Woodbourne?'

'Avril is leading her new nanny quite a dance,' replied Meg.

'She really is awfully difficult. Losing her father can't have helped.'

'Poor little thing. Though I can't say she's a particularly engaging child. Oh, by the way, Paul called yesterday evening. He said to remind you about a cocktail party you're going to tomorrow night.'

'Oh, Lord – so we are. The Cunliffes. They came to stay at Woodbourne for a couple of weeks in August. He's that poet, Gerald Cunliffe. I've half a mind to make some excuse.'

'Why? It's lovely, going to parties at Christmas time. Always so jolly.'

'Oh, I shall probably go in the end. If I said I had a headache or some such, Paul would just fuss. Anyway' – Meg got to her feet – 'if I have to go, I'd probably better get a good night's sleep. I've had a tiring two days.' She kissed her mother and went to bed.

9

THE CUNLIFFES' HOUSE in Hampstead was new and large, set in its own grounds, and built in the arts and crafts style. Elizabeth Cunliffe prided herself on her fashionable taste, and the rooms were decorated in the very latest, with cream and ivory walls contrasting smartly with dark green and red furniture, art deco lamps and rugs, and large mirrors framed in chrome and inlaid wood hanging on the walls. The hallway was decorated with wreaths of holly, fir and ivy, and a tall, splendidly decorated Christmas tree stood in the curve of the large staircase.

By the time Meg and Paul arrived, a large number of guests were already thronging the drawing room, and at a baby grand piano in the far corner someone was playing an Ivor Novello show tune. To one side of the room a long table draped in white linen was set out as a cocktail bar, where two effeminate young men were dispensing cocktails and silly banter.

Meg sidled near to receive a champagne cocktail and enjoy the repartee. Paul ordered a whisky sour and retreated to the edge of the room. Meg joined him after a moment.

'Aren't they fun? I wouldn't have expected the Cunliffes to have friends like that.'

'Nor would I,' replied Paul flatly. 'I can't say I'm very keen on pansies.'

'Well, I think they're very amusing.' Meg found Paul's tone unaccountably annoying. She took another sip of her cocktail. If he didn't feel like enjoying himself, she certainly did. At that moment some man accosted Paul, so Meg took the opportunity to wander over to join the group by the piano. The piano player was a friend of Diana's, an actor in a current West End musical, and he had a lively and appreciative audience.

'Come on, Freddie, shove up!' exclaimed Diana, popping herself down on the piano stool. She deftly picked up the left-hand part of 'Let's Face the Music and Dance', and soon a ragged chorus of singing was in full flow.

As he came into the room, Dan caught sight of Meg standing by the piano. She was wearing a scarlet dress, cut low at the back, her dark hair curling to her shoulders. She looked more grown-up than he remembered from summer. Seeing her now, remembering what had passed between them at the house party, he couldn't believe she hadn't answered his letter. He followed Harry in the direction of the cocktails, got himself a drink, and then made his way over and tapped her lightly on the shoulder.

'Hello, stranger.'

Meg turned, and her heart gave a little jolt. 'Dan! How lovely to see you.' She hadn't expected the sight of him to affect her quite as it did, but she recovered quickly and added, 'If I'm a stranger, it's entirely my own fault. I'm sorry I didn't answer your letter.'

He shrugged and smiled. 'When did you get back from Surrey?'

'Two months ago. Something like that.'

'You need another of those.' Dan caught the eye of a passing waiter and swapped her empty glass for a fresh cocktail. 'So, tell me all the gossip from Woodbourne House.'

Meg was about to tell Dan about Madeleine, when suddenly Diana appeared.

'Dan! How divine!' She kissed him lightly on the cheek. 'Isn't this fun?' She glanced around. 'Where's Paul? I know he'll be longing to see you. Let me fetch him.'

Meg smiled at Dan and shrugged. 'I'll have to tell you later.'

'I'll hold you to that,' said Dan.

Diana reappeared with Paul.

Paul shook Dan's hand. 'How are you, old boy? I say, do you know who I've just been chatting to? Guy Hitchens – you remember him from school?' As he spoke, Paul slipped his arm around Meg and drew her to him, stroking her bare shoulder with his thumb. The proprietorial gesture was not lost on Dan.

'We shared a study,' replied Dan.

'Of course you did. He might be putting a little capital into a racing car venture of mine. We met a fellow by the name of Clements at Brooklands last year, and he's come up with some very exciting ideas.'

Diana disengaged Meg from Paul. 'Let's leave these men to talk about their motor cars. Come and meet some chums of mine.'

It was almost another hour before Dan got the chance to speak to Meg again.

'I'm still waiting the hear that gossip you promised me.'

Meg laughed. 'Let's find somewhere quiet. '

They went out and down the hallway. Dan pushed open the library door and glanced in. The room was empty. He and Meg slipped inside, closed the door, and settled themselves down on a sofa. Dan lit a cigarette and offered one to Meg, but she declined.

'I love parties, but it's nice to have a breather.' She leaned her head back and closed her eyes. 'And I do believe I've had rather more to drink than is strictly good for me.' After a moment she shook her head and opened her eyes. 'Anyway, you remember Madeleine, Avril's nanny? Well, you simply won't believe what has happened.'

Meg recounted the story. Dan said nothing, merely smoked thoughtfully. 'You don't seem very impressed with my gossip,' said Meg.

'Oh, I am. More than you can imagine. I feel pretty sorry for the kid.'

'Well, I do too, of course,' said Meg hastily, slightly ashamed at having treated Madeleine's story as so much conversational fodder. 'But she says she'll have the baby adopted. Which is probably for the best.'

'Do they know who the father is?' He asked the question, though he knew no one could have the faintest inkling of the truth.

'She refuses to say. I suppose it's that fellow, Charles Asher. I can't think who else it could be.'

Dan said nothing. He could tell no one what he had seen in the studio on the day of Haddon's death, least of all Meg. Whatever she thought about her uncle, she would certainly not want to hear that. If the baby was to be adopted, then it was, as Meg had said, probably for the best. The world must be littered with the bastard children of famous men; another would make no difference. Dan could think of no one who would benefit from the truth being known.

Somewhat unnerved by Dan's silence, Meg said impulsively, 'You know, I truly am sorry I didn't answer your letter. I thought it was wonderful. You write terribly well.'

'It's really not important.' Dan drew an ashtray towards him and stubbed out his cigarette. 'Besides, I hear you've been busy.'

A faint blush touched Meg's cheeks, and she looked away. 'What have you heard?'

'About you and Paul. Are congratulations in order?'

'No, nothing of the sort.' She leaned forward and began to fiddle with the cigarette box, opening and closing the lid.

'Really? So it's not too late? Maybe I should write you another letter.'

She turned to stare at him. Too late for what? She looked away. It was probably the kind of silly line he gave to every girl. Dan put out a hand, brushing aside the dark curls of hair from her neck, and began to stroke it. It was the same intimate, sensual gesture he had used that last night of the summer house party.

Meg shivered and stretched her neck languorously, without moving away. She felt more than a little drunk, and the touch of his hand was so delightful that she didn't want it to stop. She closed her eyes, and before she knew it, Dan had pulled her gently back on the sofa and was kissing her. The kiss was deep and passionate in a way that Paul's kisses never were. Desire flooded her body, and she clung to him, returning the kiss. Then after a few seconds she pulled away.

'I'm sorry – I shouldn't have let you do that. I've had too much to drink.' She pressed the palms of her hands against her cheeks, as if to cool them.

Dan lay back against the cushions, regarding her. 'Do you love Paul?'

Meg hesitated. She put one hand over her eyes.

'If you did, you wouldn't hesitate to say so.'

'That's not true. I do love him.'

'Yes?' Dan pulled her down on the cushions and kissed her again, and despite herself Meg responded, body and soul. Paul's gentlemanly caresses never made her feel like this. She embraced Dan as fiercely as he did her, returning his kiss with equal passion, melting at the touch of his hands on her body. At last she said, 'We must stop. Someone might come in.'

'I don't care.'

'I do.' Meg pulled away and stood up, brushing down her dress, smoothing her hair. 'I can't do this to Paul. He loves me.'

Dan lay back on the cushions and regarded her. 'The truth is that Paul wants a wife. A sweet, charming wife who will be dutiful and look after him and never make any trouble. Maybe he thinks he loves you because you're easy to love, and you fit the bill. Is that really enough for you?'

Meg drew a breath. 'What a beastly thing to say! You know nothing about Paul and what he feels about me. Nor what I feel about him.'

'The way you kissed me just now told me everything I need to know on that score.'

'I wouldn't read so much into a kiss, if I were you. No' – she snatched her hand away as he tried to take it – 'don't.'

He shrugged. 'You'd be mad to throw yourself away on him.'

'Throw myself away?' She gave a laugh. 'What a peculiar thing to say.'

And with that, Meg left the library. Dan remained on the sofa, his senses still ablaze from the softness of her mouth, the warmth of her body. He was conscious he hadn't handled the situation as well as he might, but of one thing he was certain – she didn't love Paul. She might be attracted by the idea of being Mrs Latimer, of having a comfortable life with a wealthy husband, never having to worry about money again, but she wasn't in love.

Meg left the library in a state of utter confusion, her skin tingling with the electricity of Dan's kisses and caresses. She retreated to the lavatory in the cloakroom nearby to collect her thoughts. She locked the door and leaned against the cold tiles. It wasn't what was meant to happen. She loved Paul. He was everything she had ever admired and wanted in a man. Why did Dan have to come along and wreck it all by making her feel these things? She felt a kind of despair at the thought that Paul didn't have this effect on her. He was so circumspect, so kind and cautious. He would never have behaved as Dan had done, as though he couldn't help himself, as though nothing else mattered except for kissing her, holding her. She felt the blood rush to her face at the thought of Dan's mouth on hers, his hands on her breasts, her thighs. She closed her eyes. Maybe Paul would make her feel like that in time. But that possibility shrivelled and died even as the thought was born. Feelings like that didn't grow gradually. They were either there at the very beginning or they weren't.

After a few moments she turned the tap and splashed water on her face, telling herself that feelings of sexual desire were expendable, short-lived and worthless compared to genuine depth of affection and companionship. She dabbed her face with the towel and stared at herself in the mirror. But love – what about love? Wanting someone the way she discovered she wanted Dan – was that love? Or was she confusing love and desire? She leaned her hands on the basin, her mind a hopeless jumble of thoughts and emotions.

There was a light tap on the door, and she heard Diana's voice. Meg straightened up, tidied her hair, and opened the door.

'I saw you dive in here and wondered if anything was the matter,' said Diana.

'No, I'm fine.'

At that moment Mrs Cunliffe bore down on them. 'There you two are! Come – I want to show you my portrait.' She led Meg and Diana along the hall, and into the library. Dan was still there on the sofa, smoking a cigarette. Meg avoided his eye.

'Dan, what are you doing hiding away in here?' said Elizabeth Cunliffe playfully.

'I wanted a few quiet moments to contemplate the great man's work,' said Dan with a smile. It was only in the past minute, while his mind was disentangling itself from thoughts of Meg, that he had noticed the picture of Elizabeth hanging over the fireplace.

This pleased Elizabeth enormously. 'It is rather fine, isn't it? That sounds immodest, but I do think he has caught something.' The girls gave murmurs of agreement, then a silence fell as they all contemplated the picture. Elizabeth gave a little sigh. 'To think it was his last work.'

Dan thought of the painting of Madeleine, the one he had turned to the wall on the day of Haddon's death. Why had he done that? To obliterate the events, shut them out, so that nothing need be acknowledged.

'Well, now,' said Elizabeth, 'I believe some of my guests are leaving, so I must go and say farewell.' She made her exit from the library.

'I think that was our signal to get going,' said Diana. 'What say we go and find dinner somewhere? It's past nine and I'm simply starving. Let's see what Paul says.'

Paul was all for the idea, as were a few others. 'We'll have to take a couple of taxis,' said Paul. 'How about Kettner's?'

'I think I might sit this one out,' said Dan. 'I've had something of a long day.' The thought of having to see Paul and Meg together was too much. He realised he was absurdly jealous. How was it possible that she had this effect on him?

'Oh, Dan, darling, please do come!' urged Diana. 'It won't be half as much fun without you.'

Dan shrugged and gave in. He saw Meg say something to Paul in a low voice, and wondered if she, too, was trying to duck out. But Paul murmured something reassuring in reply and gave her arm a squeeze, which seemed to settle the matter.

Kettner's, it turned out, was full to bursting, and without a reservation they had no hope of a table before midnight. The story was the same at the Criterion and the Café Royal.

'I vote we chuck this and go back to ours for a supper. We have plenty of eggs to scramble, and heaps of champagne,' said Diana, as they stood on Regent Street, cold and disconsolate. 'What do you all say?'

Everyone was tired of traipsing from restaurant to restaurant, and agreed enthusiastically. More taxis were found, and they headed to Diana and Paul's Kensington apartment. Diana took immediate charge of the gramophone, and Paul went in search of champagne and glasses. Chairs were pushed back, and a few people began to dance.

'Come on, Dan.' Diana slipped her hand into Dan's and they drifted into an easy foxtrot. Meg, who had retreated to a sofa with the beginnings of a headache, watched them as they danced. They made a handsome couple, moving in careless harmony, murmuring and laughing. She stared at Dan's long, strong fingers resting on Diana's willowy back, and suddenly she longed to feel them again on her body. She jumped up restlessly from the sofa and went in search of Paul, almost bumping into him as he came through with two bottles of champagne.

'I say – watch out!' he laughed.

'I thought I might make a start on those scrambled eggs.'

'Wonderful! Eggs are in the larder, I believe. You know where everything else is?' Meg impulsively drew him towards her and kissed him. He didn't resist, but his response was mechanical. 'What was that for?' he asked with amusement as they drew apart.

Meg shook her head. 'Nothing.' She let him pass with the champagne and glasses, and went into the kitchen.

She was glad of something to occupy her, and tried not to think of Dan as she beat the eggs, found plates and cutlery, and put bread on the grill to toast. While she was in the middle of her work, Paul reappeared. He held out a glass of champagne. 'For the busy cook.'

'Thanks.'

'I like to see you in my kitchen, in your apron. It makes me feel happy. It looks right.'

Meg pushed a curl of hair from her eye and wiped a hand on her apron. She set the glass down. She came close to Paul, running her hands beneath the lapels of his jacket. 'Paul, do you love me?'

'You know I do.' He kissed her forehead lightly, then the tip of her nose. 'I've told you so a hundred times.'

'But I mean – do you love me passionately, madly? Would you die without me?'

'I say – steady on.' He gazed into her eyes, as if trying to decipher what she wanted. 'My dearest, darling girl – if that's what you want me to say, I'll happily say it. I love you so much I would die without you. There – that do?'

Meg moved away. 'I'm sorry. I'm being silly. Too much champagne. Or maybe not enough.' She picked up the glass and drained it quickly.

'Your toast's going to burn if you don't watch out,' added Paul, nodding in the direction of the grill.

'Oh!' Meg darted to rescue it. She bent down and took warm plates from the oven, and then a big bowl of scrambled eggs. She handed Paul a heap of cutlery. 'There – you can put those on the dining-room table and tell everyone supper's ready.'

People fell on the eggs and toast with relish. The meal was haphazard and jolly. Diana had lit candles around the dining room and in the centre of the table, and the atmosphere was that of a midnight feast. The available champagne had been finished, and Paul opened bottles of wine. Diana dragged people back to the drawing room and wound up the gramophone in preparation for more dancing and fun.

At the table, over the mess of toast scraps and eggy plates, Meg yawned. 'Doesn't Diana ever get tired?'

'She'll keep going till dawn,' said Paul. He and Meg were alone at one end of the table. A few others, including Dan, were chatting at the other end. Paul absently stroked the back of Meg's hand. Meg gazed at his fingers on her skin, thinking how she would feel if the touch were Dan's, the fire it would light within her, whereas Paul's touch awoke no such response. The gesture was friendly, reassuring, possessive perhaps, but it contained no sexual current. A feeling of cold despair, such as she had never felt, hit her hard. It shocked her, and for a moment her mind went horridly blank. She pulled her hand away and began to pile up the dirty plates.

'No need to do that just yet,' said Paul. 'Stay and talk.'

'I hate to see dirty plates lying around,' said Meg. 'I'd much rather clear them up now than later.'

She took the plates to the kitchen and dumped them by the sink. For a few seconds she stood there, motionless, waiting fearfully to see if that bleak, empty feeling would return. She saw a half-full bottle of gin standing on the side and, remembering the fiery comfort it had given her that night when Paul first brought her here, she opened it and poured a couple of inches into a glass. She knocked back half of it, then gasped, shaking her head. She leaned against the sink, feeling the warmth of the alcohol pool in her stomach. That was better. Her thoughts seemed clearer, stronger. To hell with the washing-up. She had done enough for one evening. She went back through to the dining room. Paul had moved to the end of the table to join Dan and the others, and

Meg came up behind him, slipping her arms round his shoulders, and leaning down to nuzzle against him. Paul reacted with slight embarrassment; sensing it, she said, 'Come and dance with me. You never dance with me.'

'Excuse me, chaps,' said Paul, getting to his feet with a smile. 'Duty calls.'

Dan watched them go. If she wanted to carry on deluding herself about Paul, then let her. No doubt she would get what she wanted out of it – social position, money, an easy life. If she was shallow enough to content herself with that, he was better off without her. He reached for the wine bottle and refilled his glass.

A moment later, Diana came in search of him. 'Come on, my absolutely favourite dance partner. I can't let you hide away in here with these rotters!' To exclamations of protest from the others, Diana hauled Dan back into the drawing room, where the gramophone was blasting out Dixieland music.

'I can't dance to this,' Paul said to Meg. 'I'm afraid I'll have to sit it out.'

Meg quickly found another partner, and threw herself into the dance. She felt exhilarated; the gin had given her energy, and blotted out the cold anxiety she had felt earlier. From the corner of her eye she saw Diana and Dan dancing together, Dan leaning in to say something over the music, and Diana throwing her lovely head back in laughter. Meg was hit by a sudden painful spasm of jealousy. When the song ended, she left the room and went back to the kitchen. The piles of plates and cutlery still stood by the sink, and the gin bottle was where she had left it. On impulse Meg uncapped it, and toppled another couple of inches into the glass. This time she drained it all. She stood with her hands on the sink, breathing heavily, letting the liquor sink down and then float her upwards. When she moved, she stumbled a little, and had to steady herself against a chair. Then she took a couple of deep breaths and went back to the drawing room. The music had stopped; people were taking a breather from dancing. Paul was deep in earnest talk with one of his friends. Meg thought of joining them, but she knew she would only be interrupting some discourse about politics, or business, or high finance, and that they would simply, in their well-meaning way, change the subject to something more suitable for a brainless young woman. She was tired of being patronised. She felt a sudden regret about Dan; she wanted to say something to him – what, she wasn't quite sure, but something to put things right. She looked around the room, aware that her brain wasn't quite keeping up, and that she was rather drunk. In fact, she felt faintly nauseous. Objects swam in her view. She leaned against the door frame, aware that Paul was looking in her direction. She didn't want to be with him or talk to him right now. She turned around quickly and left the room, hoping to find somewhere she could sit and be alone, and wait for this feeling to pass.

Further down the corridor she saw the door of a room ajar, a light on inside, and she pushed it open. What she saw heightened her nausea. Dan and Diana were together on a bed, half-sitting, half-lying, locked in an embrace, kissing. Diana's skirt was pushed up – Meg could see her stocking-tops – and Dan's hand was caressing her breast through the bodice of her dress. Neither of them was aware of Meg's presence; they were too lost for that.

Meg stepped back into the passageway, and lurched quietly in the direction of the lavatory, where she was copiously sick.

When she woke the next morning, it took Meg a few minutes to work out her surroundings and recall the events of last night. Never in her life had she felt so ghastly. She recognised the room she was lying in as one of the spare rooms in Paul and Diana's flat. She lay for a long time staring at the pattern on the curtains, hazing it into faces and animal shapes as she had done as a child, trying to let her mind go blank so that she wouldn't have to reflect on her disgrace. Her eyes felt gritty and her mouth dry. After a while she hauled herself up and put her feet on the floor. She sat inert, heavy-limbed, gazing down at the nightdress which, she recalled, Diana had lent her. At least she could remember that much. She also remembered being violently sick, and that recollection induced a new wave of nausea. She lifted her head, wondering if she was going to be sick again, then swallowed, waiting. She could hear the faint sounds of a radio somewhere in the flat. Shivering, she got up and took from the hook on the back of the door a dressing gown which Diana had thoughtfully hung there, then opened the bedroom door and ventured out.

She found Diana in the kitchen. When she saw Meg she exclaimed, 'Gosh, you look rather the worse for wear. Would a cup of tea help? I've just brewed some.' She poured cups of tea, and the two of them sat down at the table.

Diana lit a cigarette. 'Hung-over?' she asked sympathetically.

Meg nodded. 'Too much champagne.' She wasn't going to mention the gin. She glanced across the kitchen and saw the bottle, one-third full, still on the counter. She gave an involuntary little shudder and looked away. 'I'm sorry. My behaviour last night was unforgivable.'

Diana laughed. 'My dear, it was immensely forgivable. You're hardly the first person to get a bit tight within these hallowed walls. Let's face it, we did make rather a night of it.'

'Where's Paul?'

'At his club. He's meeting some racing car chappie for lunch.'

Meg looked up at the kitchen clock and saw that it was past noon. She suddenly remembered that today she and her mother were meant to be taking Christmas presents to relations in Reigate. 'Oh Lord, I must get home. I'm catching a train at half one.'

Diana put out her cigarette and untied her apron. 'I'll drive you back. I have some errands to run anyway. Off you go and get dressed.'

In the car Diana chatted about the Cunliffes' party. 'So many people I hadn't seen in an age. Dan Ranscombe, for instance – it was fun to catch up with him.'

'You certainly seemed to be making the most of one another.'

Diana gave her a glance. 'What do you mean?'

'I happened to see you both – you know, later on,' replied Meg shortly. 'In one of the bedrooms.'

'Oh.' She didn't like the idea of having been observed by Meg one tiny bit. But she merely shrugged. 'Well, that's Dan for you. He takes his pleasure where he finds it. As do I. I'm afraid we're both probably rather shallow creatures by your standards.'

'I didn't mean—'

'Oh, for heaven's sake.' Diana shifted gear somewhat crossly. 'It's what people do at parties. Dance. Get drunk. Kiss. As you've discovered.' They drew up outside Meg's house. 'Here you are. Now, don't forget you've promised to come to supper at the flat on Christmas Day. Apparently Paul has some wonderful present for you – I'm sure I can't think what.'

'I won't forget. Thanks for the lift.'

Diana watched her make her way to the front door. That nonsense last night with Dan had been very much a spur-of-the-moment thing, provoked by her own flirtatiousness and too much to drink on both their parts. A kiss and fumble in the dark didn't exactly amount to much in Diana's book, but evidently it had upset Meg – if upset was the right word. Perhaps she harboured some crush on Dan from last summer. In which case, it would be best all round if she was safely married off to Paul sooner rather than later.

Dan lay in his bed in Bloomsbury, reflecting on the events of the previous night. That interlude in the bedroom with Diana had been a bad idea, a very bad idea. He blamed the fact that he'd been half-cut and somewhat fired up from those moments with Meg on the Cunliffes' sofa. Every time he thought about it, about her, he struggled to make sense of what he felt. It was more than mere desire. No girl had ever had this effect on him. Was it possible he had fallen in love with her? He'd never been in love with anyone before, and had always taken the view it was something best avoided, if one could help it. But what if it was something one couldn't help?

He closed his eyes, reliving those erotic moments in the library. The thought of her marrying Latimer was ridiculous, unbearable. If he wanted her, he was clearly going to have to fight for her. He would undertake a sustained campaign, and he would start tomorrow by going round and apologising for the way he'd behaved and the things he'd said, even though what he'd said had been true – Paul was utterly the wrong man for her. She couldn't possibly be foolish enough to marry him. But then, there was no end to the foolish things women could do.

Meg was alone in the house, kneeling on her bedroom rug and struggling to wrap Paul's Christmas present, when the maid came to announce that a Mr Ranscombe was downstairs to see her. Meg thought of asking Dora to tell him she wasn't at home, but instead she said calmly, in spite of her racing heart, 'Thank you, Dora. Show him into the drawing room, would you? I'll be down in a moment.'

Meg waited for a few minutes, trying to compose her thoughts. She put down the scissors and Scotch tape and got to her feet, checked her hair briefly in the mirror, and went downstairs.

The drawing-room door opened, and Dan, who had been inspecting Christmas cards on the mantelpiece, turned round. He hadn't quite known what kind of reception to expect, but the chilly look on Meg's face wasn't promising.

'Hello,' he said.

'Hello,' replied Meg, closing the door. 'Why are you here?'

'I came to apologise.' She gazed at him, saying nothing. 'For my behaviour on Saturday.'

'Your behaviour with me or Diana?' The question took Dan aback. 'I saw you together, in one of the bedrooms. I suppose you just move from one girl to another, don't you?'

This wasn't helpful, but he tried to brush it aside. 'It meant absolutely nothing. It was just – well, flirting, I suppose.'

'Flirting? It looked like rather more than that. And to think that only an hour earlier you were trying to seduce me, to persuade me that Paul – who is a more decent man than you could ever hope to be – doesn't love me. You're unspeakably low.'

'It wasn't like that. When Diana and I... Look, I was drunk. Everyone was drunk – even you.'

'I was not!'

'Speaking of which, do you think I could have a drink?'

Meg, her expression still cold, moved to the drinks trolley. 'What would you like?'

'A Scotch and soda would be fine.'

Meg poured him his drink. She hesitated, then poured herself a small sherry and sat down in an armchair. Dan, taking his cue, sat down opposite.

'I'm sorry if anything I said upset you.'

'I couldn't possibly care less.'

Dan took a swallow of his whisky. 'I don't believe you.'

'Don't you? Frankly, Dan, when it comes to believing people—'

'Look, I love you. I'm in love with you. And I think you're in love with me.' He hadn't meant to say the words. They had come from nowhere, but now they were spoken, he realised how true they were.

Meg gave a gasp of laughter. 'You are beyond belief. You're shallow, casual, you'll say whatever you think will get you some sex—'

'That is preposterous.'

'No, what is preposterous is that you tried to make love to me, and then when that didn't work, you went off and got what you wanted somewhere else. It was a beastly way to behave.' She paused, then added, 'Paul would never dream of behaving like that.'

'Bloody Paul!' Dan swallowed the remains of his Scotch and banged down his glass. He stood up. 'You know, Meg, you're in danger of becoming just as much of a prig as he is. I told you I love you, and I meant it. That business with Diana was ridiculous. It wasn't even my idea.'

'You didn't seem to be very much against it, from what I could see.'

'There's clearly nothing more to say. I'd better be going. It was a mistake to come here.' Things had not gone as he had imagined. He'd made a complete mess of it all.

Dan crossed the room and opened the drawing-room door. Meg followed. She called to Dora to fetch Mr Ranscombe's coat.

Dan paused on the doorstep. He turned to Meg. 'Everything I said is true. But I can't make you see it if you don't want to. Happy Christmas.'

10

MEG SPENT CHRISTMAS Day with her mother, and in the evening Paul came to pick her up to take her back to the flat for supper with Diana and a few other friends.

'What's on earth is that?' asked Paul, as Meg came downstairs with the wrapped-up gramophone in her arms.

'It's your Christmas present. You can open it later. Here – would you mind taking it? It's rather heavy.'

'I'll say it is.'

Paul put his present in the boot of the car, and they set off. Snow was falling. The car was warm, Meg was wrapped in her fur coat, and Paul was humming some Christmas song as he drove. Meg watched the wipers swish back and forth, over and over, sweeping the snow away, and fell into a trance of thought. Here she was with Paul, safe and loved, travelling through the dark night. If only she could travel like this for ever, never having to arrive, never having to think about what lay beyond.

After several minutes she realised they weren't taking the usual route.

'Why are we coming this way?'

Paul pulled over to the side of the road, at the edge of the park. The broad street was deserted. Beneath the arc of the street lamps the snowflakes floated down in constant, hurrying drifts.

'I wanted a romantic spot, and I'm afraid there's a dearth of them in London on a cold Christmas night.' He switched off the engine and turned to her. In the half-light his strong features had never looked more handsome and reassuring. 'Open the glove box,' he said.

Meg pressed the button on the glove box and it sprang open.

'Look inside.'

Meg reached in and drew out a little leather box, wrapped with thin gold ribbon. She stared at it, then at Paul.

He smiled. 'Go on – open it.'

Meg untied the ribbon and opened the box. Nestling on a bed of dark blue velvet was the loveliest ring Meg had ever seen, a square diamond surrounded by smaller diamonds and sapphires. She drew a breath. 'Oh, Paul!'

'Happy Christmas, and please, darling Meg – will you marry me?'

She gazed at the ring. She felt utter relief. Now she would be safe. Paul would build her a new world, and there she could take shelter from all doubt and anxiety. She was marrying a man who wanted only the best for her. How could she fail to be happy?

'Yes,' she said. 'Of course I will.'

He kissed her, and when he drew away she was touched and astonished to see his eyes were damp. 'God, I was so afraid you might say no. You have no idea...' He kissed her again, then looked down at the ring. 'I hope you like it – it's an Asscher cut. Quite unusual.' He began to talk, saying something about Africa, and diamonds, and things a friend of his in the diamond business had told him. Meg didn't listen. She was concentrating on the conviction that this was entirely what she wanted, and that from now on nothing else would matter in the world but Paul and her, and their future together.

'Won't you put it on?' said Paul at last.

'Gosh, yes – I hope it fits.' Meg lifted the ring from its little cushion of velvet.

'It will,' laughed Paul. 'I borrowed one of your rings from your mother to make entirely sure.'

'You mean – my mother knew all about this?'

Paul nodded. 'I'm afraid a chap can't leave a thing like this to chance. Besides, I had to ask someone for your hand.'

If this thought disturbed Meg just a little, she didn't show it. She slipped the ring on to her finger. It looked beautiful, the most incredibly beautiful thing anyone had ever given her. Impulsively, relieved at her own happiness, she flung her arms around him. 'Oh, Paul, thank you. Thank you, my darling.'

They sat together for a little while longer, talking in low voices under the glow of the street lamps, happy in their own world.

At last Paul turned the key in the ignition. 'Come on, time we got back. The others will be waiting for us. Diana is on tenterhooks.'

'What – she knows too?'

'Of course she does! There's very little about my life that Diana doesn't know.' Paul changed down the gears as they rounded a corner. 'Actually, everyone at supper tonight is waiting with bated breath.'

Did it trouble her that others had known Paul was going to propose to her, as though her engagement had been public property beforehand? If so, she put the thought aside. She stared down at her ring, turning her hand this way and that, gazing with pleasure at its elegant sparkle, shivering with pleasure at the thought of the adventure ahead of her.

When supper was over and their friends had departed, and Diana had decided to have an uncharacteristically early night, Meg and Paul were left alone. They sat together on the sofa, talking, watching the remnants of the fire burning low in the grate. Meg nestled in the crook of Paul's arm, feeling safe and content. She twisted the ring on her finger, making it catch the light.

'I'm glad you like your Christmas present,' said Paul, kissing her forehead lightly.

'I love it. The best present anyone ever gave me.' She suddenly remembered. 'You still haven't opened my present to you!' She got up and went to the hall, where the wrapped-up gramophone had been deposited earlier. She bore it back into the room and set it on the table near the fire. 'Come on!'

Paul tore off the wrapping paper. He studied the gramophone with a bemused smile. 'Thank you. It's topping,' he said. 'But we already have one.'

'But this is one you can carry about. You can take it on picnics and things.'

Meg had included four brand-new records in their cardboard sleeves, and Paul studied them. '"The Sun Has Got His Hat On"? "Lullaby of Broadway"? I'm not sure if I know these.'

'You'll love them, I'm sure you will,' said Meg enthusiastically. She selected one and took it from its sleeve. 'This is my favourite – "Cheek to Cheek". It's from that Fred Astaire film.'

'I'm not actually terribly keen on the cinema, you know.'

Meg remembered, with faint misgiving, the few times she and Paul had gone together to films she had enthusiastically wanted to see. Had he really gone on sufferance?

'Well, maybe not, but you can't help liking the song. Here.' She inserted the gramophone's little metal handle in its side and wound it up, then placed the record on the turntable and set it spinning. Carefully she lowered the needle, and the strains of music filled the room. She took Paul's hand. 'Come on. Let's have a dance!'

Not entirely willingly, Paul got to his feet and took a few steps round the room with her. Then he stopped. 'You know dancing's not my thing, darling. Let's just sit and listen, shall we?'

'Oh.' Meg was disappointed. They sat together on the sofa. Paul listened to the record in a self-conscious way, tapping his fingers on the arm of the sofa, not quite in time to the music. Meg could tell he was only listening to please her. It wasn't that he disliked the music, she realised – it simply meant nothing to him. She felt a tiny anguish; she loved popular songs, films too, for that matter, and she wanted to double her pleasure by having Paul enjoy them just as much. That wasn't likely to happen. Still, no two people could share absolutely everything.

The record came to an end, and Paul took the record from the turntable and put it back in its sleeve. Then he closed the gramophone. 'Thank you,' he said. 'It's a lovely present. Now, it's time I drove you home.'

That was Paul all over, thought Meg. They might be engaged, but he was still going to behave entirely properly until they were married, of that she was sure.

A week later, on New Year's Eve, Dan was in a Soho pub with Harry when a mutual friend at the bar happened to mention Meg and Paul's engagement. Dan feigned casual interest, but in fact he found the news intensely painful. He went back to the table with the beers he had bought for himself and Harry.

'Who was the chap you were talking to at the bar?' asked Harry.

'Just a friend, delivering a not very good piece of news.'

'Oh?'

'That girl I told you about, the one I met last summer. She's engaged to be married.'

Harry took a reflective swig of his pint. 'Ah, well.'

'I don't believe she even loves the man. He's wealthy, of course.'

'Love is like any other luxury, Danny boy. You have to be able to afford it.'

'He can't possibly make her happy.'

'Who knows what makes women happy? They're complicated creatures. Or so I've always been given to understand. I really wouldn't know.'

Dan shook his head. 'I could never tell anyone but you, Harry, but I think I was – am – sort of in love with her. I feel as though someone has just dug a very deep, dark hole and chucked me in it.'

Harry gave his friend a wry smile. 'Dan Ranscombe, the London Lothario – in love? There's hope for you yet, my boy.' He picked up his pint. 'Come on, drink up. Thanks to my superb social connections, we have any number of New Year's Eve parties to go to, where you can drown your sorrows.'

A few minutes after midnight, in the midst of a sea of uproarious New Year revellers, Dan put both his hands on Harry's shoulders and stared at him intently. The gesture helped to steady Harry, who was very tipsy. For a worrying moment he thought Dan was going to kiss him, but instead Dan shouted over the noise of the party, 'I've made a decision!'

Harry shook his head. 'Not a good thing to do when you're drunk!' he shouted back.

Dan tried to speak again, but the din was too much. He waved a hand in the direction of a doorway, and led Harry into another room which, though busy with drinkers and partygoers, was away from the music and somewhat quieter.

'I'm only a bit drunk, and this is something I've been thinking of for a while. The business with that girl has made up my mind. I'm going to Spain.'

Harry groaned. 'Not you, too. Why? To fight?'

'God, no. I thought perhaps I could be a correspondent – you know, reporting back on what's happening there. Might make a name for myself.'

Harry shook his head again. He leaned against the wall and lit a cigarette. When he looked up at Dan, it was with tears in his eyes. 'Well, if you must go, try to bring Laurence back to me, there's a love.'

PART II

1937

1

MEG AND PAUL spent the months of spring looking for a suitable house. Paul was intent on finding a sizeable place in Berkshire, similar to his own childhood home.

'I want our children to grow up in the countryside, just as Di and I did. We had a glorious time. London is all very well for single people, but a family needs room to grow. The kind of place I'm thinking of would have stables, a paddock, perhaps a lake and some woodland.'

'Paul, we don't need a stately home! Besides, I don't ride.'

Paul was mystified. 'I don't think I've ever met anyone who doesn't ride. But not to worry. We'll have you in the saddle and out in the hunting field in no time. My father used to hunt with the Old Berks, as did I, once upon a time. Can't wait to get back to it.'

At the end of April the house agent sent Paul the particulars of a house that seemed to fire his enthusiasm.

'It's called Hazelhurst, just outside Alderworth village, a few miles from where we used to live,' he told Meg. 'Looks pretty much ideal. There are even some outhouses and barns which are perfect for conversion into a garage and workshop.'

Meg leafed through the particulars. Seven bedrooms, two drawing rooms, a billiard room, library, stable block – golly. The prospect of running such a place was daunting, but thrilling, too. She didn't even have to ask Paul if they could afford it. One of the wonderful things about marrying Paul, she had to admit, was that she would never have to worry about money again; she would have more than enough to spend on all the things that made life worthwhile.

'Guy and I have to go to France tomorrow to see a fellow in Le Mans,' Paul went on, 'but why don't you drive over and see what you think?'

Motoring on her own to Berkshire to look over a mansion seemed to Meg a splendidly grown-up idea. Of course, as Mrs Paul Latimer she would soon be doing any number of grown-up things. She had a vision of her newly married self in some pleasant morning room, going through daily menus with her cook, then perhaps wandering to the garden with a trug and secateurs to cut flowers for the house and discuss seasonal planting with the gardener. Soon there might be a nursery to furnish; she pictured herself decorating a sunny room with pastel friezes of animals and nursery rhymes, taking trips to Heal's to buy furniture, perhaps staying in a little London flat that she and Paul might keep for trips to town...

'Are you paying attention, goose?'

Meg emerged from her daydream. 'Sorry, I was miles away. What were you saying, darling?'

'That I can ring the house agent in Reading first thing tomorrow, and he could meet you there with the keys.'

'That's all right. I'll ring and make the arrangements myself. You have your trip to France to think about.' Now that she had started to think in a grown-up way, she was determined to behave in the same fashion.

Hazelhurst was perfect in every way. Meg had feared that the house might be dauntingly large, but in fact the rooms, with their airy windows looking out on to the gardens and the surrounding woodland, were delightfully proportioned, and the atmosphere was warm and welcoming. It was built over three floors, and had a charming gallery of carved oak on the first floor overlooking the spacious entrance hall. The stable block was set at some distance from the house beyond the formal gardens and a large paddock. At an angle to the stables stood a large, disused barn. The barn was reached by a track branching off the main driveway and curving round a stand of elms. It would be perfect for Paul's racing car workshop. Just what he wanted. They could – would – be very happy here.

'It's absolutely ideal,' Meg told the house agent. 'My fiancé is away at the moment, but he'll be back at the end of the week. He can come down then and look around. I only hope he likes it as much as I do. Has there been much interest in the place?' Meg's heart began to beat a little harder at the thought that someone else might buy it before them. How she wished she could clinch the deal on the spot, here and now. But it was Paul's money, and it would be Paul's decision.

The house agent told her that the house had been on the market for two months, and that so far only two prospective buyers had been to look around the property. 'I rather think the high asking price is putting people off. The gentleman who owns it is in no hurry to sell, so he's unlikely to drop the price. He's gone to live in Italy, and is happy to rent out, if he can't sell it.'

'Well, let's hope we'll be in a position to make an offer.'

Meg drove into Alderworth and went for a walk around. She knew she was counting her chickens somewhat, but she couldn't help indulging in a little hopeful speculation. She had fallen in love with Hazelhurst, and she could happily envisage herself living there. Over lunch of soup and a roll in the Alderworth Arms, she studied the map she had brought with her and saw that they were close to the Surrey border. It dawned on Meg, whose grasp of geography and distances had never been very good, that Woodbourne House was only fifteen or so miles away. Delighted at this discovery, she decided to drive over and pay Sonia a visit.

*

Meg found Sonia in her sitting room, answering correspondence.

'My dear, what a lovely surprise!' She rose from her desk and came to embrace Meg. Two slumbering pekes scrambled from their places on the hearthrug to join her.

Meg crouched down to pet them. 'Where's Monty?' she asked.

'Oh, he died, poor thing. Now I have just Domino and Rufus.'

Meg straightened up. 'I hope you don't mind my dropping in unexpectedly. The fact is, I drove down this morning to look at a house Paul and I are thinking of buying, just a few miles away, and it seemed silly not to call on you.'

'I am always delighted to see you. And how wonderful to think of you and Paul coming to live nearby! I must hear all about the house. We can have a nice long talk over tea.' She glanced at her wristwatch. 'That won't be for another hour or so.'

'I can see you have letters to finish, so I'll leave you in peace till then. I'll go and hunt down Mrs Goodall and catch up on the local gossip.'

She found Mrs Goodall in the kitchen with items of household silver arrayed on sheets of newspaper on the table, polishing a candlestick with a rag.

'Oh, mercy! You made me jump!' she exclaimed, as Meg put her head round the door. Then she smiled. 'Whatever are you doing down here? Your aunt never said a word.'

'Surprise visit. How are you, Mrs G?'

'Well enough, thank you,' said Mrs Goodall, resuming her polishing, 'but not exactly best pleased to be doing this chore.'

Meg unpinned her hat and chucked it aside, then sat down at the table. 'I thought William did the silver?'

'He's gone to visit his mother in Hove. She's very ill. He's been gone a week.' Mrs Goodall shook her head. 'She's not expected to live.'

'Oh, dear, I'm sorry to hear that.' Meg picked up a rag and the silver polish, and set to work on the lid of a chafing dish. 'What other news?'

'Well…' Mrs Goodall gave Meg a look, 'Madeleine is still

with us. Big as a barn, and about as talkative. I don't know what your aunt was thinking of, letting her stay on here. It's raised a few eyebrows in the neighbourhood, I can tell you.'

'She's being kind. Where else would Madeleine go? Her grandmother turned her out.'

'Ah, well – I understand there have been a few words between Mrs Haddon and *that* lady.'

'Really?'

'More than a few.' Mrs Goodall nodded and set the candlestick aside. She folded the rag. 'There, that's all I'm prepared to do. I told Mrs Haddon, I said, I'll do the dining-room silver, madam, but I cannot and will not clean every piece in the house. The rest will just have to wait till William gets back.' She watched as Meg finished the chafing dish. 'It's nice to see you back. Your aunt misses you, I can tell you. She's that lonely with your uncle gone.'

'Well, I may be around more often in a few months. Mr Latimer and I have been trying to find a house for when we're married, and this morning I went to see the loveliest place, just over the border in Berkshire. If we buy it, I can visit regularly.'

'Madam must be pleased to hear that.' Mrs Goodall folded her hands in her lap. 'Now, tell me all about the plans for the wedding. I want to know every detail.'

Meg stayed in the kitchen for another half an hour, talking. She enjoyed the grown-up feeling it gave her to be discussing her wedding. The last time she had sat here, she had felt little more than a schoolgirl.

When it was time for Mrs Goodall to start preparing tea, she went out to wander round the gardens, which were looking at their very best in the spring sunshine. Yet it seemed to Meg that there was an odd inertia about the place, as though nothing was expected of it any more. With Uncle Henry gone, the life of the house had somehow receded. She strolled across the lawn and stood in silence beneath the big chestnut tree. She couldn't imagine there ever being another summer house party, with people gathering here to take tea, laughing and talking on the terrace over evening cocktails, days passing in games of tennis and croquet. That had been only last August, yet it seemed long ago. An unbidden memory came to her, of Dan sitting just feet away from where she stood now, feeding her strawberries. For some reason, she remembered the golden hairs on his suntanned arms, not something she even recalled noticing at the time. She put her hands to her cheeks, which were suddenly hot. She didn't want to think about any of that. She would be glad when she was married to Paul, and everything of that kind could be laid to rest.

She was about to turn and go back to the house when she caught sight of Madeleine coming through the orchard. Mrs Goodall was right. She was very large. The baby must be due any day. She waited as Madeleine drew nearer, then hailed her. Madeleine came over.

'Hello. I didn't know you were visiting.'

'Neither did I till this lunchtime.' Meg explained about Hazelhurst, hoping it didn't sound tactless to be talking about her possible new home in the face of Madeleine's less comfortable prospects. 'How are you? The baby must be due soon.'

Madeleine shrugged. 'I suppose so.'

Meg got the distinct feeling that she didn't wish to talk about it. Perhaps she was frightened. They walked together towards the house.

'What will you do?' asked Meg. 'Afterwards, I mean.'

'Go away. Find work somewhere. Mrs Haddon is going to sort out having the baby adopted.'

'You're absolutely sure that's what you want to happen? I mean, I'm sure there are ways…'

Madeleine turned to Meg, her expression stony. 'I just want the whole thing over and done with.'

*

Over tea with her aunt, Meg talked about Paul and their plans. Sonia listened avidly, seeming to take nourishment from everything Meg had to tell her, asking questions here and there.

'How wonderful to be starting out, to have the adventure of your life ahead of you.' Sonia poured the last of the tea, and set the tea strainer aside. 'And here I am – at the end of mine. Without Henry, there are no more adventures.'

'But you're still young, Aunt Sonia. I mean...' Here Meg faltered, suddenly realising how tactless it would be to touch on the possibility of her remarrying.

'I know what you're thinking. But when you have loved once, and that love was entirely perfect, there is no point in looking again. And I could only ever marry for love. No one should marry *except* for love. I'm not saying that Henry was perfect – far from it. Everyone knew that, I most of all. I had to turn a blind eye to many things. But my love for him was perfect. I imagine you feel that for Paul.'

Meg smiled uncertainly. Was what she felt for Paul the most perfect thing in the world, a love above all loves? Goodness, how could she possibly know? How did anyone know? Perhaps only when they had the chance to look back, as Aunt Sonia was doing now.

'I'm sorry,' said Sonia. 'I don't often speak about my feelings.' She took a morsel of sandwich from her plate and fed it to one of the pekes. 'I shouldn't feed them scraps, I know. They're getting far too fat.'

Meg was on the one hand glad that her aunt had moved away from the subject of love, but on the other she wished she could hear more, find out exactly what it was that she was supposed to feel at this important stage in her life. She needed to know that her feelings for Paul measured up to whatever standard of perfection was required of them. She supposed she would just have to hope for the best, to strive to be happy and perhaps, one day, she would be able to look back and congratulate herself on having... On having what? Chosen the right man? Loved him enough? Been loved enough? Her aunt's voice broke through the confusion of her thoughts.

'I won't pretend that your visit hasn't been a godsend, Meg. Life here is quite difficult at the moment, what with Madeleine, and so on.'

'Mrs Goodall told me you've spoken to Madeleine's grandmother.'

'Mrs Goodall should not gossip.' Sonia stroked Domino's silky head, and Domino responded with an ecstatic shiver, for which he was rewarded with a morsel of cake. 'But yes. I felt it really was too bad of her simply to turn her back on the child. We had words. No doubt she overheard me on the telephone.'

'Maybe she'll come round once the baby is born.'

'I very much doubt that. The words "bastard offspring" don't sound terribly promising, do they?'

'No, I suppose not. Have any plans been made? About the adoption, I mean?'

Sonia waved the question away. 'Oh, we shall see to all that when the time comes.'

Meg glanced at her watch. 'It's nearly five. I'll have to be starting back to London soon.'

'Already? But we have so much still to talk about! Why don't you stay for dinner, and go back tomorrow? Your old room is ready and waiting.'

Sonia's hunger for company was so evident, her expression so imploring, that Meg felt she couldn't say no. Besides, there was no pressing need for her to be back in London that evening.

'Of course. I'd love to stay.'

By the time Meg went up to her old room, Effie, the oldest of the housemaids, was smoothing down the sheets and tucking in the blankets. She was a wiry woman in late middle age, and had been with Sonia ever since Meg could remember.

'Nice to see one of the guest rooms being put to use,' Effie remarked. 'It's that sad, dustsheets everywhere. When I think how busy the house used to be, so many visitors coming and going.'

'It's only nine months since Uncle Henry died. I think it will take my aunt a while to get over his death. But I'm sure in time she'll feel more sociable.'

'I hope you're right. Mrs Davenport is doing her best, trying to get her involved in this and that in the neighbourhood, but your aunt never was much one for that kind of thing.' Effie plumped the pillows and smoothed the counterpane. 'There, Miss Margaret, you should be nice and comfy. I've laid out a nightgown for you on the chair over there, and you'll find fresh towels in the cupboard by the bathroom – but you know all that.'

'Thank you.'

Meg opened the window and gazed out at the terrace and lawn leading to the gardens beyond. She loved Woodbourne House; it had warmth and beauty, and managed to be imposing without being excessively grand. She hoped Hazelhurst could be such a place. Leaning out on the window sill, she could glimpse the tennis court through the trees. Hazelhurst didn't have a tennis court. They could make one. It would be a project. Everything would be a project. Life itself was a project, and Paul had enough money for anything she took it into her head to do. That thought, exciting in theory, failed, for some reason, to stir her. She wondered why. Probably because she was tired. She was glad she wasn't driving back tonight.

In an idle half-hour before dinner, Meg wandered into the drawing room. She noticed a photograph album lying on one of the tables and opened it. It was filled with photographs from the house party last summer. There was one of them all on the picnic, Daphne Davenport with her enormous parasol. Meg recalled the walk in the woods they had taken that day, the embarrassment of stumbling on Charles and Madeleine together,

Paul's indignation – an indignation she had thought rather overworked and silly at the time. Given Madeleine's present predicament, it had probably been justified. She took the album to the sofa and leafed through it, conjuring ghosts of last summer. There was a picture of Diana posing with a cigarette by the summerhouse, pretending to be Bette Davis, one of the Cunliffes lounging in deckchairs, Sonia with Avril by the fountain, feeding the fish, Paul standing by the lake in his shirtsleeves, pipe in mouth, in the manly posture he always adopted when being photographed. She smiled and gazed at the photo for a moment, sure in her heart of her feelings for him. She turned the page, and there was a picture of Dan, sensuously stretched out in the sun on the broad stone terrace wall, eyes closed, hands folded behind his head. She could tell from his smile that he was aware he was being photographed and of how handsome he looked. Meg studied the photograph dispassionately. How easy to be taken in by those looks, that charm. She nearly had been. A lucky escape.

Sonia came in to the drawing room and sat down next to her. 'Ah, you've found my album. You know, after Henry died, I couldn't bring myself to do anything about all those photographs. I only got round to it recently. I'm glad I did.' She inspected the photograph of Dan. 'Look at Dan. Like a golden cat in the sun.' She gazed at the picture for a moment, musing. 'He's gone to Spain. I don't know why they do it, these foolish boys.' She shook her head.

Meg was startled. 'He's gone to fight?'

'No, as a war correspondent – still fearfully dangerous.'

'I thought he was dead set against people going out there.'

'Well, evidently he changed his views. I wake up each day wondering whether he's alive or dead. At least he writes regularly, which is something.'

Dead. Dan dead. The image quite shocked Meg. It felt as though someone had thrust a sharp blade into her. But of course, the idea of anyone so young dying was dreadful.

She and Sonia leafed through the rest of the pictures, then Sonia laid the album aside and rose to her feet. 'Now, I don't generally drink these days, but I think your visit is a cause for a celebration. As is this new house of yours.'

'We haven't bought it yet, remember.'

'Ah, but I have a happy presentiment.' Sonia unstoppered the sherry decanter and poured out two small glasses. She handed one to Meg with a smile. 'Just as I did about you and Paul. My presentiments are generally right.'

After dinner Meg and Sonia played a couple of games of cribbage, and then Meg went to bed, determined to make an early start for London.

But sleep wouldn't come. Meg lay there, listening to the rising wind rattle the window, which she had left ajar. She got up to close it. A hard rain was falling outside, drumming on the gable roof. Meg hoped it would be over by morning. She detested driving in bad weather. On her way back to bed she caught sight of the little bookcase, and decided she might as well read for a while, rather than toss and turn. She recognised the novel which she'd started last August, and plucked it out. It hadn't wholly gripped her, but it was something to wile away a sleepless hour.

She got back into bed. The book fell open, not at the page she had last read, but where she had put the wild rose that Dan had given her last summer. She lifted it from the pages. It was desiccated and brittle now, but the unexpected sight of it filled her with the recollection of their first kiss beneath the trees, the dappled light between the leaves, the drowsy sound of the wood pigeons. She shut her eyes as if to hold the memory back, then let it come. It didn't matter that he had turned out to be worthless, he had given her that. Her mind drifted to the night he had visited her here in this very room, and then to the Cunliffes' party, and those moments in the library, those kisses on the sofa. The recollection seemed to set her senses on fire. She lay there for a long, indulgent moment, remembering, then abruptly opened her eyes. She shouldn't be doing this. It was a betrayal. It had meant nothing. It was all just about sex, and that was treacherous, too. It had nothing to do with love, only with gratification.

The rose lay in her palm. She closed her fingers, crushing until there was nothing left of it but tiny fragments and a thin, dried stem. She dusted them from her hand, then closed the book and chucked it across the room. That was done with. She put out the light.

Sleep took a long time to come.

2

WHEN SHE AWOKE a few hours later, it was to a tapping on her door. In her sleepy state she was transported back to that night when Dan had come to her room, and she sat up, startled, trying to make sense of it. Then she grew properly awake, and realised the tapping was in fact an urgent rapping.

'Yes?' she called out, swinging herself out of bed.

'Meg?' Sonia's voice was urgent. 'Can you come, please? I need you.'

Meg hurried to the door. Sonia stood there in her dressing gown, her hair in a plait over one shoulder.

'It's Madeleine. The baby isn't due for another fortnight, but I think it's starting.' They hurried together along the passage, and Meg became aware not only of shrieks and moans coming from Madeleine's room, but also of Avril crying at the top of her voice in the nursery on the floor above.

'Avril heard Madeleine and came down to her room,' explained Sonia. 'I don't know how the rest of us slept through it. She must have thought Madeleine was dying. Now she's having a blue fit up there. I told Miss Bissett to keep her in the nursery.'

Effie, the only other servant who lived in, appeared on the stairs, clutching her robe, startled from sleep by the commotion.

'Effie, we shall need your help. The baby is coming. All hands to the pump.'

They went into Madeleine's bedroom. She was writhing and moaning in a tangle of bed sheets and blankets, a sheen of perspiration on her face, her blonde hair in sweaty tendrils. When she saw Sonia she reached out and clutched her hand.

Meg was shocked. She knew nothing of the realities of childbirth. In the rare moments when she thought about it at all, she had a hazy, sanitised conception of a little puffing and panting, and then a baby being placed in the arms of a smiling mother. She had not expected to witness such pain, such naked desperation.

'I don't know what to do!' she said to Sonia.

'Don't worry. I shall tell you what to do. Dr Egan is out attending another patient, unfortunately, but his wife says he will come as soon as he gets back. With luck he will be here before things get very far along. At the moment we must just help her manage her contractions.'

Meg didn't even know what a contraction was, and said so. Sonia explained, in between murmuring soothing words to Madeleine, who writhed like an anguished animal.

'I'm just going to give my hands a good wash,' said Sonia, and left the room.

After a few moments, Madeleine grew quieter. She lay on her side, panting.

Sonia came back, dressing gown sleeves rolled to her elbows. 'Madeleine, dear, I need you to lie on your back. I have to see whether the baby is coming.'

Madeleine gave a groan and rolled on to her back, her knees up. Sonia lifted Madeleine's nightgown. 'Dear me, this is so difficult. There isn't enough light in here. Effie, can you bring that bedside light round here?'

'How do you know what to do?' Meg asked, watching as Sonia repositioned the lamp and peered at Madeleine's nether regions.

'I was in the VAD in the war. And it helps to have had a baby oneself.'

Meg looked on anxiously as Madeleine clenched her teeth and grasped the sides of her swollen belly, giving vent to unearthly groans and shrieks. Meg was convinced there must be some problem, some enormous difficulty – surely it wasn't always like this?

'I can see the head,' said Sonia. 'This is going to happen faster than I had thought.' She dropped the edge of Madeleine's nightgown and turned to Meg. 'I need you to go to the kitchen and boil some water and bring it up here in a basin. Scissors – we shall need scissors. And towels, plenty of towels. Effie, you can fetch those.'

Meg left the room and went down to the kitchen. She had to fumble around for a few moments till she found the light switch. She filled the kettle, lit the gas, and set it on the range. It seemed to take an age to boil. Then she poured the water into the largest metal mixing bowl she could find and took it carefully upstairs.

Back in Madeleine's room, things had reached a disturbing pitch. Madeleine was clutching the rails at the head of the bed and crying out in what seemed to Meg like the distress of one dying. Sonia stood at the end of the bed in a half-crouching position, alternately coaxing and soothing. Effie, having deposited what seemed like all the towels in the house by the foot of the bed, stood anxiously by.

'Wait, wait,' Sonia was saying to Madeleine. 'Not yet. Breathe as deep as you can, there's a good girl.' She looked up and saw Meg. 'Excellent. Set the basin down here.'

As Meg placed the basin on the floor next to Sonia, she looked up. The sight was unearthly. She had no idea female private parts could look so grotesque. It was horrible. She realised the blueish bulge must be the baby's head. Madeleine was groaning and crying even more terribly than before.

'Now, go and fetch some scissors.'

Meg dithered; she had no idea where to find scissors.

Sonia caught her hesitation. 'My sewing box. In my bedroom. Quick, now!'

Meg hurried off. Sonia fixed her gaze intently between Madeleine's legs.

'Right, my dear – push, push with all your might. Take some deep breaths and give a big push. Excellent!'

It took Meg some moments to locate Sonia's sewing box, and when she returned with the scissors it was to hear Sonia exhorting Madeleine, 'Come on, Madeleine! One last time, and we're nearly there!'

She stood by the end of the bed, transfixed, and watched as a tiny purplish head emerged, its features screwed up. Sonia held the head lightly, and then suddenly the rest of the baby slithered out. It looked to Meg like a slimy human grub on the end of a bloody rope.

'A girl!' exclaimed Sonia. 'Madeleine, you have a baby girl. A towel, if you please, Meg.' She sounded satisfied and businesslike. Meg knelt down and swiftly unfolded a towel, and Sonia placed the new infant in it, wrapping it loosely. With her little finger she parted the baby's tiny lips very lightly and circled the inside of its mouth with the tip of her finger. The baby let out a raw, shivering cry. The sound pierced Meg to her very core.

'Effie, take the basin to the bathroom and empty it – quickly, now!'

Effie hurried off and returned with the empty basin a moment later, and handed it to Sonia. She was just in time. The afterbirth slithered out, followed by a gush of blood, most of which Sonia managed to catch in the basin. As she knelt cradling the baby, it seemed to Meg's horrified eyes that there was blood everywhere – was Madeleine haemorrhaging, dying? But Sonia seemed calm. She mopped up with towels and then took the scissors and cut the cord, not without some difficulty, murmuring, 'These really are not the sharpest scissors in the world.'

Down below the front doorbell pealed, and Rufus and Domino began to yap.

'That will be Dr Egan,' said Sonia. 'Better late than never, I suppose. Effie, go and show him up, please. Goodness, what a mess. But I think we have done rather well, all in all.'

Dr Egan arrived, shaking the rain from his coat. He examined Madeleine, neatly and expertly tied up the cord, then took the baby from Meg and unwrapped her.

'Mother and baby both seem healthy.' He smiled at Sonia. 'Well done to you all.'

This professional praise was very gratifying. Dr Egan approached the bed with the baby. Madeleine lay looking exhausted. Deflated was the word that came to Meg's mind.

'Madeleine?' said Sonia gently. 'Your baby.'

But Madeleine simply shook her head and closed her eyes.

'You must take her,' said Sonia. 'She needs you. She will need to feed soon.'

'I don't want it,' muttered Madeleine, and looked away.

Sonia's eyes met the doctor's.

'Give her a little while,' murmured Dr Egan, and handed the baby back to Meg. 'I'll call again tomorrow afternoon.'

'Would you like some refreshment, doctor? Tea? Or something stronger, perhaps?'

'Thank you, Mrs Haddon, but I can hear my bed calling. It's been a busy night.'

When the doctor had gone, they set about changing the sheets on Madeleine's bed, then Sonia sent Effie back to bed, and tried to do the same with Meg. But Meg, still cradling the baby, refused.

'You see how Madeleine is, Aunt Sonia,' said Meg, speaking in a low voice. 'I'll stay with her. I couldn't sleep, anyway.'

'Well, I certainly could. I feel quite exhausted.'

'As well you might – you coped wonderfully. Go to bed, and I shall see you in a few hours.'

'The baby will need to feed, you know. It isn't easy, the first time.'

'Don't worry about it. I'm sure we'll be fine. Get some rest.'

Meg drew a chair near to the window and pulled up the blind

so that she could watch the dawn come up. While Madeleine slept, she sat gently rocking the baby, musing on the tiny, sleeping face, glancing up occasionally as morning light began to pearl the sky behind the dark trees. Towards dawn the baby began to mew fretfully, and Madeleine stirred. She rolled over and gazed dispassionately at Meg and the baby.

'I think she needs to be fed,' said Meg.

'No.'

'Don't be so heartless. She's your baby. How else is she meant to survive?'

Madeleine sat up slowly, and Meg brought the baby over.

'I don't know what to do,' said Madeleine, unbuttoning her nightdress.

'Neither do I. But the baby probably does. We'll just have to muddle through.'

There followed a frustrating ten minutes in which Madeleine and baby battled with the task. Madeleine grew tearful and was on the verge of giving up, but the baby's hungry determination prevailed, and through a combination of luck and good timing she managed to latch on and began to feed.

Meg sat contemplating them, thinking what an artlessly perfect tableau they made, mother and child, bathed in the first early rays of the sun. Madeleine looked up, and the expression in her eyes startled Meg.

'I won't do this again. I'm only doing it now because... because I suppose there aren't any bottles anywhere. But there's no point. I don't want it, and the sooner everyone else understands that, the better.'

Meg looked at the baby's face, absorbed in suckling, the tiny fingers instinctively kneading Madeleine's breast, and could not imagine how Madeleine could feel anything but utter devotion to this helpless little thing. Surely if one had been discarded oneself, the instinct to protect and nurture would be stronger? But maybe the reverse was true. She had no idea what it was like to be Madeleine, what she had been going through these past nine months, but if she had been inuring herself to giving her child up for adoption, perhaps that meant she could not allow herself to feel anything for it from the very first.

The baby began to squirm in Madeleine's arms, pulling away, and Madeleine looked up at Meg. 'I think we need nappies.'

'Nappies?' said Meg in alarm. 'Where would they be?'

'I don't know. In the linen cupboard, possibly.' The truth was, whatever preparations Sonia had been making for the baby's arrival, Madeleine had refused to be either interested or involved.

Meg went to look, and met Sonia emerging sleepily from her room. Sonia dug out a bale of nappies and a packet of pins, and Meg watched as she cleaned the little bottom and managed, after a few false starts, to encase it in an ill-fitting nappy.

'I'm not terribly expert at this,' sighed Sonia. 'The nursemaid attended to all this kind of thing with Avril. But it will have to do. Madeleine, you must attend to this from now on.'

'No. I told Meg. You all know I don't want it. I just want it taken away.'

'Don't be ridiculous, child!' said Sonia sharply. 'It will take time for arrangements to be made, and until then you must look after your baby as best you can. You must learn to feed her and change her. You're her mother.'

'I don't want to be anyone's mother. I hate what's happened.'

'Then you should have thought of that nine months ago!'

Sonia left the room abruptly. Madeleine burst into tears. The baby lay in its enormous nappy, gazing benignly at the world. With a sigh Meg wrapped her in the towel. Presumably there were baby clothes somewhere, too, but the towel would do for the moment. She sat on the edge of the bed, holding the infant. Eventually Madeleine stopped crying.

'She's so pretty,' said Meg, smiling down at the baby. 'You'll have to think of a lovely name for her.'

'I don't want anything to do with it,' said Madeleine. 'You can have it, if you like it so much.'

Meg's heart jumped at the thought. But that would never do. Besides, it was one thing to like a baby, and quite another to take responsibility for it. She wasn't ready to be a mother quite yet. She stroked the baby's satin cheek with the tip of her finger.

'Let's think of a name.' Meg mused. 'Laura – what about Laura? I've always thought it such a pretty name.'

'I don't care.' Madeleine rolled over on to her side, gazing fixedly at the window.

Meg decided she was heartily tired of Madeleine's petulance and indifference. She took the baby back to her bedroom and laid her carefully on the bed, bunching the eiderdown around her so there was no danger of her rolling off – although the baby admittedly didn't look as if she was capable of that – and then washed and dressed. She kept glancing at the baby, feeling every time she did so a little surge of wonder at the fact of this tiny new life lying there on the bed, absorbing the world with grave grey eyes. Did all babies look so wise?

She took the baby down to the kitchen, where Mrs Goodall was busy preparing breakfast. Mrs Goodall's surprise and mild disapproval at the baby's overnight arrival rapidly mellowed, and she was soon declaring her a dear little mite.

'She is sweet, isn't she?' said Meg. 'It's just sad that Madeleine doesn't want anything to do with her.'

'That's probably for the best,' said Mrs Goodall briskly. 'No point in getting overfond of it.'

'She says she won't even feed her.'

'Well, there's always bottles. I'm sure we have a few around from Miss Avril's time. Madam was never one for nature's way. Now, I'd best get breakfast on the table.'

Sonia appeared in the breakfast room with a straw bassinette which had once been Avril's, some sheets and a small, handmade quilt, and a tiny gown. Meg dressed the baby while Sonia prepared the bassinette, and then laid her in it. She and Sonia sat down to breakfast. Meg recounted Mrs Goodall's remarks.

'I suppose it's true,' said Sonia. 'There's no use her forming an attachment. It's just that she's rather the obvious person to be feeding and changing the baby. Still, I was wrong to lose my temper.' She rubbed her temples with distracted fingers. 'I really haven't thought this through.'

'How does one go about having a baby adopted?'

'My dear, I have no idea. I know I should have made enquiries. It's very remiss of me.' Sonia sipped her tea. 'Still, time enough for that.'

A tiny cry rose from the bassinette, and Sonia got up. She lifted the baby into her arms and brought her back to the breakfast table.

'Now, now,' she said, smiling tenderly at the baby, 'that's a great deal of noise for such a little scrap to be making, isn't it?' She continued to murmur affectionate, reproving nonsense, and the baby grew calmer.

'Madeleine isn't interested in giving her a name,' observed Meg. 'I thought Laura might be rather nice.'

'Laura – how perfectly sweet!' She contemplated the baby. 'Yes, we shall call you Laura. Just for the time being, of course.'

Meg, watching her aunt cradle the baby happily, felt a faint misgiving. Perhaps it wasn't just Madeleine who had to be wary of forming affection for this new person.

'One more slice of toast,' said Meg, 'and then I really must be getting back to London. This visit has been quite an adventure.'

'It certainly has. I wish you could stay longer, but I know you have a busy time ahead of you. As do we.' She smiled down at the baby. 'Don't we, Laura?'

When Paul came back from France, Meg was bursting with news, both about the baby and Hazelhurst.

'Well, I'm delighted that you like the house so much. I'll ring the agent chappie and we can go down together first thing next week. As to the baby, it might have been better for all if it had died at birth.'

'Paul! What a perfectly dreadful thing to say! She's adorable. And I named her. She's to be called Laura.'

'Let's hope she grows up to have more sense and morals than her mother.'

'You can be quite insufferable at times,' said Meg. 'It's a terribly sad situation for both of them. I suppose if things were otherwise, Madeleine would dote on her baby. But because she's decided to give it away, she won't let herself feel anything. She even offered to let me have her.'

'No, thank you very much!' exclaimed Paul. 'I certainly don't want charge of someone else's bastard offspring.'

'That's exactly how Madeleine's grandmother described her,' observed Meg sadly. 'Poor Laura.'

Paul, conscious that he had said something to displease Meg, though not quite sure what, said, 'You have a very generous heart, my child, feeling so much for other people. But you can't lead their lives for them. You have your own to think about. And I intend it to be a very happy one. Now, tell me more about the house.'

3

IN THE SAME hour, Dan was sitting in his third-floor bedroom in his hotel in Madrid, finishing his latest report for the *Graphic*. He worked to the sound, beyond his window, of constant gunfire and shelling – a sound to which he had become so accustomed that he scarcely paid attention, unless the threatening whine of the approach indicated the shell might land closer than most. Even then, he would only pause to listen and wait for the explosion, further or closer as it might be, and carry on tapping at the typewriter keys. Like most of the hotel's residents, he operated on a level where fatalism, nonchalance and recklessness rubbed weary shoulders. Since the last shell had not struck, why should this? It was in the same stoical spirit that the citizens of Madrid went about their daily business, knowing that at any moment a rifle bullet might send them, newspaper or shopping basket in hand, sprawling into sudden death on the street. Who knew? No one. So who could possibly care? But if they had no say over the larger issues of life or death, everyone still tried to exercise such mundane control as they could over the detail of their daily lives, hence the hotel manager's insistence that Dan keep his windows open so that the glass wouldn't blow out if a shell landed close by.

Dan spooled his finished report out of his typewriter and glanced through it, then went downstairs, left the hotel and took it over to the *censura*. When he came back, the clerk at the reception desk plucked a letter from one of the pigeonholes. 'For you, Señor Ranscombe.'

Dan took the letter up to his room and opened it. It was from Sonia, dated two weeks ago, telling him that Charles Asher had been wounded while fighting with the International Brigade's 15th Battalion, and had been sent to hospital in Madrid for treatment and recuperation. She asked if Dan would spare some time to visit him. Dan weighed this up. He hadn't much cared for Charles, but the chap would probably welcome seeing a friendly face, so it seemed the decent thing to do.

The next morning, Dan went to the hospital, but was told that Charles had been discharged the previous day and was in temporary accommodation in a local barracks. He made his way to the barracks and found Charles sitting on his own at a table in the shabby mess, reading a dog-eared copy of *Right Ho, Jeeves*. A pair of crutches rested against the table. He glanced up as Dan came in, and after a second's hesitation, recognition dawned.

'Dan, isn't it?' He hesitated, embarrassed. 'I'm sorry, I don't remember your surname.' He stuffed the book in the pocket of his jacket and held out a hand. Dan shook it.

'Ranscombe. Sonia wrote and told me you were in the hospital here. How are you?'

'So-so, thanks. I caught a bullet in my upper thigh and one in my ankle. My leg was a bit of a mess at the time, but it's not too bad now.'

Dan nodded and glanced at the crutches. 'Reckon you can make it as far as the bar round the corner?'

Charles smiled thinly. 'I can try. I'm actually pretty nifty on these things.' The two of them left the barracks and made their way down the street, Charles swinging along on his crutches.

'It's nice to see someone from home,' he said, glancing at Dan. 'Decent of you to look me up.'

They had reached a scruffy bar with a few tables scattered outside. 'This do?' asked Dan.

Charles nodded. They sat in the spring sunshine at a table under an awning, and ordered a couple of beers. As the waiter set down the bottles and glasses, Dan looked Charles over, trying to assess how much the events of the last few months had changed him. He was dressed in corduroy breeches, dusty leather boots, and a battered leather jacket over a thin shirt, a red kerchief knotted round his throat. With his hair cropped short beneath his cap, he seemed a leaner, older version of the young man Dan had met at Woodbourne House just a few months before, but the look in his dark expressive eyes was still boyishly earnest. He knocked two cigarettes from a packet and lit them while Dan poured the beers. He handed one to Dan and leaned back in his chair, pulling off his cap as he took the first drag.

'What are you doing out here?' asked Charles.

'I'm here as a reporter for the *London Graphic*.' They smoked in silence for a few seconds. 'So,' said Dan, 'you've seen action. Where was it?'

Charles blew out a plume of smoke. 'Jarama.'

'Would you care to tell me about it? I'd be interested.'

Dan listened as Charles talked about the battle, about the day that had dawned clear and sunny over the olive groves, and had ended in rain and mud and blood. He described the onslaught by the Nationalists, the pitiful carnage wrought among the young Republican recruits as they were mown down by Franco's elite fighters. 'I don't know how many died,' said Charles, taking a long pull at his beer. 'And I don't know how or why I wasn't among them. The miracle is that in the end we won, we saw them off. And I'm proud to have been part of it. Though how much good it will do in the long run is anyone's guess.' He shrugged and took a last drag of his cigarette, then ground out the butt in the little tin ashtray. He picked up his box of matches and turned it over. 'Funny, when I was living in those trenches, I would have sold my soul for just one match. What good's a fag without a match? You can't imagine a more beastly existence than living in a muddy trench.'

'Still, you're out of it now.'

'I'm being sent back to the front in a week.' He glanced at his surroundings, then at Dan. 'Last summer seems a lifetime ago, doesn't it? That house party. Tea on the lawn, everyone dressed up for dinner. Fishing for trout by moonlight.' He shook his head. 'I liked Mrs Haddon. How is she?'

'She's well, I believe. I haven't seen her since. Just letters.' Dan knew only too well the implausibility of Meg's theory that Charles was the father of Madeleine's baby, but since he was here, he might as well put it to the test. After a pause, he said, 'That girl, Madeleine – do you remember her? The nanny?'

Charles nodded. 'Yes.' He reached for his cigarettes and lit another.

'She's having a baby. But she won't say who the father is.'

Charles was about to say something, then he caught the expression in Dan's eyes. 'What?'

'I just wondered – you know, you and she, that day in the woods – whether—'

'You think I might be the father?' Charles pinched his cigarette between finger and thumb and took a sharp drag, shaking his head. 'Good God, no. I kissed her once, that's all.' There was something so simple and dismissive in the way he spoke that Dan believed him. 'I must say, she didn't really strike me as that kind of girl. Don't you have any other candidates?'

Dan took a sip of his beer. 'I didn't mean to insult you. But no, no one has a clue.'

'I don't feel insulted. The truth is, I've never slept with a woman. Sad, isn't it? But there it is.'

There was an embarrassed silence, and Dan turned the talk to other things. After half an hour they had finished their drinks. Dan paid, and they walked back to the barracks.

Dan pointed to the book stuffed in Charles's jacket pocket and smiled. 'That's the one where Gussie Fink-Nottle gets drunk at the prize-giving, isn't it? And P. K. Purvis wins the Scripture Knowledge prize.'

'G. G. Simmons.'

'G. G. Simmons, that's right! I don't know when I've read anything funnier.' He shook his head. It seemed bizarre, and rather touching, that someone of Charles's political and social views should seek escape in the world of Jeeves and Wooster.

They stood together in the spring sunshine for a moment, reflecting, then Charles said, 'Well, so long.' He shook Dan's hand. 'Thanks for coming to visit me. It was kind.'

'I would offer to come again, but I'm making arrangements to leave shortly. Perhaps we'll meet in London.'

'Perhaps we will.'

But after saying goodbye to him outside the scruffy little bar, Dan never saw Charles Asher again.

A week after he returned from Madrid, Dan went to visit his godmother. Over lunch he talked about his exploits in Spain.

'I'm just glad you're back safe and sound,' said Sonia. 'I think anyone who goes there, soldier or journalist, is either brave or foolish.'

'I certainly wasn't brave. Not like some of the journalists, who went right into the thick of the fighting to get their stories. I had no intention of risking my life. It makes me wonder whether I'm not rather a coward. I wonder if I would feel differently if England went to war.'

'But you were living in Madrid. By all accounts it's a dreadfully dangerous place.'

'It's strange – a lot of the time it didn't feel like it. There was rather a sense of...' Dan paused, looking for the right word, 'of fun, if that doesn't sound too trivial. Fun and adventure.'

'The young take most things in that spirit, which is either all to the good or most regrettable, depending on how one chooses to look at it. Certainly it makes wars possible. Helen tells me that your pieces in the *Graphic* were first-rate. She said everyone talked about them.'

'That's nice to hear. My bosses seem happy, at any rate. Being a foreign correspondent is a sight more interesting than writing up the Summer Exhibition.'

'And did you manage to visit Charles Asher? When I heard he'd been wounded I thought he might be grateful to see a friendly face.'

Dan nodded. 'I saw him just before I left. He was on the mend, but he's going back to the front line.'

There was silence for a moment, then Sonia said, 'You'll have heard all about Madeleine's baby, I suppose?'

'Yes. Meg told me at Christmas.'

'Did she tell you that Charles Asher is probably the father?'

'I'd heard something like that. But I can tell you that he's not.'

'Can you be certain?' Sonia gazed at him intently.

'Pretty much. I asked him, and he said he couldn't be. I believed him.'

Sonia nodded slowly, as though settling something in her mind. After a pause she said, 'The intention was always to put the baby – her name is Laura – up for adoption. But when Meg told me about these speculations that Charles Asher might be the father, it seemed to me he should be told, in case... in case he chose to be involved. But if you're sure he's not...'

'I'm quite certain.'

'... then it makes all the difference.' She paused. 'You see, Madeleine is going away in a matter of weeks. For good. Daphne Davenport helped to find her a situation in Yorkshire, a large family in want of a young nanny. She's very lucky to be making a fresh start. And I want Laura to stay here.'

Dan was taken aback. 'You're going to adopt her?'

'I've grown so attached to the little thing, and it seems pointless to send her to strangers when she could have the best of homes here. She would want for nothing, and she'd be company for Avril when she's older. Having another child around might do her the world of good.' Sonia glanced through the open French windows and saw Effie wheeling the pram across the lawn. She put down her napkin and got to her feet. 'Come with me.'

Dan rose and followed her out to the terrace, and down the steps to the lawn. Effie had pushed the baby's pram beneath the shade of some trees, and was settling her blanket over her.

'I thought she could do with some fresh air, ma'am, seeing as it's such a nice day.'

'A very good idea. Thank you, Effie.'

Sonia bent over the pram. 'Isn't she a darling?'

Dan looked down at Laura. She really was the most extraordinarily pretty infant. She had large, expressive grey eyes, with well-defined brows, a soft thatch of golden hair, and a rosebud mouth. She wriggled and stretched tiny hands.

'I can see why you're smitten. What does Madeleine think? About you keeping the baby, I mean.'

'Well, that's just it. For some reason I can't fathom, she doesn't seem happy with the idea. She won't say why exactly.'

'Perhaps she feels it would be harder for her to cut her ties.'

'I don't see what possible difference it can make to her. She's been utterly indifferent to the baby since the day she was born. I just wish I could persuade her that it would be in Laura's best interests for her to remain here. I've even offered to let her stay here with Laura, but she won't hear of that. I'm worried that she'll take it into her own hands, speak to an adoption agency, and then Laura will be taken away.' Sonia sighed. 'But it's Madeleine's choice.' She bent and stroked Laura's cheek, then straightened up. 'Let's go inside and have coffee.' They walked back across the lawn. 'I have a few things I must attend to this afternoon. Can you amuse yourself till teatime?'

'Absolutely. I'll loaf about here for a while and then go for a walk.'

'Splendid. Then we can have tea on the lawn.'

Dan idled away an hour in the library with the newspaper, then took a stroll into the village. On his way through the orchard he caught sight of Madeleine sitting beneath a tree, reading a book.

'Hello there,' said Dan.

Madeleine regarded Dan apprehensively. They hadn't seen one another since the day of Henry Haddon's death. Everything about that day in August last year lay between them.

'Hello.'

He dropped his jacket on the ground and sat down next to her. 'What's the book?'

She closed it and showed it to him.

'*Villette*? Can't say I've ever read it. Any good?'

'It takes a bit of getting into, but yes.'

He nodded. They sat in silence for a few moments, insects humming in the warm air around them. Dan knew that Madeleine was thinking about those moments in the barn, the final moments of Henry Haddon's life, and their shared secret.

'You know,' said Dan at last, 'I have never told a soul about you and Henry Haddon.' He met her eye. 'And I never shall. You have my word on that.' Her gaze held his. 'Do you believe me?'

She took a moment to answer. 'Yes.' She laid the book down, put her hands over her eyes and drew her knees up. The posture was childlike. Then she took her hands away and let out a long breath, as though rid of something.

'I've just had lunch with Mrs Haddon,' Dan went on. 'She says you're going away soon.'

'I've got a job in Yorkshire. Mrs Haddon says she doesn't want me to go. She says the baby and I can stay here. She's grown very fond of Laura.' She shook her head. 'If she knew the truth, she wouldn't want either of us here for a second.'

'And what do you feel?'

'I just want to get away, pretend none of it happened. Before the baby was born, I thought people were going to do things – to have her adopted, to make it all disappear. Then when she came, no one did anything. Mrs Haddon kept fussing over her, and buying her things.' She shook her head. 'The last thing I want is to stay here and look after a baby I never wanted.' She turned to look at Dan. 'You may think that's heartless, but it's true.'

'Then why not leave the baby here with Mrs Haddon? It's what she wants.'

'I know it is, but how could I, after what I did? It would feel like an even worse deceit. And she's been nothing but kind to me.'

Dan plucked and chewed on a stalk of grass. 'Well, there is another way of looking at it, you know. Laura is her father's daughter, as well as yours. Some would say she belongs here. That Woodbourne House is where she should be. She is a Haddon, after all. If no one ever knows' – he turned to meet her gaze – 'then no ill can ever come of it. Can it?'

She looked away. 'I hadn't thought of it like that. But I still feel it would all be a horrible lie.'

'Madeleine, only two people know the truth. You and me. And neither of us will ever say anything.' He chucked the chewed grass stalk away. 'I think you should let Mrs Haddon look after the baby. Let her have a good home. Let her stay where she's loved.'

Madeleine pondered this, and at length said, 'Perhaps.'

Dan picked up his jacket and got to his feet. 'I'm going into the village. Perhaps I'll see you later.'

She watched him go, shading her eyes with her hand, then sat for a long while, thinking.

When Dan reached the village, he went into the Swan, bought himself a pint of beer, and took it outside to a table overlooking the village green, where he settled himself comfortably with his book.

Ten minutes later he looked up and was mildly astonished to see Meg coming out of the post office. She was wearing a dark blue suit with a nipped-in waist, and a little hat with a fetching brim that dipped over her brow, her dark hair neatly pinned up. Dan thought, with a pang, that if she was trying hard to appear grown-up and sophisticated, she had succeeded. She was busy putting her purse away, and as she snapped her handbag shut and looked up, he was ready with a smile. She hesitated for a moment, then crossed the green.

'What an extraordinary surprise,' she said. 'You're quite the last person I expected to see in Chidding.'

'I came down for the day to visit my godmother.'

'That's a coincidence. I was going to pop in and see her. I just stopped in the village to buy some stamps.'

'Congratulations, by the way. You and Paul.'

'Thanks.' They gazed at one another for a long moment, then Meg added, 'Paul and I have bought a house just a few miles away, in Berkshire.'

Dan nodded. 'I see.'

'It keeps me very busy, decorating, furnishing and so forth. And we're building a tennis court. Such upheaval. I have to come from London on a regular basis to keep an eye on things. Paul is so busy with his racing car business, it all seems to be left up to me. Driving back and forth is so tiring.'

'I can imagine.' She was clearly still trying on for size her new role as the future Mrs Latimer. It amused him to see her so determined to be grown-up.

'Won't you join me?' he asked. 'The pub does a very good beer.'

She gave a little grin, looking more like the Meg he knew. 'I'm not much of a beer-drinker, but perhaps a cider would be nice.'

Dan disappeared inside the pub. Meg sat down, quelling her mixed feelings of pain and pleasure at seeing him. The last thing she wanted was to feel anything at all. She told herself firmly that what had happened was in the past, and quite inconsequential, and this was a good opportunity for them both to behave like civilised people, and re-establish themselves as nothing more than friendly acquaintances.

Dan returned a few minutes later with a glass of cider.

'Cheers.' Meg picked up Dan's book and glanced at the cover. '*Plato Today* – what's this all about?'

'Just a review copy I found lying around the office. I thought it looked rather interesting. Some chap imagining Plato coming back to today's world to see how the ideas he sets out in *The Republic* are being used – or rather, misused. I'm at the bit where he visits Nazi Germany and weighs up what's going on there.'

'Sounds terribly dry. Give me a good detective novel any day. Frankly, I hear quite enough from Paul about the Nazis. He seems to enjoy scaring everyone with the idea that there's going to be a war.' Her eyes sought Dan's. 'Do you think there might be?'

'Perhaps.'

'I so don't want there to be.'

'It's not worth thinking about. Tell me about yourself instead.'

Meg talked about the coming wedding, and about her new house, and about Paul. As he listened, Dan could tell how much she wanted to be kept safe, to shut out the wider world and focus on her home, her kitchen garden, her tennis court, and the needs of her husband, so that she need never unlock the gate in the garden wall and peep out at the savagery of the wild woods beyond. A war, for Meg, would simply mean the spoiling of all that was agreeable. It wasn't that she was shallow – she was like a child asleep. He watched her face, her lovely eyes glancing around as she spoke, occasionally skirting his gaze but never quite meeting it. He wanted to put out a hand and catch her chin, hold her face still, level with his. He fantasised about bending forward to kiss her, gently unpinning her hat, letting down her hair, pulling off her clothes and taking her across the pub table in full view of the scandalised village. The savage sexuality of his thoughts, in the face of her chatter about Diana's intractability over the matter of bridesmaids' dresses, made him smirk.

Meg caught his expression. 'I'm sorry, going on about myself. When did you get back from Spain?'

'A week ago. I saw Charles Asher when I was out there. You remember him?'

Meg nodded. 'Of course. I suppose you know that Madeleine and her baby are still at Woodbourne House?'

'Yes.'

'Madeleine says Charles Asher isn't the father, but I don't see who else it could possibly be.'

'It isn't Charles. He told me so himself.'

'Well, he would say that, wouldn't he? If he wanted to avoid responsibility, I mean.'

'I believe he was telling the truth. And I think it's quite irresponsible to gossip about it.'

Meg lifted her chin, then said, 'You know, you seem different, Dan. You don't seem very… friendly.'

'Don't I?' There was a moment's silence. Dan lit a cigarette and asked, 'Tell me, are you happy?'

She paused in surprise, her glass halfway to her lips. 'Of course I am. Enormously.' She laughed. 'What a question.' She sipped her cider, then added, 'Are you?'

'On one level, yes. My career is going well, I'm earning more money – nothing by Paul's standards, but at least I do work I'm proud of now – and life is amusing. I have good friends, and the world is an exciting, interesting place. But on another level – the one where I have to watch you marry someone you don't love, and who doesn't love you in the right way – no. Not happy at all.'

'Oh, don't start all that nonsense again. You don't understand the first thing about me, or about Paul, or what we feel for one another.' She paused and added in what she thought was a kindly manner, 'I hope you'll come to the wedding. I know Paul sent you an invitation.'

'What a bloody silly thing to say.' He ground out his half-smoked cigarette. 'But your capacity for being bloody silly no longer astonishes me.'

She stared at him. 'How incredibly rude! There is absolutely no need to swear at me.'

'There is every need. You are hell-bent on being so utterly, tediously conventional – but maybe that's all you're capable of.'

'How can you pretend to love me and say that kind of thing?'

'Because it's the truth, and that is what love is about – something you have yet to discover.'

'What would someone like you know about love?' Meg got up. 'You've turned into something unforgivable, Dan – a bore.'

'I suppose you think that's a smart, grown-up thing to say – like all the other smart, grown-up things you've been practising lately.'

This was too close to the truth. 'Now you're just being nasty.' She got to her feet. 'I think I'll drop in to see my aunt another time. Goodbye.'

He watched her as she walked away. She was right. He was boring – boring and bitter. And it was all pointless, because no words he could use would change what she was going to do. He'd have been better off following his urges and trying to kiss some sense into her. But she had taken herself to a place beyond his reach.

4

ON THE DAY that Madeleine was to leave Woodbourne House, she waited until she knew that Miss Bissett and Avril were safely out of the nursery, and that Laura would be alone in her cot. She opened the door and went in, and approached the cot and looked down at Laura, lying fast asleep. From the day the baby was born – no, months before that – she had trained herself to feel nothing, to leave her care to others, and so for an instant Laura looked nothing more than another indifferent scrap of life. It was a good thing she'd never permitted herself to have any feelings for her, otherwise she wouldn't be able to leave, as she was doing now. Yet the knowledge that this was her daughter, an ineradicable part of her, filled her with a painful sense of loss. She put out a hand and rested it on the blanket. Laura stirred, and Madeleine slipped her finger into the baby's hand and felt the tiny fingers curl tight. All she had to do was pick her up and take her with her. Laura was hers. No one could stop her. The impulse was intense. But she was going to Yorkshire, to a job, to a life where she had no daughter, where she could be free to pretend all this had never happened. And that was just as well.

She drew her hand away. What Dan had said was right. There was no better place for Laura than here. It was where she belonged, though no one would ever know why. She gazed at the baby, her sense of dispassion returning, then left the nursery and went downstairs to say goodbye to Mrs Haddon, and to leave Woodbourne House for good.

*

The news that Madeleine had agreed to leave Laura with Sonia, rather than have her put up for adoption, met with mixed reactions in the rest of the family. Meg thought it a wonderful arrangement, but Helen disapproved.

'Sonia has allowed herself to get far too fond of the child,' she told Meg. 'What if Madeleine changes her mind in a few years?'

'I hardly think that's likely. As far as I know, she wanted to get away and make an entirely new life for herself.'

'You can never be sure about these things. Besides, Avril won't like having a rival for her mother's affections. You may not know this, Meg, but after Avril was born, your aunt was terribly ill – not in a physical way, you understand. Henry tried all kinds of doctors, but none of them could help. It was months before Sonia would have anything to do with Avril. It did untold damage, of course. They're not close in the way a mother and daughter should be. Avril is a difficult child, I grant you, but seeing her mother dote on this baby is hardly going to help. You mark my words.'

Helen's presentiments turned out to be correct. Two weeks later, when Helen was staying at Woodbourne House, Paul and Meg were invited to lunch. It turned out that Avril had not taken kindly to the news that baby Laura was now to be a permanent presence in her life.

'Effie actually found her putting stones into the pram the other day,' Sonia told them. 'Not large ones, of course, but large enough. And I've caught her pinching Laura. I really don't know why she behaves so badly.'

'She's jealous,' said Helen. 'One can see why. Her position as the only child in the household has been usurped.'

Meg glanced at Paul, who had been displaying signs of mild boredom ever since the subject of Laura had been introduced.

'Anyway,' Sonia continued, 'I've decided to send Avril away to school. She'll be seven this autumn, quite old enough. She needs to be with children of her own age, and to learn to socialise. It will be a wrench, of course, and I shall miss her dreadfully, but I am sure it will be good for her.'

'Frankly, I'm not sure that's a good idea,' said Helen. 'You may find that sending her away only makes things worse.'

'Well, my mind is made up,' replied Sonia firmly. 'There have been times when I've thought Laura was hardly safe around Avril. I can't have that.'

'I think my mother's right,' said Meg, as she and Paul drove back to London. 'I'm not sure it's wise of Aunt Sonia to be thinking of sending Avril away. It's bound to make her even more resentful of Laura.'

'What I do not understand,' replied Paul, 'is why that brat is afforded any recognition at all by Sonia, or by anyone else. It's utterly beyond me.'

Meg sighed. 'She's a baby, not a brat. Just because she was unfortunate enough to be born out of wedlock—'

'It's not a matter of misfortune. It's a matter of loose morals.'

'Babies don't have morals.'

'Don't pretend you don't know what I mean. You know perfectly well I'm talking about her mother.'

'Madeleine is not the first unmarried girl in the world to become pregnant. People do have sex, you know.'

'I'd rather not talk about these things, but if we must, we must. Having sex outside marriage is simply wrong. That is a matter of Christian teaching.'

'So that's why we never have?'

Paul was so astonished by this that he swerved into the side of the road and stopped the car. He turned to her. 'I can't believe you would contemplate such a thing. Would you really want to degrade yourself in that way, bring yourself down to her level?'

Meg hesitated. This conversation had turned into the nearest thing they had ever had to a row, and while she was a little frightened of where it was going, she was also, in a clumsy way, quite sure of what she meant.

'Would it really be so degrading? We love each other, and we're going to get married, so why would it be wrong?'

'Because sex belongs within marriage. Being able to wait for that sacrament, that day, is a measure of our restraint. We're not animals, we don't slavishly give in to our impulses.'

Meg gazed at him. Never at any time, when he had kissed her, when they had lain curled up together on the sofa in his flat, had she felt the slightest danger of any uncontrollable impulses surging within him.

'What impulses are you talking about?' she asked.

Paul looked away, turning the key in the ignition. 'The normal kind. The ones men have.'

'*Men* have?'

The engine coughed heavily, then wheezed into silence. Paul turned the key again, and the engine coughed and laboured again. 'Damn and blast!' He gritted his teeth, turning the key over and over.

'Women have impulses, too, as you call them. You know, Paul' – she had to raise her voice above the labouring of the engine – 'I sometimes wish you would stop being so jolly honourable and... and... Christian about everything! I wish you would just tear my clothes off and make love to me, right here and now! I wish you even wanted to!'

'For God's sake, I simply cannot have this ridiculous conversation now! I have to start the car!' He got out and slammed the door, then rummaged in the boot for the starting handle. It had begun to rain. Paul inserted the starting handle and began to crank it. After a couple of turns he stood back, and the engine gave a promising chug, then died. Swearing, Paul cranked again, and after ten minutes in the rain and several more abortive attempts, the engine fired into life. Meg felt the tension in her body relax. Paul threw the starting handle into the boot and got back in. They sat in silence, the engine thrumming, rain pattering on the windscreen. Paul let the choke in, then turned on the windscreen wipers. Meg watched them as they swished back and forth. He put an arm around her shoulders, speaking gently.

'My darling, this isn't something we should quarrel about. I can wait for you. We will both be better people for having waited. I don't want anything to spoil our marriage. I want it to be perfect.'

He leaned across and kissed her. She returned the kiss, which was the usual pleasant, but decorous affair. The one time when she had sought to kiss Paul as Dan had once kissed her, his response had felt like a faint withdrawal, almost a reproach, and she had not persisted. If only he would show just one flicker of ardour, of genuine desire. She wanted so much to be wanted. But perhaps he meant what he said. He was a man of such genuine decency that for him, desire was probably not a thing he would allow himself to feel until their wedding night. This prompted another thought.

She pulled away from him, looking candidly into his eyes. 'I know a bit about life, Paul, and about men. Hasn't there been anyone before me?'

Paul let go of her. Without looking at her, he said, 'Please, Meg, have some delicacy.' Then he put the car in gear, glanced in the rear-view mirror, and pulled away from the side of the road. Nothing was said for the remainder of the drive to London.

Meg and Paul were married in early June at Chelsea Old Church, not far from Meg's home in Cheyne Walk. Meg wore a dress of white silk, with a long veil falling from a headband of tiny rosebuds, and carried a bouquet of mixed white and pink roses and lily-of-the-valley. Her bridesmaids – Diana, Avril and two other cousins – continued the theme in dresses of rose silk. Avril threw a tantrum outside the church just before the service, which caused a delay of several minutes. After that, the service, with Guy Hitchens in attendance as best man, and Meg's uncle to give the bride away, proceeded without a hitch. Dan did not attend.

Paul and Meg were to travel to Scotland for their honeymoon, to spend a week at a Perthshire castle owned by a friend of Paul's, so the wedding night was spent at the flat in Kensington. Diana had tactfully absented herself, but had ordered a few things in from Harrods and seen to it that the maid had prepared and left in the pantry a delicious cold supper and a bottle of wine.

It was a relief for both of them, after the pressures and rituals of the wedding, to sit at the kitchen table in intimate solitude, eating supper and toasting their own happiness. They talked over the day, reflecting on its challenges, its absurdities, its pleasures. Both were glad it was behind them.

'Heaven knows how Di got hold of this Semillon,' said Paul, holding his glass up to the light. 'It's outstanding. I wouldn't expect my sister to know one vintage from another.'

Meg stirred the contents of the ice bucket. 'The ice is melting already. It's going to be a hot night.'

This inadvertent reference to the hours that lay before them, freighted with the weight of sexual expectation, brought a brief silence, which both pretended not to notice. Paul reached out and caught Meg's hand in his, rubbing the new wedding ring lightly with his thumb. 'Mrs Latimer.'

Meg smiled. 'Mr Latimer.' She reached across and kissed him, then sat back, studying his face. Such a serious, kind face. She had married a man of utter dependability, a man who could never commit a cruel deed or think a dishonourable thought. He would be a wonderful husband and father. In her mind, the future spread itself out like a sunny landscape, with Hazelhurst at its heart.

'We should go to bed soon,' remarked Paul, pouring the remainder of the wine into their glasses.

Meg's thoughts returned to the here and now, and she felt a little tinge of fear. She so wanted tonight to be perfect. If only she knew what Paul expected – or what she herself expected. No doubt Paul was experienced to some degree, which would make up for her own ignorance. She had often wondered at the anachronism which required that women should remain virginal until their wedding night, whereas men were expected somehow, somewhere, to have acquired sexual experience. It seemed to Meg that this gave men a somewhat unfair advantage.

Paul stroked her hand again. 'Meg?'

'Mmm?' She roused herself and smiled at him. 'Yes, of course.'

'Perhaps you'd like to go ahead of me. My dressing room is somewhat masculine, I'm afraid, but I hope it will do for tonight. Shall I take your case through?'

'Thanks.' Meg thought about the mysterious, unbroached sanctum of Paul's bedroom, and suddenly wished that all this was happening somewhere, anywhere else.

He leaned across and kissed her, then left the kitchen.

Meg rose and went through to the drawing room. In the beautiful emptiness of the room, lit by the evening sun, she felt an unexpected sense of possession – not just of Paul, but of everything that came with him. This room, this spacious flat, a whole world beyond it, was now hers. But of course, it was as much Diana's. For the first time, she weighed her position against Diana's. She knew that Diana was entirely dependent on Paul. Their father, a man of antiquated views, had left his entire estate – which was a considerable fortune – on his death to Paul. Until such time as she married, Diana looked to Paul for a home, clothes, an allowance, all of which Paul gave generously and freely. These thoughts dwelt idly in Meg's mind as she crossed the room and opened the long windows which looked out on to the garden square, letting in the warm summer air.

Paul came into the drawing room and saw her at the window. He came up behind her and rested his hands on her shoulders, stroking his thumbs lightly across the nape of her neck. She dipped her head, inviting further caresses; in the same instant she retrieved and put away the memory of Dan. But Paul merely patted her shoulders, dropped an affectionate kiss on her head, and said, 'Give me a call when you've finished.' He crossed the room and sat down on one of the sofas, picked up a copy of the *Telegraph*, and began to read. Meg gazed at him for a moment, then left the room.

Paul's dressing room was, as he had said, very masculine. On one wall was a closet full of suits, both town and country, with hats, scarves and gloves on a shelf above. Shoes were neatly ranged on a rail at the bottom, and cravats and ties hung on another rail inside the closet door. The tallboy, into which she also peeped, held shirts, underwear and socks, and on top of it sat a leather box containing studs and cufflinks, a pair of ivory-backed brushes, and a wooden rack of pipes. On the walls hung prints depicting the interiors of various London clubs.

Meg opened her suitcase and took out her nightdress. It was of palest lemon chiffon, trimmed with lace, with a matching peignoir. She laid both garments across a nearby chair, and fished her toilet bag from the suitcase. She took off her going-away dress and hung it on a spare hanger in the closet, making space among the suits and overcoats. She paused there for a moment to inhale the tweedy fragrance of Paul's clothes, and smiled. Then she kicked off her shoes and padded to the basin in her slip, where she washed her face, cleaned her teeth, and unpinned and brushed her long, dark curls. A feeling of excitement and nervousness lay in the pit of her stomach. Something about the size of the basin and taps reminded her of boarding school, and getting ready for bed on her first night there. She hesitated over face cream. She hated her skin to feel dry, but she didn't want to go to bed with a greasy face. Not the best look for a wedding night. She made do with putting a couple of small dabs lightly on her forehead and cheeks and rubbing them well in.

She gazed in the mirror at her reflection. Paul's shaving brush and razor stood on the glass shelf beneath, part of the picture.

They helped to make her look like someone's wife, she thought. She looked down at her wedding and engagement rings, twisting them on her fingers, then shrugged off her slip, took off her underwear, unfastened her stockings and suspenders, and stood naked. The air was warm enough for her to feel no chill, and the feeling of nakedness was delicious. She smoothed her fingers down over her hips, closing her eyes and relishing the sensation. She thought for a moment of going now, as she was, down the corridor and into the drawing room, offering herself to Paul. But in the same instant she could imagine him lowering his newspaper, and looking at her with an expression of quizzical surprise. No. Maybe some other time, when they had got to know one another in that way. But not tonight.

She slipped on her nightdress, and the kiss of chiffon on her skin was almost as delightful as being naked. The folds of the nightdress floated about her as she turned, and she felt both sexual and graceful at the same time. This was better. She opened the closet door to admire her reflection full length. She knew she looked very lovely. She was not ashamed of enjoying the moment; she might never look this lovely again, might never be so intensely, physically aware as she was tonight.

She slipped on the peignoir and went into Paul's bedroom. It was spacious, carpeted in dark green, with a desk against one wall and a tall Chinese lacquer cabinet against another. The bed was a large four-poster with no canopy. At its foot stood a blanket box. Next to the desk was a bookcase; two of its shelves were entirely lined with copies of Wisden, and a series of hunting scenes decorated the walls. On the desk itself stood two framed photographs. One was of a handsome couple in Edwardian garb – Paul's late mother and father, she guessed – and the other was of a group of young rowers on a jetty, some standing, some sitting, laughing in the sunshine. Paul was among them, his arm slung affectionately around the shoulders of a dark-haired young man. On the wall above hung a number of framed photographs of sporting teams from school and university. Meg studied these with interest. Paul appeared in them all, more often than not as captain, either holding a rugby ball, muddy and muscular, or looking dashing in cricket whites with a bat planted between his feet. Dan was in one of the cricket photos, standing in the back row looking diffident. Meg studied his features with interest, then realised what she was doing, and glanced away.

When she had had enough of the photos, she went and sat on the bed. It was neatly made, the white linen pillows plump and inviting, a crisp sheet turned over the blankets and dark green silk bedspread. Everything was expensive and tasteful and very masculine. It didn't look or feel like a bed which was expecting a girl in a lemon chiffon nightdress. Paul's slippers stood neatly on the rug. On the bedside table lay a copy of an Edgar Wallace novel with a pipe cleaner as a bookmark, an ashtray next to it, together with a flask of water and a glass. She could imagine Paul climbing between the sheets at night, reading for a while, switching off the light and sleeping his blameless sleep, and then the maid coming in to clean and tidy the next day, arranging everything in the same way, just as Mr Latimer liked it.

It struck Meg, as she looked around, that no concession had been made to her presence here tonight. It was as though the room did not wish to acknowledge her.

She went to the windows and opened two of them, setting them carefully on their hasps. She drank in the evening air, letting its freshness fill the room, and noticing the tinges of dusky red in the sky. She was acutely conscious of how vivid everything seemed, and how alive she felt.

It occurred to her that she should call to Paul, tell him she was ready for bed. She crossed the room, a tremor of excitement shuddering through her, and just then Paul appeared in the doorway. On the end of one forefinger he held the undergarments she had shed several minutes ago, and in the other hand he held her shoes. He smiled and raised a playful eyebrow.

'I hope, Mrs Latimer, that this doesn't mean I will be constantly tidying up after you. I'm a creature who likes order.'

Meg managed to smile back. 'I can see that.' She took the undergarments and shoes from him. 'I'll put these away.'

He smiled in mock reproof. 'Please see that you do.'

She understood the cumbersome joke, yet it jarred with her that he should care or bother about such things, tonight of all nights. She put the shoes in the bottom of the closet and stuffed the underwear into a corner of her suitcase. When she returned to the room, Paul had drawn the curtains and was loosening his tie. He stopped, caught her by the wrist, and drew her towards him.

'You look very beautiful.' He traced a finger inside the lace at the top of her nightdress. She felt something inside her relax, and happiness returning.

'Thank you.' She waited to be kissed, but he turned away, took off his tie, and disappeared into the dressing room.

Meg sat on the edge of the bed in a state of uncertainty. Should she get in, or wait for him? She stood up, slipped off the peignoir, and sat down again. She glanced around, wishing she knew what to do. She could hear the sound of water running, and Paul humming. She thought about him reading the paper in the drawing room while she got ready for bed, and the way he had brought her shoes and underwear to put away. Surely it shouldn't be like this, so matter-of-fact, with this unmindful distance between them. At this moment, on this night, they should be everything to one another, completely absorbed, physically and mentally, nothing else mattering. That was the way she had always pictured it. But everything felt so detached, pragmatic.

Hoping that doing something decisive might soothe her anxieties, she pushed back the heavy lip of the bedclothes and got into the tightly made bed, tugging out the sheet at the side. Even the bed didn't approve of her. She glanced at the bedside table with its paraphernalia. This was probably the side of the bed Paul liked to sleep on. She switched on the bedside light, then shuffled herself over to the other side. She lay back against the pillows, and wondered if she was the first woman ever to sleep in this bed. Had Paul ever had lovers? She would never know. It had been made clear to her that it was not something that would ever be discussed. But why? Surely there should be no secrets between them. They should reveal absolutely everything to one another.

Paul came in to the room. Even in his striped pyjamas he looked to Meg thrillingly masculine, his tall, muscular body a tantalising degree closer to hers. He closed the door and padded to the bed. To her surprise, he dropped suddenly to his knees, rested his elbows on the counterpane, and clasped his hands. He closed his eyes, took a deep breath, and began to pray.

Meg sat staring at his dark, earnestly bent head. What was he praying for? Guidance? Fortitude? Her sense of exclusion was extreme. At last he unclasped his hands and looked up at her. The impression of some divine approval having been bestowed was inescapable.

He got into bed, and moved against her. They put their arms around one another and smiled, then kissed. Paul was normally not given to kissing with tongues, but clearly this occasion permitted it. The kiss was deep and long, and Meg found herself searching for something in it, and searching in vain. She thought of Dan, but only to try to remember that blazing sensation of feeling, to try to rekindle it now with Paul. She wanted it so badly to be there. That Paul desired her was evident; he was physically very aroused. She could feel it. He tugged down the bodice of her nightdress and caressed her breasts clumsily with his hands, one after the other, mechanically, all the while murmuring that he loved her. She said 'I love you' back, but the faintness of her own voice seemed to echo not desire, but despair. She thought she might cry, and felt suddenly afraid. It was that same drenching fear which had washed over her the night of the Cunliffes' party. His right hand moved down her body, tugging up the hem of her nightdress, pushing her legs apart.

'Please don't be afraid,' he murmured. 'My poor, poor child.'

Then he was fumbling with his pyjamas, and she felt him jabbing and pushing into her. She gasped and tried to move, to make it easier for him, to reach down and help, but he pushed her hand away, clamping her wrists at either side of her head. She felt a tearing pain, then he was fully inside her, and she felt an enormous relief. She could feel a tear trickling on her cheek and wanted to wipe it away, but he still held her wrists fast as he moved rhythmically within her. She wanted to say something, to ask him to slow down, to make her part of it, but wherever he was, he was not with her. His eyes were squeezed shut, and his mouth was slack and open, panting. He looked momentarily grotesque, unlovable, and Meg averted her eyes, waiting for it to be over.

When it was, when he had subsided, pulling together his pyjama trousers and rolling away, Meg lay inert. She tugged her nightdress down and surreptitiously wiped the tears from her face. She could feel the sticky dampness pooled between her legs and knew she couldn't sleep like this.

'I have to go to the bathroom,' she murmured. She got out of bed, went through the dressing room, and down the corridor to the lavatory. She cleaned herself, then sat and wept for a moment. She stared at the tiled wall opposite. Perhaps if they had gone to bed together months ago, and learned more about each other, things would have been different tonight. But she knew this wasn't true. Lovemaking had never happened between them, not because of any sense of propriety, or Christian restraint on Paul's part, but because he had never wanted it, not really. There was no shared passion. It was probably beyond him to acknowledge that any woman could have sexual desires and feelings. She certainly couldn't go back now and make him talk about it. For Paul, sex was evidently something that had to happen, that women must accept and endure, and that he would perform with her because she was his wife.

She got up and went back to bed. Paul was waiting for her. She lay down, trying to return his tender smile.

'Have you been crying?' he asked gently, stroking her face. 'I'm told it hurts the first time. Poor darling. It will be better next time, I'm sure.' He put up a hand and stroked the carved bedhead. 'I suppose you've been wondering where I got this marvellous piece of furniture. It's an Italian rococo tester bed. I bought it in Arezzo three years ago and had it shipped to London. The box at the foot of it is called a *cassone* – actually, it's what the Italians call a marriage box, which is rather appropriate in the circumstances...'

Meg closed her eyes and stopped listening. She heard nothing, thought about nothing, and eventually Paul fell silent. He dropped a kiss on her forehead.

'Sleep tight,' he murmured, then rolled over and switched off the light.

5

THE SUMMER WHICH unfolded at Woodbourne House that year was very different from previous ones. During Henry's lifetime, the summer months had been busy ones for Sonia. Regular parties of visitors from London – artists, writers, actors, musicians, politicians, fascinating people both young and old, some beautiful, some less so, some downright eccentric, but all offering something by way of interest and charm – had enlivened the days. Now the days were quiet. Last summer's daily deliveries of large parcels of meat and poultry from the butcher, and tubs of cream and milk from the local farm, had dwindled to modest amounts, and the wine cellar went unreplenished. Much of the produce from the kitchen garden was sent to the cottage hospital. The guest bedrooms and reception rooms were shrouded in dustsheets, and Woodbourne's immaculately kept gardens and empty lawns had an air of unfulfilled expectation about them, almost as sad as if they had lain neglected and overgrown. No one played on the tennis court.

But Sonia barely noticed this social depletion. The focus of her time and attention was now Laura, and while Effie combined the duties of a nursemaid as well as housemaid, Sonia took an abiding interest in everything connected with the baby. When Laura was wheeled out in the afternoon to take a fresh-air nap in the shade of the trees by the terrace, Sonia would sit beside her with a book until she woke. Occasionally she would excuse Effie from the business of giving Laura her bath, on the pretext that some other domestic duty was required of her, so that she herself could have the pleasure of gently soaping and towelling the little body. It became her custom, too, to give Laura her bottle at teatime, and to go each night to the nursery for a final glimpse before she was settled for the night.

None of this was lost on the servants, nor on Avril.

Avril had always had her mother's dutiful affection and attention, but the ties between them were not close, and now that she was no longer a baby herself, those attentions were confined to bedtime stories and the occasional outing. By and large Sonia left Avril to her own devices and to the care of Miss Bissett. Accustomed to being a solitary child, Avril would probably have been content enough, but to witness her mother's attentive delight in Laura aroused in her painful feelings of jealousy. She had dimly understood that when Madeleine's baby was born, both it and Madeleine would leave Woodbourne House. But although Madeleine had gone, the baby remained. Its very helplessness seemed liked a provocation. While she herself received regular scolds and reprimands for perceived misdemeanours, only coos and smiles were bestowed on the baby. Avril began to hate its very existence.

'Madam's setting up a store of trouble for herself, you mark my words,' observed Effie to Mrs Goodall. 'She's that taken with the baby she doesn't see the damage she's doing. The pity is there's no one to tell her otherwise. Maybe you could say something?'

'It's not my place. What could I say?' Mrs Goodall shook her head. 'They should have had it adopted in the first place. I don't know what Mrs Haddon was thinking.'

Sonia's vague plan to send Avril to school became concrete one afternoon – Laura had been left unattended in her pram in the garden, and Effie found Avril slapping the baby with a spray of nettles, raising a bright red rash on her tiny face and setting her screaming.

'I cannot have Avril hurting the baby like that. It's high time she learned to behave and acquire some discipline. She is quite beyond my handling,' Sonia told Helen in a telephone call.

'Surely you can see why she does such things? She's jealous. It's not too late to change your plans and put the baby up for adoption, you know,' Helen replied.

'That is not the solution. Avril will be sent to board in September. Daphne Davenport has highly recommended the school that Constance attended, and I'm going to have William drive me there next week so that I can look around.'

At Hazelhurst, Meg was struggling to get to grips with married life. She found the business of running a large house intimidating, particularly in the matter of employing servants. Paul was no help, as his time and attention were constantly taken up by his racing car enterprise, and although Meg had hoped to cope without enlisting Diana's aid, she turned to her for advice during one of Diana's visits.

'I managed to find my cook, Mrs Runcie, through an advertisement – she seems fairly competent, though it's early days – but I simply can't for the life of me find any decent maids. I thought there would be no shortage of suitable girls hereabouts, but it seems they'd rather go off and work in the towns. I'm making do with the daughter of the farmer down the road. She's meant to be a maid-of-all-work, but she's really not up to it. It takes her all day to get through work she should have finished in a morning.'

Diana's eyes widened. 'My dear, a place this size calls for at least two live-in maids. I daresay one of them could double up as a table maid when you have people to dine. And I'm surprised your cook hasn't demanded a kitchen maid. There's bound to be a domestic agency in Reading. I suggest you ring them up. I only need a house-parlourmaid now that Paul's gone, and she lives out, thank heavens.' She lit her third cigarette of the morning. 'So, how are you enjoying wedded bliss?'

'Immensely.' Meg said it with genuine enthusiasm. She wasn't thinking about – and certainly wouldn't have dreamt of mentioning to Diana – the business of sex. Nothing there had improved, mainly because Paul didn't seem to think anything was wrong. And although Meg herself knew something was, she didn't quite know what. For Paul, the act of love seemed to be a duty, and the sounds that escaped him when engaged in it reminded Meg of nothing so much as the grateful groans of one relieved of some frightful torment. She never felt so remote from him as when they were having sex. It felt like the least loving of all the things they did together, and she was at a loss to understand how to make it better. She was beginning to think that perhaps it was an aspect of married life which must simply be endured.

So she didn't think of any of this as she answered Diana's question. She thought only of the simple, easy pleasures of shared domesticity and the novelty of their new home, breakfasts together, walks in the woods, drives into Alderworth, sending Cook home for the evening and making supper by themselves, listening to the wireless as dusk fell. When his racing car friends weren't visiting, that was, or when Paul wasn't away at yet another Grand Prix. She smiled at Diana. 'Being married is fun. You should try it.'

'Not for a while yet, thanks. I like my freedom too much. And London. Don't you find it a bit of a yawn out here in the sticks? I imagine bridge with the local gentry is about as exciting as it gets.'

'No, the house gives me so much to do. And I'm getting to know people hereabouts. Some of them are awfully nice. I've already been enlisted by the vicar's wife into hosting a stall at the Alderworth fête next month. And I'm learning to ride. Paul says he'll have me out in the hunting field next season.'

'How simply ghastly.' Diana glanced in the direction of the French windows. Paul and two friends had settled themselves in wicker chairs on the terrace outside. Mingled snatches of their conversation drifted through to Meg and Diana.

'You can't deny Mercedes-Benz did miraculously well.'

'There's no competing with the Germans, given the amount of money their government throws at racing car manufacture.'

'What about the French? I don't call one and a half million francs small change.'

'Sad for Alfa Romeo's works team, though.'

'Mmm, there are lessons to be learned there. We need to be looking at hydraulic brakes and box section frames. The standard mechanical ones are no good.'

Diana threw Meg an agonised look. 'My dear, how *do* you bear it?'

'I have tried to take an interest, but somehow...'

Deftly Diana lifted the curtain aside and craned her neck to look out. 'Who is the divine man with the red hair?'

'Roddy MacLennan. He's the team's new driver.'

'I do hope he's staying to lunch.'

Meg suppressed a sigh. 'Probably for the entire weekend.'

'Do I detect a faint note of pique?'

'Oh no, it's not that I mind. It's just that it's all so – so *masculine.* None of Paul's friends seems to be married, or ever brings a girlfriend to stay. It would be nice to have a bit of female company. But they're all simply wedded to their racing cars. The worst of it is, they strain to be polite at mealtimes, chatting about trivial things, when I can tell they're simply *dying* to get back to desperately important topics like piston rods and engines.' After a moment's hesitation, Meg added in a burst of candour, 'I sometimes feel utterly superfluous.' Then she laughed to show she took it lightly. 'But men need their interests, I suppose. Women can't hope to have their husbands all to themselves. Speaking of lunch, I'd better go and see how things are coming along. I only hope the poached salmon isn't getting the better of Cook.'

When Meg had left the room, Diana took a quick glance in her compact mirror, then stepped through the French windows on to the terrace.

'Hello, sis!' exclaimed Paul. 'When did you get here?'

Guy and Roddy hastily stubbed out their cigarettes and rose to their feet.

'About an hour ago, while you were busy with your cars,' replied Diana, exchanging a kiss with her brother. She held out a hand to Guy. 'Guy, how lovely to see you again.' She turned to Roddy. He was even better standing up. Six foot two, or thereabouts, slim-hipped and broad-shouldered, just the way she liked them, with a thatch of soft red hair, keen blue eyes, and a nicely chiselled, somewhat foxy face. He was very freckled, and very handsome.

'Diana, this is Roddy MacLennan – Roddy, my sister Diana.'

Diana shook hands with Roddy. 'How d'you do? Meg tells me you're part of the racing team?'

'That's right.' He glanced down apologetically at his oil-stained overalls. 'Sorry about the rig.' Despite his Scottish surname, Roddy's voice and accent were impeccably English, and he spoke with a slight stammer, which Diana found charming.

'Please don't apologise – awfully workmanlike.' She gave a smiling glance at Paul's faultless tweeds. 'I see my brother doesn't propose to get his hands dirty.'

'Hardly fair,' replied Paul in mock resentment. 'Roddy's our new driver. It's his job to get mucky. As Latimer-Hitchens' team manager I need to look immaculate.'

'We're taking the car over to Chalvey airfield tomorrow,' said Guy. 'Roddy's test driving the new engine. Why don't you come?'

'How very dashing.' Diana gave Roddy a smile. 'Unfortunately I have to be back in London this evening.'

Meg came out to the terrace. 'Lunch will be another half-hour, I'm afraid. Cook is struggling rather with the mayonnaise.'

'Fine,' said Paul. 'That gives Roddy time for a wash and brush-up. But first I have something to show you all.'

'Not a car, I hope?' said Diana.

'Not a car.' Paul led the way from the terrace across the lawn in the direction of the paddock and stables.

'Morning, Dixon,' called Paul. The young groom-gardener, who was busy in the yard, touched his cap to the party. Paul led the way in.

'Allow me to introduce you to The Commander.'

In the loose box stood a magnificent chestnut. He whinnied and nickered as Paul approached with a handful of hay, lowering his muzzle to take it.

'Isn't he a beauty?'

There were murmurs of admiration. Roddy stepped forward and ran his hands appreciatively over the horse's neck and flanks, making Diana wish she could do the same to Roddy. 'He's perfectly built for steeplechasing. What is he – sixteen hands?'

Paul nodded. 'And a bit. I paid a hundred guineas for him, I don't mind telling you. I can't wait to get him out in the field next season. I bought a nice-tempered little mare for Meg at the same time. It was love at first sight, wasn't it, darling?'

Meg nodded. 'She's called Grisette. You can see her in a moment. I don't pretend I'll ever be the world's greatest horsewoman, but Dixon says I'm making good progress. And from Dixon, that's high praise indeed, I can assure you.'

After Grisette had been duly inspected and admired, they set off back to the house for lunch.

'It's such a nice day, I propose we have it on the terrace instead of inside,' suggested Paul.

'What a lovely idea,' said Diana. She glanced at Meg's face, and fell back a step beside her. 'You don't seem keen,' she murmured.

'Oh no, it's an excellent idea. I'm just worried that it will inconvenience the maid to have to re-lay the table outside. I hate putting her out.'

Diana could see it was going to take Meg some time to acquire the necessary confidence to make her the supreme mistress of her household. 'My dear, you mustn't worry about putting the servants to trouble – it's what they're for.'

'Yes, you're right,' said Meg. 'I'll speak to her.'

As she crossed the springy turf of the paddock, her arm linked in Diana's, Meg lifted her head and looked around her, reminding herself how extraordinarily lucky she was. She had Paul, and Hazelhurst too, and with a little practice she would learn to manage them both.

The constraints that Meg usually felt when lunching with Paul and his friends were lifted by Diana's presence. Diana evinced a lively interest in all things to do with racing cars, and the Grand Prix season in particular; Meg found it hard to tell whether it was genuine or not, but she found Diana's enthusiasm transformed the subject, making it more interesting than she had hitherto found it. Perhaps the key was to encourage men to talk about what interested them, rather than endure the awkwardness of forcing them to look for polite alternatives.

'Switzerland and Monaco – how grand! If I were you, Meg, I would insist on going too. There's something terribly thrilling about powerful motor cars – and if it got too tiresome, you could always go shopping.'

'We're not quite ready for the championship circuit yet,' said Guy. 'The non-championship venues aren't quite so glamorous, I'm afraid.'

'Besides, I'm not sure Paul would welcome my presence,' said Meg. 'I'd just get in the way.'

'I would think any man would be delighted to have such a delightful distraction,' said Roddy gallantly.

Paul smiled and helped himself to mayonnaise, but said nothing to encourage the idea.

As the meal progressed, and the talk turned to London and the season, Meg gradually became aware that surreptitious flirting was going on between Diana and Roddy. It was driven mainly by Diana, but Roddy's subtle responses were unmistakable. Given that the two of them had only just met, Meg was somewhat surprised, but she couldn't help admiring Diana's technique. Paul noticed too, and registered his mild disapproval with glances and a couple of marked silences. But neither Diana nor Roddy seemed aware, and the flirtatious banter continued. Why, Meg wondered, did Paul have to be so stuffy at times?

When the meal was over, Guy and Roddy announced they were going back to the workshop to carry on with the engine modifications. Paul rose to join them, but Diana laid a detaining hand on his arm.

'I insist you stay and entertain me for a little while longer, brother dearest. I haven't seen you in a month, and I have a few things I need to talk to you about.'

Meg took this as a cue to make herself scarce. She guessed that Diana had need of money, as she so often did, and would want to make any application to Paul in private.

'I have some letters to attend to, so I'll leave you in peace. I'll tell Mary to clear lunch away.'

Meg was halfway to the morning room when she realised that she had left her letters in the drawing room. She went back to retrieve them, and as she did so she heard Paul's voice from the terrace saying, 'The way you behaved towards Roddy was, quite frankly, nothing short of embarrassing.' There was a harshness in his voice which she had never heard before, and it made her pause.

'Oh dear, do I detect a note of jealousy?' she heard Diana reply. 'I hope you're not in love with him, the way you were with that Bettany boy.'

'Don't be disgusting.'

'Who says it's disgusting? You men are so wrong-headed about that kind of thing. Anyway, thanks for the cheque, brother dearest. I don't know where the money goes.'

'I think I do.'

Meg moved away from the window and quickly left the room, shocked. She thought anxiously for a while about what Diana had said, but came to the conclusion that referring to Paul being in love with a man was simply another of her careless turns of phrase. Paul was devoted to his friends – everyone knew that. He was, as Meg often found herself saying to people, 'very much a man's man'. It meant nothing, she decided, and resolved to think no more about it.

6

AS THE MONTHS passed, Meg began to feel she was making headway. The tennis court was finished, and she had succeeded in recruiting a couple of respectable housemaids, Gwen and Enid, and a kitchen maid, Maud, to help Mrs Runcie. She had begun to make friends in the area, although the women whom she had befriended, such as the vicar's wife and Anna Kentleigh, the wife of a wealthy neighbouring landowner, both had young families, which kept them busy at times when Meg was not. She had hoped that there might by now be signs that she and Paul would soon have a family of their own, but so far she was disappointed. She told herself that it was hardly surprising, since they had only been married a few months, but at the same time she couldn't help thinking that the chances might have been a little higher if Paul had been at home more. He seemed preoccupied with his business, and was away more often than she had anticipated.

Finding time hanging heavy on her hands that autumn, she invited her mother to stay while Paul was abroad with his racing team. When he arrived home at the end of the week she hurried out to meet him.

'I thought you'd be home last night,' she said, as she kissed him. 'I was getting worried. You should have called.'

'The boat train got in very late, so I stayed at the club and picked up the car this morning. Sorry, I didn't think to call.' He came inside with Meg and greeted his mother-in-law. 'How are you, Helen? I'm glad someone's been keeping Meg company.'

'How was Czechoslovakia?' asked Helen.

'The racing was fine. We had an excellent time, though we didn't come anywhere. The Germans saw to that. They win pretty much everything, and they're insufferably arrogant about it, too, I can tell you.'

'And about a lot of other things besides car races. Mr Hitler is getting far too big for his boots, if you ask me,' said Helen.

'I'm so glad to have you back,' said Meg. 'Promise me you won't be going anywhere for at least a month?'

'I promise.' He dropped a kiss on her forehead. 'I'll come and join you shortly. I just need to freshen up. Oh, by the way, I ran into Dan Ranscombe at Bellamy's last night. I asked him if he'd like to come down next month. James Kentleigh has invited us to shoot on his estate on the eighteenth. I'll probably ask Guy and Roddy as well.' He caught Meg's expression. 'You don't look best pleased. I thought you liked having people down.'

'I'm perfectly happy about it,' replied Meg, searching for an excuse for her reaction. 'I just sometimes wish we had some female company as well.'

'Then why don't you invite Diana? She knows everyone. And she's a pretty good shot.' As he turned to go back to his study, Paul added, 'Guy could bring Amy along, I suppose, and Roddy and Dan are bound to have girlfriends on the go. I might ask them to bring a female guest or two. Then you won't feel so outnumbered.'

Meg wished she could have greeted Paul's announcement that he had invited Dan to stay with calm indifference, but somehow it bothered her. She tried to rationalise her feelings, and eventually decided that the heart of the problem was the way things had been allowed to get out of hand last year. She should have kept the relationship on a friendly level and never let things go any further. She and Dan had got themselves tangled up in a silly mess over a few kisses, and his behaviour had become unkind and rather absurd as a result. The last conversation they'd had in spring had demonstrated that. A pity, really, because they'd got on so well in the beginning, and when he wasn't being marvellously conceited and presumptuous about certain things, he was fun to be with. So the best thing to do was to put it behind her – none of it could possibly matter, after all, now that she was married – and start things over again, on a sensible level, when they next met.

A fortnight later, Meg decided to go to town and do some shopping. Her mother had gone on her annual sojourn to Biarritz, so Diana invited Meg to stay at the flat. She arrived a little after seven, and Diana answered the door in her petticoat.

'There you are! I couldn't remember when you said you were arriving.' She gave Meg a kiss and ushered her inside. 'I've given the maid the evening off. Come and chat to me. I'm just getting ready to go out.' Meg set down her overnight case and followed Diana through to her bedroom. 'I'm meeting some friends at the Ritz for cocktails, and then probably going on to some club or other for supper,' said Diana, bending towards her dressing table mirror to dab make-up on her face. She glanced at Meg's reflection. 'You're most welcome to come along, if you'd like.'

'Sweet of you, but to be honest, I'm most awfully tired.'

'If you're sure. The spare room is all in order, and you know where everything is. Do help yourself to a drink, if you like. I'm just going to finish getting ready.'

Meg dropped her bag in the spare room, then wandered through to the drawing room. Ten minutes later Diana appeared in the doorway, swathed in an elegant grey coat with a high fur collar, silver evening bag in hand.

'Are you sure you'll be all right? There's a set of keys in the left-hand drawer of the hall table. Don't forget to take them with you if you go out. I'll see you tomorrow. Nighty-night!'

A moment later Meg heard the front door slam, and silence descended. As she sat leafing through the latest copy of *Harper's Bazaar*, it occurred to her that the last time she had been here in the flat was on her wedding night. She tried to dismiss that memory. She had become used by now to compartmentalising her relationship with Paul, concentrating on the interest and amusement of its daylight hours, and relegating sex and the hours of darkness to a place that didn't matter. Yet after a few minutes some impulse made her get up and wander through to his bedroom. She gazed round the starkly masculine interior, and allowed herself to admit the disappointment of the sexual relationship which she endured, rather than enjoyed. Perhaps if their marriage had started somewhere else – a neutral room in a foreign hotel, a place not freighted with Paul's bachelor past, and whatever it held – they might be different people to one another now. *We were never lovers*, thought Meg. *We became husband and wife without ever having become lovers.* She knew in her heart that that had been a mistake, but it was one that couldn't be undone now.

She crossed the room, and inspected again the sixth form and university sporting pictures that hung above the desk, glancing along the rows of young faces, and the names below. This time, one of the names rang a bell. She concentrated for a moment. Then it came back to her, the fragment of conversation between Paul and Diana that she had overheard a few weeks ago after lunch. She counted along the row until she found the face that matched Arthur Bettany's name, and studied it. He was undoubtedly attractive, his features marked by a certain soft-lipped petulance and dark-eyed arrogance. He was dressed in cricket whites, gazing challengingly at the camera with a hint of a smile. Paul, as team captain, stood a couple of places away from him in the centre of the photograph. Meg's gazed shifted between the two, as if trying to detect some connection. Then she glanced at the photograph of the university rowing team on the desk and realised that the young man in the affectionate embrace of Paul's arm, his own arm around Paul's waist, was also Arthur Bettany. She was suddenly struck by the intimacy of their pose. Ridiculous, she told herself. She recalled schoolgirl crushes from her own adolescence; probably much the same thing happened with young men. She turned away from the photos and went back to the drawing room to pour herself a drink.

Diana and Meg spent the following morning clothes shopping in the West End.

'I can't imagine how you'll get through the winter with just five new dresses,' remarked Diana, as they left Harvey Nichols.

'It's more than enough,' said Meg. 'Social life in Berkshire is a lot quieter than London. There's not much to dress up for. Except Paul, and he scarcely notices what I'm wearing most of the time.'

'I'm sure he does really. It's just that my brother is a typically undemonstrative Englishman. I'm glad that you both like living in the country so much. When I was younger, I couldn't wait to get away. Even now I can only bear it in small doses, or if there's some jolly house party with lots of guests.'

'Oh, that reminds me,' exclaimed Meg. 'Paul has invited a few people down for a day's shooting on a neighbour's estate the weekend after next, and we want you to come. So far the guests are Guy and his fiancée, that fellow Roddy MacLennan, and Dan Ranscombe. Please say you'll come – there could be a scarcity of women otherwise.'

'I don't *think* I'm busy,' replied Diana, though her mind had been made up the moment she heard Roddy would be there. 'It's just a question of whether I want to go tramping through muddy countryside taking potshots at pheasants. Paul won't let me off the shoot, I can assure you.'

'Well, I've never shot a thing in my life, so perhaps you can stay home and keep me company.'

'My dear girl, Paul will still expect you out in the field, even if it's just to carry a thermos of coffee. You can expect to be unwrapping a nice Purdey shotgun at Christmas. My sister-in-law will have to be able to shoot as well as hunt, and no doubt become proficient at fly-fishing, too.' Diana glanced at Meg and laughed. 'Don't look so worried. Shooting isn't difficult – which is just as well, given the number of dimwits who do it. And pheasants are pleasingly slow-moving targets.'

'It's just that I'm not especially keen on killing things.'

'You're not likely to, on your first time out,' said Diana briskly. 'Now, shall we find somewhere for tea?'

'I don't think so, thanks. I know Paul would prefer it if I'm home for dinner, so I'd better set off soon.' She scanned the street for a taxi. 'So, will you come for the shooting?'

'I wouldn't miss it for the world,' replied Diana.

In the days running up to the shooting party, Meg was in a fluster. She and Paul had never had so many people to stay, and she was anxious first of all about whether or not there was enough linen for the beds, and then about whether Mrs Runcie would be able to cope with cooking meals for a large number of people.

'I shouldn't fret about it,' said Paul. 'Kentleigh will provide lunch on the shoot. Breakfast more or less takes care of itself, so she'll only have to concern herself with dinner on Friday and Saturday. I expect most people will want to get back to town at a decent time on Sunday. We shan't be more than eight, which isn't a great many.'

'Do we know yet exactly how many are coming? It will help Cook to have definite numbers.'

'Guy is bringing his fiancée, and I told Diana and Dan to bring friends, if they liked, but I'm not entirely sure what's happening on that front. So we'll just have to see who turns up.'

That, thought Meg, was about as useful as saying that breakfast would take care of itself. However, Mrs Runcie didn't seem particularly put out by the uncertainty over numbers.

'We can make dinner on Friday stretch, if needs be,' she said. 'And by Saturday we'll know how many we are. I'll look out some nice recipes. And Maud will put her shoulder to the wheel, won't you, Maud?' Maud nodded nervously. 'We'll be fine, madam, never you worry.'

Meg was not entirely reassured. She knew that Mrs Runcie was prone to overestimating her own capabilities and was quite liable to succumb to mild hysteria over a collapsed sponge or a curdled sauce. And Maud's talent didn't extend much beyond peeling vegetables and washing pots. Still, barring disasters, they would probably get by.

Half an hour before the other guests were due to arrive for dinner, Meg, Paul, Roddy, Guy Hitchens and his fiancée Amy were assembled in the drawing room for cocktails.

'I can't think what's keeping Di,' Paul murmured to Meg. 'She said she was getting a late-afternoon train. She should have been here ages ago. As for Dan – well, he's a law unto himself.'

'We can't wait dinner. Cook will have a fit. She's making a cheese soufflé as a first course.' Why, oh why, thought Meg, had she not scotched that idea? How ridiculous, on an evening when people might arrive late or piecemeal, to be having soufflé.

Shortly after eight, when there was still no sign of Dan or Diana, Meg went to the kitchen.

'Mrs Runcie, some of the guests are late. I've no idea when they'll get here. Will the soufflé keep?'

Mrs Runcie's pink cheeks grew even pinker. 'No, madam. A soufflé does not keep. If it doesn't come to the table in five minutes, I can't answer for the consequences.'

Meg swithered. It seemed rude to start dinner without Dan and Diana – but it was rude of them not to turn up on time. And then there was the matter of the soufflé. 'Very well, Mrs Runcie, we shall have dinner now.'

The soufflé was a success, and was followed by lamb cutlets and fondant potatoes and vegetables. One of the housemaids, Gwen, was waiting at table, and doing so with great proficiency.

Apart from the vacant places at the table, Meg felt things were going not badly.

'You're so lucky to have a good cook,' said Amy, a willowy girl with an eager manner. Meg guessed she had only come out this season. 'I've heard servants are a veritable minefield. Frankly, the idea of running a household terrifies me. I only hope I can do as well as you when I'm married.'

Paul directed a gratified smile at his wife.

'I'm very much a beginner,' said Meg, 'but thank you. When are you and Guy—'

Her words were interrupted by three extremely loud horn blasts and the sound of car tyres slewing on the gravel outside. Paul put down his knife and fork.

'Our late arrivals, I presume.' He got up and left the room.

Meg carried on chatting to her guests, but with one ear on the commotion and conversation in the hallway. A moment later Paul returned to the dining room, looking a little grim, followed by Diana, Dan and Eve Meyerson. Diana, still in coat and hat, swooped on Meg with an apologetic kiss, managing to knock cutlery to the floor in the process. Meg could smell gin on her breath.

'Darling Meg, I'm *so* sorry we're late! Utterly unforgivable, but entirely Dan's fault. He offered me a lift, you see, and when I went to meet him he was drinking with all these people, and it took me simply ages to drag him away.' Diana caught sight of Gwen hovering uncertainly with the serving dishes. 'Oh, cutlets, how heavenly. I'm simply ravenous. Let me take my coat off.' She turned to Amy. 'Oh, how do you do? I don't think we've met...'

Meg watched Diana carefully, trying to assess how drunk she was. After introductions had been made, Dan said to Meg, 'Diana is completely right – it's my fault we're late. I'm afraid we got caught up in a farewell drinks party for one of my colleagues, and I hadn't realised how long the drive from London would take.' He had evidently had a few drinks, but didn't seem to be too much the worse for wear.

'That's quite all right,' replied Meg. 'I'm just glad you're here in one piece. There's still plenty of food.'

Food was served to the new arrivals, and the meal resumed, enlivened now by Diana's tipsy high spirits. Meg watched Eve and Dan discreetly. She told herself she was glad to see Dan so evidently happy with someone. It would make it easier to get their friendship back on to a sensible footing. She couldn't help thinking how well he was looking – she always forgot, until she saw him, how vividly handsome he was.

When the meal was over, Paul gave Meg a glance. Taking her cue, Meg rose and caught the eye of first Amy, then Eve. 'Ladies, shall we go through to the drawing room and leave the men to their brandy and cigars?'

Diana, who was now more than a little drunk, her eyes sparkling and her cheeks lightly flushed, laughed and exclaimed, 'Oh, must we have all that tosh? Nobody does it in London now. It's so… so…' Diana waved her glass, 'divisive! Don't you think? It's much chummier if everyone stays together. I was dining with the Goodmans just last week, and the ladies all stayed put. I'm sure Roddy agrees with me – don't you, Roddy?'

Appealed to in this way, Roddy had no choice but to reply gallantly, 'If it means not being deprived of your company, of course I do.'

Paul began to speak. 'I think—'

Diana shushed him. 'No, dearest brother, Roddy agrees. And we girls are perfectly comfy where we are – aren't we?' Diana smiled round at the other women.

Amy gave an uncertain little laugh and glanced at Guy. Eve raised her eyebrows and said in a comically husky voice, 'Well, if we're to stay put with you chaps, I for one insist on a brandy and a cigar.' She sounded so droll and sharp that everyone laughed; then she added in her ordinary voice, giving Paul a sweet smile, 'But only if my host will allow it.'

Taking his cue, Paul smiled in return and inclined his head in a little mock bow. 'How can I refuse such a charming request?

So be it. For tonight, the ladies shall be honorary gentlemen. Brandy and cigars for all.'

Meg sat down, relieved that the situation had been rescued – Paul was such a stickler for convention – but slightly bewildered by the realisation that she would have been incapable of doing what Eve had done. But of course, Eve was always cool and quick-witted. No wonder Dan liked her. By the looks of things, more than liked her. She sat for a wistful moment, then, recalling her duties as a hostess, rang for coffee while Paul attended to drinks.

Later that night, when everyone had gone to bed, Meg lay awake, Paul asleep next to her. The dinner party had gone well, by and large – everyone seemed to have fun, which was the main thing. Diana and Dan and Eve arriving late had seemed to help, in an odd way, relaxing the sense of formality which had pervaded the meal till then. That was probably the result of her trying too hard. She so wanted to do everything properly, to make Paul proud of her. She lay thinking about her guests, hoping they were comfortable, trying to envisage how the day would unfold tomorrow. At least the weather forecast was reasonable. She listened to the house in darkness giving its usual settling creaks and sighs, and found herself thinking that one of those sounds might be Dan treading softly in the direction of Eve's bedroom. The recollection of the night he had come to her room at Woodbourne House rushed upon her before she could stop it. She shut her eyes and gripped the bed sheet tight, willing it away. Her mind ranged furiously in search of some other image, some favourite thing, and she concentrated hard on thinking about Grisette, about cantering her through the autumn woods, and succeeded in thrusting the memory back, back into the depths of her mind. She rolled over and pushed herself into the warmth of Paul's back. He woke, and groggily reached out a hand to cover one of hers, nothing more. After a moment she moved away, turned over, and closed her eyes.

7

'KENTLEIGH HAS FIVE guns as well as our seven, so we'll be a decent-sized party,' said Paul, as everyone assembled in the hallway the following morning. He glanced at Meg. 'Darling, are those shoes entirely suitable? Some of the drives are a very long walk, and it's been raining a fair bit recently. I suggest you find some stout boots.'

Meg went to hunt out something sturdier, and when she returned, Paul was fretting over the time. 'It simply isn't done to keep one's host waiting. Come on, let's all get a move on.'

Chastened yet again, Meg was in a mild sulk as they got into the cars to drive to Alderworth Hall, where the Kentleighs lived. Her mood was not improved when Paul murmured to her in what he thought was a consolatory way, 'Don't feel bad, chump. You just need a bit of training. What we need is to get you some shooting lessons and the right equipment. Today you can watch and learn.'

As Paul had predicted, the first drive was a long way away, and it seemed to Meg extremely dull sport to have to tramp so far in the freezing cold just to blast off a shotgun at a few clumsy birds. The beaters drove the birds from cover, and the pheasants, in their panicky, ungainly flight, hurled themselves over and over at a fence, before finding their level and rising in flight. The stuttering crash of the guns was deafening. She watched in pity as the birds dropped from the sky. It seemed too easy, more a massacre than sport.

On the walk to the next drive Dan noticed Meg looking cold

and miserable as she trudged along. She'd hardly spoken to him since he'd got here. Probably to do with the argument they'd had outside the pub in Chidding last summer. He saw her fall behind the others as she tried to bring to heel Paul's new young retriever, who still couldn't quite resist the scent of a rabbit, and slowed his pace to fall into step beside her.

'Hello, there. I haven't had the chance to talk to you properly yet.' He was glad of an excuse to be within touching distance of her. He marvelled at the translucence of her skin, the dark, wayward softness of her hair.

She smiled. 'No, it's been awfully busy. This is the first kind of thing Paul and I have hosted.' Meg's gaze slid sideways to Dan's fingers flexing nervously on the stock of his shotgun.

'Actually, I want to apologise for the way I behaved last time we met. I had no business saying what I did.'

'Please don't worry – I'd entirely forgotten about it.' They walked on in silence. Meg fought to find some impersonal, commonplace remark, and remembered something. 'By the way, I meant to ask – do you remember someone called Arthur Bettany from your schooldays?'

Mildly surprised by the change of tack, Dan replied, 'Yes, we were in the same form.'

'What sort of a boy was he?'

'Ridiculously clever. Somewhat arrogant. He got a scholarship to study mathematics at Cambridge. Good bat, too.' Hardly fair to mention his effeminacy, Dan thought; he'd been a schoolboy, and people changed. 'Why do you ask?'

'No reason. His named cropped up. I just wondered.'

They had reached the next drive, and the guns were lining up. 'Well, I'd better go and join the others. See you later.'

'Yes. See you later.'

And they parted, both feeling faintly unhappy, neither quite sure why.

*

So far the day had been unsatisfactory for Diana. She was peeved to find that Roddy was so intent on the day's sport that he wasn't paying her as much attention as their last encounter had suggested he might. In fact, his attentiveness merely extended to bringing down any bird she missed – which she did rather often, thanks to her hangover.

'I say,' she said crossly, 'must you keep wiping my eye?'

Roddy just laughed and carried on bagging whatever came within range of his gun.

'Ass!' muttered Diana to herself, though she was unable to resist a lingering glance at the muscled thighs stretching the tweed of his plus fours as he bent to retrieve his cartridges, which wasn't lost on Eve.

'He's quite an eyeful, isn't he?' she murmured.

'Roddy's the only reason I'm here,' confided Diana, as they waited for the beaters to raise more birds. 'I loathe shooting, but I'm hoping this weekend will provide some rather more interesting sport.' She glanced at Eve. 'How are things with Dan?'

Eve sighed. 'I'm a glutton for punishment. I know perfectly well he doesn't care as much about me as I do about him.' She hesitated, then decided to confide. 'A few weeks ago when he was drunk he told me that he's harbouring an unrequited passion for some married woman. He won't say who she is. A glamorous, rich beauty, no doubt. So there's room for me in his bed, but not his heart.'

'Hmm. With Dan, it's probably more a case of wanting what he can't have, rather than really being in love.'

'Perhaps that's my problem. Maybe I should play harder to get.'

'My dear, you can't afford to get too soppy about Dan. He really isn't the faithful type. Anyway, I remember last summer you said you weren't interested in anything more than a fling.'

'It's become a bit more than that – for me, at least.'

'That's too bad. No cure for love, I'm afraid.' She gave Roddy another glance. 'I have no intention getting bogged down in all that emotional stuff. I simply take my fun where I find it.'

The atmosphere at dinner that night was relaxed and convivial after the day's shooting, and Mrs Runcie's food was excellent. One of Paul's current projects was the stocking of his new cellar, where he had already laid down some excellent vintages, and the wine was first-rate and plentiful. Meg surveyed the table as her guests sat over coffee and liqueurs, the low light sparkling on the wedding-present crystal and Minton porcelain, and felt supremely happy and secure. The weekend had given her a new confidence. There would be many more successful weekend parties such as this. She would learn to shoot, become a good enough horsewoman to join the hunt, be everything Paul wanted her to be. She looked across at Paul, and they exchanged smiles.

Roddy, who had been conversing with Paul, suddenly turned and spoke across the table to Dan. 'What do you think, Dan? You're well up on politics these days. Paul reckons that Mosley's support is growing in London.'

'Well, it's true the BUF is trying to move back to mainstream politics,' replied Dan, after a moment's thought, 'but you can't ignore the fact that it's essentially an anti-Semitic movement. You only have to look at what happened at Cable Street to see that the British people won't stand for that.'

'Really?' said Guy, as he passed the port. 'In the local elections last spring Mosley got over twenty-three per cent of the vote in Limehouse.' The general chatter round the dinner table subsided in deference to a serious subject. 'And only heads of household were allowed to vote – the dads and granddads, so to speak – so who knows how much higher the figure would have been if his younger supporters had had their say?'

'The real point,' said Paul, lighting a cigar, 'is that, like it or not, we have a Jewish problem. It's the failure to face up to it that's the cause of all the trouble in Germany. Perhaps if it had been openly addressed and debated, we wouldn't be in the mess we are now. Look at the numbers of Jewish refugees flooding into this country.'

'They're an industrious lot, at any rate,' observed Roddy, taking the port from Guy. 'The entire Leipzig fur trade seems to have transferred itself to London. That can't be bad for business.'

Dan glanced at Eve, wishing he could think of a way to stop what he thought might be coming next.

'I'm not saying some of them can't be useful. The important thing to ensure is that we take only those refugees who can contribute something to the country, the cream of the milk so to speak,' said Paul. 'I was speaking to a friend in the Foreign Office just last week, and he agrees an open-door policy is out of the question. We can't just let a wave of foreign Jewish rabble swarm in.'

Eve, who had been listening quietly up to this point, suddenly looked up, her dark eyes intent. 'A swarm of rabble? Each one is a human being, just like you. I think the attitude of the government is deplorable. I'd go so far as to describe it as anti-Semitic. Too many people think, oh, how much can Hitler do to the Jews with the eyes of the world looking on? But we know what's happening to Jews there.' She looked round the table. 'We all do. It's just not something that civilised people in English dining rooms wish to talk about – why discuss the German boycott of Jewish businesses or the Nuremberg laws when you can talk about pheasant-shooting or vintage wines?'

'My dear Eve,' said Paul, 'I feel as sorry for them as the next person, but we cannot simply open the floodgates and allow anyone and everyone on to these shores—'

Eve put down her napkin and stood up. She turned to Meg. 'I'm sorry. I'm spoiling your dinner party, but I think I should go to bed.'

A more accomplished hostess might have defused the situation somehow, but Meg was too dismayed to know what to say.

'I say,' stammered Roddy, 'I'm sure Paul didn't mean anything, you know.'

'No, honestly – I'm tired.' She tried to smile. 'Please excuse me. Meg, that was a wonderful dinner. I shall see you all in the morning.'

There was a pained silence after she had left the room.

'Oh well, it just goes to show the old adage is right,' murmured Guy. 'No politics or religion at the dinner table.'

'Perhaps you didn't realise that Eve herself is Jewish,' said Dan. He glanced at Paul. 'I thought you might have picked that up from her surname.'

'Good Lord, I had no idea. I say—'

Dan rose from his chair. 'I'll just go and see that she's all right.'

When Dan had left, Diana got to her feet and announced that she intended to have an early night, too. Her glance met Roddy's briefly.

'I think I might do the same,' said Amy.

Meg rang for Enid to clear the table.

'If the ladies are retiring, how about we three have a game of billiards?' said Paul, swallowing the remains of his port.

Guy seized on the suggestion with relief, but Roddy, tilting his chair back and yawning, said he would pass. 'A day in the open always leaves me rather pooped. I'll head for bed, if you chaps don't mind.'

Diana glanced at the clock as she undressed. Only a little after eleven. Would Roddy wait until Paul and Guy had finished their game of billiards, and the household was asleep? That might be an age. She lay down on the bed, sexual longing flooding her with a delectable urgency. She closed her eyes, lifted her nightdress, and ran her hands over the satin flatness of her stomach. She thought of Roddy, imagining undressing him, touching him.

Deciding she might as well get ready for bed, she put on her silk robe and picked up her wash bag. As she left her room she could hear from downstairs the clatter of the maid clearing the dinner table. The landing was in darkness, and though she felt about for the light switch she couldn't find it. Still, there was just enough light from the hallway below for her to see her way to the bathroom. As she reached the bathroom door, she was startled by a tall figure looming next to her in the half-darkness. Roddy, also in his dressing gown, had arrived at the bathroom at the same moment.

'Good lord, you gave me such a fright!'

'You rather surprised me, too,' replied Roddy. 'Please' – he gestured to the bathroom – 'after you.'

'I have a better idea.' She opened the door and took his hand. A moment later they were in the bathroom together. In the darkness he slid the bolt and drew her towards him. Then his arms were around her, his mouth on hers. In a matter of seconds their robes were on the floor and she was flattened against the wall as he thrust into her. It was over in a few delirious moments. Their breathing grew slower.

'I think we both needed to get that out of our systems,' murmured Diana, running her hands over the smoothness of his chest, then down his muscled thighs.

'Yes, indeed.' His mouth found hers, and to her astonishment Diana felt him hardening inside her again.

'Oh, God,' she muttered, arching her back lightly. At that moment, the landing light came on outside, and the doorknob rattled. They both froze; Diana clapped a hand over Roddy's mouth to stifle his laughter.

'I shan't be long!' called Diana to whoever was outside the door. 'I think the bulb must have gone.'

'Oh, how annoying for you,' replied Meg's voice. 'How can you possibly see to do anything?'

As though in response, Roddy began to move gently inside Diana, at the same time sliding the tips of his fingers between her legs. She gave a tiny whimper, and reached out, fumbling for the tap. She turned it, and water splashed noisily into the basin, just in time to drown the shuddering sigh that escaped her as Roddy's fingers began their work.

'I'm sort of feeling my way,' she gasped, trying to keep her voice normal.

'It's too silly,' replied Meg. 'You should have told me about it. I'll go and tell one of the maids to come up with a replacement.'

They waited for a breathless moment until they were sure she had gone. Then very slowly Roddy began to thrust into her once more, gently at first, then harder. They came in the same instant, water still gushing from the tap next to them.

Diana let her breathing slow, her head still thrown back, her eyes closed. Then she gasped, 'We'd better get out of here before the maid comes.'

'My room,' said Roddy.

They fumbled on the floor for their robes, turned off the tap, and emerged hesitantly on to the darkened landing. Stifling their laughter, they padded their way swiftly to Roddy's room and locked the door.

Enid arrived at the bathroom with a spare bulb, then went back downstairs a few moments later. 'I couldn't find nothing wrong with the bathroom light, ma'am. The bulb's working fine.'

'How odd,' said Meg. 'Perhaps it's the switch. I'll have it looked at first thing.'

The next morning Meg was woken at half nine by the sound of the phone ringing. The shrill, insistent sound carried through the interconnecting door from Paul's study. Paul stumbled out of bed to answer it.

A few moments later he came back in a state of excitement, plucking his dressing gown from its hook. 'That was Bunny Warren. They've cancelled an event at Brooklands. The clerk of the course says we can take the new car on the mountain circuit today, if we want. It's the perfect place to test its acceleration and road-holding.'

Meg yawned. 'Why leave it till Sunday morning to let you know?'

'Bunny knew on Friday, but apparently he had rather a heavy weekend and forgot till this morning. I'll go and tell Roddy. If he has plans to go back to London this afternoon, he'll have to forget them.'

Paul left the room. Meg lay in bed trying to work out what difference this would make to the day's arrangements. Everyone had been due to leave before lunch, but now it looked as though Guy and Roddy would be staying on. Perhaps Dan and Eve could take Amy back to London. Or maybe she would want to stay and go back later with Guy. No matter, everyone's plans would become clear over breakfast. She got out of bed, and had just put on her dressing gown when Paul came back into the room. Meg could tell from his face that something was wrong.

'What's the matter?'

Paul simply shook his head and disappeared into their dressing room, closing the door.

Meg was alarmed. The expression in Paul's eyes had been intense, raw, as though something had pained him deeply. It wasn't a look she had seen before. She approached the dressing-room door, hesitated, and after a moment turned and went out on to the landing. There she met Eve on her way to the bathroom, and at the same moment Diana emerged from Roddy's bedroom, her blonde hair tousled, clutching her robe together. Meg's surprise must have been evident, for Diana glanced at her and muttered crossly, 'Oh, not you, too!', then swept into the bathroom, banging the door behind her.

'I should have been quicker off the mark,' said Eve, trying not to laugh.

'Gosh,' said Meg. 'Oh well, there's another bathroom on the next floor. You'll find the stairs at the end of the corridor.'

'Thanks.'

Meg stood there for a moment, bemused. Given Paul's views on sex outside marriage, he must have been more than upset to find his sister in Roddy's bedroom. Though Meg couldn't help thinking that Paul's expectations of people were somewhat unrealistic, in this day and age. Though the fact that Diana had been in Roddy's room, and not the other way around, suggested that she had gone to him. No doubt that made it even worse in Paul's eyes.

She went back to their bedroom and knocked gently on the dressing-room door. Paul opened it, half-dressed, his face blank. 'Yes?'

'Are you all right?'

'Why?'

Meg faltered. 'I saw Diana coming out of Roddy's bedroom. It's upset you, I can tell.'

Paul said nothing for a moment. He looked down at the tie he held in his hand. Meg could see a muscle working in his jaw. Then he said in a low voice, as though he could barely contain himself, 'I am more than upset – I am totally disgusted. Why must my sister pollute every man she meets? She's like a bitch in heat.'

'Well – I think maybe Roddy played his part, too. It seems hardly fair to blame Diana – if blame is the right word. Which I'm not sure it is.'

'Don't defend her! Don't make it worse by reminding me that you subscribe to her low values. You made me aware of that before we were married. At least one of us was sufficiently—'

'Paul, stop it!' exclaimed Meg. 'Don't take it out on me! If you're disappointed, upset, or whatever, then go and deliver your sermon on sexual morality to those two – though frankly your attitude seems quite absurd.' She couldn't help adding, 'If you want to know, I think it might have done us a lot of good if we had gone to bed with one another before we married.'

'Meaning what?'

'Meaning – oh, I don't know! Nothing. Please let's not row. I hate it. I'm not the one you're upset with.'

She closed the door on him before he could pursue the argument further, leaving him to get dressed.

The mood at breakfast was confused. Although Meg did her best to be cheerful and talkative, it was clear to all that Paul was put out about something. Roddy had tactfully stayed in his room, and Diana made short work of tea and toast then left the breakfast table briskly.

'So,' asked Meg, glancing from Paul to Guy, 'are you going to test drive the car at Brooklands?'

'I haven't made up my mind,' replied Paul curtly.

'Well, hadn't you better, dear? I'd like to know how many we might be for lunch.'

To this Paul made no reply. Guy gave Amy a glance, then said, 'It would help to know sooner rather than later, old man. Because if we are taking her out, I might ask Dan to drive Amy back to London – if that's all right with you, Dan?'

'Absolutely.'

Paul muttered something about checking gaskets, and left the table. Dan glanced at Meg. Despite her brightness, he could tell there was something wrong. Perhaps she and Paul had had a row. He said as much to Eve as they left the breakfast room.

'I don't know about that,' replied Eve, 'but I *do* know that Diana spent the night with Roddy, and word seems to have got out. Maybe Paul doesn't like such shenanigans under his roof. Did you notice Roddy didn't come down to breakfast?'

'Paul can be something of a prude,' remarked Dan, 'but he's also a stickler for good form, and it's hardly good form to make one's guests feel awkward.'

'Well, let's not concern ourselves overly with our hosts' domestic squabbles. I'm going to pack. Let me know when you've found out if we're giving Amy a lift. I should like to be in London before lunchtime.' She paused at the top of the stairs. 'I assume we're taking Diana?'

'I imagine so. I'll check.'

Dan went to Diana's bedroom, but found it empty. He went downstairs to the morning room, thinking she might be there, but the sound of Paul's angry voice made him halt outside the door.

'I cannot believe that you would come to our home and behave in such a disgusting way!'

'Oh, stop it, Paul,' came Diana's voice in reply. 'Do you have any idea how perfectly ridiculous you sound?' Dan heard the snap of a lighter. 'I will behave any way I choose.'

Dan retreated a couple of feet to the round polished table in the centre of the hallway, making a pretence of examining the local paper which lay there, staying close enough to listen.

'Not in my house, you won't. And I absolutely forbid you to have anything more to do with Roddy.'

'What cheek! Who are you to forbid me anything?'

'I'm the person who pays your bills, gives you a generous allowance, and allows you to live rent-free – that's who.'

'Are you threatening me?'

'If you choose to take it that way. I'm telling you what to do for your own good.'

'Don't you think Roddy might have a say in this? Are you going to forbid him to have anything to do with me as well? Do you think you can control everyone?'

'Roddy is my employee. I can make it clear to him where his best interests lie.'

'You are quite outrageous!' There was a moment's silence; Dan could hear the click of Diana's heels on the parquet floor. 'I know what's behind this. You want Roddy all for yourself. And you can't bear to think that Roddy would rather have me.'

At this point Dan decided it might be wise to absent himself, since the row had reached a pitch where one or other of them was likely to come storming out at any moment. He didn't wish to be caught eavesdropping, fascinating though it all was. What on earth had she meant about Roddy? So far as Dan knew, Paul had a deep and abiding loathing of homosexuality. Perhaps she was just goading her brother out of spite. Siblings could be foul to one another in argument. Dan imagined that the real cause of Paul's anger was his sense of outraged decency, and the fact that it was his own sister who was behaving badly, flinging her wanton behaviour in his face. Added to which, Diana had put Paul in an embarrassing situation vis-à-vis Roddy. He wondered how Paul would deal with that.

In the end it was Roddy who dealt with it. Realising that someone had to say something, he went to Paul half an hour later and addressed the issue in a frank fashion, apologising for the indiscretion, saying that he could see how he had caused Paul personal embarrassment, and that it might be best if he were to leave the racing team. Roddy had a good understanding of the workings of Paul's mind, and the suggestion was more a gesture of appeasement than a serious proposal. It enabled Paul to respond in a reproving but magnanimous spirit.

'I can't pretend I'm not disappointed, Roddy. There are certain standards, and you and Diana fell well short of them. But you're both grown-ups. Let's say no more about it.' Roddy, relieved not to be threatened with a horse-whipping, put out his hand, and Paul shook it, adding, 'But you do understand the problems it will cause if things continue? With Diana, I mean?'

This surprised Roddy, and also presented him with a slight difficulty. At present he had no serious intentions regarding Diana, but it would be insulting to say as much.

He cast around for a suitably oblique response.

'I can assure you nothing of the kind will happen again.'

So Paul and Guy and Roddy took the car to Brooklands, and Dan, Eve, Amy and Diana returned to London, leaving Meg to ponder the events of the weekend and try to work out whether it had been a success or not. She eventually decided that, whichever, it had at least been interesting.

8

DAN WAS AT his desk, going through an article he had written on an exhibition of Degenerate Art in Munich, and wondering how much of it would escape Mr Hitchcock's blue pencil, when a call came through to him from Harry.

'Harry, how are you?'

'Ecstatic, my dear. Laurence is back, and not a mark on him!'

'That's good news. You must be very happy.'

'I'm so extravagantly relieved that I'm throwing a supper party at Panteli's this evening by way of celebration, and you have to come. Brian Hawthorn will be there, and Gavin Henderson.'

'Is that the downstairs place in Frith Street?'

'The same. Corkage is free, so if everyone brings a bottle or two, we can have an excellent night of it.'

'I'll be there. What time?'

'I told Stavros nine o'clock, around seven or eight people.' He added, in a voice that trembled with warmth, 'God, Dan, it is so good to have him back. I have had a year of hell. Night and day the gates of dark death stood wide...'

'And you've retraced your steps to the upper air. Or Laurence has.'

'Homer, was it?'

'Virgil.'

'Ah, yes, of course. Well, see you tonight.'

Dan put the phone down, glad for Harry. Just yesterday he'd

had a telephone call from a deeply distressed Sonia, telling him that she'd heard Charles Asher had been killed in an attack on a bridge. Poor Charles, with his Wodehouse paperback stuffed in his jacket pocket, and his dogged belief in the fight against Fascism, and who had never even got to sleep with a woman before his short, troubled life had ended. How pointless and random it all seemed.

Panteli's was a small and formerly obscure Greek restaurant in a Soho basement which Harry, perpetually on the lookout for good, cheap food, had discovered six months ago. He had advertised its delights to his wide circle of friends, and now it was on its way to becoming a fashionable bohemian hangout. This, coupled with the fact that Harry was something of a grecophile, having travelled much in Greece during his university years, endeared him tremendously to the patron, and when Dan came downstairs into the restaurant a little after nine, Stavros Panteli and Harry were engaged in raucous conversation at a table crowded with Harry's friends.

Dan sat down between Brian and Gavin, two of Harry's magnificently effeminate chums. Brian, a poet with dark, soulful eyes, was already fairly drunk, and regaling the table with an outrageous story of a recent encounter with an Irish navvy. Gavin, a wealthy aristocrat who had fought in Spain the previous year, was explaining to Laurence his plan to house a number of Spanish child evacuees on his estate. Dan helped himself to a large glass of wine and joined in the conversation.

Two women, Laurence's sister and a friend who was an avant-garde painter, joined the party. Eventually the food arrived, each dish proudly announced by Stavros as the waiters set them on the table – youvetsi, souvlaki, spanakopita, keftethes and quantities of excellent bread. The feast commenced, Laurence's return was toasted by a tearful Harry, and someone was sent out to get more wine.

After a couple of hours Dan, fairly drunk, left the table and made his way to the gents at the back of the restaurant. As he came out he noticed a man in conversation at a corner table with two older men. The lighting in the corner was poor, but Dan felt he knew him. He paused, trying to work out where he had seen him before. The man sat back abruptly in his chair, dismissing something one of his companions was saying with an impatient wave of his hand, and Dan realised that it was Arthur Bettany. The gesture contained all the restless arrogance that Dan recalled from their schooldays. How strange to have heard Bettany's name for the first time in six years just recently, and now to encounter him in a Soho restaurant. For a drunken moment he thought of going over and saying hello, but there was an intensity about the conversation which told him he might not be welcome, and besides, he had no special wish to renew the acquaintance. He and Bettany had got on well enough, but they hadn't really been friends. Suddenly Arthur turned and glanced in Dan's direction, and Dan moved away, back to the rowdy table where the wine was still flowing and Brian was singing 'Mad About the Boy' in a throaty impression of Marlene Dietrich.

An hour later, when it was nearly midnight and Dan was thinking of leaving, Bettany passed their table, now alone. He was immediately hailed by Brian.

'Arthur! My little Tartur! Tarty darling, come and say hello!' Arthur paused somewhat unwillingly. Brian grabbed his hand. 'No, you're not a tart at all, you're a dear, sweet thing, aren't you?'

Arthur forced a smile and managed to shake Brian off. 'Good to see you, Brian – don't let me interrupt your party.'

'Come and sit with us, dear boy! We're having a shockingly good time. Laurence here is back from the wars and we are celebrating.'

'I'm on my way to meet someone.' Arthur glanced around the table and caught Dan's eye. He put out his hand. 'Ranscombe. I thought it was you.' Dan shook his hand and murmured a greeting. 'Sorry I can't stay,' said Arthur to the table in general. 'Enjoy yourselves.'

'Who was that?' asked Harry.

'Chap I was at school with,' said Dan. 'Arthur Bettany. I haven't seen him for years.'

'Were you at school with darling Arthur? I'm sure he wasn't so utterly exclusive then as he is now,' drawled Gavin, lighting a cigarette from a candle stuck in a bottle.

'What do you mean?'

'There's a rumour he has some secret wealthy lover, but no one knows who the man is.'

'I heard it was an MP,' said Laurence's sister.

'It's too sad that he's so utterly off limits. Completely naff.'

'Naff?' Dan hadn't heard the word before.

'Not available for—'

'Gavin!' screeched Brian. 'Remember there are ladies present!' The table collapsed in hoots of laughter, and Brian closed his eyes and in a wobbling falsetto began to sing, '*Last night I dreamt my lover came to me...*'

A few moments later Dan leaned across to Harry and said, 'I have to go, I'm afraid. I've got an article to finish and I'm already past the deadline. Need to be up bright and early.' He rose and left to a ragged chorus of farewells.

The night was frosty and clear as Dan emerged on to the pavement. The streets were quiet, just a few people leaving or heading for clubs, a couple of sailors on the prowl. He turned the collar of his coat up and began to walk in the direction of Bloomsbury and home, pausing by the railings of Soho Square to light a cigarette, ignoring the invitation of a passing street-walker. As he flicked a match into the gutter he glanced up, and saw Bettany beneath a street lamp on the other side of the square. He was pacing in small circles, hands in pockets, clearly waiting for someone, his breath pluming on the frosty air. He was directly on Dan's route home, and as Dan had no wish to encounter him again he decided to go the long way round the square. When he reached the far side, curiosity made him glance back. Whoever Bettany had been waiting for had arrived. The two were close together, the other man gripping the lapels of Bettany's raincoat. Dan stopped and stared for an anxious instant, wondering if Bettany was being threatened. But it didn't look that way. Bettany dropped his head for a moment on the shoulder of the other man, who relaxed his grip and placed his hands on Arthur's chest. They were speaking, but were too far away for Dan to hear their voices, let alone anything that was being said. Arthur's companion turned his head slightly, and Dan could see his face clearly by the light of the street lamp. It was Paul Latimer.

When he got back to his rooms, excited and appalled, Dan threw off his coat and sat down to think about what he'd seen. Gavin was hardly the most reliable of sources, but if what he'd said about Arthur Bettany having some mysterious wealthy lover was true, could it possibly be Paul? It might seem ludicrous, but it would make sense of what he'd overheard Diana say when she was arguing with Paul, and of what he'd just seen in Soho Square. Dan began to reassemble fragmentary recollections from school and Cambridge, suddenly seeing Paul's avuncular friendships with younger men, all that tactile, manly affection, in quite a different light. Was it beyond the bounds of possibilities that he had married Meg, not for love, but to establish a respectable façade for some double life? Yet Meg seemed so happy. He remembered the stab of pure jealousy he had felt seeing her exchange smiles with Paul over the dinner table a few weekends ago. It had killed him, seeing that warmth between them. How could that be fabricated?

This revelation, if true, sent everything tumbling into chaos. It made all the difference in the world if Paul was using her. It would be appalling. She might be happy enough now, but a deceit like that couldn't last. The longer it went on, the worse the consequences would be for her.

So what should he do? He sat revolving the matter in his mind, considering it from every angle. To speak to Meg, with or without proof, would be insanely destructive. She would hate him for ever. To speak to Paul would achieve – what? What would he say to Paul that couldn't simply be denied? He would make a fool of himself without accomplishing anything. He realised, in the end, that there was absolutely nothing he could do.

Meg had never expected to find life at Hazelhurst as dreary as she did that December. In the short, dark days of winter the world seemed to shrink in on itself, and the countryside, so full of life in spring and summer and fruitfully pleasant in autumn, lay dank and still. The house, with its cook and maids, gave her little to do domestically, and with Paul away for days on end, she felt very lonely. She made occasional expeditions to Woodbourne House to see Sonia, but she came away from those visits feeling envious of how happy and busy Sonia seemed, looking after Laura.

A few days before Christmas, things reached a peak. In an attempt to spin out the afternoon, Meg had gone into Alderworth to pick up some things from the chemist's, and on the way back decided to drop in on Anna Kentleigh, in the hope of a cup of tea and some company. She found Anna in the nursery with her three children, making Christmas decorations. All was lively chaos. The table was littered with bits of card and tissue paper, and there was much squabbling over glue and glitter. Anna was sitting at the end of the table, smoking and supervising matters with mild indifference. She seemed pleased to see Meg.

'Thank heavens you dropped in – I was just trying to invent an excuse for having a drink. I gave Nanny the day off to do some Christmas shopping, most of the maids are out, and being in charge of these three has left my nerves completely frazzled.' She got up and tapped her eleven-year-old son smartly on the crown of his head. 'Frank, don't hog the glitter. Esme, share the scissors with your sister. If you'll keep an eye on them,' she said to Meg, 'I'll rustle up some sherry and some of Mrs Ruddock's heavenly mince pies.'

Esme, the five-year-old, turned to Meg with serious eyes and held up a card on which she'd drawn a fat angel, its wings daubed with glue and silver glitter. 'This is for Grandma. She's spending Christmas with us, and I'm going to leave it in her room as a surprise for her.'

'I'm sure she'll love it,' said Meg. Esme, gratified, returned to her labours.

Meg surveyed the scene wistfully. This was what she had envisaged for herself, a warm, busy household, a family to love and care for. She and Paul had only been married for half a year, so it was ridiculous to feel this way. It had probably been fanciful, too, to move to the countryside and expect a life like Anna's miraculously to spring into existence. If it ever came, it would be a long time in the making.

When Anna returned, she announced, 'Mince pies, troops!' and the children scrambled from the table. Anna handed Meg a glass of sherry.

'Cheers. How are your Christmas preparations coming along?'

Meg knew that Paul fully expected to have a quiet Christmas at Hazelhurst, but she said, 'They're a bit up in the air at the moment. What about you?'

'Oh, we have a full house every year. James's mother always comes – she never quite lets me forget that Alderworth Hall was her home once, and always manages to imply that it was better run in her day. And my sister and her husband and their brood generally spend a few days with us. It's rather tiring, but tremendous fun.'

Meg sipped her sherry and watched the children. She remembered her own childhood Christmases in London, going to Selfridge's to see Father Christmas, the brightly lit shops, the carol service at Chelsea Old Church. She came to a decision. She was not going to spend Christmas in deepest Berkshire, alone with Paul.

When Paul came home the following afternoon, she told him so. 'I think we should spend Christmas in London. My mother's away, but we could stay with Diana, and maybe go to some parties. It would be more fun than being on our own here.'

Paul, who was standing by the mantelpiece cleaning out his pipe, seemed astonished. 'But we've spent half a year making our own home perfect. Why should you want to leave it at Christmas, of all times? I was looking forward to a quiet few days, just the two of us.'

'But I have quiet days all of the time, Paul! You can't imagine how dull it is when you're not here. And it's not as though we have a family of our own to make Christmas for.'

'Am I not your family now?' He knocked the contents of the pipe bowl into the fire. 'Besides, I don't find the idea of being in London as attractive as you evidently do.'

'Then why do you spend most of your time there?'

'Because, as you well know, I have business to attend to.' He opened a tobacco tin and began to fill his pipe, adding, 'I'm sorry you're bored with your life.'

'Oh, Paul, of course I'm bored! There's nothing to do here!'

'Dear me, you sound like a petulant child.'

Anger welled up in Meg. She had noticed Paul using this tactic increasingly – if she said or asked something to which he objected, he would become chilly and critical, knowing she hated any antagonism between them, and depending on that to make her back down. Which she generally did. But today she didn't feel like backing down.

'Perhaps that's because you treat me like one. Sometimes I feel you like having me cooped up here, your obedient wife, waiting for you to come home, with no purpose in life except to provide you with meals and company, and perhaps one day to produce some children.'

'Which you show precious little sign of doing.'

Meg was genuinely shocked, but a little bit of her was glad he had said it, glad of the chance to have a fight. There were things inside her which, if she didn't say them, might burst her heart. 'Are you surprised, given the way… the way…' But here she faltered, unable to find the words.

'The way what?'

'The way we make love. It's all wrong! It's… it's… oh, I don't know!' She knew she was about to become tearful, and hated herself for being weak. 'It's so unloving!'

She gazed at him, and in a transfiguring instant his expression of aloofness became one of concern. He put his pipe on the mantel and came and put his arms around her.

'My darling, what a thing to say!' She returned his embrace longingly, wanting so much to be reassured, yet knowing at the same time that it would be dangerous to let things rest there. 'You know I love you. I don't understand what you mean.'

Yes, you do, she thought. She lifted her eyes to his and said quietly, 'I mean there is no passion. No desire. Sometimes, Paul, it's as though you just…' from somewhere, nowhere, she dug out a word that she knew was closest to what she felt, 'as though you just fuck me, not because you want to, but because you have to.'

He recoiled as though she had slapped him. 'I never expected to hear that kind of language from you. Never. Do you realise how it defiles you? How utterly repellent it makes you?'

She grasped his arm, instantly sorry, her anger forgotten. 'Oh, Paul – I didn't mean to! I was only trying to say, to make you understand—'

He shook her off. 'Stop it! This is worse than disgusting. You say a thing like that and then try and abase yourself – good God, Meg, show a little control.' He picked up his pipe. 'If things are so unsatisfactory for you, I will sleep in my dressing room until you say otherwise.'

He left the room. Meg stood by the hearth, letting her emotions subside. Her instinct was to follow him, make everything all right, but she steeled herself not to. The despair she felt had nothing to do with having displeased him; its source lay in the knowledge that something was deeply wrong, but that Paul refused to admit it. Refused, not just because he didn't want to, but because he felt he didn't need to. She thought, too, of what he had said about her showing precious little sign of having a baby. It was the kind of cruel remark she had never thought to hear from the Paul she knew and loved. Did he really blame her?

After a few minutes she left the room. The glow of the light under the library door told her where he was. She made a phone call to Diana, then went upstairs and packed a small case. She went downstairs, put on her coat and hat, and knocked on the library door. Paul was sitting in his leather armchair by the fire, reading a copy of *Horse and Hound*, his pipe in the ashtray next to him.

'Paul?'

He glanced up.

'I really would rather spend Christmas in London,' she said calmly. 'So that's where I'm going now. I've rung Diana. You and I just seem to be getting on each other's nerves, and I can't bear feeling lonelier than I already do. If you would like to come with me, of course, that would be nice. Besides which' – she glanced at the window, where rain had begun to patter – 'it would mean you could drive.' She couldn't resist the desire to placate, to make things sound again.

Paul sighed. 'You are a chump.' He stretched out a hand. 'Come here. I've already forgotten that awful thing you said earlier. It wasn't like you, and I forgive you.' She approached the chair and let her hand be taken. 'Now, go and take off your coat and hat and let's hear no more about it. This is your home, and we shall spend Christmas here, just the two of us.'

'No,' replied Meg. 'You're not listening. I don't want to spend Christmas here. I want to be with people, with friends. I have been unbearably lonely recently. The last thing I want is to hate being at Hazelhurst. I need a change of scene. If you come too, we can have a lovely time.'

Paul withdrew his hand and picked up his magazine. 'You're being tiresome. I suppose you think marching off to London like this somehow wins you the argument.'

'Paul, it isn't as petty as that. I wish you would listen sometimes. Anyway, I'm going. If you don't want to come with me now, I hope you decide to join me soon. I would rather not spend Christmas without you.'

'Then stay here.'

Meg closed the door without a word, picked up her case, and left the house.

9

DIANA WAS OUT when Meg arrived at the flat in Kensington, but had left a key with the hall porter. The following morning she and Meg met at breakfast.

'Have you and Paul had a row?' asked Diana.

Meg explained what had happened. 'The last few weeks have been so lonely. I couldn't face Christmas there, just the two of us.'

'I can't say I blame you. I remember what winter is like in deepest Berkshire. My brother can be very stubborn, but I bet you anything he'll be here in the next couple of days.'

'I hope so.'

'Don't look so glum. Unless you have plans, I vote we go and do some Christmas shopping. Then tonight you can come with me to Ava von Hoffmanstahl's do. She throws quite the best parties. I'll telephone and tell her I'm bringing you along. Paul, too, if he sees sense. Have you something to wear?'

'I've brought a couple of dresses, but they're not exactly party attire.'

'Then you can raid my wardrobe. Go and have a look while I run my bath.' Diana disappeared to the bathroom with her tea.

Meg wandered into Diana's bedroom. Diana's clothes from the night before lay on the floor where she had dropped them. If it weren't for the maid tidying up every day, Meg suspected the place would be chaos. As it was, when she opened the doors of the wall-long wardrobe, garments were neatly arranged by type and hung on padded satin hangers. Diana seemed to have any number of cocktail and party dresses. Meg drew out a couple of shorter ones. Diana was taller than she was, and anything floor-length would swamp her. One was a halter-neck dress in rose chiffon with bead trimming on the bodice; the other was black, made of silk, with diamond-shaped panels and thin shoulder straps. She went to Diana's long cheval glass and held each one in front of her. She had just decided that the rose chiffon was safer, when Diana wandered in, in search of some cosmetic. As she passed, she pointed to the black one.

'Try that. It looks nothing hanging up, but it's divine on. Chanel – I picked it up in Paris last summer.' She took a pot from the dressing table and disappeared.

Meg took off her clothes and wriggled into the dress. She was slightly curvier than Diana, but it still fitted beautifully. Glancing down, she realised it wouldn't do with a brassiere. She slipped the black straps down, unhooked her bra and tossed it aside, then pushed the straps back up. Black was not a colour she generally wore. She had always thought it too sophisticated, something for older women. But as she gazed at her reflection, she knew she looked stunning. The diamond-shaped panel on the front of the dress moulded itself to her figure, and the bodice was cut so that it cupped her breasts perfectly. She caught up her hair and half-turned her head. Worn with the diamond necklace and earrings Paul had given her, it would look simple but dramatic. She felt a delicious thrill such as she hadn't experienced for a long time – the pleasure of wearing beautiful clothes, and knowing she looked wonderful and would be admired. Carefully she took off the dress and put her own clothes back on. Then she put it back on its hanger and carried it back to her room.

Diana lay soaking in her bath. In some ways it would be beastly inconvenient having Paul and Meg here. She was having a tricky enough time with Roddy without Paul finding out they were still seeing one another. If only she could exercise more self-control where Roddy was concerned. She knew how off-putting it was for a girl to appear too keen on a man, and in the past she'd never had any trouble playing the game perfectly, making herself unavailable and then available at precisely the right moments. Somehow Roddy got to her in a way that other men never had, and it probably showed. Maybe she was a bit in love with him. It was an interesting, if worrying, thought.

The last person Dan expected to see at the von Hoffmanstahls' party was Meg, and certainly not looking as she did. She was wearing diamonds and a backless black dress, with her hair up, and she looked more beautiful and sophisticated than he had ever seen her.

'I'm glad to see you,' she said. 'I don't know a soul here, and everyone seems terribly grand. Diana brought me, but she's otherwise occupied, as you can see.' Dan followed the direction of Meg's glance and saw Diana with a group of young men, Roddy MacLennan among them.

'Where's Paul?' asked Dan. A waiter passed with a tray of glasses of champagne, and Dan took two, handing one to Meg.

'He's still at Hazelhurst. But he'll be here any day.' She took a sip of her champagne. 'How well do you know our hostess?'

'I don't know her at all, actually. I'm a friend of her husband, Raimund. I reviewed some book about his father a year ago, and he got in touch. We've met up a few times. Very interesting chap.'

'Is Eve with you?'

'No,' he replied, then added, 'There's nothing serious between us, you know.'

'That's a pity. You're well suited. She's so clever. I'm quite a dunce by comparison. Those things she said that evening at our dinner party, about the Jews in Germany. She was right, of course. I'm too busy leading my own safe life to know or care.' Her expression grew pensive. 'Sometimes I feel like a child. A privileged, spoilt child. That's what being married to Paul is like. I thought marriage would be transforming, a way of growing up and into the world. But it's not like that. I sometimes wonder what on earth the point of me is.'

'Are you saying that being Mrs Paul Latimer isn't point enough?'

Meg coloured, lost for a reply. He realised the remark had been hurtful, but he didn't care. He wished he could tell her what he'd seen that night in Soho Square. Then maybe she'd realise what a mistake she'd made. But it wouldn't achieve anything. It would simply destroy her.

Though he knew it was childish, Dan decided to spend the rest of the evening flirting and gossiping with Diana. Towards midnight, Roddy took Diana to one side.

'Can we go back to yours? I'm sick of the way that Ranscombe fellow has monopolised you all night.'

'Perhaps,' replied Diana, enjoying the subtle change in the weighting of things. 'Though I'm not entirely sure you've earned the privilege.'

Roddy was leaning against the wall. He glanced around quickly to see if anyone was watching, then drew his finger down the length of Diana's bare back and slipped his fingers into the waistband of her dress, stroking her buttocks. 'You don't know what it does to me to see you flirting with some other chap. I've been lusting after you all evening.'

Diana pretended to consider. 'Well, if I do let you come back, you'll have to behave very discreetly. My sister-in-law is staying.'

Roddy removed his hand. 'In that case, perhaps it's not such a good idea after all.'

'Why ever not?'

'You know very well why. Because it will probably get back to Paul. And frankly, I want to keep my place on the racing team.'

'What? Rather than see me?'

'I just don't see the sense in jeopardising either.'

'What a ridiculously craven attitude,' said Diana, angered by the thought that her entire life seemed to be run according to the wishes of her brother. 'Do you always dance to my brother's tune?'

'I don't intend to argue about it, Di. I'm sure you'll find someone else to see you home.' And with that, he left.

Diana felt close to tears. Just when the momentum had swung her way, everything had gone wrong. Blast Paul.

At that moment Meg came up. 'I think I'm ready to go home, if you are.'

Diana nodded. 'More than ready.'

Having said their goodnights, they found their coats and departed in search of a taxi. Dan watched them go. When he went to take his own leave of his hosts a few minutes later, he found Ava holding a silver evening bag, which he recognised as Diana's.

'Someone left this by the cloaks,' Ava said. 'I think they must have forgotten it.'

'It's Diana Latimer's,' said Dan. 'I know where she lives. I can drop it round to her tomorrow, if you like.'

'Oh, would you? That's very kind.'

Dan bade his hosts goodnight and went in search of a taxi. He sat in the cab, brooding on his conversation with Meg, wishing he could simply douse his feelings, the way one might a fire, and achieve some peace. It was not to be, apparently.

Over a late breakfast the following morning, Diana announced her plans for the day. 'I'm lunching with my uncle and aunt in Belgravia, then I have more Christmas shopping to do, and after that Lydia Esmond and I are going to the theatre. What are you up to?'

'I thought I'd stay here, in case Paul arrives.'

'It'll be too ridiculous if he sits sulking in Berkshire. Oh, by the way, if Roddy MacLennan rings while I'm out, tell him… tell him I shall be busy for the next fortnight, and simply won't have a free moment.'

Diana left shortly before one. Meg dismissed the maid for the day, and sat in the kitchen, fiddling with the remains of yesterday's *Times* crossword. After a while she laid down the pencil and wondered what on earth she was doing. The more time went by, the wider the gulf between her and Paul was growing – and there shouldn't be a gulf at all. On impulse she went to the hall and telephoned Hazelhurst. Paul was out, one of the maids told her. Thinking perhaps he was on his way to London, Meg asked if he had taken the car. But no, Mr Latimer had gone for a walk with the dogs.

Meg pictured Paul tramping unhappily on his own through the woods, then returning to an empty house. He was being ridiculously stubborn, but she hated the idea of him being all alone over Christmas. She would go back. She went to her room and began to pack.

Ten minutes later, as she was scribbling a note to Diana, the doorbell buzzed. She put down the pen and went to the door, and was surprised to see Dan standing there.

'Oh – hello.'

'Hello. I've come to return something to Diana. Is she here?'

'No, she's gone out for the day, I'm afraid.'

'No matter.' He held up Diana's bag. 'Perhaps you can give it to her. She left it at the party last night.'

Meg took the bag. 'Won't you come in for a moment?'

As he stepped into the hallway Dan noticed Meg's coat lying folded across her suitcase.

'Would you like some tea?' asked Meg.

'Thanks.' Dan took off his hat and followed her into the kitchen, and she filled the kettle and set it on the gas. He sat at the kitchen table, still in his overcoat, and watched Meg moving around the kitchen, fetching cups and saucers, filling the milk jug. Minutes passed, the silence between them growing into something potent, but at the same time peaceful. He thought of a dozen things to say, but uttered none of them. One by one she brought the tea things to the table.

'We can go into the sitting room, if you like.'

'I'd rather be in here. I like kitchens.'

'So do I.' She sat down and poured the tea, passing Dan a cup.

'Thanks. So, you're on your way back to Hazelhurst?'

'How did you know?'

'I saw your things in the hall. I thought Paul was coming here for Christmas?'

Meg stirred her tea, deciding she might as well tell Dan. 'The truth of it is, we had a disagreement. I didn't want to spend Christmas stuck in Berkshire. So I came up to London on my own. But he hasn't called, or made any move to join me here, so I think I might as well go home.'

Dan said nothing as he fished in his overcoat pocket for his cigarettes and lit one. He rose and looked round for an ashtray, found one and brought it back to the table. He studied the glowing tip of his cigarette in silence as Meg drank her tea. She found she couldn't take her eyes off his hands, fascinated by the movement of his fingers, the tendons in his wrist as he tapped off the ash, the light golden hairs on his wrist beneath the shirt cuff. She had an overpowering urge to reach out and feel the warmth of his hands.

She went on, 'I don't want you to think Paul and I are unhappy. It isn't like that.'

'Why should you care what I think? You either are happy or you aren't. It's none of my business. Though from what you said last night, I take it marriage isn't everything you expected?'

She met his gaze, feeling the change in the atmosphere between them. There seemed no point in anything but complete honesty. 'I don't know.' She looked away, adding slowly, 'In some ways it is. The house, domesticity, companionship – certain things are as I hoped they would be. But sometimes it feels as though those things are…' she hesitated, 'superficial. That makes it sound like they don't matter. They do. Oh, I don't know.' She pushed her cup away. 'Can I talk to you as a friend? We are friends, aren't we?'

'Yes, we are. And yes, you can.' He felt his heart tighten.

'I thought that loving Paul and being married would somehow be sufficient purpose in life. That we would be everything to each other. But he has his affairs of business in London, and his racing car project to occupy him. It's as though he has a world, and I merely have an existence within it. I seem to have no purpose beyond him. At first I thought that was simply the nature of love. But sometimes, when he's away for days on end, I think about a thing you once said…' Her voice tailed off.

Dan waited as the seconds ticked by. 'What thing? If it was something beastly, it's not worth dwelling on. I was jealous, that's all.'

Meg got up and carried her cup to the sink. She stood with her back to him, hands resting on the sink, saying nothing. Dan ground out his cigarette. Then he rose and went over to where she stood. He leaned back on the work surface and tried to look into her face. She wouldn't look at him. He reached out and gently turned her face to his. The mere touch of his fingers electrified her. 'Tell me.'

'You said Paul simply needed a wife, and I fitted the bill. That he didn't really love me.'

'I'm sorry. I should never have said that.'

'Why? You were saying what you thought was true. Are you saying now it wasn't true?'

'Oh Lord – look, I didn't want to believe you were in love with him. I was still hoping I had a chance.' He paused. 'When did I say this, anyway?'

'At the Cunliffes' party. In the library.'

'Ah, yes. The library.' Was she remembering, as he was, the way they had kissed, clinging together, burning with need for one another? He searched her face, but could read nothing.

'So, sometimes I think of that, and I wonder if you were right. That I'm just another feature adorning Paul's life. The little wife waiting at home.'

'I'm sure he loves you,' said Dan, knowing he only said this so that she shouldn't be unhappy.

'I wish I were sure,' murmured Meg. 'I want so badly to be loved.' She turned to Dan, straining with every effort of thought to resist the impulse to touch him, to put her hand against his face and feel the warmth of him. The longing that blazed within her seemed kindled simply by his nearness, by some mysterious chemistry.

'But you are,' said Dan. 'You know you are.'

They gazed at one another, overpowered by something utterly beyond their control. He took hold of her and kissed her. After a slight tremble of resistance, she sank against him and let it happen, all sensible thought drifting from her mind. Then after a few seconds her senses returned and she pulled away. 'This is wrong. We mustn't do this.'

'Don't you want to be happy? Ever? Even just for an hour?' The intensity in Dan's voice took her aback.

'But it's—'

'Christ, don't say it's wrong. Of course it's not wrong. What's wrong is that you married him, and I couldn't stop you.' His mouth found hers again, and she kissed him back hungrily, feeling something give way within her. He slipped his hand inside the bodice of her dress and caressed her breasts. He felt no guilt at what he was doing. Her marriage was a sham, even if he couldn't tell her that, and besides, she wanted him as much as he wanted her.

'Does he make you feel this?' muttered Dan. 'Does he?'

'No,' she gasped. The last vestiges of restraint fell away. She drank in the harsh tweed scent of his coat as she pushed it from his shoulders, tasted the roughness of his chin as she dabbed it with kisses, felt the thickness of his hair as she ran her fingers through it, holding him, striving to bring her body as close as possible to his. She tugged at his shirt and tie and he worked at the fastenings of her dress as they fought to find each other's skin. Dan slipped a hand between her legs, lightly thumbing the damp crotch of her knickers, and she let out a small gasp. He stopped. They gazed at one another for a second, their breathing hard and urgent.

'Not here,' muttered Dan. 'Much as I like kitchens.'

Meg took his hand and led him out into the hallway. Her mind was a blazing blur, the urgency of her desire dictating everything. She had no coherent sense of betrayal; none of that mattered. She led him to Paul's bedroom. The room, with its dark green walls and solid furniture, sat in its customary manly silence, the sheets and bedding smooth and tight, as they had been on that first night of her marriage. She went to the bed and began to pull at the closely tucked sheets and blankets, hauling them back from the pillows, tugging and wrenching everything into disorder. She turned to Dan, who stood in the doorway, tieless, his shirt halfway unbuttoned, looking uncertainly around, understanding where he was. Meg felt crazily in control, exultant in what she was doing. She put out a hand, and as he came towards her she kicked off her shoes and unfastened the remaining buttons of her dress, letting it slip to the floor. She lay back on the bed, and then his mouth was on hers, and she was sliding his shirt from his back as he pulled off the remainder of his clothes. She ran her hands over the muscles of his chest, back and arms in a kind of ecstasy of pleasure, vaguely aware of the deftness with which he was removing her underwear. Then the warmth of his skin was close against hers, and she could allow herself to feel the hardness of him, brush him with her fingers and feel the spasm of his longing in a way which she could never allow herself with Paul.

He lowered his head to kiss her shoulders, then her stomach. Where his hands went, his mouth followed. Meg closed her eyes and let her senses lift her into some place where she was barely conscious of anything beyond her own pleasure. As she reached a moment where she could scarcely bear it, she felt him enter her; his mouth was on hers again, and she tasted herself. A shudder ran through her and he moved as far inside her as he could, and she arched her back slightly, giving herself up entirely to a sense of completeness she had never thought possible, and the knowledge that it was Dan filled her with an inexpressible happiness. He seemed utterly attuned to her, as though his body was listening to hers, waiting, feeling, following.

For Dan the intensity was something he had never experienced with any woman. At moments he would pull away, almost leaving her, simply to experience the pleasure of gazing at her face, blurred with anxious desire, before pushing himself into her again, feeling her relief as his body locked once more to hers. The rhythm between them mounted to a place of slow pleasurability, until at last Dan could hold back no longer. A few seconds later, he felt a tremor of pleasure rock her body, and she cried out, her thighs tight against his.

They clung together, their breathing slowing, their passion ebbing, their senses separating, retreating from each other into their own minds until eventually they lay side by side in a state of stillness. They lay that way for several minutes, wordless.

Suddenly Meg's eyes grew alert. She glanced at the doorway.

'What?' asked Dan.

'I don't know. I just thought...' Then she closed her eyes. 'Diana said she'd be out all day and evening. But even so, this is madness.'

Reality seemed to pool and congeal in the room. The coldness of it made Dan reach for the blankets and pull them up around their shoulders.

'It's not madness. It's the sanest thing anyone has ever done. I love you. And now you know what that means.'

She opened her eyes and looked into his. 'Yes. Yes, I do. All those months ago I told myself I shouldn't pay any attention to the things I felt for you. That I could train myself out of them.'

'Tell me, then.'

She was silent for a long time, her eyes searching his face, her fingers toying with his hair. 'I love you. I always have. From the first time you gave me a cigarette. We'd just played tennis, and I didn't really want it.'

'You didn't really smoke.'

She laughed, and the feeling of her body trembling against his was delightful. 'No, not really. But I wanted you to think I was sophisticated.'

'I thought you were sweet. And not in the least sophisticated.'

They lay in the warmth of the bed, the afternoon deepening outside, talking for a long while. They made love again, and then, amazed at the perfection of it, yet again. At a little after four o'clock Meg turned her eyes to the darkness beyond the window. She remembered standing at that window a few months ago on her wedding night, aware of her heightened self, the prepared responsiveness of her body. She remembered, too, how it had met with nothing. Not like this. For the first time, she was aware of an ache of guilt. Whatever she felt for Paul, her husband, it was genuine, and she had betrayed it. She searched in herself for a reason to care, and found it – found the knowledge of Paul's kindness and trust. Maybe it wasn't his fault he couldn't love her as Dan did. She turned away from Dan's arms.

Instinctively Dan said, 'Don't think about him.'

Amazed that he had guessed, she turned back to him and kissed him. 'I can't help it.'

'It mustn't stop here. I love you too much. You love me. Something has to be done.'

'Don't. This is bad enough.'

'You don't mean that.'

'Not like that. I mean it's too soon, too... Oh, I don't know what happens next. I can't think.'

The ringing of the phone in the hall jarred them both. Meg flung back the covers and stood up. She glanced around hastily, then picked up Dan's shirt and put it on. Dan lay back, enjoying the sight of her in his shirt as she ran to the hall. He heard her pick up the phone, then her voice in low, staccato conversation. Her words were inaudible. He heard her replace the receiver, and a moment later she returned to the room. She sat down on the bed, not looking at him. Dan reached out a hand and caressed her shoulders.

'That was Paul.' Meg's voice was toneless. 'He's coming to London this evening. He said he was sorry about what happened. His train gets in at eight o'clock. I said I would meet him.' She burst into tears.

'Hush,' said Dan. 'Come here.' He drew her towards him. 'You needn't feel guilty. We've put right what was wrong. Don't you believe that?'

She wiped her eyes and shook her head. 'No. We've just made things even more wrong.'

'Don't say that. Are you sorry it happened?'

'No!' She turned to look at him, then fell against him, kissing him. 'No, no! What terrifies me is to think that it might never have. But that doesn't make it any better. I'm married to him, Dan. I made promises. And he has never been anything but kind and loving to me.'

'Don't think about it.' He slipped his shirt from her shoulders and on to his own. 'Come on. We're going to get dressed, then go and have an early supper somewhere, and after that you will go to the station and meet Paul. We have a lot of time to think about what happens next. But I will be thinking about you' – he kissed her – 'every minute of every day that I'm away from you.'

They dressed in silence. Dan could sense she was already removing herself from him. As she slipped on her shoes, she glanced at the bed. Hurriedly she began to tug and smooth the rumpled sheets into place, plumping and arranging the pillows, pulling up and straightening the blankets, then the counterpane, moving round the bed and tucking things in firmly and snugly. When she had finished she stood back, her hand to her mouth, her expression uncertain, almost fearful. Dan watched her and knew that she was thinking of tonight, when she and Paul would be in this room, in this bed. His heart gave a lurch of dismay. This was not going to be in any way straightforward. In fact, it was probably the path to hell.

Over the next few days Meg felt as though she were living some other woman's life. On the evening when she went to Paddington to meet Paul, her lips still soft and burning from Dan's kisses, she was convinced it would be impossible for her to behave normally. But she found smiles and words came easily, the more of them the better. There was a kind of terrible giddiness about her emotions, and her happiness made it easy to pretend she was pleased to be with Paul again. It was the perfect disguise, not least for guilt.

Christmas and New Year passed, and still she felt as though her life had become a fiction. She regarded Paul with a kind of impervious detachment, weighing her feelings and wondering. She saw it all with a terrifying clarity now. Paul had always been a wise friend who could be trusted to look after her, the hero of her childhood, and she had blindly gone into marriage thinking that was enough. She had known nothing, nothing. She now felt indivisible from Dan, body and soul. She saw now that everything that had gone before, since the moment he had stepped off the train last summer, had been leading inevitably to this. Why had she spent so long pretending otherwise? The happiness of her life lay in being with him, and the sooner they could be together, the better – the guilt that haunted her day in, day out in every living moment with Paul, demanded the same thing. She couldn't go on letting Paul believe in her.

Perhaps in an attempt to make sense of her divided situation, she found pretexts for avoiding sex with Paul. Some peculiar carnal fastidiousness would not allow her to continue with what she saw as the charade of their sex life, after what she had known with Dan, and to whom she now felt she belonged. If Paul minded, he didn't show it. He was as affectionate as ever. As the days of early January went by, she could feel the rhythm of domestic life at Hazelhurst forcing her back to her old reality, and there were times when the light of the few precious hours that she and Dan had spent together seemed like that of some receding star. The time till she could see him again seemed unbearably far away. When they had parted, they had agreed that he could not write to her or ring her, and Meg did not want to write letters to which she could receive no reply. It had been left that she would make an excuse to come up to London in January and stay for a weekend – where and on what pretext, without the possibility of Diana finding out, was something she would have to work out. What happened after that, she had no idea.

Dan waited impatiently for Meg to get in touch to say when she was coming to London. Every day he expected a call or a letter. But the first days of January passed without any word.

Late one morning his office phone rang, and as usual he snatched it up, hoping it might be Meg. It was Eve. His heart dropped. Their relationship had been bumping along in a casual way before Christmas, but it couldn't carry on any more.

'Hello, stranger,' said Eve. 'I'm at a loose end, and wondered if you'd like a bite of lunch.'

'If you like.' It would be an opportunity to explain to her that things had to end. 'Will the café round the corner do?'

'I'll see you there in five minutes.'

They established themselves at a corner table with sandwiches and tea, and chatted for a while about work and colleagues. When the small talk had dried up, Eve said, trying to keep her tone light, 'I've missed you. I rather hoped you would be in touch over Christmas.'

'I'm sorry. I meant to call, only things got a bit busy.'

There was a silence. Eve could tell from his manner that

something had changed. 'Dan, if you have something to tell me, just come out with it.'

'It's the married woman I told you about.' Eve appraised him with cool eyes. She took a cigarette from her bag and lit it, waiting. 'Something happened over Christmas, and the upshot is, I believe now that she cares for me as much as I do for her.' He looked up and met Eve's gaze. 'I think she may leave her husband. In fact, I'm hoping she will. I mean, the last thing I want to do is to break up anyone's marriage—'

'But you will if you have to.' Eve's face and manner were so composed that Dan found it impossible to know what she was thinking, but he caught her caustic tone.

'You're disappointed in me, evidently.'

'It's not my place to judge you. You've always been honest about your feelings for me. I knew from the start that it was hopeless ever to expect you to love me—'

'I never intended to hurt you.'

Eve gave an abrupt laugh, but he could see that her dark eyes were bright with tears. She tilted her chin, trying to blink them back, taking a hard drag of her cigarette. 'I imagine those are words you say a lot, Dan. No doubt you'll go on saying them to people, believing that somehow they make everything all right, that you can use them to excuse everything you do.'

'I never pretended with you. I was honest from the beginning. You chose to accept it. I value what we have. I don't want to lose your friendship.'

'Fine, and I can keep your bed warm while you wait for your wonderful married lady to end her marriage?'

'That's an absurd thing to suggest. And the last thing I want.'

'Then you have more scruples than I supposed.' She opened her bag and fished for some change and dropped it on the table. 'That's for my share of lunch.'

'Don't be silly. I don't want—'

Eve rose, interrupting him, and pulled on her coat. 'Goodbye, Dan. At least you've always been candid. I can't fault you there.'

The bell on the café door tinkled as she left. Dan sat staring at the remains of the plate of sandwiches. He shrugged, picked one up and ate it. It was true, he'd always been strictly honest with her. Was he to blame if she felt more for him than he did for her? He didn't think so. She'd known what she was getting into. He would rather not have hurt her, but in a situation like this people were bound to end up being hurt. At least now he could focus on Meg, and not feel guilty about anyone. Not even Paul, who was living a lie of his own, God help him. He finished the sandwiches and went back to the office.

At the beginning of the second week of January Meg began to feel unwell. She was listless and queasy, and wondered if she might have the beginnings of flu, which was doing the rounds locally. She made an appointment to see Dr Carr at his surgery in the village, but mentioned nothing to Paul.

Dr Carr examined her, and asked her questions, nodding thoughtfully at her replies. At the end of his examination he folded up his stethoscope. 'Pop your things on, and come out when you're ready,' he said, and left the curtained cubicle.

Meg dressed herself, then slipped out from behind the curtain and sat down. Dr Carr was busily writing. He finished his notes and looked up with a smile.

'I'm happy to say that I don't think there's a thing wrong with you, Mrs Latimer. In fact, it's nothing more than the early stages of pregnancy.'

Meg's mind blazed with shock. She sat staring at him. Rational thoughts began to fall into place. 'How long? I mean, how many…?' She faltered, an agonised part of her longing for it to be Dan's, and that very thought feeling like the worst treachery against Paul.

'The uterus is quite full, so by my reckoning, seven to eight weeks. Which would account for your queasiness.'

Meg sat rigid on the chair. 'But it can't be that many weeks. I mean, I had some bleeding just two weeks before Christmas.'

'That isn't necessarily significant. It can happen even when one is pregnant. But it's something to keep an eye on. You must let me know if it happens again, even a little. Now, we must look ahead and think of arrangements for your care.'

Meg was aware of Dr Carr's mild voice as he continued to talk, but she wasn't listening. The baby was Paul's. The thing they had both wanted and hoped for had finally happened, just when she was on the verge of destroying their marriage. Maybe this was God's way of resolving everything. She didn't have a strong faith, but she believed in fate. And this one seemed inescapable.

Her mind returned to the here and now, and she heard Dr Carr saying, 'Your husband will be delighted, I'm sure.'

'Yes. Yes, I'm sure he will be.'

She could feel doors closing around her. And Dan was on the other side of them all.

PART III

1938

1

JANUARY PASSED WITHOUT any word from Meg, and a sick feeling of doubt began to grip Dan. He refused to believe that she had had a change of heart. He had only to recall that afternoon in Diana's flat to know beyond doubt that she loved him. Certainly her situation was far from simple. Paul had claims upon her; the life that she had created for herself at Hazelhurst wouldn't be easy to shed. She was probably afraid of many things if she were to abandon her marriage – the reaction of her family and financial uncertainty not least among them. But that monumental step didn't have to be taken yet. Why had she failed to arrange to come up to London, as she had promised? That surely couldn't be so hard to manage.

In the first week of February, when he was sitting in his office, he suddenly decided he could bear it no longer. He would telephone her at Hazelhurst. If Paul answered, he would be ready with some reason for calling him up, a request for investment advice or some such easy excuse. But when the operator put him through it was one of the maids who answered. Dan asked to speak to Mrs Latimer.

'Who shall I say is calling?'

'Tell her it's Mr Ranscombe.'

Time ticked by, then the maid returned to the line. 'I'm sorry, but Mrs Latimer isn't able to come to the telephone.'

It was as though his heart had been plunged in ice. She was there, but she wouldn't speak to him. Dan thanked the maid and hung up. He pushed his typewriter away, leaned his elbows on the desk and ran his fingers through his hair, wondering what had happened, and what he could do to put it right.

In the drawing room at Hazelhurst, Meg stared at the fire, waiting for the thudding of her heart to subside. The struggle not to take the telephone call, to hear his voice, had been intense. Thank God Paul was out. She would have been hard pushed to find a lie to excuse the fact of Dan ringing her here. If only he would stay away, make no contact. The pain of falling in love and losing him so quickly would never die, but it might gradually become tolerable. If she didn't see or hear from him, then thoughts of him would inevitably retreat to the furthest corner of her mind, and she could get on with her real life. For this was real life. The fact of the baby made her glad now, and Paul's delight and the prospect of being a proper family, and of having busy, filled days, made it all bearable. She was lucky, so lucky. That was what she had to keep telling herself.

The arrival of a card from Sonia on his twenty-sixth birthday at the end of March, sending affectionate greetings and reminding Dan that it was a while since he had been to Woodbourne House, filled him with guilt. He had been trying to obliterate the fact of Meg's inexplicable withdrawal with savage amounts of work, and he had neglected a number of people, including Sonia. He rang and thanked her for the card and promised to come to Woodbourne that Saturday for lunch.

His earnings as a journalist had risen over the past year, and with the extra income he made from freelance articles he had recently splashed out seventy guineas on a second-hand MG, which he reckoned something of a bargain. Lovelorn though Dan might be, like any young man he had a natural youthful resilience, and it restored his vanity and his spirits to speed through the Surrey countryside in his sports car. He understood himself sufficiently well to know that egotism was one of his chief weaknesses, and had lately begun to wonder whether the state of his feelings where Meg was concerned might not merely be a matter of wounded pride, and all he needed to do was teach himself not to care. Perhaps it was as simple as that.

Over lunch he and Sonia exchanged gossip and discussed the political situation in Europe.

'I think I may try to persuade my paper to send me to Berlin as a correspondent. It's where the news is being made at the moment.'

'Do you think war is inevitable?'

'I'm afraid I do, rather.'

'After the folly of the last one, it seems unthinkable that it should happen again. I'd only just become engaged when that war broke out. My fiancé, Gregory, died at Neuve Chapelle. All the beautiful young men. My aunt lost her four sons, my childhood cousins. For what? And here we are, starting it all over again.'

'Well, there's some way to go – maybe it won't happen.'

Sonia put down her napkin. 'Let's pray it doesn't.' She got to her feet. 'Come and take a look at my garden. It's looking quite wonderful now that spring is here.'

Laura was brought down from the nursery and put in her pram, and Sonia and Dan set off for a stroll around the grounds, Sonia pushing the pram. Dan, who had noticed that so far Sonia hadn't mentioned Avril once, asked how she was getting on at school.

'Oh, quite well, I think. I had a letter from her last week. Her handwriting has certainly improved.' Sonia pointed to some scillas coming into bloom beneath the trees in a carpet of blue. 'Exactly the colour of Laura's eyes.' She smiled and touched the baby's cheek. 'Don't you think she looks well?'

'Thriving,' replied Dan. 'Do you hear from Madeleine at all?'

'No. When she left, she made it clear she was cutting her ties completely. She said she was grateful for everything I'd done, but that the baby could only stay here on condition that she need never have contact with her, so that she could put all this behind her for ever.'

'It's not easy to pretend the past never happened.'

'I imagine it's easier if one has no reminders. I don't honestly expect to hear from her.'

Dan wondered if this wasn't so much an expectation as a hope. They wandered through the gardens, talking of this and that, and eventually came back to the courtyard, where Dan's car was parked.

'I'm afraid I'll have to be getting back to town,' said Dan.

'Well, it's been lovely to see you. Don't leave it so long next time.' As they walked to his car, Sonia asked, 'Have you seen anything of Paul and Meg lately?'

'I haven't seen Paul since last autumn. The last time I saw Meg was just before Christmas.' It had only just occurred to Dan that Sonia might know something which would give him a clue as to Meg's silence. 'How are they?'

'Oh, very well. Meg was here just the other day. Paul is in Germany for a fortnight, so there was the usual gripe about how lonely she gets, but I assured her she'll have plenty to keep her busy when the baby comes.'

The news hit Dan like a blow. So Meg was pregnant. He stared at Sonia in shock, then asked abruptly, 'When is it due?'

'Next August, I think – or was it September? I'm not entirely sure.'

Dan glanced distractedly at the pram. 'Would you like me to help take the pram into the house?'

'Don't worry, I can manage.'

'Right. Well, thank you for lunch. It was lovely to see you, as always.' He kissed his godmother hastily and got into the car.

He did the calculations as he drove, covering the miles to Hazelhurst. Why hadn't she told him? How could she have kept this from him?

Meg, who was in the morning room going through brochures for nursery furniture, heard the sound of a car on the driveway and went to the window. When she saw who it was, her first panicky thought was to tell the maid to say she wasn't at home. But Dan was already heading towards the front door. The doorbell pealed through the house, and as she went out into the hallway, Enid appeared from the nether regions of the house.

'It's all right, Enid. I'll attend to it.'

Enid disappeared. Meg hesitated for a moment then opened the front door.

'May I come in?' Dan's face was grim.

Meg said nothing. She left the door open and went back into the morning room, her heart thudding. When she turned round he had closed the door and was leaning with his back against it. His expression was still the same. Then a second later he crossed the room towards her, flinging his hat on to a chair, and took her in his arms and kissed her.

Meg tried for a moment to resist him, but failed. She kissed him back, and they clung to one another.

'Why didn't you tell me about the baby? I've been going out of my mind with unhappiness, not knowing why I hadn't heard from you. And why in God's name are you still here, with him? If this is my baby, you should be with me.'

Meg gazed at him with miserable eyes. 'Oh Dan,' she said slowly, 'it isn't yours. I'm sorry.'

He gripped her shoulders. 'You can't be sure about that.'

'Yes, I can. The doctor is. I was pregnant before you and I...'

He absorbed this. 'In God's name, why didn't you write and tell me? I've been in hell, not hearing a word from you.'

She faltered. 'Cowardice. I knew you would find out eventually from someone. I thought it would be best just to let it all – die away.'

'*Die away*?'

Tears filled her eyes. 'Dan, everything has changed. I'm having Paul's baby. I married him hoping for that, and now it's happening. I can't change that, even if I wanted to.'

'You can't stand here and say you don't love me. Tell me you don't love me.'

She gazed at him helplessly. 'It doesn't matter whether I love you or not, because I'm going to stay here and do my duty to Paul. I'm going to have his child, and that is the way my life will go on. I will be without you, and eventually I'll be able to bear that.'

'It won't be enough. As long as you know I'm alive, it won't be enough.'

'I will have to make it enough.' She pulled out a handkerchief and wiped away her tears.

He drew back a little, studying her face as though he hadn't looked at her properly until this moment. 'You're unassailable, aren't you? That's what this has done to you. The fact that you're having a baby has put you in some kind of fortress.'

'If you like. Having a child is one of those inescapable things.'

He turned from her again and walked to the window, reassembling his thoughts. He had his card, and he had no choice but to play it.

'What if,' he said at last, turning to look at her, 'I were to tell you that your marriage to Paul is a sham?'

She shook her head. 'I know you think I'll be living a lie, but you're wrong – I'm very fond of Paul. Even if I don't love him the way I love you, we can make it work.'

'I don't mean it in that way.' There was a moment's silence. 'Paul has a lover.'

Meg stared at him. 'Don't be absurd.'

'It's true.'

She drew a shaking breath. 'Do you really think that making up ridiculous lies about Paul is going change my mind?'

'It isn't a lie. A lie would get me nowhere. Your entire marriage is a travesty, and you need to know the truth. Paul has a lover. Not a woman. A man. I've seen them together.'

'Who is it? Who is the man?'

'His name is Bettany. Arthur Bettany. You asked me about him, remember? But I didn't tell you everything.'

She wrapped her arms around herself, as though cold. 'I refuse to believe it. I know Paul, the kind of man he is. He's not capable of that kind of cruelty.'

'Isn't he?'

'No, he's not. He's honourable. And he's kind and good. That's why I don't believe you. That's why, when I found out we were to have a baby, I decided to stay with him.' Something in her expression told him he had made a mistake. Everything he said now, no matter how true, was going to push her further and further from him.

'Even though you love me, not him?'

'Yes.' She barely whispered the word.

'And what happens when you find out I'm right?'

She shook her head. 'You can't be right. You just want it to be true so that you don't have to feel guilty about what you did. What we did.'

'Oh, for God's sake, stop deluding yourself! Leave him. Please. Leave him and come with me.'

She shook her head slowly. 'You are so selfish, Dan. So incredibly selfish.' He came towards her again, but she flinched from his touch. 'You came here to damage me.' Even through her tears, her voice was cold. 'And you succeeded. Now just go away. I mean it – leave.'

Dan knew there was nothing more he could achieve. He took his hat from the chair and left the room without a word. Meg heard the front door close once more, then the car engine. Eventually the sound died in the distance, and she was left alone and in silence.

Paul was due home from Berlin in three days. In that time Meg went over everything, piecing together evidence that might lend truth to what Dan had said. The jibe she had heard Diana fling at Paul, about his being in love with Arthur Bettany. The photographs in Paul's bedroom. His long absences in London.

But then there was Paul himself. Never once had he done anything to make her doubt that he cared deeply for her. She couldn't believe that he had married her as a smokescreen for some seedy secret life. The Paul she knew wasn't capable of that. Yet since their wedding night – and before, if only she had allowed herself to read the signs – their marriage had been passionless. Where was that finding its outlet? Or was Paul simply a sexual ascetic to whom such feelings were foreign, but who would muster the outward demonstration of them in the marriage bed when required? The doubts and questions went back and forth in her mind.

Paul came back at the weekend bearing gifts, full of affection and telling Meg how much he had missed her. She had intended to confront him with what Dan had said as soon as possible, but now, with his solid, affectionate and utterly normal presence filling the house, the idea of articulating Dan's allegation seemed as unimaginable as the allegation itself.

That evening at dinner, though, she knew she had to find a way. She couldn't sit talking and smiling with these hellish thoughts racing around in her mind. Paul was giving a mundane account of the inadequacies of the hotel he had stayed in, and Meg could feel the state of her attention and nerves growing more and more fragile. He must have sensed something was wrong, for he stopped and asked, 'I say, darling, are you all right?'

Meg said abruptly, 'I have something to ask you.'

'Ask away.'

'I want to know about Arthur Bettany.'

It seemed to Meg that her words resonated in the silence that followed. She had been looking down at her scarcely tasted dinner, but now she raised her eyes to his. Paul had paused in the act of cutting up his mutton chop and was regarding her with a curious expression, one she couldn't read. He set down his knife and fork. She had the sense, one she often had, that while his face gave nothing away, his mind was working rapidly.

'Well, let me see.' Paul sat back in his chair. 'We were at school together. He was my fag for a year. Exceptionally clever chap, first-class cricketer. We sculled together at Cambridge a bit.' He affected to laugh in puzzlement. 'But please, what is all this about? I didn't even know you were aware of the fellow's existence.'

She could tell he was perturbed and trying not to show it; that, for Meg, spoke volumes. Yet his affectedly casual tone gave her a way back. She could shrug and make up some story about how she had heard Bettany's name and was simply curious to know more about him. But to do so would solve nothing. She had come this far, and she must find out the truth.

'What is he to you? I know you see him in London. Is that who you spend all your time with while you're away?' Her voice was as taut as her nerves.

Paul stared at her in silence for a long moment. Still she could not read his expression. Was he angry? Was he playing for time, trying to think up some excuse?

When he spoke, his voice was low and level, and he had dropped any pretence at lightness. 'Meg, why are you asking about him?'

'Please, Paul – just answer my question. Do you see him when you're in London?'

He shook his head. 'Look, for reasons you don't understand, this is deadly serious. I must know why you're asking me and what you know about him.'

His tone alarmed her and put her slightly on the defensive. She felt instinctively that she was on the wrong track. She said nothing for a long moment and then, feeling a little foolish, her voice faint, she said, 'He's your lover, isn't he?'

Paul stared at her in shock. 'What? Why would you think such a thing?'

His reaction took her by surprise. She had fully expected a blustering tirade of disgust and outrage. But his puzzled surprise seemed entirely genuine. The feeling crept upon her that this had all been some hideous misunderstanding. Of course Dan's suspicion was wrong. She could see that now. In fact, she began to wonder why she had given it the slightest credence. She leaned her elbows on the table, kneading her forehead with her fingertips.

'Where has all this come from?' asked Paul.

'It doesn't matter.'

'Meg, you must tell me.' When she didn't answer, he added gently, as though talking to a child, 'It is vitally important that I know.'

Meg was at a loss to understand why she now felt so utterly wrong-footed. But at least she had a lie prepared for this question.

'You'll think me a fool. But last summer, when – oh, I don't know, it was one day when Diana came to lunch, and Roddy and Guy were here as well. I overheard you and Diana talking, and she said something – something about you having been in love with someone called Bettany. It troubled me horribly. I thought it meant that, well, that you'd had some sort of love affair with him. What else was I to think? And then last autumn when you kept going up to London, spending days away, I began to wonder if you were seeing him. You have photos of him in your room in London. I tried to put it out of my mind. It seemed ridiculous. But I couldn't help it.'

'Surely you didn't really imagine that I would have married you as some kind of pretence?'

She shook her head. 'I didn't know what to think. I just had this idea – you know how ideas build up. Especially when one is lonely.' She took her fingers from her brow. 'It's not true, any of it – is it?'

Paul rose from his chair and knelt next to her, drawing her hands down into his. 'Of course not, you goose. I should probably be supremely insulted that you should believe me capable of such a thing. But perhaps we should both make allowances for hormones at a time like this – don't you think?'

At the easiness of his manner her mind faltered. Perhaps she had believed him too easily. She tightened her fingers around his. 'Probably. Paul, you'll think me ridiculous – but I need you to swear – swear on the life of our baby, that none of it's true. That you'd never deceive me, or have an affair with… with anyone?'

'I swear. I have never deceived you. I would never deceive you. You are the only woman I have ever loved, and I will always love you. And our baby.'

She closed her eyes, and wearily rested her head on his shoulder. Of course she believed him. Here she was, living the life she had chosen, and here she would remain.

2

AS THE SUMMER months passed, Meg spent a good deal of time with Anna Kentleigh, who seemed to treat Meg's pregnancy as a rite of passage which would gain her admission to some private members' club. One warm late afternoon in June they were sitting together on the terrace at Hazelhurst, Meg with lemonade and Anna with a G and T, while Anna imparted such wisdom as she had concerning the rearing of infants, which, since she had left most things to the nanny, was not a great deal.

'Absolutely the first thing I did with all of them was to get them to take the bottle.'

'Really?' said Meg with faint dismay. 'I had thought I would nurse my baby myself.'

'Oh my dear, there's no more certain way to destroy your figure. And think what a bind it will be, having to be about all the time. They feed every couple of hours, you know – well, in the early days certainly. I would have missed an entire season's hunting if I'd breastfed Frank. And you shan't be able to go anywhere without taking it with you. Parties will be impossible.' Meg thought she would happily forgo parties and fox-hunting to be with her baby, but said nothing, for fear of Anna's mild scorn. Much as she enjoyed their friendship, it was marked with a degree of bossiness on Anna's side. 'You'll have a nanny, of course?'

'I suppose so. I haven't really given it much thought.'

At that moment Paul joined them on the terrace. He sank into a chair and poured himself a glass of lemonade. 'Just what I need. Blasted hot in the workshop in this weather.'

'Do you have a race meeting coming up?' asked Anna.

'Not till August, when we go to Italy, but we have a good deal of preparation to do before then. That reminds me, darling' – Paul patted Meg's knee – 'Dick Seaman has invited me to go with him to Germany next month for the Grand Prix. He's driving for Mercedes-Benz.'

'For the Germans? Why not the British team?' asked Anna.

'We're not fielding a team. Too flannel-footed at the moment, and not enough money. Mercedes-Benz scouted Dick after he won the British Grand Prix, and I don't blame them. He's a hell of a driver.'

'Seaman.' Meg pondered the name. 'I don't think I know him. Was he at our wedding?'

'Most certainly. I can't believe you don't remember him.'

'Heavens, there were so many people, I can't recall half of them. Is he one of your Cambridge friends?'

'Yes. I owe him a lot. It was through him that I learned to fly. His American chum, Whitney Straight, kept a plane at Cambridge and gave us both lessons. And he and Dick had Rileys that they used to race, which is what got me interested in cars, too.'

'Isn't he Lillian Seaman's son?' asked Anna.

'That's right. Do you know her?'

'We've met a few times. She's the most frightful snob – stiffest corsets in all England. Fearfully rich, though.'

'I'll say, and she spoils Dick rotten. I remember when she bought him a brand-new Bugatti for his twenty-first birthday, and he ploughed it straight into the side of a bus outside Victoria coach station. Now she funds his racing team, even lets him run his workshop out of her London town house.'

'He sounds quite a character,' observed Anna.

'You should invite him down here before you go to Germany,'

said Meg. 'I'd like to meet him properly. In fact, why don't we have a bit of a summer party? I'm terribly proud of how lovely the garden's looking, and it's an age since we've done any entertaining. Are you and James going to be away in July?' she asked Anna.

'We don't go to the South of France until August.'

'Then you must come. And I might ask you to help me with arrangements, if you wouldn't mind. I'm a bit of a novice at entertaining a large crowd.'

'More than happy, my dear.'

'What do you think, Paul? Shall I draw up a guest list?'

'With my blessing.' Paul drained his glass of lemonade and stood up. 'Now, if you'll excuse me, ladies, I must get back to the workshop.'

When Meg next went to Woodbourne House, her plans for her July garden party were well in place, and she told Sonia all about them.

'I do hope you'll come.'

'Thank you. Of course I shall. It sounds delightful. If you would like any produce from the kitchen garden, just say so. There is far too much these days.'

'That's kind. My own vegetable plot is still in its infancy. I don't expect anything much from it till next year. I'll consult Mrs Runcie about what food we're to have and let you know. Oh, and do bring Avril. Our neighbours' children will be there.'

'I'm sure she would love to come. She's about somewhere,' added Sonia vaguely. 'Home for the summer holidays. I must say, I think I did the right thing in sending her to board. She seems, well, more agreeable than she used to be.' At that moment Avril appeared in the doorway. She was eight now, taller, looking less of a little girl, and wore her dark hair in two stubby plaits. 'Ah, there you are! Darling, come and say hello to Meg. I'm sure it's been ever such a long time since you saw her.'

'Not since my wedding,' said Meg with a smile. 'How is school, Avril? I hear you're enjoying it.'

'It's all right.' She clambered on to her mother's knee and picked up the remains of Sonia's cake and ate it.

'Do you have a best friend?' asked Meg.

'No. Millicent was my friend, but then Vera Burton told her beastly things about me, and she stopped being my friend.' She shrugged. 'I don't care.'

'Oh well, I'm sure you have lots of other friends,' said Meg, though as she regarded Avril's closed, sullen little face, she somehow doubted it.

Avril swung round and began to tug in a babyish way at Sonia's long necklace of amber beads. 'Mama, will you give me my bath tonight? And sing to me while you dry me, the way you do with Laura?'

'Darling,' said Sonia gently, 'don't pull so – you'll break them.' She unwound Avril's cake-sticky fingers from her necklace. 'Don't you think you're rather big to be bathed these days? I haven't given you your bath since you were very little.'

'You do it for Laura.'

'Laura's a baby. She can't bath herself.'

'But you're not her mother.' Avril began to whine in a silly, petulant way. 'You're *my* mother, *my* mother!' She tugged hard at Sonia's necklace, and suddenly it gave, sending amber beads rattling and rolling across the floor.

Sonia clapped her hands to her bosom in an attempt to prevent any more from falling. 'Oh, Avril! Look what you've done. I told you not to.' She eased Avril from her lap, trying to contain the broken ends of the necklace. 'Come and help Mama pick them up.'

'No,' replied Avril stoutly.

'Oh, Avril,' said Sonia reproachfully.

Avril said nothing, merely turned and walked out. Meg stared after her. Did Sonia really think school had made her more agreeable? If anything, she seemed worse. She put her teacup aside and knelt on the floor with Sonia to pick up the scattered beads. Sonia spread a clean handkerchief on the floor and they dropped the beads on to it, one by one, as they found them. Sonia gathered up the handkerchief and sat down again with the little bundle in her lap.

'Such a shame. Henry gave me the necklace for my birthday the year he died. Still, I can have them restrung. But they won't be the same. I had to have some pearls restrung and they've never sat properly since.' She sighed. 'Don't think badly of Avril. She's had a very tiring term. And of course when she sees Laura having her bath it makes her want to be little again.'

'I'm sure,' said Meg. 'How is Laura?'

'Oh, quite delightful. Would you like to see her? We always have a little play together around this time of day.'

They made their way upstairs to the nursery. Miss Bissett was busy with a basket of sewing, and fifteen-month-old Laura sat on a large quilt in the middle of the floor, surrounded by playthings. She held up her chubby arms in delight when she saw Sonia, who bent to pick her up.

'She's quite a big girl now, isn't she?' Sonia beamed with pleasure as she held her.

'What a difference a month makes.'

'It certainly does. She's almost walking now. Watch.' She lowered Laura to the floor, and Laura took a few unsteady steps, tottered, and sat down with a plop.

'What a darling!' laughed Meg. After watching the baby for a moment she asked, 'What will she call you – when she's old enough to speak, I mean?'

'I've thought about that – aunt, I suppose. Aunt Sonia. That will probably do.'

'And will you tell her about who she is, and so on?'

'I suppose so – someday. Goodness, don't spoil this nice moment with such speculations!' Sonia knelt down and handed Laura a rattle, which she began to shake vigorously. Meg knelt down to join the two of them, wondering if Sonia had thought things through as clearly as she ought to.

At that moment Avril came into the nursery. She sat down at the table and picked up a crayon to finish the drawing she had begun earlier. But after a few minutes she put it down. She rested her chin on her hand, chewing the end of one pigtail, and contemplated the trio on the floor.

Sonia glanced up. 'Come and play with us, darling. We're having such a lovely time.'

Avril gave no sign of having heard her mother. When Meg beckoned to her a moment later, Avril merely shook her head.

For the next ten minutes, every time Meg glanced in her direction, Avril was sitting exactly as before, watching Laura intently, her expression inscrutable.

The last person Dan now wished to encounter, after all that had happened, was Paul, but it was inevitable they would run into one another, and they did so at Bellamy's, their club, one evening in July.

Paul was friendliness itself. 'How are you, old fellow? I can't believe I haven't seen you since the shoot last year. Let me buy you a drink. I'm meeting Guy for dinner, but not till eight.'

Dan, loafing in an armchair without any appearance of having to be elsewhere, could hardly refuse.

Paul ordered a couple of whiskies and sodas. 'So,' he asked Dan, 'how's the world of journalism?'

'Not bad, thanks. I've moved on from the arts pages – well, I still do the odd review – and now most of my time is spent reporting the political situation in Europe.'

'Well, that's fertile ground, certainly. The Germans seem to be arming at a feverish pace. I said at the time of the Anglo-German Naval Agreement that it was a mistake to let them arm beyond Versailles. All done in the name of stability, but look what's happened. Now Hitler's taken Austria, there'll be no holding him...'

Dan only half-listened; he was busy trying to puzzle out his feelings towards Paul. The strength of his conviction that Paul was deceiving Meg had weakened. He had talked it over in confidence with Harry, and Harry, playing devil's advocate, had pointed out that Dan's suspicions were based mainly on gossip and conjecture, and that he was probably placing undue significance on what he had seen that night in Soho. Now here was Paul, airing his political views in his usual bluff, somewhat patronising manner, being so like the Paul Dan had always known, that it was hard to think of him as a man who had cheated a woman into marrying him just to conceal his secret homosexuality. A fellow's manner could disguise all kinds of secrets, but Dan had to accept that he had perhaps formed his suspicions too easily, and had been mad to voice them to Meg.

'... and of course it leaves Czechoslovakia utterly exposed. I have no doubt there's going to be a war. But Meg hates all that kind of talk. Understandable, really. Women don't like anything that threatens their peace and security, especially when they're nest-building.'

Dan had no choice but to ask after Meg.

'She's very well, thanks. Baby's due in a few weeks and, touch wood, all is going well. I'm being a good, attentive husband.' Paul lit his pipe. 'Actually, we had a bit of a tiff around Christmas time about my spending too much time in town, so I've had to mend my ways there. Though I'm granted special exeats where racing is concerned.'

'How's the business coming along?'

'Pretty well, thanks. Slowly getting into shape, though we're not ready for the big league yet. As a matter of fact, I'm off to watch the German Grand Prix in a couple of weeks. Should be interesting. Chance to see Herr Hitler at first hand. Say what you like, one can't help admiring the man, the way he's taken Germany by the scruff of the neck. By the way, I take it you're coming to our garden party on Saturday? Can't tell you the commotion Meg has made over the organising of it.'

'I'm not sure I got the invitation.'

'Really? I'm certain I told Meg to put you on the list. Oh well, come along anyway.'

'I'd love to, but I'm afraid I'll be at Trent Bridge.'

'The Australia–Nottinghamshire match? Should be a good day's cricket. Well, that's a pity. I'm sure Meg would have loved to see you.'

How far from the truth that was, thought Dan, and was struck by the realisation that by rights he should be feeling deeply ashamed of his behaviour. He had callously tried to destroy Paul's life, and here he was, feigning friendship. But the fact was, he didn't care. He would gladly have trampled over Paul's happiness and felt not the slightest guilt, if he could have Meg. But that had been tried, and it had failed.

'Yes, it is a pity. Do give her my best.'

Dan left the club shortly before eight and walked along Piccadilly, wondering how it was that all the people he knew seemed to be settled and content in their lives, while his restless soul struggled to find a purpose. By the time he reached the Strand he had come to the firm decision that he needed to get away. He would ask the paper to let him travel to Europe as a correspondent, and report on the events which, it seemed to him, were unfolding with an ominous rapidity. The work he had done in Spain should stand him in good stead, and the *Graphic* needed someone on the ground out there if they wanted to keep up with their rivals. He would rent his rooms, get out of London, and leave the business of Meg behind. She had her own life to get on with, and he had to start his again.

Buoyed up by his decision, he had just decided to seek out Harry in the Wheatsheaf, his regular Soho haunt, when he heard a woman's voice call his name. He turned and saw Eve emerging from her office. She gave him a smile that could have meant many things, but mainly that she was prepared to be friendly.

'Working late?' he asked.

'Writing up a piece on the Evian conference.'

'Oh, that thing Roosevelt's organised in France.'

'He may have organised it, but he hasn't bothered to go himself. Sent some businessman as the US representative. That's how important he thinks the Jews are. Do you know, they haven't even let the Palestinian representative sit with the delegates?' Her dark eyes shone, something Dan had always liked about her when she was angry.

'You sound like you need to get this off your chest. How about a drink?'

She sighed. 'Why not?'

Dan steered her towards the Cheshire Cheese and they settled at a table with gin and tonics.

Eve quickly resumed the topic of the conference. Dan observed her as she talked, thinking how fresh she looked in her blue dress, her silky black hair framing her sternly pretty face. 'No one cares, that much is clear. Every country protests that it's doing as much as it can already – believe us, we feel sorry for the Jews, but our country is already overcrowded, taking refugees will mean more economic hardship for our people. The truth is, no one wants the Jews. Anti-Semitism is everywhere.' Eve had been drinking quickly as she talked. Now she put down her empty glass.

Dan picked it up. 'Another?'

'Make it a double. I've had a lousy day.'

When Dan brought the drinks back to the table, Eve asked, 'So, how are things with you?'

'A bit up in the air. As a matter of fact, I've just made up my mind to ask the powers-that-be to send me to Germany as a foreign correspondent. I have personal reasons for wanting to get away from England for a while.'

'Your married lady?'

Dan nodded. 'She's out of my life. She chose her husband over me. In fact, she's having a baby soon.'

'Oh, I see.' There was a silence, then Eve said, 'I'm sorry our last meeting was unpleasant. I'm afraid I was upset.'

'You had every right to be. I behaved badly.'

She shrugged. 'When you're in love, there is no good and bad behaviour. You just do what you have to.'

Dan sat back in his chair, sighed, and stretched out his legs. 'Yes. So, that's all over.' He inspected his glass. 'And I feel like getting drunk.'

Eve smiled at him. 'You know what? So do I.'

Two hours later they left the pub. In the street Dan kissed Eve.

'Come back to my place,' he murmured. 'If you think that's selfish and insulting, say so. I have no excuse, other than that I want you.'

'I suppose it's both those things. And I suppose I don't care. I want you, too.' She kissed him and they clung drunkenly to one another in the dark street for a moment, then turned and walked towards Bloomsbury.

The next morning Dan lay in bed, smoking, watching Eve as she dressed. She sat down on the edge of the bed and began to pin up her hair, turning to glance at Dan.

'Don't get the idea that last night meant anything. I can't afford to be hurt again. It was what it was. Nothing more.' She stood up, brushing down the front of her dress and slipping on her shoes. 'God, I drank too much.' She picked up the flask of water from beside the bed, splashed some into a glass, drank it back, then filled it again.

'Perhaps we could see each other now and again – on an unofficial basis, obviously.'

She gave him another sharp glance as she sipped her water. 'Hm. We'll see. Anyway, I have to go.' She picked up her bag and hat from the chair.

'I'll call you,' said Dan.

'If you like.' She bent and kissed his head, then left.

*

'I ran into Dan Ranscombe in town yesterday evening,' Paul remarked to Meg at breakfast. 'Seems he didn't get his invitation to the party, for some reason. I told him to come along anyway.'

Meg's heart tightened. 'He's not coming, is he?' She blurted it out before she had time to think.

'No, he's going to Nottingham for the cricket. You sound like you don't want him here.'

'It's not that,' said Meg hastily. 'It's just that it throws things out, having extra guests at the last minute. I entirely forgot to put him on the list.'

'I shouldn't have thought one more here or there would make much difference.' Paul folded back his newspaper and helped himself to more coffee. 'But it's rather beside the point, since he won't be coming. Anyhow, he said to give you his best.'

'That's nice.' Meg was more composed now, but her heart was hammering. It would be like this for a long time, she supposed, whenever his name was mentioned. She rose from the table.

'No more breakfast?' asked Paul. 'You've hardly eaten a thing. Got to think of the baby and keep your strength up, old girl.'

'I'm not hungry,' replied Meg shortly. She hated it when he called her 'old girl', but she couldn't say so. He was only being affectionate. And affection was what their marriage was built on now.

3

MEG'S PARTY WAS the success she had hoped for. The sun shone, the guests enjoyed themselves, and Avril managed not to fight with the Kentleigh children.

Sonia came splendidly attired in a dress of ecru silk, a gamboge chiffon scarf tied around the crown of her wide-brimmed sun hat, and her elegant arms tinkling with silver bracelets.

'Dear Sonia must be the most expensively dressed bohemian ever seen,' Diana remarked to Meg. 'She puts us all to shame.' She watched Sonia gliding among the guests, pausing to talk to Dick Seaman and a group of other racing enthusiasts who were seated under a large elm. 'I'm going to go and help her break up the racing clique. They're being very anti-social.'

'Do – I must see if Mrs Runcie and the maids need a hand with laying out the food. I hope the wasps won't be a bother.'

Meg disappeared into the house and Diana wandered over to the group beneath the tree. She bent to kiss Sonia and slipped into the seat next to her.

'Sonia,' she murmured, 'you are far and away the best-dressed person here. I utterly adore this fabric.' She lightly touched Sonia's dress.

'Thank you, my dear,' replied Sonia, reminding herself that young people no longer tended to observe strict social niceties, such as not discussing personal appearances. 'I had it made up from some silk which Henry brought back from a trip he made to the Far East some years ago.' She was unable to add that he had in addition brought back a most unpleasant venereal disease, which had required no end of treatment before it could be got rid of. That incident had almost ended their marriage.

'Most unusual,' said Diana.

Sonia turned to acknowledge some remark made to her by one of the young men, and Diana glanced across the garden to where Roddy and Guy, who had just finished a game of tennis, were sitting chatting on the lawn by a bank of rhododendrons. Roddy was lounging on one elbow, his shirt open at the neck, his racquet next to him. He had let his red hair grow rather long, and kept tossing it out of his eyes. Paul was passing nearby and Guy called out to him, but to Diana's bemusement Paul affected not to hear and carried on walking. She knew Paul was infatuated with Roddy. She had known it for months, though he himself would never have acknowledged the truth of it. She felt sorry for her brother. A couple of years ago, when Paul had singled out Meg as a suitable wife, Diana had been relieved that he had fixed on a decent girl, and not some gold-digger. But perhaps it would have been better had he married a hard-nosed society beauty who understood the bargain she was making, looked for her own pleasure elsewhere and let him get on with leading the life he should with whatever men he wanted. But no, that would never have worked. Paul seemed utterly without self-knowledge. The sexual step was one he would doubtless never take with any man. It simply wasn't in him.

The chatter and buzz of people making their way towards the al fresco luncheon tables made Diana turn her head. Meg was shepherding her guests, directing them towards plates and cutlery, bidding the maids replenish the jugs of lemonade and punch. She looked 'blooming', thought Diana, to employ that well-worn expression generally applied to pregnant women. But it really was the right word. Her skin and hair shone, and her face was happy. The marriage seemed to be a success. Perhaps Paul was one of those unusual creatures who could love women as well as men. Though she'd never, until Meg, seen any evidence of that.

Diana watched as Roddy got to his feet, brushed down his trousers and made his way across the lawn with Guy. He looked in her direction and caught her eye. She winked at him, and he gave her a knowing smile. That was a promise. After lunch, when Paul was otherwise occupied, they would steal away into the surrounding woods and enjoy themselves.

When she felt that all her guests were settled, Meg helped herself to some food and headed with her plate towards the table where Sonia was seated with Paul and Diana and Roddy and others. She'd been so busy that she hadn't yet had a chance to talk to her aunt. Paul found her a chair and placed it next to Sonia's.

'Oh, what a relief to sit down!' said Meg.

'You shouldn't be rushing around so in your condition,' said Sonia reprovingly, then added, 'Though this is a most splendid party. You're to be congratulated, my dear.'

'I couldn't have done it without Anna's help. I don't think you've met her, have you? I'll introduce you after lunch. She's been such a brick.' Meg craned her neck to get a glimpse of the table where the children had been put. Avril was seated next to Frank Kentleigh, and giggled as Frank tried to put a cube of ice down the back of his sister's frock. 'Avril seems to be having fun.'

'I'm just relieved she's behaving herself. She does seem to be so much better around other children these days. Though she can still be rather difficult where Laura is concerned. No doubt she'll get over that in time.'

Sonia turned to Dick Seaman. 'Tell me, how is your mother? We were such friends when we were debutantes together, you know, and I was often at Kentwell Hall. I haven't seen her for a few years. I hope she's well?'

Dick, a restless, pleasant-faced young man with brilliantined hair, nodded. 'As indefatigable as ever, Mrs Haddon. She's the reason I'm in England at the moment. Though I probably shouldn't admit it, I'm trying to get her to stump up some money.'

'Yes, I understand motor racing is something of a costly business. In any event, do give her my very best regards and tell her that I shall call on her when I'm next in London.'

'I shall.'

'So, do you live permanently in Germany now, Mr Seaman?' asked Meg.

'Oh, Dick, please. Yes, I have a house at Ambach on Lake Starnberg, just outside Munich. The lake is stunning. I do a lot of water skiing. Bit of a novelty to my German friends, but they've become very keen. Paul came to stay there on his last visit. You must come, too, sometime.'

'And how do you find Germany in general?' asked Sonia. 'One reads so many reports, it's hard to make one's mind up about Herr Hitler. Are you an admirer, or not?'

Dick glanced around, slightly self-conscious, aware of being the focus of the table's attention. 'That's a bit of a poser. Well – there's no denying Hitler's shaken the place up. He stands no nonsense. Doesn't have time for slackers or Communists. Everybody's got to work. I think the German people admire the way he's reorganised everything, galvanised the country, so to speak.'

'And his treatment of the Jews?' asked Meg. 'What are your feelings about that?'

Her tone was gentle, far from aggressive, but Paul cut in with a light laugh and said, 'My darling, don't spoil your lovely party with questions of race and politics. About which I'm sure you don't know as much as you think you do.' He turned to Dick. 'You know, I'd like to hear more about Uhlenhaut's design for the new W154. A five-speed gearbox, that's very clever.'

'Oh, the V12 engine is a complete triumph. As a matter of fact, I was there when Hitler unveiled the car at the Berlin Motor

Show last March. Quite a spectacle. The government backs the team to the very hilt.'

The talk now turned entirely to racing and the forthcoming Grand Prix, with Dick fielding excited questions from the enthusiasts present. Meg turned and signalled to Gwen to clear the plates. She was trying to maintain a calm, bright demeanour, but her heart was thumping with rage.

Diana sighed inwardly. Really, her brother could be appallingly condescending where women's intellects were concerned, if not downright rude. He probably had no idea he sounded exactly like their father. Still, it was Meg's problem to cope with, not hers. She met Roddy's glance across the table, held his gaze for a fraction of a second, then turned to Meg.

'Darling, do you mind if I go and explore a little? I haven't seen enough of your heavenly garden.'

'Of course not.'

Sonia, bored by the turn the conversation had taken, was about to offer to join her, but Diana was already up and away, crossing the lawn with her elegant stride.

A few minutes later Roddy slipped away from the table and disappeared in the direction Diana had taken. He found her waiting for him on the fringes of the wood by the paddock, where Grisette and The Commander stood nibbling the grass. He took her hand, and they made their way into the woods along a narrow path dappled with sunlight. When they had gone as far as seemed safe, they stopped against a tree and kissed hungrily. Roddy began to unbutton the bodice of Diana's dress.

'Not here,' murmured Diana. 'Someone might still come along. A keeper or someone.'

They turned off the path and made their way through shrubs and undergrowth, side-stepping bramble shoots and nettles, until they came to a small glade smothered in ferns. Roddy stepped into the centre and began to trample them down. He put out a hand to Diana and she slipped between the waist-high ferns into the space he had made. Roddy sank to his knees, drawing Diana down with him. They kissed for a long while. Diana glanced around. They were perfectly hidden from view, even in the unlikely event that someone should stray far from the path this deep into the woods.

'I only hope we can find our way back,' she murmured.

'I don't care if we never do,' said Roddy, kissing her neck, easing her dress from her shoulders and kissing her breasts in turn. She closed her eyes and arched her neck in pleasure.

'Let's take everything off,' said Roddy, beginning to unbutton his shirt. 'I want to make love to you in the open air, entirely naked.'

'Dare we?'

By way of reply he pulled off his shirt, then the rest of his clothes. Still on his knees, he watched as Diana took off her clothes one by one, until she too was naked. They laughed at the same moment, then embraced and kissed, sinking against the coolness of the bruised ferns.

Some time later, Diana sat astride Roddy's stomach, the sunlight warm on her back. She reached out a hand and drew her fingers lightly through his hair.

'Such a colour.'

'From my mother's side. Strawberry blond, so she says.'

'Rather more ginger, if you ask me,' replied Diana, tossing back her own fair hair.

'If we had children,' said Roddy, 'they'd have the most marvellous colouring. My magnificent tawny hair—'

'Ginger.'

'—your green eyes—'

'Your preposterous freckles.'

'Your ridiculous ears.' He reached up and pulled her hair back from her face.

She pushed his hands away. 'My ears are not ridiculous!'

Roddy leaned back on his elbows, surveying her.

'Seriously. If we had children.'

She met his level gaze. 'What are you saying?'

'I'm saying' – he sat up, pulling her towards him, and kissed her – 'that it would be rather ripping.' His slight stammer as he said this touched her heart. He kissed her again. 'Don't you think?'

'Yes,' she whispered. 'Yes, I do. But you do realise it would mean—'

'It would mean getting married, and all that nonsense, I know. But if that's what it takes...'

Diana, for once in her life, was at an utter loss. She wanted nothing more in the world than to marry Roddy. She loved him with a desperation that frightened her, but until now she had refused to address the problems that marriage to him would entail, not least the fact that Roddy had scarcely two ha'pennies to rub together. Not much of a problem while he was a single, adventurous young man with an indulgent mother happy to fund his bachelor lifestyle. But marriage was quite another thing.

'But we fight half the time. What if we find we don't get on at all, being married?'

'We fight because we can't be together enough, and that's all the fault of your ridiculous brother. It puts me in a bad temper. If we were married, we could do this any time we like, instead of constantly sneaking away, trying to make sure he doesn't find out.'

'But that's the point. We've been trying to make sure he doesn't find out so that you won't lose your place in the racing team. You know how he feels about us.' She paused. 'And you know why, too – don't you?'

Roddy shrugged. 'He's fond of me.'

'More than that.'

'Even if he sacked me, there are other teams to drive for.'

'But do you... I mean, do you think you feel...?' She broke off, not quite sure how to finish the question.

'Do I love you? Is that what you mean? You are the most maddening girl alive, but to my astonishment, and entirely against my better judgement, I find I love you. Truly.' He put a finger beneath her chin and tipped her head up so that she had to look at him. 'So shall we?'

Diana regarded him doubtfully. She ran light fingers through his mane of red hair. 'What would we live on? You know I'm not a girl who can starve in a garret for love, don't you?'

'We would manage somehow.'

She did a swift calculation. Paul had always been fiercely conscious of the inequity brought about by their father leaving the entire estate to him, and he had never been anything but generous with her when she needed money. It had been understood, too, that when she married he would settle a decent sum on her. But given how he felt about Roddy, how jealously he guarded his friendship with him, could she take that for granted? He might not recognise his infatuation for what it was, but the events of the shooting weekend suggested that he would be far from happy if she and Roddy became engaged.

'You still haven't given me an answer,' persisted Roddy. 'And you still haven't said if you love me or not.'

'You know I do. You're an ass if you don't. But...' she touched his neck, then drew her finger down across his chest and kissed him, 'are you sure it isn't all about – well, just this?'

'No, I don't think it's simply about – just this.' He kissed her back, slipping his fingers between her legs. 'But it's undoubtedly a consideration, you have to admit.'

'Yes,' she gasped, closing her eyes. Thoughts of money completely fled her mind.

'An impartial onlooker might say I'm taking advantage of the situation, but I'm going to assume that "yes" means you'll marry me.' He kissed her again. 'Which makes me very happy.'

Fifteen minutes later, as they made their way back through the woods to the path, Diana remarked, 'We've been gone ages. I wonder if anyone noticed.'

'I doubt it. And even if they did, who cares? We're a respectably engaged couple now.'

She turned and gave him a radiant smile. 'How sick-makingly conventional.'

'I know. Who would have thought?' After a moment he added, 'Why don't we tell people today? I mean, it's rather a convenient moment, so many of our friends together in one place.'

Diana hesitated. Her instinct was to speak to Paul first and make sure of the money, but on second thoughts, perhaps it would be better to present him with a fait accompli, and then talk him round, if needs be. He might be absurdly jealous of her relationship with Roddy, but surely he wouldn't cut her off without a bean just because of it.

She nodded. 'Let's.'

They crossed the lawn, hand in hand. Luncheon had been over for an hour, but people still sat in groups at tables, sipping coffee. The children, led by Frank, were cartwheeling competitively at the far end of the garden. Diana and Roddy sat down next to Meg, who had absented herself from the general conversation and was staring into the distance.

'Oh, hello,' she said, as they sat down. 'Sorry, I was miles away.' She caught Diana's expression. 'What's that mysterious smile for?'

Diana told her, and Meg gave a gasp of delight. 'Oh, but how marvellous!' She glanced around the garden. 'Do you want people to know, or are you going to wait? Because if you do…'

'No time like the present,' said Roddy firmly. He lifted up a coffee spoon, about to rap a glass.

'Wait,' said Meg, 'Paul's taken a few people off to the workshop – oh, look, here he comes now.' Paul was coming round the house from the workshop with Guy and two others in tow.

Roddy tapped the spoon against the wine glass, and clear, light chimes rang through the air. Conversation died away. Those further off in the garden gradually stopped talking and began to make their way towards the table. When all were gathered, an expectant hush fell, broken only by the shouts and laughter of the children. Roddy rose to his feet. Paul stood, uneasy and puzzled, at the edge of the gathering.

'First of all, I'm sure you would all like to join me in thanking Paul and Meg for hosting such a splendid party today' – there came a rippling murmur of appreciation – 'and secondly' – Roddy looked down at Diana, and they exchanged smiles – 'I hope you'll also join in congratulating me on the fact that I have...' he hesitated, stammering over his words, 'asked Diana to be my wife and, I am thrilled to say, she has consented.' This produced cries of delight, and several of the guests clapped. People came forward to add their personal congratulations. Meg stood by, hands folded beneath her chin, smiling in delight. Her eyes sought out Paul, and she saw him standing a little way off, looking on, his expression inscrutable. Whatever he was thinking, he didn't seem to share the general pleasure. She couldn't understand why he was so absurdly proprietorial where Roddy was concerned. Oh, well, he would just have to get used to the fact that Diana had a greater claim on his affections now.

Later, when the guests had gone, Meg was sitting in the drawing room with Diana, who was staying over.

'Gosh, I'm absolutely bushed,' said Meg, yawning.

'I'm not surprised, in your condition.' Diana stretched her arms above her head and closed her eyes briefly. 'What a perfectly lovely, lovely day.'

Meg smiled across at her. 'Happy?'

'Immensely. I couldn't be happier. I just wish Paul was.'

'Oh, he'll come round, I know he will.'

'The thing is,' Diana dropped her hands into her lap, 'I can't afford for him to disapprove. Roddy doesn't exactly have a lot of money, and I'm entirely dependent on Paul, as you know. He always said he would settle a decent sum on me when I got married, but what if he decides not to?'

'Why would he do that?'

'Oh, I don't know. He resents what I have with Roddy. His male friendships have always been a bit of a thing with him. Paul's not always as straightforward as one might imagine.'

'I'm absolutely sure he's not going to leave you high and dry. I'll have a word with him, if you like.'

'Would you? It might set my mind at rest. In theory I'd be happy to marry Roddy and live on bread and margarine–'

'But in fact, you'd rather not,' laughed Meg.

'Well, quite.'

'Rest assured, I'll make sure you don't.' Meg rose, running a hand over the swell of her stomach. 'I'm going to get to bed. But first, I need to find my book. I think I left it in the summerhouse.'

Bidding Diana goodnight, Meg went out and across the garden in the direction of the summerhouse, and was surprised to find Paul in there, smoking his pipe.

'I was looking for my book,' she said. The two had scarcely spoken since the party, and the smell of his pipe smoke filling the summerhouse irritated her. She remembered his cutting put-down earlier, and felt a smart of rekindled anger.

Paul glanced around, saw her book, and handed it wordlessly to her.

'You know,' she said, fingering the book, 'I still haven't forgiven you for your beastly behaviour towards me.'

Paul regarded her emptily, almost without interest. 'My behaviour?'

'When I was talking to your friend Dick today, asking him about the situation with the Jews in Germany. You were unspeakably rude.'

Paul tapped the cinders from his pipe into a nearby ashtray and laid his pipe on the table. 'It was hardly the time or the place to raise the subject. In fact, in the circumstances, I thought you were the one who was ill-mannered. At least I spared you embarrassment.'

'You did nothing of the kind. You belittled me, as you always do.'

'Don't be absurd. I simply didn't wish to see you attempt to discuss a subject you know nothing about.'

She felt anger tightening her heart. 'And as for the way you looked when Roddy and Diana announced their engagement – that was too horrid for words. Couldn't you at least have seemed pleased?'

Paul got to his feet. 'Shut up! I don't want to discuss anything with you! Not that, or what I said at lunch, or anything else! Stop meddling in things you don't understand!'

He strode out of the summerhouse and across the garden in the direction of the workshop. Meg stared after him. She sat down, working back over the conversation, willing her righteous indignation to die away. He could be absolutely insufferable, but whatever the rights and wrongs, she couldn't bear animosity between them. She had come to realise how fragile the edifice of kindness and affection which she had built to sustain her marriage was, and any damage needed to be repaired swiftly. Even if she were not the one in the wrong, she had to make amends, to ensure they didn't go to bed feeling hateful and angry at one another. Paul's pipe lay on the table. She picked it up, smoothing its still-warm bowl with her thumb. Holding it, she rose and went out of the summerhouse to the workshop. She knocked lightly on the door, but when there was no reply, she went in.

Paul was poring over some plans on the bench. Meg went over and put a hand on his arm, and laid his pipe on the bench.

'Let's not argue. I'm probably over-tired. I'm sorry I got cross with you.'

He sighed and looked up. 'I'm sorry, too.'

Meg waited for a moment, then said, 'I don't know why you're not happy about Diana and Roddy.' This was a lie; she was all too aware how passionately fond Paul was of Roddy. She believed his feelings fell far short of the kind of thing Dan had once suggested, but she guessed his reaction to their engagement had probably been prompted by male jealousy of some kind. 'Is it because he doesn't have money?' The question offered Paul an excuse and at the same time gave her a chance to plead Diana's cause.

Paul was silent for a moment, then said, 'I suppose it is.'

'Well, for goodness' sake – the poor man can't help it if he's hard up. But can't you help them? You've always said Diana was hard done by when your father died. Now's your chance to be generous and put it right.' She didn't wait for his response. Instead she leaned forward and kissed his cheek lightly. 'I'm going to bed. Don't stay out here too long.'

4

DAN WASTED NO time in petitioning Mr Hitchcock about being sent to Europe, and was in his office first thing on Monday morning. As Dan laid out his proposal, Mr Hitchcock sat frowning and doodling on his blotter.

'I can cover political developments in Europe generally, send regular pieces on German economic and military policy, and of course there would be human interest pieces, too.'

'Hmm.' Mr Hitchcock capped his pen and sat back. 'A European correspondent, in effect? I suppose the Reuters' reports we get lack a personal touch. Your despatches from Spain were first-class. And certainly there's enough going on to warrant having someone there to report first-hand.' He glanced sharply at Dan. 'I take it your languages are up to scratch?'

'I studied German and French at university.'

Mr Hitchcock pondered for a moment. 'Leave it with me and I'll let you know in a few days.' Dan rose and was about to leave the room when Mr Hitchcock added, 'If I do say yes – and that's not a given, mind – you won't be rushing off straight away. We have too many staff on holiday in the next few weeks. I probably couldn't let you go until mid-September.'

'Of course.'

Dan left the office feeling hopeful. If Hitchcock recommended something, the paper's proprietor generally went along with it.

By the end of the week, Mr Hitchcock had given his official blessing to the project. Now that there was no danger of getting involved too deeply with Eve again, since he had a ready-made exit, he telephoned her and arranged to see her. Over dinner he told her about his move.

She smiled wanly. 'It will be good for your career. I envy you. A big adventure. Do you know anyone in Berlin?'

'I have a friend, Rudi Lange. I met him in Germany during my Cambridge years. He's a reporter with the *Berliner Morgenpost.* But that's about it.'

'I can put you in touch with an old schoolfriend of mine, Alice Kingsley – well, she's Alice Bauer now, married to a diplomat. She works for the German Broadcasting Corporation. She could be useful.'

'Thank you. I need all the contacts I can get.'

Throughout the rest of the meal Dan could sense that the news that he would be leaving London soon had prompted some kind of withdrawal in Eve. When they left the restaurant, he suggested going back to his rooms for a drink.

'I have some new gramophone records. And of course,' he added, leaning in and kissing her ear, 'there are other things we can do to amuse ourselves.'

She stopped on the pavement and turned to him. 'I don't think that's such a good idea.'

'Really? That's not what you said last time we were together.' He put his arms around her. 'I thought we'd renegotiated terms.'

Her dark eyes were sad. 'They always have to be your terms, Dan. That's the problem. I suppose I hoped things might turn out differently this time. If you weren't going away, if we had more time… well, maybe they would. But you just want someone to keep your bed warm until you leave. After me it'll be some *hübsches Mädchen* in Berlin.' She shrugged. 'Admit it.'

He was silent for a moment. 'You want too much from me. I can't offer anything more.'

'Because you're still in love with her? Even though she's rejected you?'

'It's not a matter of choice. That's the nature of being in love with someone. It doesn't let go just because you want it to.'

'That's so true.' After a pause she added, 'I'll write to Alice, and send you her details. I'm sure she'll be happy for you to get in touch with her.' She kissed him lightly. 'Good luck, Dan. And be careful. Germany's not a kind place these days. You'll stay in touch, won't you?'

'I will. So long.'

She smiled. 'So long.' A cab was cruising the street with its yellow light on, and she hailed it and jumped in.

Dan watched the cab until it was out of sight, then turned and walked back to Bloomsbury.

As the date of his departure drew near, Dan realised he would have to negotiate with his landlady the possibility of having a friend take over his rooms while he was away.

When asked, Mrs Woodbead raised a doubtful eyebrow. 'I don't know, Mr Ranscombe – it's not something I normally allow, not in a regular way.'

'I promise to provide an impeccable substitute. I'd hate to have to give notice and find new digs when I come back. I doubt if I'd find such a wonderful landlady anywhere else in London.'

Dan's flattery and winning smile had the desired effect. She folded her hands beneath her bosom, gratified. 'Well, it's nice to be appreciated, Mr R. There's not many as does. I always try to do my best by my tenants, and you've been a good one, by and large. Better than some I've had.' She affected to consider. 'I suppose this once I could make an exception. Whoever it is would have to be respectable and quiet, and prompt with the rent, mind.'

'You needn't worry on that score. You're a treasure, Mrs Woodbead. Thank you.'

But when he asked around his immediate circle of friends, no one was in need of digs. So he bought Harry a pint at the Wheatsheaf and asked him if he knew of anyone.

'Bound to be someone,' said Harry, taking a sip of his beer. 'How much rent do you pay?'

'Four pounds a month.'

Harry stuck out his lower lip. 'That's a fair bit.'

'They're decent rooms, as you know.'

'I'll ask around.'

'No riff-raff, mind. Someone my landlady can stomach, and who's good for the rent.'

'I'll see what I can do.'

'And if you can find someone who wants to buy an MG Midget, that would help.'

'All right, all right. At this rate I should be charging you commission.'

'You still owe me five guineas for that article on Giraud.'

'If I find you a tenant by the end of the week, are we square?'

'I suppose so.'

Harry fished for his cigarettes. 'So,' he proffered the pack to Dan, 'our man in Berlin, eh?'

'I can't wait. I'm itching to get where the story is. Europe's a veritable powder-keg, if you'll pardon the hackneyed expression. The governments of just about every nation are all kowtowing to Hitler, mainly because they don't really understand what he's up to.'

'And you do?' Harry lit their cigarettes.

'It's all there in *Mein Kampf*.'

Harry shrugged. 'Never read it.'

'Of course you haven't. You're not likely to, if you don't know any German. There's no decent English translation. Some Irish fellow was working on one, but the Nazi Ministry of Propaganda wouldn't let it go ahead. They probably decided it would hinder their cause rather than help it. Anyhow, it's quite an eye-opener. Hitler comes right out and announces that the Nazi goal is domination. The Master Race wielding a mighty sword to bring the lost regions back into the Reich, that kind of stuff. The aim is to annihilate France and then start the great drive eastwards. No one here seems to realise how serious he is.'

Harry looked thoughtful. 'You could do a piece on that for *Ire*. You know, in the form of a book review.'

'*Mein Kampf* was published over a decade ago, Harry.'

'I only meant as a sort of framework. Actually, if you can find time to do the odd article for the mag while you're over there, that would be much appreciated. Art, music. There must be a nice little cultural underground movement in Berlin right now.'

'I don't especially want to attract adverse attention from the authorities by writing about anti-German art and music, old man. When the Nazis don't like a book they burn it, and you know what Heine said about that – a society that burns books will one day burn people.'

Harry gave a snort. 'I doubt if even the Nazis would go that far.' He got to his feet and picked up Dan's empty glass. 'Same again?'

Harry was as good as his word. Before the week was out, he informed Dan that he'd found the perfect person to take over his rooms.

'Matter of fact, it's someone you know. Arthur Bettany. I met him at Kleinfeld's last Monday, and he told me he was being hoofed out of his digs soon. He seemed the ideal candidate, so I mentioned your place.'

Dan was mildly taken aback, but he couldn't really find a reason to object to Bettany. In many ways, he was ideal, since Dan knew him and could vouch for him to Mrs Woodbead.

'I suppose he'll do. Thanks.'

'Think nothing of it. He said he'd call you at your office to fix it all up. Now listen, don't bugger off to Berlin without telling me. We need to arrange a farewell drink.'

*

Arthur Bettany telephoned Dan two days later, and arranged to see the rooms. He arrived a little after seven, dressed in a long gabardine mac and a trilby, and carrying a small, battered leather attaché case. He inspected the rooms, which consisted of a small bedroom-cum-study, a large, well-furnished sitting room overlooking the street, and a small back kitchen.

'I share a bathroom with another chap on the landing, a rep for some cosmetics firm, and he's away a lot of the time,' Dan told him. 'The landlady is better than most. I'll introduce you to her later. As long as she gets the rent on time, she'll leave you pretty well alone. She'll give you an evening meal for sixpence extra, as long as you let her know in the morning. She always makes sure there's a fire laid in the evening if the weather's chilly, and she's not stingy about coal. All in all, it's not a bad billet. Here, have a seat.'

Arthur sat down in a red plush armchair by the window and surveyed the room. Dan studied his face. The fresh, boyish handsomeness of his school years had changed into something leaner and more angular, but with his dark, curling hair and large, intelligent eyes, he was still undoubtedly attractive. Dan couldn't help noticing how lustrous and long his eyelashes were, almost like a girl's.

'How is she about visitors?' asked Arthur. 'You know, at night.'

'She's fine about that, as long as you don't make a row. Just keep it discreet.'

Arthur nodded. 'I think the place will do very well. When do you leave for Europe?'

'In a fortnight. I'm not sure how long I'll be gone,' said Dan. 'Six months at the very least, I should think. I'll give you plenty of notice when I'll need the rooms back.' Dan glanced into the street. 'It's a pretty handy area. I can walk to most places – work, Soho, that kind of thing.'

Arthur smiled. 'Yes, you're something of a Soho habitué these days.'

'Most journalists seem to be.' Dan paused. 'What's your line of work?'

'Civil service.'

'Funny, at school I always had you down to become a boffin, or an academic. You know, Cambridge don, that kind of thing. You were always so damned clever, picking up the mathematics prize year after year.'

Arthur smiled again, dropping his eyes to the attaché case on his lap, but made no reply.

A silence fell. Dan was very conscious that Arthur was keeping his distance. There was none of the familiarity and friendliness he might have expected from an old schoolfellow. Perhaps it was just as well. He had no real wish to know him better now.

'Come on,' said Dan. 'I'll take you to see Mrs Woodbead.'

They went downstairs to the ground floor of the house, which Mrs Woodbead occupied. Dan introduced Arthur, and as though at the flick of a switch Arthur's reticence disappeared, and he became bright and charming. Mrs Woodbead was very taken, and the matter was settled. Arthur would move in the day after Dan left.

A couple of weeks later Dan ran into Guy at Bellamy's.

They chatted for a while over drinks, exchanging news about Guy's racing venture and Dan's forthcoming departure for Germany.

'By the way,' remarked Guy, 'I heard yesterday that Meg Latimer has had her baby. A boy. To be called Maximilian, apparently.'

'Really? I must send my congratulations.' Dan drained his whisky. 'Another drink?'

So, there it was, thought Dan as he signalled to the steward. The final door had closed. Being a mother would now be the most important thing in her life. He and Meg might as well never have been. She and Paul and Maximilian – what a name; he only hoped they would have the sense to refer to him as Max – were a family now, and Meg would do her utmost to make it all work, and to keep her son safe and secure. Good luck to the little blighter. If it weren't for the baby, he reflected, he and Meg would probably be together now, instead of at an unbridgeable distance.

Three weeks later Dan arrived in Berlin. He had arranged to meet his old friend Rudi Lange in the bar of the Adlon Hotel. Rudi was a stocky, cheerful, sandy-haired twenty-six-year-old, wearing a Bavarian-cut sports coat and a squat hat worn at a jaunty angle. The two hadn't met for five years and had a lot to catch up on.

After a couple of drinks, Rudi announced he was hungry. 'The dining room here is too expensive. I know a little place not far away. Come on.'

Rudi took Dan to Café Protze, a shabby little restaurant in the shadow of the S-Bahn railway viaduct, and ordered beers and plates of pig's knuckle with sauerkraut.

'Not bad grub, eh?' said Rudi, wolfing his food down.

Dan had to agree that the fatty hock in its thin gravy tasted better than it looked. He glanced around as he ate. On one wall of the café hung a large picture of the Führer, and on another a printed notice with the admonition, *Always give the Hitler Salute!*

Rudi caught his eye and winked. 'There's a police station just round the corner. The Kripo come in here a lot.' He nodded in the direction of the fat, balding proprietor cleaning glasses behind the counter. 'Old Protze has to play up his commitment to National Socialism. He used to be a Kozi in the old days – you know, a bit of a red. He doesn't want anyone to remember.' Rudi wiped his plate with a piece of bread. 'Everyone in Germany was someone different before March nineteen thirty-three.'

When their plates had been cleared away they ordered coffee and sat talking over the times, old and new.

'Berlin seems to have changed a lot since I was here as a student,' observed Dan. 'All that Nazi regalia, loudspeakers on lamp-posts. And everyone looks so poor.'

'It's a dump, if you ask me,' said Rudi. 'There's no good food in the shops, everyone is fed up queuing for everything. You can't even get a decent suit – all the cloth is made out of wood pulp. They make petrol out of coal, rubber out of coal and lime.' He shrugged. 'That's the price you pay for trying to become a self-sufficient nation.'

'So why do people go along with it all? Can't they see that Hitler and Göring and the rest of them are just thugs?'

Rudi glanced at nearby tables. '*Nicht so laut*. That's the first lesson you need to learn, my old friend – always speak well of *der Führer.* You don't want the Gestapo opening a file on you.' He signalled for the bill. 'Come on, let's taste a bit of nightlife.'

They walked the damp streets in search of a taxi.

'I used to go to the cinema in the evenings,' remarked Rudi, 'but not so much now. I can't stand those endless newsreels of the rallies. It's bad enough having to salute when the fucking Reichswehr march past. You know we have radio wardens who go round checking people are listening every time there's a party broadcast? It's our civic duty to listen.'

'Where are we going?' asked Dan.

'The X Bar. It's an illegal jazz club that I know.'

'Illegal how?'

'The Nazis don't allow what they called negro jazz. But there are still bands who play it. That is, they sandwich American hits in between the opening and closing chords of acceptable Aryan numbers. You just have to know the right places. I'm a big jazz fan.'

Dan refrained from telling Rudi that he wasn't.

Rounding a corner they passed a glass magazine display, and Dan glanced at its contents and stopped dead in his tracks. There on the cover of a newspaper was a crude drawing depicting a white-coated doctor with a swarthy, hook-nosed face, gloating over the fainting form of a naked blonde girl. In his hand was a gigantic syringe, and above in bold script were the words **GERMAN WOMEN – THE JEWS ARE YOUR DESTRUCTION!**

'*Der Stürmer*,' said Rudi. 'Pretty sick propaganda, eh? I've seen worse covers than that. What's funny is the SA took all these display cases down in the summer of the Olympics, so as not to shock the sensibilities of foreigners. Yet it's the kind of thing my Jewish friends have to see day in, day out.' Rudi caught sight of a taxi and whistled it down. 'Here we go! Jump in. Let's go and have some fun.'

After the jazz club Dan invited Rudi back to the Adlon for a nightcap. At eleven, the bar was still busy. Rudi spotted someone he knew, and disappeared for a moment, returning with a bespectacled, balding man with a moustache and a round, serious face.

'Dan, I want you to meet a very illustrious man – Bill Shirer, of CBS News. Bill, this is my friend, Dan Ranscombe of the *London Graphic*.' The two men shook hands, and Rudi signalled to the bartender for three beers.

'Are you planning to cover Hitler's meeting with Chamberlain at Godesberg?' Dan asked Shirer.

'Of course.'

'What do you think will happen?'

'I think the British and the French will sell the Czechs down the river, ask them to surrender unconditionally to Hitler and turn the Sudetens over to Germany.'

'The Czechs won't accept it. They'll fight alone,' said Rudi.

'I hope you're right,' said Shirer. 'I'm pretty disgusted with the whole mess. Watching the mighty British Empire going begging to Hitler is not an edifying sight.' He caught Dan's expression. 'Not my words. It's what the papers are saying.' He raised his glass. 'Anyway, here's to the Czechs, good luck to them. But they should prepare for a sell-out.'

They talked on, discussing the events in Prague, trading views on whether war was imminent or not, all agreeing it was inevitable. Dan warmed to Shirer. He was shrewd and knowledgeable, and clearly a journalist of great integrity.

'How long have you been in Germany?' Dan asked him.

'Four years,' replied Shirer.

'There's no one Bill doesn't know,' said Rudi proudly. 'And that includes Hitler's top brass. He even goes drinking with them.'

'Really?' Dan was surprised. 'Hardly the most salubrious company.'

Shirer gave him a sharp look. 'Without knowing those men, you can't begin to understand what's happening here.'

'Of course, as a reporter one naturally has to be close to the heart of things. But – socialising?'

'If you want to be an effective correspondent, you can't be choosy. For instance, when I found out that Rosenberg, the head of Nazi Foreign Affairs, was holding regular beer evenings, I made a point of going along. Rosenberg himself is a crack-brained, doughy-faced dolt, but thanks to his *Bierabende* I've got to know Göring, Hess, Ribbentrop, Himmler, the whole clambake. They're a repulsive bunch of misfits, but they're the men closest to Hitler. They execute the Führer's every command, and those commands determine every facet of life in the Third Reich.'

Shirer's hard-boiled approach was chastening. 'So, what are they like?' asked Dan, genuinely curious.

'Göring's a fat swashbuckler who likes dressing up and throwing big parties. But he's powerful – probably the most powerful man around Hitler. He's a crude kind of a guy, but the people love his sense of humour. It makes them think he's genuine and down-to-earth.' Shirer pulled a pipe from his pocket, along with a tobacco pouch, and began to fill it. 'And he's well connected, knows all the right people, which is something Hitler needs.' He tamped down the tobacco with his thumb. 'He's also a morphine addict.' He wagged the stem of his pipe at Dan. 'You don't get to find out these things without a little fraternisation, no matter how distasteful you might think it.'

'No, I see,' murmured Dan. 'And von Ribbentrop?'

Shirer laughed. 'Let's just call him Ribbentrop. The "von" is a fraud. He persuaded some aunt whose husband was knighted by the Kaiser to adopt him, just so he could stick "von" on the front of his name. That tells you a lot.' He flicked open his lighter. 'In fact, everything about him is phoney. The way he talks, the way he acts – behind all that, the man's a nincompoop, a simpleton. Granted, his English and French are pretty good, but he has not' – Shirer clicked several times at his lighter to get a flame – 'he has not the slightest understanding of France and the French, or of Britain and America. In fact, I can't think of a worse man to be Hitler's foreign minister.' He pocketed his lighter and puffed reflectively for a few seconds, then added, 'Göring loves attention, he likes talking to the press. But I never get much out of Hess.'

'What about Himmler?' asked Rudi. 'What's he like?'

'The chicken farmer? Pretty unimpressive. Looks more like a middle-ranking *Beamter* than a chief of the secret police. Basically the man's just a characterless thug – but he's important and he's powerful. He gets things done.'

Rudi signalled to a passing waiter. '*Noch drei Bier, bitte.*'

'Not for me, thanks,' said Shirer. 'I need an early night.' When the waiter had disappeared, he went on, 'The one person you never see at the beer evenings is Goebbels. He hates Rosenberg. But I've managed to get to know him pretty well through press conferences and parties. He's an educated man, but you'd never guess it to listen to him. Every word he utters is banal. For my money, he's simply a neurotic, club-footed dwarf. I can't stand the guy.'

Though fascinated, Dan couldn't help feeling a tinge of scepticism. 'These men are Hitler's closest advisers. They run Germany. Surely they can't be so...' Dan struggled for a word, 'so mediocre?'

Shirer shrugged, inspected his pipe, which seemed to have gone out, and sighed. 'They're just gangsters. And gangsters don't need to be intellectually gifted, or scintillating orators. Or even great thinkers. All they need to be is in control. On which note' – Shirer drained his beer glass and pocketed his pipe – 'I shall bid you folks goodnight.' He rose and shook hands with them both, and smiled at Dan. 'Nice to meet you, Mr Ranscombe. Good luck in Berlin. I hope we meet again.'

'I'll be listening to your broadcasts,' said Dan. He watched Shirer go. 'Quite a fellow,' he said to Rudi.

'Isn't he? I'm glad you two hit it off. Some people think he's a touch arrogant, a bit of a know-all, but that's because he *does* know all. And everyone.'

Dan was about to say something, but stopped in astonishment. Crossing the bar in their direction was Paul Latimer. In the split second that their eyes met, Paul's expression seemed to Dan momentarily appalled, but the next moment he was smiling and shaking Dan's hand.

'Dan, what a surprise! Though I suppose I should have known I might bump into you. I heard on the grapevine that you were working out here. Is this your regular hangout?'

'I've only just arrived. But it seems to be a regular watering-hole for journalists. Let me introduce my friend, Rudi Lange – Rudi, Paul Latimer.'

Rudi shook Paul's hand. 'A journalist also?'

'No, no – racing car enthusiast. I'm here visiting my friend, Richard Seaman.'

'*Mein Gott!*' exclaimed Rudi. 'Seaman is a big hero here! Winning the Grand Prix last year, that was truly something. And he's your friend?'

'Yes.'

Rudi smiled, narrowing his eyes at Paul and taking a swift drag of his cigarette. 'You a Nazi, too?' There was a frozen pause, and then Rudi broke into laughter, slapping Paul on the shoulder. 'Hey, just a joke! Your friend gave the Nazi salute on the podium, you know – not just once, but twice. Think how that must have delighted our Führer!'

'Rudi has a very German sense of humour,' murmured Dan. 'Will you join us for a drink?'

'I won't thanks,' said Paul. 'I've had rather a tiring trip, and I need to be up early.'

'Staying long?'

'Just a couple of days. Anyway, I must push along. See you back in Blighty.' He nodded to Rudi. 'Nice to meet you.'

'*Ebenfalls*,' murmured Rudi. Then he added, after Paul had departed, 'He didn't like my joke, did he?'

'Nobody likes being called a Nazi, Rudi. Except the Nazis.'

But Rudi wasn't listening. He had spotted some more friends on the other side of the room and invited them over to the table. The conversation expanded and continued, more drinks were bought, and it was after one o'clock by the time Dan made his way to bed, wishing he could stick to his resolution not to drink so much.

A few days later a letter came from Sonia. Dan read it over breakfast. His godmother had an enjoyably eccentric style, with much underlining, and the world of home which she conveyed seemed, against the backdrop of all that Dan was witnessing in Berlin, impossibly serene.

> *I trust the goings-on between Czechoslovakia and Germany are giving you plenty of copy. I do try hard to pay attention and follow it all in The Times, but – and I know you'll forgive your ridiculously frivolous godmother for saying this – it seems so very complicated and dull! I am hosting a dinner in a fortnight's time – quite a large one, I may say – and have invited several of Henry's old friends. They are all such frightfully clever people – the Brenans and the Raviliouses especially – and if I can't say anything particularly intelligent about what is happening in Germany, it would be wonderful to be able to come up with some first-hand gossip!*

Dan could just imagine the satisfaction it would give Sonia to be able to regale her guests with details not generally available to the newspaper-reading public. He would have to see what he could do. He folded up the letter and put it in his pocket, and went off to catch the train to Godesberg.

PART IV

1939–41

1

IT WAS A Monday morning in late June, and Meg had come to London to spend a few days with her mother while Paul was abroad.

Helen sat at the breakfast table with Max in her lap, feeding him mashed banana. She ran a tentative finger along the line of her grandson's gum. 'I think he's got a top tooth coming, Meg.'

Meg put down her teacup and leaned over. 'Where? Let me see.'

Ten-month-old Max began to crow and babble and shake his head from side to side. 'It's not exactly easy to show you,' laughed Helen.

'He's always in a good mood at breakfast.' Meg smiled fondly at her son, picking up one fat little hand and kissing it. 'Are you sure you'll be all right on your own with him?'

'Dora will be on hand if the need arises,' said Helen briskly. 'She adores babies. I do think it's high time you found yourself a nanny, though. When your aunt Sonia and I were girls your grandmother employed a nursery maid as well as a nanny. And here you are, trying to cope on your own.'

'It so happens I've found one. She starts a week today. I've interviewed her and taken up her references. She seems perfect.'

'Well, that's good news. Where did you find her?'

'A friend of Anna Kentleigh's works for the Jewish Refugee Committee. She gave me the names of girls from Germany looking for domestic work. That's how I found Lotte.'

'Oh, my dear – a Jewish refugee. Is that wise? What does Paul think?'

'He wasn't at all keen. I can't think why. She's gentle and sweet, and her English is really quite good. She's from a professional family in Vienna. Anyway, I put my foot down – not a thing I often do. Now' – Meg got to her feet – 'I should make a move.'

'Where are you having your outfit for Diana's wedding made?'

'I'm trying a new dressmaker over in Kensington that Anna recommended. Paul says he doesn't understand why I can't wear the same outfit to Diana's wedding that I wore to Muriel Leatham's. Men really have no idea.' Meg glanced out of the window. 'Drat, it's starting to rain.'

'It won't last long. It's been showery all week. A pity, after we had such a glorious start to June. You can always take a taxi.'

'No, I'll catch the bus. I much prefer it. Gives me time to think and I don't have to talk to the cab driver.'

'I don't blame you. All cabbies seem to want to talk about these days is whether there's going to be a war.'

'The *Express* says there shan't be, and that's good enough for me,' said Meg.

'I wish I could share your optimism,' replied Helen. 'But all those posters about how to recognise a mustard gas attack, and the sandbags at the Ritz – someone is taking it seriously. Rachel Whigham has been complaining that so many young men are joining up that there aren't enough to go round at debutante parties.'

'Mother, I refuse to think about it,' said Meg. She put on her hat, found her bag and an umbrella, kissed her mother and set off for town.

The shower was already passing, and the summer day was breaking serene and fresh, but above the greenery of Hyde Park the lolling, silver bulk of the barrage balloons struck a threatening note. The incongruity of the scene seemed to reflect Meg's own state of mind. All was ostensibly content in her life, but it held unsettling facets – facets which she did her best to ignore. She lived her life from day to day, hoping that companionability, and the fact of Max, would sustain her marriage. She reassured herself that lots of people's marriages were probably the same.

Meg had, without realising it, become adept at self-deception. She measured the bearability of her life in increments of fulfilment; Max was the greatest of these, then the running of her home, then, strangely, the diligent work she performed to sustain her marriage, which involved manufacturing affection, friendliness, and an enthusiastic show of interest in Paul's affairs. The sense of keeping something alive had its own rewards. She never allowed herself to think of Dan.

The dressmaker's took the better part of an hour, after which Meg went to Bond Street in search of a hat. As she emerged from a milliner's she heard someone call her name. She turned and saw Eve Meyerson waving from the other side of the street. Meg felt a sense of misgiving as she watched her cross the road through the traffic.

'I thought I recognised you,' said Eve with a smile. 'How nice to bump into you like this.' She pointed to Meg's hatbox. 'I see you've been shopping.'

'It's a hat for Diana's wedding.'

'Of course – it's only a few weeks away, isn't it? Lovely to have a wedding to look forward to, with everything as grim as it is. Is Paul in London with you?'

'No, he's gone to Belgium for the Grand Prix.'

There was a pause, and then Eve asked, 'Are you going anywhere special? Because I was just thinking of having some lunch. Would you like to join me?'

'Yes, of course.'

'Come on. There's a little place in South Molton Street that I know.'

They settled themselves at a table in the corner of the restaurant, and the waiter brought menus. They ordered, and then Eve said, 'Diana tells me you have a little boy now. Tell me all about him.'

Over lunch Meg talked about Max, and life at Hazelhurst House, but eventually, feeling that all this must be too domesticated for Eve's taste, she said, 'Of course, country life is somewhat sheltered. I mean, Paul gets *The Times* every day, and one reads all the frightening things about how war is inevitable. But somehow, on drowsy summer days in Berkshire, none of it seems quite real. Even here in London all the sandbags and barrage balloons seem like... oh, I don't know, props for a film.'

'It's all too real, I'm afraid. And while I hope it won't happen, I do think we shall have a war. It's not so much what the British papers say as the German ones. They had a field day over the Japanese blockade of the British and French concessions in Tientsin recently.'

The waiter took their plates away, and Eve offered Meg a cigarette.

Meg shook her head. 'No, thanks.' She hadn't the vaguest notion what Tientsin signified, and couldn't decide whether conversation with Eve made her feel more intelligent, or more stupid. 'How do you come to read German newspapers?'

'Dan sends them to me.'

'Oh, yes. He's working there as a correspondent, isn't he?' Asking after him could not be avoided. 'How is he?'

'He seems to be wonderfully well, from his letters. Don't you ever hear from him?' asked Eve. 'I thought you were friends.'

'No.' Meg's voice faltered, and she added, 'He's really more Paul's friend than mine. There's really no reason why he should be in touch with me.' She looked away, feeling herself blushing fiercely, a girlish affliction she could do nothing to prevent.

Eve was puzzled by her sudden embarrassment. Then, from nowhere, an astonishing notion came to her. Could it really be possible that Meg was the married woman Dan was in love with? She did quick calculations. The timing certainly fitted. Dan had been convinced she was going to leave her husband to be with him. Then it turned out she was having a child, and the affair had broken down. She felt certain she had hit upon the truth. There was only one way to find out.

'Don't look so coy.' Eve gave Meg a cool smile. 'I know you and he had an affair.'

This was so unexpected that Meg was unable to disguise her shock, and Eve knew instantly she had hit the nail on the head. It had been Meg all along – not some cold-hearted femme fatale, as she had imagined. Jealousy seared her. How could he possibly be in love with someone so tediously insipid, so utterly conventional?

'Dan told me all about it,' Eve continued smoothly. 'I'm used to his minor infidelities. Perhaps I have too forgiving a nature – but we all have our weaknesses. Dan's weakness is that he can't resist a challenge. He always had quite a thing for you – remember the house party in Surrey? And when Dan sets his sights on someone, he doesn't like to fail. Even a little thing like a marriage won't get in his way. You were quite a conquest.'

Meg was stupefied. Had it really meant so little to him? It didn't seem possible that he would betray her in such a way.

'He told you that?'

Eve shrugged. 'He got what he wanted. It's all in the past, and I forgave him.'

The suggestion was that she had been merely an interlude in his relationship with Eve. Meg could hardly believe it. If that was all she had meant to him, why had he come to Hazelhurst that day, thinking he was the father of her child, begging her to leave Paul?

She struggled for words. She didn't want to discuss with Eve any part of her relationship with Dan, but she had to say something. 'It's true there was something between us, but I don't believe I meant so little to him as you say,' she said in a low voice. 'He asked me to end my marriage so that we could be together.'

'Just as well you didn't. It's all part of the game with Dan. I think he rather liked the idea of putting one over on Paul. You're well out of it.' Eve blew out some smoke, watching Meg's face. 'It wouldn't have lasted, you know.'

Meg sat in silence, recalling how Dan had tried to persuade her that Paul was deceiving her with some male lover, that her marriage was a sham. How absurd that had turned out to be. Perhaps it was evidence of the lengths he would go to.

'You don't know Dan very well, do you?' Eve went on, stubbing her cigarette out in the ashtray. 'Anyway, we've probably dwelt on this long enough. You should count yourself lucky. You had the pleasure of a little fling – he's rather wonderful in bed, isn't he? – and you kept your marriage intact.' She smiled at Meg in an entirely friendly fashion. 'Shall we get the bill?'

Meg fumbled in her handbag. She took a couple of pound notes from her purse and dropped them on the table. 'I'm sure that will more than cover my share.' And with that she rose and left the restaurant as quickly as she could. Eve watched her go. It had been a petty piece of vengeance, but she had thoroughly enjoyed it.

When Meg returned to Cheyne Walk, her mother handed her a telegram. 'This came while you were out.'

Meg opened it and read its contents.

'Oh.' She put her hand to her mouth. 'Paul's friend Dick Seaman has been killed. His car caught fire in the Grand Prix.'

'How ghastly!'

'Paul says he has to stay on for a few days.' She crumpled the telegram. 'Dick and his wife had only been married a few months. Simply dreadful for her.'

'Do you want to change your plans and stay on here for a while?'

Meg sighed and shook her head. 'Thanks, but I should get back. I have a million and one things to do. Our train is at five. I must go and pack."

The journey home was difficult and tiring. Max was a

restless, fretful handful, and although the other people in her compartment were politely forbearing, Meg desperately wished he would stop crying and fall asleep. In the brief interval when he did, her thoughts immediately reverted to the conversation with Eve. She was tormented by the idea that she had been no more to Dan than a mere conquest, as Eve had put it. It shouldn't matter, since there was nothing between them now, and never would be, but somehow it did. She had stored away the memory of the afternoon they had spent together as lovers like some precious jewel, and now it turned out to be tawdry and worthless. The thought that she had meant so little to him shrivelled her soul. She felt a fool. Worse still was the knowledge that it wasn't secret, as she had supposed. If Dan had told Eve, might not the information make its way to Paul? Her heart contracted at the thought. What a fool she'd been to have trusted and loved Dan. He had deliberately tried to destroy her marriage, and now he might do so carelessly. She must make sure that didn't happen. Somehow the news of Dick Seaman's death made everything feel fragile. The security of her marriage felt more important than ever.

Diana and Roddy were married a few weeks later at St Peter's in Belgravia. Diana looked ravishing in a sheath-like wedding dress of white satin with a decorously high neckline.

'How she manages to look sophisticated and virginal at the same time is a wonder,' murmured Sonia to Meg.

'Doesn't Roddy look proud?' said Meg under her breath, as Paul and Diana reached the altar. She glanced at Paul, standing at Diana's left side, looking immensely smart in his morning dress, a white rose in his buttonhole. His expression was wooden. *Oh, for heaven's sake, Paul, do buck up*, she prayed. He looked as though he were at a funeral, rather than about to give his only sister in marriage. At least he'd done the right thing and settled a very generous amount of money on Diana. He'd seemed fine lately, this morning he'd been in a good humour, and last night – last night, for the first time in almost ten months, he had made love to her. It had been no better and no worse than on previous occasions – the same wordless intensity, without tender prelude or aftermath – but the fact of it had made her grateful. The fabric of her world was patched and mended. It looked and felt roughly normal again.

As though he heard her unspoken words, Paul, like one coming awake, suddenly smiled at Diana, then at Roddy. Meg's anxiety fell away.

'There's Dan, late as usual,' murmured Sonia. 'Did you know his father died? He came back from Berlin for the funeral. So sad. I was very fond of Edwin.'

Meg glanced round to look at Dan. Despite everything Eve had told her, the sight of him brought a pang to her heart. How miserable for him, his father dying while he was abroad.

'Oh look,' said Sonia, as the priest stepped forward, 'we're about to begin.'

The wedding luncheon went well. Paul's speech was stiff and somewhat perfunctory, but Roddy's elder brother, the best man, was a splendid success. Roddy, with only the slightest and most charming of stammers, bestowed thanks where due and fulsome compliments on the bridesmaids. Meg kept a close eye throughout the afternoon on Paul. He conducted himself with his usual ponderous politeness, and clearly made an effort to be cheerful, but there were moments when she caught him watching Roddy with miserable intentness.

That evening, changed out of their wedding attire, Paul and Meg sat in the kitchen in the Kensington flat, drinking tea. Paul had spoken very little since the wedding, and seemed morose.

'Do you remember how we sat here on the night of our

wedding?' said Meg. 'When Diana left us food and a bottle of wine?' Paul said nothing. 'It seems a long time ago.' After a moment Meg dropped her attempt at lightness, and said, 'Oh Paul, I wish I knew why you're so unhappy.'

Paul stared at her. 'I'm not unhappy. What on earth gives you that idea?'

'You've hated the whole business of Diana and Roddy getting married. Don't pretend you haven't.' When he didn't answer, unable to keep her suspicions in check any longer, she added, 'If you must know, it seems to me you have a liking for Roddy that isn't healthy.'

'Don't speak about things you don't understand.'

Meg's heart began to beat hard. 'Do you love him? Is that what this is all about?' Paul stood up and walked to the other side of the kitchen. Meg persisted, 'Why do you look at him the way you do? I watched you this afternoon. Like a hungry child!'

There was a long silence. At last Paul shook his head. 'You reduce everything to your own crude terms. I don't expect you to understand. But since you are so intent on trying to find some obscene truth to fit your suspicions, I will tell you.' He looked angrily at her. 'Yes, I'm jealous of my sister because she has supplanted me in Roddy's affections. You're a woman. You have no idea of the strength of feeling of one man for another. It's deeper than anything you could ever feel. You women fill your heads with notions of love and romance, but you couldn't begin to comprehend male friendships. They are finer and more wholesome than anything between a man and a woman. If I am unhappy, if I have any regret, it's because something between Roddy and myself has been sundered, lost, sacrificed to a relationship much less pure and – yes, laugh if you like – less noble. There – are you happy?'

Meg listened aghast. 'You mean you really think – is that what you think of marriage? Of our marriage? That any one of your men friends is worth more to you than I am?'

'Don't you see that simply by making that comparison, that

odious comparison, you show how little you understand? A woman's comprehension of what it is to love rests in emotional triviality. And sex. She frames everything in terms of physical love. That is natural, for she wants children. But friendship between men is deeper than that, richer than that. Diana, like all women, uses sex for her own ends. And yes, I resent the way it has blinded Roddy to the value of his friendship with me.'

This was worse than anything Meg could have imagined. 'So that's the way you see it. Your feelings for me are second-rate, imperfect. And you see Roddy and Diana's love in the same terms.'

'I told you, the two don't bear comparison. What men feel for one another is different.'

'Better?'

He shook his head. 'I didn't expect you to understand.'

'Because I'm a woman.'

'If you like.'

She let out a long breath. 'At least this is the most honest we've ever been with one another.'

'Yes.' He had grown calmer. 'Meg, nothing I say is meant to devalue any marriage, particularly ours. That is a sacrament.'

'Just that you and Roddy have something holier and more pure.' She paused. 'What about Arthur Bettany? Did you lie to me about him?'

'Stop this, Meg. I told you, these are things no woman could possibly understand.'

Meg rose from the table. 'I'm going out.'

'Where?'

'Just out. To get away.'

'Don't run away every time—'

'Every time what?'

'Every time you lose an argument.'

'Paul, this isn't an argument. There is nothing to lose or win.' She gazed at him, feeling further apart from him than she ever had. 'Absolutely nothing.'

She left the flat. The warm evening had a surreal air. The shock of what Paul had told her had left her feeling light-headed. It wasn't that she didn't believe him. She did, entirely. It laid bare the basis on which he had married her, the shallowness of his feelings for her, expectations that went no further than... no further than what? Than her own feelings for him, if she was honest. Perhaps Dan had been right in the very beginning. Perhaps Paul had decided he needed a wife, and because he placed no special value on any woman's love it had only mattered that the person he chose loved him – or thought she did – and that he could be fond of her. She genuinely believed that, so far as he could, Paul cared deeply for her. But only because she was his wife, and the mother of his son, and the laws of life dictated that one must and should love and protect that person. Did Paul actually have any idea what real love was? Presumably in relation to men, whom he evidently considered superior to women. *What a bargain we have made*, she thought.

She walked all the way down through the park to the Serpentine, trying to untangle the confusion of her thoughts. Paul had laid bare a truth about himself that Dan had suspected, and tried to warn her about, but that she had refused to believe. She sat down on a bench and stared across the river at the evening summer sunshine filtering through the trees. Perhaps she should leave him. But where would she go? She knew, thanks to Eve, how little she had meant to Dan. That had been a ridiculous fantasy. No, leaving was impossible. She was too afraid to unpick the fabric of her comfortable life and face the consequences. Not just afraid for herself. Afraid for Max. A fearful thought came to her – if it ever went as far as a divorce, might not Paul try to take Max from her? No, no – anything was better than that. Their marriage, she now saw, was deeply flawed, but in the end it was a contract, like all marriages. So far, and for the sake of her son, it was one she was prepared to honour.

After a long while she rose from the bench and made her way back through the park to the flat. Dusk was falling. She let herself in and found Paul in the drawing room. He was sitting on the sofa, his hands cradling a crystal tumbler of Scotch. He gazed at her as she stood in the doorway.

'I thought you might not come back.'

'I had to come back. Where else would I go?' She went to the drinks trolley and poured herself a sherry, then sat down next to him on the sofa.

'I thought you might have gone to your mother's.'

She sipped her drink and sat back with a sigh against the cushions. 'Of course, because that's where slighted wives always go.'

'Do you feel slighted?'

'I suppose I do, Paul. You told me my true value. I thought I was worth more.'

He put his glass down sharply on the table and turned to her, grasping her shoulders and pulling her towards him, surprising her. 'Don't say that. You're worth everything to me.'

'Not everything. Come on – compared to someone like Roddy, or any one of your real friends?'

'Please don't twist my words. You're my wife, and I love you. I have never loved any other woman.'

'It might have been better if you had,' replied Meg bitterly.

His response wasn't what she expected. He let go of her and sat back. 'I know.' There was a silence. 'I haven't led that kind of life. School, university – everything for me has been a masculine world. I've learned how to behave with women, but it's not an instinctive thing. I couldn't… I mean, I never wanted to be with any woman in what you might call a romantic way. I didn't know how. If any of Diana's friends tried to – I don't know, seduce me, I suppose – I simply withdrew. I wasn't interested. Or I was scared. With you it has always been different. We've known one another since we were children. Nothing was difficult. I knew you hero-worshipped me. Don't smile like that – you know it's true, and you must let me be honest. I knew you could love me. I knew I could love you. I thought it would be ideal.' He closed his eyes. 'If I have done things badly, Meg, for God's sake teach me how to do them better.'

Touched, bewildered, she moved closer, put her mouth to his and kissed him. 'This has been a long day,' she said. 'Shall we go to bed?'

'No,' she said, when he came to bed. 'No pyjamas. Take them off.' A moment later, when he slipped naked between the sheets, she said, 'And don't put out the light. You always put out the light. This time it will be different. I will show you what to do.'

Half an hour later, Meg lay in the dark. She could tell from Paul's breathing that he was already falling asleep. It had been awkward, but better. She had tried, and she must keep trying. Her heart shrank when she thought of everything Paul had said that evening. He scarcely understood himself, and she couldn't help him. Perhaps he had twisted every natural tendency within him to become the kind of man he thought he should be. Perhaps the result was some dreadful lie in which they were both trapped. All she knew was that this marriage was the only security she had, and she must convince Paul as well as herself that it was normal and worthwhile. Above all, they must go on being kind to one another.

2

DURING THE FINAL few days of August, the weather was warm and thundery. As tension wound in Europe, as diplomatic efforts grew more frantic by the hour to find a bloodless means of fulfilling Germany's irreducible demands, as threats and warnings flew to and fro between the nations, the last hours of careless pleasure for ordinary people ticked slowly by. Each evening they tuned in to the news bulletin to learn which way the wind of war, whispering ever closer, was blowing.

Dan managed to speak to Rudi, who was pessimistic.

'They've started food rationing here, which is a sure sign it's coming. Who knows, though? Perhaps it's just Hitler trying to impress London and Paris. Everyone's grumbling. No one wants this war. All the correspondents have left. The Adlon bar is very lonely without you boys.'

In London, sandbags were piled high, notices about air-raid and gas-attack warnings plastered walls, paintings and artefacts in every museum were being surreptitiously moved to storage, and hospitals were being quietly evacuated. Yet against this backdrop Londoners idled away Bank Holiday Monday with their customary round of picnics and pleasures.

The next day Meg spoke to her mother. In response to Helen's mood of gloomy anxiety, Meg remained resolutely optimistic. 'The *Express* still says war isn't inevitable.'

'I believe that's known as having one's head in the sand. If you could see everything that's happening in London.'

As she held the receiver to her ear, Meg turned and glanced out of the window. Lotte had spread a rug out on the lawn and Max was crawling about happily in just a vest and nappy. The day was warm and tranquil. A picnic lunch was planned. 'But surely there's still a chance for us to make the right decision?'

Helen sighed impatiently. 'Meg, the decision has already been made. We've given our pledge to fight at Poland's call, come what may. Anyway, I'm glad you and Max are out of harm's way in the country. How is Paul?'

'I hardly know. He went away on Monday on urgent business and he's only telephoned once. I don't know when to expect him back. He's been frightfully mysterious these past weeks.' Some tension within her broke suddenly. 'Oh, I know you're right and that I'm deluding myself. I just... I just don't want it to happen.'

'Well, well – perhaps Mr Beaverbook's optimism is justified. There's still time, I suppose. Cheer up. I shall come and visit soon. Give little Max a kiss from me.'

All that day and the next, Europe held its breath. Diplomatic exchanges continued to wing back and forth between the British ambassador and the powers in Germany, glimmers of optimism flickered, but the sands were running.

Then on Friday, just as Dan arrived at the office, he was greeted by a breathless colleague with the news that Hitler had invaded Poland, and the bombing of Polish cities had begun.

Dan met Harry for a hasty lunch in the Wheatsheaf.

'So, what now?' asked Harry.

'War, I imagine. I spoke to my friend Rudi in Berlin just before I came out. Hitler gave a speech at the Reichstag this morning and apparently he seemed nervous and depressed, as if he didn't quite know what he'd done. He's probably hoping that Britain will back down from its promise. And France. But that won't happen. Hitler said once that the greatest mistake the Kaiser made was to fight England, and that Germany shouldn't ever repeat that mistake. I rather think he's about to find out how right he was.'

*

Meg stood in the drawing room at Hazelhurst and watched Paul, on a stepladder, pasting broad strips of black paper down the edges of the windows.

'We could have got one of the maids to do that, you know.'

'I'm sure I'll be a darn sight quicker,' replied Paul. 'Kentleigh said taping strips crossways would stop the glass falling in if a bomb explodes.'

'If a bomb falls on Hazelhurst, I'm sure we'll have other things to worry about. Please just do the edges. It will look so dreadful otherwise. This is all such a bother. Mrs Runcie told me this morning that Gwen is already talking about going to work in some factory that makes aeroplane parts.'

'Well, we're at war now. All hands to the tiller. You can't expect to run a house with the same amount of staff.' Paul stepped down from the ladder. 'There. That should do the trick. Was that your mother on the phone a moment ago?'

'Yes. She's in quite a state. Says she and the maids spent all yesterday sewing blackout curtains, the air-raid sirens are playing havoc with her nerves, and she can't decide whether it would be better to be bombed or gassed. London sounds so foul at the moment that I invited her to stay with us for a while, but she won't contemplate leaving Cheyne Walk.'

'Helen is very independent.'

'Yes,' sighed Meg. 'She is.'

The telephone rang, and a moment later Gwen knocked and put her head round the door. 'Please, 'm, it's Mrs Haddon for you.'

Meg went to the hallway and picked up the receiver. 'Sonia, how lovely to hear from you. How is everything at Woodbourne?'

'My dear, we're in such a state. I've spent most of the afternoon at the village hall. Daphne Davenport is the local billeting officer, and I've been helping her to organise the evacuees. Five hundred of them arrived today from some place called Lewisham.

We have taken two boys, Colin and Sidney Jennings. Colin is eleven and Sidney is nine. They seem very lively, but they're polite and clean. You wouldn't believe the nonsense the village people talk about how London children are crawling with lice. I've put them in the nursery. I do hope Mrs Goodall and the other servants don't make too much fuss about the extra work.'

'It sounds as though you'll be busy, certainly. I wonder if we shall have evacuees here? I haven't heard anything.'

'Not every place is getting them. You may be lucky. People seem prepared to do anything to avoid having them. Poor Daphne used to be a most welcome visitor in all the houses hereabouts, but being a billeting officer has transformed her into a figure of terror. She says that when her car approaches, people positively flee through side doors and gardens. The authorities have evacuated simply thousands of people, so they must be expecting bombs and gas raids any day. It's all quite terrifying. I wish your mother could be persuaded to close up the house and come to the country. So much safer.'

'Paul and I were just saying the very same thing. But she says she's determined not to let Hitler disrupt her social life. It will take nothing short of a direct hit on Chelsea to persuade her to leave.'

'Such changes. All the men seem to be joining up. Dan has taken a commission in some regiment or other. He can't say where he's being posted, of course, but I've told him if it's anywhere convenient, he must come and visit whenever he's on leave. I suppose Paul will be thinking of joining up?'

'I imagine so. I suppose since he can fly a plane the air force will want him. Diana's terribly upset because Roddy intends to train as a pilot. For some reason she thinks he'd be safer in the army or the navy. I can't think why.'

Sonia turned to see Colin and Sidney clattering downstairs, rucking the carpet and dislodging a carpet stair rod. 'Oh dear, I'd hoped for a nice, long chat, but the boys are coming downstairs. I think I should go. Come over soon with Max, if you can. It's been such an age. Goodbye.' Sonia put down the receiver.

'Boys, boys! You must not run everywhere. There are precious things in this house, and we must have no breakages.'

Chastened, Colin and Sidney walked sedately through the house to the back, but as soon as they reached the rear door and freedom, they were off at a run, whooping and shouting.

Lobb was in the kitchen garden, tending his tomatoes, when the boys appeared.

'What'cher doin'?' asked Sidney, in not unfriendly tones.

Lobb straightened up and turned to look at Colin and Sidney. These must be the evacuees from London. Probably never seen so much as a lettuce growing in their lives. 'I'm looking after these here tomatoes.' The boys came closer to inspect the plants. Lobb picked two small tomatoes and gave one to each.

'Thanks,' said Colin. He indicated the tapering wigwam around which the runner beans had been trained. 'What's them?'

'Beans,' answered Lobb. 'I expect you'll be having some of them for your dinner tonight. I picked a whole basin for Cook not half an hour ago.' Gratified to have an audience, Lobb led the boys along the beds, pointing out different vegetables. 'Them's radishes. Carrots. This here' – he indicated a large area full of leafy green plants – 'is potatoes. If you're good lads, I might let you fork some up tomorrow. Like digging up treasure, nearabouts.'

Colin and Sidney liked the sound of this. 'What's them 'uns with all the black stuff round 'em?' asked Colin, pointing further down the garden. They moved along the path.

'That's celery.' From the pocket of his overall Lobb produced his gardening knife with its keen, stubby blade, and bent down to saw off a couple of sticks. 'The black stuff's soot from the chimney. I piles it round the crown of the plant to bring it on.' He handed each boy a stick.

Gingerly Sidney bit off a tiny fragment, tasted it, and spat it out.

'You won't be spitting it out if the Germans come,' said Lobb. 'Might be all you have to eat then.'

Colin, understanding the challenge, crunched reflectively.

'Not bad. I never had that before.' He eyed Lobb's gardening knife. 'That's a nippy blade.'

'Is that your dog?' asked Sidney, who had caught sight of a small mongrel dog snoozing in the sun, tied to a fence post by a thin length of rope. When the dog saw Lobb and the boys it sprang to its feet, dancing about and tugging at the rope. Lobb looked at it mournfully.

'Aye. My old dog died, and the farmer's wife, she gave me one out of a litter they had. It was kindly meant, but my old dog was happy to lie in the sun and take his ease, and this 'un, he's no more'n a pup, forever scampering about the garden and diggin' and chasin' things.' He shook his head. 'So I have to keep him tied up while I work.'

'What's his name?' asked Colin.

'I calls him Star, 'cause of the little mark he has – see there, just above his eye?' Lobb cocked his head on one side. 'Looks like a star to me, any roads.'

'Star,' breathed Colin. He crouched down and repeated the name coaxingly, and the pup leapt around in a frenzy of pleasure.

'We could look after him for you,' offered Sidney. He spoke casually, but his heart was beating hard. It had been the dream of his life to have a dog. His parents wouldn't hear of it, not in their cramped two-up, two-down in south-east London.

'Yes! An' we could train him, an' everything!' added Colin.

Lobb bent down and scratched the puppy's ears. 'You could, I s'pose.'

Colin's attention had been drawn by the sight of the barn at the end of the orchard.

'Whose house is that?' he asked.

'Bless yer, that's never a house. That's the barn. Mrs Haddon's husband – her husband as was – used it as somewhere to do his painting. He was a famous artist.'

'Can we play in them trees?' asked Colin, pointing to the orchard.

'I don't see why not,' said Lobb. 'Only don't go climbing 'em. Them apples isn't quite ready yet. You wait a week or two and you can help me pick 'em.'

'Can we go in the woods, too?'

'You can just about go anywhere, I guess. But stay away from the old well. That's out of bounds for you lads.'

Colin set off, shouting to his brother, 'Bags I be the cowboy!'

Sidney hesitated, feeling the need to consolidate matters regarding Star. 'We'll be back in a bit and take Star for a walk.'

Lobb shrugged. 'You can take him into the orchard with you, if you like. He can't do much harm there. He needs a run about.' He unfastened the rope from the pup's collar, and Star bounded forward. Sidney laughed in delight and set off at a run towards the orchard, Star scampering at his heels.

Lobb watched the boys and the pup haring through the orchard, dodging in and out of the trees. Then he shook his head and stumped back down the path to his work. Nice to have a bit of boy around the place for a change.

Avril was in the nursery helping Effie pack her trunk for her return to school. Hearing shouting and laughter outside, she went to the window and saw Colin and Sidney playing in the orchard with the puppy from the farm. They were throwing him a stick, which he kept retrieving joyfully. It looked like fun. She regretted now having been horrid to the evacuees at lunch. She had thought she didn't want strange children in her house, but she saw now that maybe it would be nice to have someone to play with.

She turned to Effie. 'I'm going outside to play.'

She went to the boot room and fished around among the tennis racquets and galoshes until she found an old tennis ball, and then she went to the kitchen and begged Mrs Goodall for a bagful of the cherries which she had seen Lobb bringing in earlier.

Colin and Sidney's laughter and chatter died away when they saw Avril approaching. They'd been told by their mum that they had to be polite to everyone in Mrs Haddon's house, but so far Avril had been bossy and rude and they didn't see any reason to be nice to her.

Avril held out the bag. 'Cook gave me some cherries. We can share, if you like.'

Sidney regarded her mistrustfully, but gave a grudging nod. 'Thanks.'

'And I found this indoors. It'll be much more fun for the puppy to chase than just a stick.' She tossed the tennis ball to Colin, who grabbed it gleefully. He held it up, and Star began to jump for it. Colin threw the ball across the orchard, and Star took off at full pelt, hurling himself on to the ball and bounding back with it in triumph.

'I'm gonna race him!' exclaimed Sidney, and got to his feet. He glanced at his brother. 'Ready?'

'Ready!' cried Colin, and launched the ball again. As soon as the ball left his brother's hand, boy and dog raced after it, and a moment later both were tumbling on the ground, the ball bouncing between them, Star yapping excitedly.

When the children had exhausted the pleasures of running through the orchard with Star, they cast around for other ways to entertain themselves.

'Let's go exploring,' suggested Colin. ''There's loads of places we haven't been yet.'

'What about that well?' said Sidney, for whom any forbidden thing or place possessed inevitable attraction.

'You're not allowed to go there,' said Avril.

'D'you know where it is?'

'Yes, but I'm not telling.'

'If you don't tell us, we won't let you play with us no more.'

'That's right. And we're looking after Star, so you won't be able to play with him, neither.'

Avril hesitated, then said, 'All right. Come on.'

She led them down towards the tennis court to the old well hidden by bushes near the path. Its stone sides were partially overgrown with ivy, and its mouth had been covered with a circular wooden lid which had been roughly nailed to two wooden battens on either side. Colin tugged experimentally at one side of the lid, and the rusted nails gave slightly.

'Come on,' he said to his brother. 'Let's find something to push it up with.'

Avril watched as the boys searched around for something strong to act as a lever. They found a stout-looking stick and after much pushing they managed to prise one side of the lid from its batten. Then it was the work of a moment to unhinge the other. The three children slid back the cover and bent over, looking down into the dark depths.

'Can't see nothin',' said Sidney.

'That's 'cause it's miles deep,' said Colin. He picked up a stone. 'I read in a book you can tell how deep a well is by counting how long it takes for a stone to reach the water.' He held the stone up. 'Start counting, but not too loud, or we won't hear it.'

He held up the stone, and as soon as he dropped it, Avril and Sidney began to count in hushed whispers. They reached six before they heard the distant, faint splash. They stared at one another with wide eyes.

'See?' said Colin.

'But you still don't know *how* deep it is,' Avril pointed out.

'Jolly deep,' retorted Colin.

They amused themselves by shouting into the depths of the well and listening to their voices echoing back, until the muffled tones of the gong could be heard summoning them to tea. 'Come on,' said Avril, 'we've got to go in. We'd better cover it up.'

They lifted the wooden lid and slid it clumsily back into place, then sped off through the trees to the house.

As autumn turned to winter, the anticipated German assaults did not materialise. There was no rain of fire, no poison gas attacks. A strange lull set in, during which people began to relax and wonder what all the fuss had been about.

'To think I rushed out and bought all the things on the ARP list on the very first day,' Helen complained to Sonia in a telephone call. 'The blackout is a fearful bore – it's so difficult to get about now that it gets dark early. Delia Compton was almost run down by a man on a bicycle with no lights the other night. There have been any number of accidents. And getting a taxi is simply impossible. Apparently there's no blackout in Paris. It's quite beyond me why we have to blunder about in the dark while the French don't.'

Sonia agreed that the blackout was a nuisance, but her main complaint was with the servant situation. 'Dilys is leaving next week to work in a munitions factory, and Grace is going off to be a Land Girl. No doubt William will be joining up, too. That will leave me with just Effie and Mrs Goodall and the kitchen maid, and the whole house to run and keep clean. Mercifully Lobb is too old to be called up. All the houses around here are losing staff.'

'That makes it difficult with your evacuees, I suppose.'

'I doubt if they will be with us much longer. Mrs Jennings wants the boys back home for Christmas. To think we all thought bombs would come raining down on us first thing. I suppose we should be grateful.'

The first months of 1940 saw England's worst winter in living memory. The cold was bitter, the ground frozen solid. In late January snow began to fall; not the usual picturesque inch or two adorning the fields and trees and mantling the landscape, but heavy fleets of thick, scudding flakes that blinded the eyes and stung the skin, piling in great drifts against houses and barns, blocking roads and lanes, burying sheep. Woodbourne House was entirely cut off. The snow, which was feet deep, made the road to the village impassable and brought the telephone lines down. The lorry delivering coke couldn't get through, and so the boiler went out and the pipes froze. Without central heating the house became arctic, and its inhabitants piled on layers of clothes. Sonia wore her fur coat at all times. Domino and Rufus buried themselves beneath Sonia's eiderdown and gazed out on the world with mournful eyes. The feeble electric heaters in the bedrooms scarcely made any impact on the chill.

But with adversity came resilience and ingenuity. Sonia and Effie went out each day and broke off icicles, which they carried back to the house in pails to melt and boil in kettles and pans so that there was water for the household. Because the cisterns were frozen, jugs of melted snow had to be used to flush the toilets. In the kitchen, without Mrs Goodall and the usual deliveries of bread, milk and meat, and with Lobb's vegetables frozen in the ground, Sonia's culinary powers of invention were put to the test. She rose to the challenge with determined energy, and with the help of a cookery book and her own imagination managed to make loaves of bread with flour and dried yeast and condensed milk, and to create edible meals from bully beef and canned vegetables.

The coal supply had not entirely run out, which was a blessing, for Laura came down with bronchitis and the nursery had to be turned into a sickroom, with a fire burning day and night. On one of her forays outdoors for icicles, clad in fur coat, headscarf, woollen cap and gumboots, Sonia came across a store of logs in a shed, put there by Lobb after he had felled two diseased apple trees in the orchard the previous autumn. She carried the logs back in armfuls, stacking them up in the kitchen porch, and in the evenings they made a bright, fragrant blaze in the drawing room.

Sonia spent much of her time nursing Laura, sponging her hot little body and applying the mustard poultices which Mrs Goodall prepared and swore by. While the little girl slept, she would sit by her bedside, stroking the soft, fair curls of hair from her burning forehead, wishing with her whole soul that she could take the burden of her illness upon herself. How she longed for Dr Egan's help. Damp compresses and Friar's Balsam could only do so much. She was grateful that Avril was safe and warm in her boarding school in Kent.

On the day that Lobb managed to make his way through the snow from the village with some bread and milk for the besieged household, Laura's fever broke, her temperature came down, and everyone breathed a sigh of relief. She grew well enough to sit up and sup the little dishes of porridge and honey which Mrs Goodall made for her, and Sonia read her nursery rhymes and fairy stories, to which Laura listened with grave, attentive eyes.

The long spell of snow had a transformative effect not just on the landscape, but on Sonia, one which lasted long after the weather broke and life returned to normal. Never again, she decided, would she ring for breakfast in bed. Not while the war lasted. The business of meals being taken in three different parts of the house – the nursery, the dining room and the kitchen – must come to an end. No one had the time or energy to maintain such a state of affairs. During the snow siege, when the dining room was too cold to be inhabited, they had all eaten together in the warmth of the kitchen at the large scrubbed wooden table, the same table on which vegetables were chopped, dough kneaded and pastry rolled on a daily basis, and for Sonia the arrangement had proved enlightening. When contact was resumed with the outside world, she decreed that henceforth the household would amalgamate and everyone would eat their meals together in the kitchen. The artisanal comfort and practicality chimed with the mood of the times, and she felt liberated by its informality. She was able to observe and appreciate at first hand the work Mrs Goodall did in grim circumstances, and the conversations they had over cups of tea together had given her a perspective on life which was both humbling and inspiring.

At first Mrs Goodall was not entirely at ease with the arrangement. She had a sense of the right order of things; the mistress should reign upstairs in the drawing room and morning room, dictating the life of the household, and the servants below should put her orders into practice and ensure that all ran smoothly. The kitchen was her kingdom, and she did not welcome any intrusion, even that of her mistress. But when she saw that Sonia did not mean to interfere, and that the new arrangement meant less fetching and carrying and greater convenience for all concerned, she accepted it. Over the years she and Sonia had developed a relationship of mutual respect, and now to that appreciation was added the warmth of friendship. For the adversities of war and its effects on the household were something they had to deal with jointly.

With the advent of rationing, Sonia decided that the grounds of Woodbourne House must be put to good use to provide as much of the household's needs as possible. She set Lobb to digging up extra land to grow more fruit and vegetables, and the greenhouse, where in previous years Lobb nurtured bedding plants for the summer garden, was given over to the cultivation of tomatoes and cucumbers, and pots of vegetable seedlings for the kitchen garden.

Sonia worked alongside Lobb, planting and thinning out seedlings, tending the new vegetables, and keeping the beds weeded, while Domino and Rufus snuffled around nearby. For this she found her trailing frocks and bead necklaces impractical, and so she bought instead a few pairs of French linen trousers and workmanlike Viyella shirts, and wound silk scarves into fetching and practical turbans to wear while she toiled among the trenches of peas and rows of cabbages.

One day in early summer, after a long afternoon spent putting canes next to the new tomato plants and tying them off, Sonia went indoors, unlaced her boots and padded through to her sitting room, where Effie had laid out tea. It was the one indulgence of the old regime which she permitted herself. Teatime for

Sonia was a small, civilised landmark in the day, one which signified the proper order of things. The sight of her Meissen chinaware, with its filigree edges and delicate pattern of blue flowers, never failed to delight and reassure her. She poured a cup of tea, added milk, and put a slice of Mrs Goodall's seed cake on a plate. Then she switched on the wireless, and while she waited for it to warm up she drew up a footstool and settled into her armchair, stretching out her legs. She listened to the news while she had her tea. It was all dreadful. The Germans had entered Brussels and taken Antwerp. First Holland, she thought, now Belgium. France would doubtless be next. Soon Britain would be all alone. The idea made her feel cold and afraid. The news was followed by a broadcast by the new prime minister, Mr Churchill. Sonia drained the dregs of her tea as she listened to his growling tones.

'We have become the sole champions now in arms to defend the world cause... We shall defend our Island home, and with the British Empire we shall fight on unconquerable until the curse of Hitler is lifted from the brows of mankind. We are sure that in the end all will come right.'

Sonia closed her eyes, and repeated the words in a murmur. 'In the end all will come right.' It was what everyone had to believe now.

3

SONIA'S SELF-SUFFICIENCY DRIVE continued throughout that year and into the next. In the autumn she had a chicken run erected next to the tennis court, so that they would have a plentiful supply of eggs, and in the spring of '41 a pigsty was built near the orchard. She bought six pigs from a local farmer for fifteen shillings, and persuaded Daphne Davenport and a few other local householders to supply household scraps to fatten them, in return for a share of the ham and bacon when they were eventually slaughtered.

'We shall have all we need and to spare, I hope,' she told Mrs Goodall, 'and if we can help others in the neighbourhood, so much the better.'

In the early years of the war Meg, too, made great strides in the management of the Hazelhurst household. With the aid of recipe books borrowed from Anna Kentleigh's cook, and help from Lotte, she became a proficient cook, and she and Lotte managed all the meals between them, while Enid carried out the domestic chores. The vegetable garden which had been laid out three years earlier was now fully productive and Meg, like Sonia, enjoyed the hours she spent in it.

To everyone's surprise, Paul did not go into uniform. It was generally understood that he was being employed by the government in some capacity, but as it was all very hush-hush no one, least of all Meg, had any idea of the precise nature of his work, save that it took him away from Hazelhurst for long spells.

The dog cart was Meg's idea. She enjoyed having friends from London to stay – many of them were only too happy to snatch a week in the country, away from the blackout and the air-raid sirens – but often there wasn't enough petrol for her to pick them up from the station, and Alderworth lay just beyond the ten-mile limit imposed on taxis.

'I scarcely have time these days to ride Grisette much,' she told Paul, 'and she's getting fat munching grass out there all day. Why can't we use her to fix something up, like a pony and trap? Then the taxi can take people as far as the pub in Frimley, and I can trot Grisette out and fetch them.'

Paul was dubious at first, but he asked around, and eventually procured a second-hand back-to-back cart from a local farmer. Dixon, who had yet to receive his call-up papers, managed to find a driving harness and taught Meg how to harness Grisette to the cart. Grisette, after a twitchy start, eventually took obediently enough to the novel business of pulling something, and soon the dog cart, with Meg at the reins, was a regular sight along the roads around Alderworth.

One of its first passengers was Helen, whom Meg had invited to stay for a few days. She hadn't needed much persuading. She was down to one cook-maid – and a not very good one, at that – and the constant bombing raids meant that life in London was grim. The food would be better at Hazelhurst, she reasoned; country people had the wherewithal to make up for the inadequacies of rationing. The beds were good, too, and she hadn't seen her grandson for a while.

Helen took care to buy a first-class train ticket, but even so, she found the journey trying. The first-class carriage was full, with no room to spread one's belongings, and she was able to squeeze only her suitcase on to the luggage rack, and had to sit with her gas mask case on her lap, together with her handbag, which made reading her book difficult. The train was teeming with soldiers in their heavy boots and khaki uniforms, packing every corridor with their unwieldy kit, including that of the first-class carriage. They made such a racket that Helen had no peace at all on the journey. When she reached Ascot, she did as instructed by Meg and took a taxi to Frimley, and was deposited outside the Star and Garter public house. There she waited, and ten minutes later Meg came round the corner in the dog cart.

Although Meg had mentioned this new form of conveyance in passing, Helen hadn't expected to be met in it.

'Heavens,' she said. 'Am I to get into this contraption? I thought you'd be meeting me in the car.'

'I go everywhere in this,' said Meg cheerfully, as she stowed her mother's belongings and helped her up. 'We mustn't waste petrol, and besides, it's a lovely way to travel now spring's here.'

Helen said nothing. It might be mid-May, but in her view summer had not yet properly arrived, and it was still too chilly to make travelling in the open comfortable. Besides, she didn't feel entirely safe, perched aloft. After five minutes or so of bowling along the country road, however, she began to feel less precarious, and decided that riding in a cart was rather pleasant. She hadn't done it since she was a girl. She took a deep breath of spring air and gazed around at the countryside, the bright, new green of the hedgerows, and thought how good it was to be away from London for a while. So peaceful. So clean.

During her visit Helen was struck by how casual life at Hazelhurst had become. It seemed to her that Meg's relationships with Lotte and Enid were now unduly familiar; one would scarcely have guessed that they were the servants and she the mistress. Everyone seemed to be getting along in a most rough-and-ready fashion. Standards, she supposed, were bound to slip in wartime, but it seemed a pity.

'Don't worry, Mother, I won't expect you to pitch in,' said Meg, when on the first night Helen expressed surprise that Meg should be in the kitchen peeling and chopping vegetables for their evening meal.

'Oh, I'm only too happy to lend a hand. Everyone must do their bit,' murmured Helen. 'Though I suspect I might be better off catching up with my knitting than getting in your way in here.' She added with a touch of pride, 'I'm knitting service woollens. I've done five sleeveless pullovers in the past month.'

'How splendid. I do wish I could knit as well as you. Perhaps when you have time you can knit something for Max?'

'I'd be happy to,' said Helen. She inspected the ingredients Meg was preparing. 'This all looks very nice. What are we having?'

'Rabbit pie and spring vegetables. Dixon catches the rabbits. He's shown me how to skin and butcher them. It's quite easy.'

'Really?' murmured Helen faintly. 'By the way, where's Paul? I haven't seen him since I got here.'

'He's away. He'll be back tomorrow night.'

'Still gallivanting off and leaving you here to fend for yourself?'

'I'm perfectly capable of running Hazelhurst myself, Mother. And he's not gallivanting, as you call it. He has government work to attend to.'

'I should have thought he'd be more use in uniform. He knows how to fly a plane, and we need people with that kind of ability.'

To this Meg said nothing. The suggestion that Paul was not doing his bit rankled enormously. The admiration and respect she felt for her husband, mixed with her fear and need to be protected, had formed themselves into a defensive version of love. This in turn was tied into her feelings about her country, her sense of patriotism. She identified Paul, and all he stood for, with England. She could not bear any implied slight regarding his loyalty. Seeing that Meg was not inclined to continue the conversation, Helen departed for the drawing room and her knitting.

A visit to Woodbourne House was planned towards the end of the week.

'I hope you have enough petrol for the car,' said Helen. 'I don't think I should enjoy going all that way by horse and cart.'

'Of course we'll take the car. That is, if we've enough coupons for the petrol. Paul's been driving it quite a bit recently. I'd better go and check.'

Meg went to Paul's study and opened the desk drawer. Only two coupons remained for the rest of the month, which would buy a couple of gallons. Depending on how much fuel there was still in the tank, it should be enough for the trip there and back – just. As she was about to close the drawer, she glanced at the neat pile of buff folders on Paul's desk. She often wondered exactly what it was he worked away at. Aware that she shouldn't, she flicked open the top one, and saw a typed page headed *Memorandum* and stamped with the startling words *Top Secret*. She was about to close it when her eye was caught by a name she recognised in the first paragraph. The mysterious Mr Bettany, yet again. Feeling like a guilty schoolgirl, she scanned the memo quickly – it said something about the Government Code and Cypher School at Bletchley Park, and then something else about penetration of German intelligence. At that moment she heard footsteps in the hall outside. Paul came into the study seconds after she had closed the folder.

She closed the drawer. 'Just checking how many petrol coupons we have. Sonia has invited us to Woodbourne House on Friday.'

'The tank's half full. You shouldn't have any problem.' Paul moved towards the desk. 'I'm afraid I won't be able to join you. I have to go back up to London tomorrow.' He opened a cupboard in the desk, picked up the buff folders and put them inside, then locked it.

Meg felt a momentary guilt. Had he seen her looking in the folder? No, she had closed it before he even opened the door. She had long ago dismissed Dan's ridiculous allegations about Paul and Arthur Bettany, but there was evidently some connection. She told herself she must put it from her mind. She'd had no business looking in the folder.

'That's a pity,' she said. 'Never mind. I'll give her your love.'

*

If Helen had been taken aback by the altered life at Hazelhurst, she was even more astonished by the changes at Woodbourne House, particularly Sonia's functional new mode of dress.

'You look quite the land girl, my dear,' she observed, when Sonia came round from the kitchen garden to greet them. Sonia was wearing dark green overalls rolled to the knee, leather boots, a short-sleeved cotton shirt, and her hair was bound up in a fetching turban made out of a Liberty scarf, which perfectly matched her overalls.

'All in the name of practicality,' replied Sonia briskly. 'One can't plant potatoes in a frock and heels.'

Helen accepted this mildly snubbing reference to her own smart suit and town shoes with a sisterly smile and a fond kiss. Sonia greeted three-year-old Max with rapture. 'What a handsome boy you're becoming! Would you like to see my pigs?' Max nodded.

'Pigs!' exclaimed Helen.

'Yes, I keep three Berkshires and two Oxford Sandy and Blacks. They're quite docile breeds, which is important, since Lobb and I do all the work of looking after them. Pig-keeping can be quite a strenuous business, you know. Come along, I'll show you our wartime improvements, and then we'll have lunch.'

'Good heavens, what's happened to your lovely lawn?' asked Helen, as the party made its way round the side of the house. The perfectly manicured lawn which had once stretched from the gardens to the edge of the tennis court was now a swathe of uncut grass rippling in the breeze beneath the chestnut tree.

'It will be turned into hay for local horses in late summer,' said Sonia, who was enjoying the moral superiority which came with her self-sufficiency; she and Helen had always been competitive. 'I can tell Lobb is itching to get going with the motor mower. He was always so proud of his lawn, but I tell him that sacrifices have to be made.'

When the pigs and chickens had been duly admired, everyone went inside for lunch.

'I've closed off the dining room,' said Sonia, as they went through the back of the house into the kitchen. 'I decided there's simply no point in trekking meals from one part of the house to another. We eat in the kitchen now. So convivial, don't you think? And most of our food is *en casserole*. We are quite a by-word in simplicity, aren't we, Mrs Goodall?'

'Indeed we are, ma'am,' replied Mrs Goodall.

'Well,' said Helen, as she regarded the dishes which Lily brought to the table, 'you certainly live rather better here in the country than us poor folk in the city. Food rations go simply nowhere there.' She was secretly relieved to see that Mrs Goodall and Effie did not intend to sit down with them. That would be taking things too far.

After lunch Meg went for a walk with Laura and Max, while Sonia and Helen sat in Sonia's drawing room and had a long talk.

They drove back to Alderworth at teatime, Max asleep in his grandmother's arms.

'I know they're absolutely vital, but all these new aerodromes do rather spoil the countryside,' observed Helen, gazing through the car window. 'How is Diana? Didn't you say her husband is with the RAF?'

'Yes, he's a flight lieutenant. He's somewhere in the Midlands. Diana's staying at a hotel nearby. She goes everywhere he's stationed. She can't bear to be away from him.'

'Of course, they've only been married a year or two,' mused Helen. 'But she should give some thought to taking a job. I think I might.'

Meg glanced at her mother in surprise. 'Aren't you a bit old?'

'I'm only forty-eight, Meg. Hardly ancient. As a matter of fact, seeing what you and Sonia are doing has made me realise that I'm just sitting there in London, neither use nor ornament – except for knitting a few jumpers – when I could be doing so much more. All my energy is going to waste, now that I don't have a proper household to run any more. I think I shall join the WVS.'

'Well, good for you,' said Meg with a smile.

'I rather pride myself on organising people and getting things done. I'm sure I can make a worthwhile contribution.' Besides which, thought Helen, it would help to deflate her elder sister's balloon of moral superiority, and show her that she wasn't the only one who could roll her sleeves up and get stuck in.

4

DURING ONE OF his spells of leave, Dan decided to go round to his rooms in Bloomsbury and pick up a few items which he had been meaning to collect. He still had a key, and while he thought it unlikely that Arthur would be in at that time of day, it seemed impolite just to let himself in. He trotted upstairs and rapped lightly on the door, not expecting an answer, latchkey at the ready. A few seconds later Arthur answered the door. He was clearly surprised to see Dan and, although he made an effort to smile, not best pleased.

'Ranscombe – what are you doing here?'

'I just stopped by to pick up a few of my things.' There was a pause. 'I may come in, mayn't I?'

'Of course.' Arthur stood aside.

'Just my chess set and a few books—' Dan broke off as he came into the living room. There, seated comfortably by the window in the red plush armchair, his pipe in one hand, a glass of Scotch in the other, was Paul. He greeted Dan amiably.

'Hello there,' said Dan. 'This is a surprise.'

'I was just on my way back from the British Library when I bumped into Bettany here. He invited me up for a drink. Very decent set of rooms you have.' Dan thought he detected a faintly patronising tone. Paul took a pull on his pipe. 'Won't you join us for a drink?'

Dan hesitated for the merest second. The fact of finding Paul and Arthur Bettany alone together could have rekindled his old suspicions, but the lack of furtiveness or embarrassment, and the unforced, casual manner of both men, belied the idea that this was a sexual rendezvous. Nonetheless, it seemed curious.

'Don't mind if I do.' He took off his cap and settled himself in a chair, while Arthur uncapped the Scotch and poured out a measure. 'Just a splash of soda, thanks.'

'What's your regiment?' asked Paul, as Arthur handed Dan his drink and resumed his seat.

'Middlesex.'

'Much going on?'

'Not really. I'm stationed down in Surrey at the moment, which makes it handy for getting over to Woodbourne House on the odd leave. I suppose it's the closest thing I have to a proper home these days.' Dan caught Arthur's sharp glance. 'Don't worry. I'm not hankering to have the rooms back. Now that I'm no longer working in Fleet Street, I doubt I ever shall.'

'War's got to come to an end sometime,' observed Paul.

'Yes, but the big question is when, and how.'

'Surely you don't harbour the treasonable thought that Germany might prevail?' said Arthur, with a dry smile designed to indicate the facetiousness of his remark. 'Though I imagine there are any number of people, even in the clubs of St James's, who are privately preparing for such a possibility and quietly trying to devise ways of making a German victory work to their personal advantage.'

'I disagree,' replied Paul. 'For the British people the idea of anything short of victory is inconceivable. I think the mood of the nation is confident and strong.'

'I read an interesting article by Orwell on the subject of patriotism the other day,' observed Dan. 'He takes the view that all pacifists are essentially pro-Fascist. If you hamper the war effort you automatically help the Germans.'

'That's one way of looking at it,' said Paul. 'But you could also argue that those who fight against Fascism become Fascists themselves, in the long run. It's an interesting paradox. Rather like the way we lock up pacifists and conscientious objectors. There's a certain irony in putting a man in prison for his religious beliefs when we're at war with a totalitarian regime, don't you think?'

'I suppose so. But I don't have much sympathy with those fellows. If you're a citizen, you shouldn't be entitled simply to chuck up your responsibility to the state in time of need just because you don't believe in war.'

'Well, that's the basic issue, isn't it? Not everyone believes war is the right way to defeat Fascism.'

Arthur Bettany took out his cigarette case and offered it to Dan. 'Do you know what Benjamin Britten said when he was asked what he would do if his country was invaded?' He chuckled as he lit Dan's cigarette. 'He said, "I believe in letting the invader in and setting him a good example."'

'I can't say I share that particular philosophy,' observed Paul. 'But I'm more tolerant of the pacifists than Orwell. We're fighting for freedom of conscience, after all, aren't we?'

'The freedom of conscience to be a Nazi sympathiser?' asked Dan.

'To be Oswald Mosley, if you like. Anyhow, not all Fascists are anti-Semites. And just because you admire certain things about Germany – for instance, I think the fact they have no speed limits is quite wonderful – well, that doesn't make me a Fascist.'

'But surely it's not what you think about Germany and the Germans that matters – it's how you feel about your own country, and whether you think Britain and our way of life is worth defending.'

'Of course, that's right. Though it's a mistake to confuse patriotism with nationalism. I think most British people are deeply patriotic, but they're not nationalistic in the blinkered way of the German people. You could never rise far in politics in this country by promising the people military glories and victories, the way Hitler has. The British are fighting for things they can scarcely identify. Little things that make us who we are. Not for glory or power over other nations. Just to be allowed to get on with things the way we always have.' Paul puffed on his pipe for a moment. 'Speaking of Orwell, I remember reading something he wrote once about being English, and it stayed with me. "The suet puddings and the red pillar-boxes have entered into your soul." Perhaps he meant it sardonically, but it's true. It's not just the things you love about your country, but the things you take for granted and only ever half-notice. A way of life. That's what it's about for most of us.'

There was silence for a moment, then Arthur said, 'I say, Latimer, do you remember that time at school when you and Beeston confiscated a box of Sobranie Black Russian that I'd filched from home? Whatever happened to them? I was abominably put out about losing those.'

'We smoked 'em, of course,' said Paul. All three men laughed.

From here the conversation drifted into schoolday reminiscences, then after fifteen minutes or so Dan glanced at his watch and drained his glass. 'I'm afraid I have to be getting back.'

'Sure you won't stay for another?'

'No thanks.' He rose and picked up his cap. Arthur refilled his own and Paul's glass. 'If I might just…?' Dan indicated a cabinet on the other side of the room.

'Oh, by all means.' Arthur stepped aside to let Dan fetch his chess set and some books.

'Good to see you,' said Paul.

'Yes. Give my best to Meg and Diana.'

'I shall, thanks.'

With a nod to Arthur, Dan left the flat. Whatever the nature of Paul and Arthur's relationship, thought Dan, as he made his way downstairs, there was definitely more to it than a chance encounter at the British Library. One could sense some kind of intrigue between them. Perhaps he had been right all along. Poor deluded Meg. If only she had believed him.

*

When Dan's battalion received orders to leave for an unknown destination the following week, the general assumption among the troops was that they were being sent abroad to fight, and there was a sense of exhilaration and trepidation, heightened by the fact that the move was to be made at night and in secrecy. But their destination turned out to be to Scarborough, and coastal defence work, laying coils of barbed wire along slipways and beaches, erecting pillboxes and anti-tank gun emplacements, digging trenches, and laying landmines. Their quarters were an abandoned holiday camp, and Scarborough itself, on evenings when it was possible to go into town, offered limited attractions. Dan preferred to stay in the mess after dinner and drink with his friend and fellow soldier, Brendan O'Connell. Brendan was a twenty-five-year-old Dubliner, six foot three and built like a prizefighter, who on the outbreak of war had been a teacher in a boys' prep school. Although the tutelage of small boys might have appeared an unlikely vocation for a man with his temperament and appetite for drinking, Dan considered Brendan's gentle earnestness and abidingly savage longing to kill as many Germans as possible perfectly compatible. He was intelligent and humorous, and he and Dan had become close friends. Brendan had done a good deal of soul-searching before leaving Ireland to volunteer his services to the British army, but in the end he had decided de Valera was wrong to keep Ireland neutral. For Brendan, the Nazi menace was one that threatened all of the West, and to fight that menace with force of arms seemed not only right but necessary. He had fought with the Republicans in the Spanish Civil War, and as he put it to Dan, 'I set out to fight Fascism, right enough, and I don't bloody well intend to leave the job half-finished.'

One evening, at the end of a particularly tedious day spent counting telegraph poles and overseeing the erection of a pillbox which was to be disguised as an ice cream kiosk to house the detonator plunger for the harbour mines, they sat in the mess with their drinks, mulling over their work. The evacuation of troops from Dunkirk the previous year, and the sense that Britain was now fighting alone, added to their desperate sense of frustration at not being involved in active combat.

'I don't want to spend the rest of this war like some glorified navvy, digging trenches and carting sandbags.' Brendan shook his head in disgust. 'It's not what I joined up for.'

There was a moment's silence, and then Dan asked, 'Have you heard of a thing called special operations?'

Brendan took a swig of his beer. 'Can't say I have. Is that like, what, spying?'

'No, not that. More like raiding parties – you know, carrying out covert operations, taking the enemy by surprise, that kind of thing.'

'Like the German Storm Troops?'

'Exactly. Churchill reckoned they worked so well for them in the last war that he's ordered the formation of a similar outfit here.' There was another silence, and Dan added, 'I'm thinking of volunteering.'

Brendan nodded. 'Is that so?' He sat reflecting. 'Dangerous work. Going behind enemy lines, maybe? Guerrilla operations?'

'That kind of thing.'

Brendan raised his glass and tipped it in Dan's direction with a grin. 'Sounds like it beats putting up tank barriers at the seaside. Where do we sign up?'

A week later Dan and Brendan found themselves in a remote training camp in the Scottish Highlands. The regime was beyond anything Dan had envisaged. The volunteers were sent out with heavy equipment on punishing marches across mountain ranges, they swam icy rivers in full kit, slept in ditches, and tackled fearsome assault courses. They were trained in unarmed combat, and learned to cross terrain unseen and unheard at night, and to build bridges and rafts. A week was spent under canvas on the remoter slopes of Ben Nevis, learning to ski, prompting Brendan to observe that only in Scotland could one expect to ski in the British Isles in summer The training was relentless and continued day and night, teaching the men how to live and fight in the harshest of conditions. Every man there knew that if he failed to rise to the challenges he would be returned to his unit, and no one wanted that ignominy. Dan had thought himself physically pretty fit, but it quickly became evident to him that he would have to muster every reserve of energy and determination to succeed. Brendan, big and powerful as he was, found it less taxing; without his camaraderie and good humour, Dan wasn't sure that he could have made it through the six weeks. But on the final exercise, a simulated beach landing at night using live ammunition, Dan was exhilaratingly conscious of the level to which his powers of speed, strength and awareness had developed, and he knew he would pass muster.

When the training was over, Dan and Brendan were sent on a fortnight's leave, ahead of their first, as yet unknown operation. Brendan went home to his family in Dublin, Dan to his club in London. The relief of sleeping between fresh sheets and eating food that wasn't cooked over an open fire in a raw wind was exquisite, and Dan spent the first day relishing the comforts of civilisation before getting in touch with Harry. They met, as usual, in the Wheatsheaf.

'You've lost weight,' remarked Harry. 'And you're in civvies. Where have you been for the last few weeks?'

'Just training.'

Harry brooded. 'I've had my call-up papers, so I'll have to pack in the magazine until the war is over. Hard to find contributors these days, anyhow. Or subscribers, come to that. Oh, by the way, something you should know – Bettany's left town. I'm assuming he's been called up, but no one seems sure. Shadowy figure at the best of times. You might want to check up on your rooms.'

'Thanks, I will,' said Dan. 'Not that I've any use for them, now that I have my father's old place in Belgravia. Though frankly I prefer staying at my club.'

'Nice to have the choice,' observed Harry.

Dan left the pub an hour later and walked up to Bloomsbury. Mrs Woodbead, when he knocked on her door, greeted him with a mixture of relief and indignation.

'Mr Ranscombe! Perhaps now someone will tell me what's going on. Your friend Mr Bettany upped and left a fortnight back, without so much as a by-your-leave. I'm down two weeks' rent, and I need to know what's what. Are you coming back, or am I to find a new tenant?'

'I'm afraid I've no use for the rooms, Mrs W, not now I'm in the army. I'm sorry my friend left without notice. I'll tell you what – I'll pay you the two weeks' rent you've lost, and I'll move the rest of my things out. That way you can find a new tenant quick as you like.'

'It might not be that easy to find someone in a hurry, not the way things are.'

'All right – a month's rent. How does that sound?'

'That's very fair of you, I'm sure.' She watched as Dan took some notes from his wallet. 'We all live in straitened times,' she added, folding the notes and tucking them inside her blouse.

'Indeed we do. I'll pop upstairs and fetch my things, then drop the key off.'

'Thank you, Mr Ranscombe. It's been a pleasure having you as a tenant. Even if your friend did light off rather sudden.'

He and Mrs Woodbead shook hands cordially, then he went upstairs to his flat and let himself in. Bettany had decamped, leaving no trace of himself behind, save for a dusty trilby hat on top of the wardrobe. Dan had removed most of his belongings to the house in Belgravia before Arthur had moved in, and the furniture belonged to Mrs Woodbead. There were only a few personal items of his left, such as books and some pictures. He found a small holdall stuffed in the back of the wardrobe and put everything into it. On the way downstairs he slipped the latchkey through Mrs Woodbead's letterbox. Funny, Bettany disappearing like that, thought Dan as he left the square. No doubt the army had claimed him, as it was claiming everyone these days.

He went to Belgravia to drop off the holdall. Since his father's death he had been there only a few times, and the place smelt musty with disuse. He wandered through the rooms. Most of the furniture was draped in dustsheets, but he had managed to put up blackout curtains in the kitchen, the drawing room and his own bedroom. He had no idea what he would do with the house. It was the last place on earth he wanted to spend his leave, so it would just have to sit here, empty, for the time being. Maybe he would sell it after the war. Unless the Germans won and took over everything.

When he got back to his room at the club, he suddenly remembered the mail he had picked up from the hall porter on the day of his arrival. He'd been so tired that he hadn't even bothered to look at it before climbing into bed, and thereafter it had lain forgotten on the mantelpiece. He scanned the handwriting on the envelopes. Two from Sonia – he would have to call her, perhaps try to get down to Woodbourne House before his leave was up – and one from Eve. He felt a weight of guilt, but most particularly in relation to Eve. He had fallen into the habit of looking her up occasionally when he was on leave, taking her out, sleeping with her, fully expecting her to be there at his convenience every time. He scarcely ever wrote. It was shoddy behaviour, but she didn't seem to mind. Or if she did, she hadn't said so yet. Perhaps this letter would be reproaching him for not having been in touch for almost two months. He ripped it open. There was just one hastily scribbled page, asking him to call her the next time he was in London, and adding, 'I need to speak to you. I have something important to tell you.'

Dan was intrigued. He rang down to the hall porter and asked him to put a call through to the *Herald*'s offices.

'Eve? It's Dan. Sorry I haven't been in touch. I only came back the other day. I got your note. What's all this about needing to speak to me urgently?'

'Well, first of all, thanks for saying how much you've missed me.'

'I've missed you unbearably.' The lie was easy. And, in a way, he had. He'd missed having a woman, any woman.

'Thanks.'

'So, what's all this about?'

'Why don't you do the decent thing and invite me to dinner? Then I'll tell you.'

'Where would you like to go?'

'It's an age since I went anywhere nice. Why don't we have dinner at Quaglino's and then go on to Ciro's after?'

'You live for pleasure alone.' He glanced at his watch. 'Quaglino's at eight. I'll book a table. And look beautiful.'

'Don't I always?'

Dan ran a bath and lay soaking for a while, inspecting his now extremely well-muscled body. It was still something of a novelty to him. Smiling at the thought of how Eve would react to it, and also at his own spectacular vanity, he put out his cigarette in the soap dish, slid down the bath, and ducked his head beneath the water.

Eve scanned the menu at Quaglino's. 'Don't you simply love the fact that oysters aren't rationed?'

'I suppose there's not much mines and U-boats can do to damage that particular market,' replied Dan, lighting a cigarette. 'What will you have to follow?'

'The poached salmon, I suppose. How I wish we could have steak. I'm meat-starved. We all are. I'm sure I'm becoming anaemic.'

'You look pretty well to me.' He gave the waiter their orders, then said, 'Now, what's this important thing you have to tell me?'

'First things first.' She held up her glass. 'To us.'

'Us?'

'Britain. The war. Victory.'

'Oh, indeed. Bottoms up to all that.' He took a swig of champagne. 'Now, fire away.'

'Well, you remember my friend Alice Bauer?'

'Yes. I forgot to thank you for putting me in touch with her. She passed me a lot of useful information. At considerable risk to herself, I might add.'

'She would. She's not exactly overfond of the Nazis.' Eve reached into her handbag and drew out a piece of paper. 'She sent me this recently.'

'What is it?'

'It's a list of names drawn up by German intelligence. Some party official gave it to her. It contains the names of certain British citizens whom the Nazis regard as sympathetic to their cause. She sent it to me because I'm someone she trusts, and as I'm a journalist she thought I could make sure it reaches the right hands. I thought you should see it first.' She slid the piece of paper across the table to Dan. 'Paul Latimer's name is on it.'

Dan gave a short laugh. 'What? Paul, a fifth-columnist? I hardly think so.' He took the paper and opened it, scanning the names. There it was. Paul Hugo Latimer, co-owner of a racing car team. It couldn't be anyone else. He looked up at Eve. 'Someone's got the wrong end of the stick. He has – or had – certain connections in Germany, admittedly. But so do lots of people. Things can easily be misinterpreted.'

'I have to say I was rather surprised myself. It doesn't square with anything one knows of Paul.'

The waiter arrived with a tray of a dozen oysters. Eve squeezed lemon juice over them and helped herself to a couple, while Dan studied the list again. It was doubtless authentic. Alice's sources had always been impeccable. But there had to be some innocent explanation as to why Paul's name was there. Looked at logically, something as trivial as his friendship with Dick Seaman could have sparked the idea. Not only had Seaman, a British citizen, gone to live in Germany and married a German woman, he'd given the Nazi salute on the podium after some Grand Prix when Hitler was present, according to Rudi. Perhaps Paul had been at that Grand Prix. In fact, he very probably had. Rudi's stupid joke that night in the Adlon bar, when he'd asked Paul if he was a Nazi, showed how easily one could make a false connection. There had been more than a few people within eavesdropping distance that evening, too. Dan recalled the frozen expression with which Paul had greeted the joke, and felt a faint misgiving. He'd assumed Paul's look had been one of distaste, but it could just as easily have been something else altogether. He knew that Paul was involved in government work, but the idea that he was a covert Nazi sympathiser seemed too ridiculous. He thought of the things Paul had said a few weeks ago during the conversation with Arthur Bettany. How could his patriotism possibly be in doubt?

Eve's voice broke into his reflections. 'Hey, wake up. I'm going to polish this lot off, if you don't look sharpish.'

Dan hooked an oyster from its shell and swallowed it.

'So,' she went on, 'what do you make of it?'

'I think there are a lot of frightened people out there, prepared to make something out of nothing. The idea that Paul is a traitor is ridiculous.'

'It certainly seems far-fetched to me, but, well, someone's got to hand this thing to the authorities.'

Dan reflected for a moment. 'Look, this could make a lot of trouble for Paul – possibly undeserved trouble. There are plenty of reasons why his name could have finished up on this list. Can I take it? I want to make my own investigations.'

Eve shrugged. 'If you like.'

'Thanks.' Dan folded the paper and slipped it into his inside jacket pocket.

She indicated the oysters. 'Go on – you have the last one. I've had seven.'

After dinner they went dancing at Ciro's, then spent the night at Eve's flat in Regent's Park. The following morning, before she left for work, Eve asked him what he was going to do with Alice's list.

'I told you. I want to do some digging.'

'You can't leave it too long.'

'No, I know.'

She kissed him. 'Will I see you before you go away?'

'Yes, I'll call you.'

'Promise?'

'I promise.'

5

DAN WENT DOWN to Surrey to visit Sonia that weekend, and spent much of it helping with the construction of an Anderson shelter at the far end of the garden. It was designed to be sunk into a bank of earth and covered with turf when completed. 'I want it to keep us safe,' said Sonia, 'but not to be a complete eyesore. Practicality combined with aesthetics, that's the idea.'

Dan spent Saturday morning digging the trench for the foundations, and in the afternoon he and Lobb erected the steel arches and worked the corrugated iron sheets into place. Dan was glad of the work; he knew it was important not to slacken off too much after his training. By the evening it was almost complete. At six o'clock Lobb put away his tools and went home for the night. Dan was fastening the last of the clip-bolts into place when Sonia came out, with Avril and Laura, to inspect the shelter.

'Most impressive,' said Sonia.

'I'll put the soil and turf on top tomorrow,' said Dan. 'Though I can't guarantee it will take in this dry weather. It'll need plenty of watering.'

Avril and Laura were wandering around the dark, exciting interior, the pekes pattering behind them. 'It's like a little house,' said Avril. 'Can we put chairs and things in?'

'We'll certainly have to have some creature comforts,' said Sonia. 'Oh, Avril, don't sit down on the bare earth.'

'I'll put down some duckboards to make more of a floor,' said Dan.

'An excellent idea, but one that can wait until tomorrow,' said Sonia. 'Time for tea. We'll have it on the terrace. The grass is too long for us to sit under the chestnut tree, like the old days, I'm afraid. Laura, dear, you'll have to come out of the little house for now. You can come back tomorrow.'

When tea was over, Sonia told Dan to stay on the terrace and enjoy the evening sunshine. 'You deserve a rest. I'll join you for a sherry in a while.'

The others went inside, and Dan lay back in his chair and closed his eyes, listening to the low hum of the insects among the flowers and the bubbling coo of the wood pigeons in the summer trees. All was tranquil, and the evening sky was mercifully free of planes. One could almost believe the war wasn't happening. It was pleasant to pretend, just for a while.

After a few minutes Dan felt a light tug at his sleeve. He opened his eyes and found four-year-old Laura at his elbow. She was holding a book and regarding him with grave, grey eyes.

'Read me a story, please.' It was a gentle, but firm instruction.

Dan pushed himself up in his chair and took the book from her hand. 'Right-ho. Up you come.'

She clambered on to his knee and settled back against him as though it were the most natural thing in the world. He opened the book randomly, and was about to begin the story of Red Riding Hood. 'No, not that one,' said Laura. She turned the pages back to the very beginning, to the story of Jack and the beanstalk.

'This one?'

Laura nodded. When the story was finished, she asked for another. Dan obliged, and threw himself into the parts that called for funny voices, which made Laura laugh so ecstatically that Dan laughed, too. Neither of them was aware of Avril watching them stonily from the nursery window.

*

The next day Dan began the task of building up a two-foot layer of soil and turf on top of the shelter. Sunday was Lobb's day off, and he worked alone. As he was working, he noticed Avril standing nearby, watching. The ten-year-old had been quite chatty and interested in the project the day before, so he said to her, 'You're going to need lights in here if there's a raid. Once I've finished this, we could make some by putting night lights inside flower pots. What d'you reckon? There are a couple of chairs and an old table in the shed, too. We could bring them in here, make it more homely.'

Avril wanted nothing more than to help make flower pot lights and furnish the shelter, but seeing Dan and Laura having such fun with stories the evening before had kindled a sour unhappiness inside her, so that she now had no wish to please Dan or herself. She gazed at him sullenly and shook her head, then turned and walked away.

Funny kid, thought Dan as he resumed his work. No better now than when she was five.

On the way back to the house Avril came across Laura playing with Star on the lawn. She watched her for a moment, thinking, then said, 'Laura, do you want to see something? Something mysterious?'

The four-year-old looked up. She wasn't used to hearing Avril talk to her in this friendly, coaxing way. In fact, she wasn't used to Avril paying her any attention at all. She nodded.

'Come on, then.' Avril held out her hand and Laura got to her feet. Avril led her across the lawn to the wood, Star pattering at their heels.

When he had laid the last piece of turf, Dan stood back and admired his handiwork. He glanced at his watch. Fifteen minutes till lunch. Just time for a quick stroll and a smoke.

He wandered down to the tennis court. Lobb had kept it mown, so that it wasn't entirely neglected, but the grass was far from the pristine surface on which he and Meg had played a few years ago. He stood reflectively, summoning back memories of the summerhouse party, then after a minute or two he flung away the end of his cigarette and went back up the path.

As he walked along something caught his ear, and he stopped. The light, muffled sound of a child's voice, singing, came through the trees. He stepped off the path and through the bushes, following the sound, then stopped dead. There, leaning over the edge of the old well, her fair hair falling over her face, was Laura. The little girl was leaning so far forward that her feet were well off the ground, and with just the slightest further momentum, she could easily topple in. The wooden lid lay on the ground a few feet away.

Dan held his breath and crouched down. He moved forward as stealthily as he could. Laura was still singing softly into the echoing depths of the well. Praying she wouldn't hear him and move in surprise, he reached out and grasped her by the ankles, and pulled her backwards into his arms. She gasped and struggled and began to cry, and he tried to calm her. Eventually she quietened.

'What were you doing?' he asked. He felt shaky with relief.

Laura sniffed back tears. 'I was singing to the princess in the well. Avril told me about her. She said she's lonely, and if you sing to her it makes her feel better.'

'I see.' They were still sitting together on the ground, Laura in Dan's lap. 'Well,' he said, 'I'm sure she feels a lot better now. But you mustn't do it again. Wells are dangerous places for little girls. Come on, let's get you back to the house.'

Laura did not tell Dan how Avril had pulled the big lid off the well, then helped her up the stone sides, till she was balanced on the edge, looking in. Nor did she tell him how Avril had urged her to lean over as far as possible, right, right over so that the princess would hear her. She had been too busy singing to notice Avril run quietly away, Star following. Just as now she was too happy to be sitting aloft on Dan's shoulders, brushing the summer leaves of the trees with her hands, to care about any of it.

Ten minutes later Dan returned with a hammer and nails and some lengths of wood, and secured the lid so that no child could prise it off. No point in mentioning it to Sonia, he decided. She would just have a nervous fit, and blame Avril. It was hardly Avril's fault if Laura took literally every nursery story that Avril told her.

That evening Dan packed his kitbag, ready to leave.

'So,' asked Sonia, 'what now? Back to Scarborough when your leave ends?'

'No, that's finished with.' He wished he could tell her about SOE, but knew he couldn't. 'I might be posted overseas.'

'Well, look after yourself. I hope you'll come to Woodbourne when you have leave. Your room will always be waiting.'

'Thank you. I don't think you know what it means to me to be able to come here. It's like an oasis of sanity.'

'I don't know about sanity. There are times, particularly where the pigs are involved, when I think myself quite mad. Now, before I forget, I need you to return something to my sister Helen in London, if you don't mind. She came to stay a few weeks ago, and she left some jewellery. Apparently she can't get by without it. I'll just fetch it.'

Sonia returned moments later with a small leather jewellery roll and gave it to Dan. 'You know where she lives?'

'Yes, Cheyne Walk. I called there once, when Meg was still living there.'

'Ah.' She paused. 'Do you see much of Paul and Meg?'

'No, I haven't seen either of them for a long time.'

'Meg is quite changed. I mean, she was always a capable girl, but she has positively grown up in the past year or two. It's partly being a mother, I think, and partly the war.'

'War changes everyone.' Dan glanced at his watch. 'My train's in half an hour. I'd best be off.'

*

Dan set off across the fields to the station. He was still mulling over the business of the list that Eve had given him, as he had been all weekend. There had to be some way to find out more. Should he try to get in touch with Alice to see if she could find out more details of why Paul's name was on the list? No, that would put her at too much risk. She might cover her activities by wearing a Nazi party badge and spouting pro-Nazi nonsense at every opportunity, but the mere fact that she was British meant she must already be under surveillance. As he reached the road the idea of asking Bill Shirer came to him. With his knowledge of the tight-knit world of espionage and the German high command, perhaps Paul's name had come to his ears. It was a long shot, but it was worth trying. He would write and see what he could find out. Anything to get rid of this troublesome uncertainty.

As he turned off the path on to the road Dan heard a low droning sound and looked up to see a flight of German bombers, over twenty he reckoned, flying in formation, no more than two thousand feet above. He flattened himself against the hedgerow as the planes passed directly overhead, flying in a westerly direction through the summer sky. He watched as they gradually became specks in the distance, then carried on towards the station.

Meg was in the nursery with Max when she heard the drone of planes. She hurried to the window. Paul came in at that moment and joined her.

'Should we take cover?' asked Meg.

Paul watched the bombers rumble over the fields beyond Alderworth Hall. From further off came the stuttering sound of machine guns, and the German formation began to break up under attack from Hurricanes and Spitfires.

'No, I suspect they're heading for Bracknell. There's a squadron of Blenheims stationed there.'

The RAF planes had engaged some of the bombers, but the crump of bombs exploding further afield indicated that the first wave of the formation had got through. In the distance came the crack of anti-aircraft guns. Max ran to his mother and Meg picked him up, and the three of them stood gazing in horrified fascination as the aerial battle unfolded in the skies above James Kentleigh's estate. In the space of the next ten minutes they saw three German bombers and two British planes shot from the skies. The remnants of the German formation disappeared westwards, pursued by British planes. A Spitfire angled in on the last remaining Heinkel and let loose a burst of machine gun fire, and the German bomber lurched, then began to come down slowly at a low slant. Its three occupants parachuted to escape seconds before the plane hit the ground in a sheet of flame and black smoke on Creechurch Hill, just beyond the village, and the Spitfire barrelled low in a victory roll before disappearing westwards to join what was left of the battle.

The sound of the planes receded. They waited in silence for some minutes, then Meg set Max down on the floor.

'How horrible to see two of our own planes shot down. To think that could have been Roddy.' Paul said nothing. It was the first time Roddy's name had been mentioned by either of them in months. Meg went to the chest of drawers and took out some clean pyjamas for Max. 'Diana rang me while you were in London last week. She's terribly low. She isn't allowed to know where Roddy's been stationed, so she can't join him. She's just sitting in the flat in London, all on her own.'

'She should get a job with one of the forces, take her mind off things.'

'What, like you?' The words were out of her mouth before she could stop herself. There had been a good deal of tension in the house lately, and she and Paul were having frequent arguments. Meg could put it down to nothing in particular, though she blamed Paul rather than herself. He was preoccupied and irascible much of the time, and she couldn't help feeling that life at Hazelhurst was easier when he wasn't there.

'You know I'm engaged in government work,' said Paul quietly. 'Otherwise I'd be in uniform like a shot.'

Meg knew it wasn't fair, but the fact that she was allowed to know nothing of Paul's work made her feel it was all a bit of a sham. She told herself over and over that whatever he was doing must be valuable, just as valuable as the contribution of every active serviceman – more so, perhaps. But she was aware that the fact that he spent his time in the comfort of his country home, or up in London, reflected poorly on him in the eyes of the servants and other local people, whose husbands and sons had gone off to fight. James Kentleigh was now a prisoner of war, and Meg couldn't bear the idea that Anna should think that Paul wasn't doing his bit. She knew she should say nothing to anyone about Paul's work, but when Anna had observed that it was odd that Paul was still at home, Meg could not help telling her that Paul was working for the government. Anna had merely replied, 'Oh, a desk job,' and Meg had felt the slight keenly.

She slammed the drawer shut impatiently. 'I think I'll go up to London. I could do with getting away, and I can see my mother and Diana. Lotte will be able to look after Max for a couple of days. And of course, you're here most of the time.' She hated herself for uttering these unpleasant barbs, but somehow she couldn't help herself.

Paul left the room in silence. Meg stared at the pyjamas folded in her hands, sighed, and then called to Lotte to give Max his bath.

Meg went up to town the following week, and dropped in on Diana at the Kensington flat.

'Nice to see at least one member of my family,' said Diana. 'I've hardly seen anything of Paul this last year. Come and have some coffee – one of life's few remaining pleasures that mercifully hasn't been rationed. I get the most heavenly beans from a little man in Soho.'

'So,' she continued over coffee, 'tell me what my brother is up to. I should have thought he'd be in the RAF by now.'

'The fact is, he's working for the government,' said Meg. 'All terribly hush-hush. No one's allowed to know a thing about what he's doing. It's rather strange to have him about the place so much when every other man of his age is in uniform. Dixon – you know, our groom and gardener – couldn't wait to get his call-up papers. But it seems he has an enlarged heart, whatever that is, and the army won't take him. I'm grateful he's staying on with us, but the whole thing has made him wretched. I can tell by the way he looks at Paul that he doesn't understand why Paul hasn't joined up. It doesn't seem to bother Paul, though, what other people think.'

'He was always able to rise above other people's opinions,' sighed Diana. 'It's a kind of arrogance, but it's part of his make-up.' She stirred her coffee, then said, 'I was thinking of taking a job. I met Constance Davenport a few weeks ago – you know she's a doctor at the Royal Free now? I was being feeble, fretting about Roddy, and she said the best thing for me would be to get a job. She suggested I train as a nurse, which quite appeals.'

'And will you?'

Diana gave a half-smile. 'I'm afraid war work is out, for the time being. I'm going to have a baby. I've only just found out.'

'Oh, Diana, that's wonderful!'

'It is rather. Roddy doesn't know yet. He's due home on leave in a fortnight, and I'll tell him then. I'm just so afraid that he'll never live to see it. Fighter pilots die every day, and he's bound to be one of the unlucky ones in the long run.'

'Not necessarily.'

'That's what he says. He's so – what's that American expression? – so gung-ho. The last time I was with him, he described what it's like being up in a plane, fighting the Germans. It sounded frightful. The noise, and the fear, not knowing whether the enemy is going to come from behind you or under you. Roddy says it's all a question of nerve, staying cool under pressure. I think he enjoys it even more than being a racing driver. Well, perhaps "enjoy" isn't the right word. He thrives on it, says there's something rather wonderful about getting up at daylight and listening to the dawn chorus over a mug of tea, fighting for your life by lunchtime, and back drinking ale with the locals in some quiet country pub after sunset. To me it sounds utterly absurd.' She gazed at Meg. 'How can he possibly go on doing that, day after day, and stay alive?'

'If anyone has the right temperament to survive what he's doing, Roddy does.'

'I know, I know. And I'm so happy to be having our baby. But it's just another person to be afraid for. And heaven alone knows how I'll cope, bringing up a child on my own here. I mean, I have plenty of friends, but it's not the same as having one's mother or family on hand.'

There was a pause, then Meg said, 'Why don't you come and live at Hazelhurst? We would so love to have you. It's much safer than here. In fact, the more I think about it, the madder it seems for you to stay in London.'

Diana looked doubtfully at Meg. 'Do you think? I'm such a city girl at heart. You know how I detest the countryside.'

Meg laughed. 'It's not about all that any more. It's about being safe. Honestly, you really should consider it. Will you?'

'Yes, I'll think about it. Thank you.'

They talked for another hour or so, then Meg glanced at her watch. 'Heavens, look at the time. Mother's expecting me for dinner at eight, and she hates people being unpunctual.' She got up. 'Why don't we go somewhere special for lunch tomorrow, just as a treat? The Criterion, perhaps?'

'That would be divine. I shall book us a table.'

Meg kissed her sister-in-law goodbye and left. It had been raining hard when she got off the train, but now it had thinned to a fine drizzle. Deciding against the bus, she began to walk to Chelsea.

Dan was due to have dinner with friends that evening. He reckoned it would probably be the last evening of its kind that he'd have for some time, and he was determined to enjoy himself; in three days he would receive his orders, and God alone knew when he would next be back in London. He bathed and dressed, and was searching in a drawer for a tie when he came across the jewellery roll which Sonia had given him to deliver to Meg's mother, and which he'd entirely forgotten about. He swithered for a moment, then decided he probably just had time to make a detour to Chelsea to drop it off. He tied his tie, put on his jacket, put the jewellery roll in his pocket, and hurried downstairs.

'Rather inclement out there, sir,' remarked the porter as Dan came through the lobby. 'I'd advise you take an umbrella.' He reached behind the desk and handed one to Dan, who thanked him and hurried out into the street with it.

By the time Dan got to Chelsea the rain was petering out. He turned into Cheyne Row and was halfway down when suddenly the harsh, rising wail of the air-raid sirens filled the air. A warden in a tin hat came hurrying round the corner.

'Where's the nearest shelter?' asked Dan.

'The church down on the Embankment.' He rushed off, peeping frantically on his whistle.

Dan started to run towards the church. People began to emerge from nearby houses, heading in the same direction. Evening mass had been about to begin at almost the very moment the sirens sounded, and Dan and the others joined the handful of worshippers being herded by the priest towards the entrance to the church crypt. The air was full of voices babbling in panic and consternation, but behaviour was calm and people moved down the stone stairs in an orderly fashion. Someone had gone ahead to light lamps, and the dimly lit interior of the crypt, which consisted of a series of three brick chambers leading into one another and running the length of the church, felt ghostly and strange. As people filed in their anxious voices echoed from the arched ceilings, and at the eerie sound a few children began to cry. Dan, tucking himself next to a stone pillar, glanced around; he estimated that at least a hundred people had sought refuge within the space of a few minutes.

Down in the gloom of the crypt the sound of the enemy planes was fainter. After a few minutes a series of explosions shook the building, and then came the hollow booming of the ack-ack guns. Threads of dust fell from the vaulted brickwork, giving off a faintly acrid smell. Dan could sense the collective prayer being offered up, that the church should not take a direct hit. The useless words, 'please God, please God' were not on his lips, but running through his mind, over and over. To distract himself from the dread of the next explosion, he began to study the faces of those around him. An elderly woman in a fur coat stood nearby, her husband's arm around her, eyes shut tight. The priest himself stood a few feet away, eyes raised heavenwards as he listened, waiting, and looking, though he didn't know it, like a martyred saint in a Renaissance painting. Next to the priest, crouched on the ground, was a young woman, her head tucked down, her arms around her knees, waiting fearfully. Something about her held his gaze. He waited for her to lift her head, so that he could see her face. Another juddering explosion, nearer this time, shook the earth, and people cried out in fear. The girl looked up, and Dan saw that it was Meg. He threaded his way past people and reached her side, laying his hand on her arm. She gave a start and got to her feet. Her expression, as she gazed at him, was unfathomable.

'What are you doing here?' she asked incredulously.

'I was on my way to your mother's house. She left something at Sonia's, and I was returning it.' Whatever reply Meg was going to make was drowned by another explosion. They stood together, waiting, listening. 'That one was further away,' said Dan.

Conscious of the warm pressure of his hand on her arm, she

struggled with the confusion of her feelings, glad he was there, but at the same time reminded of the hurt and humiliation she had felt after that last conversation with Eve two years ago.

Explosions continued, but the sound seemed to be receding. After a long while they ceased altogether. People's voices rose in a hopeful murmur. The priest said he would go and take a look, and disappeared in the direction of the steps.

A moment later he reappeared. 'They're sounding the all-clear!'

In slow relief, people began to move back upstairs.

'I was going to my mother's, too. I'm staying the night,' said Meg. She scanned the faces of people filing past. 'I thought she might be here, but I don't see her.' They made their way up to the street.

They were met with a scene of devastation. A bomb had fallen on the Embankment, and the nearby houses lay in jagged, smoking ruins. The air was filled with brick dust and fires flickered among the rubble. Wardens, policemen and ambulances were everywhere. Meg hurried to the end of the street, which had been cordoned off by wardens and where teams of rescuers were working among the debris to find survivors.

'Back you go, love!' shouted a man.

Meg craned her head past the barriers to see if her mother's house was still standing. It appeared to be. The evening air was filled with smoke and drizzle and the stench of burning.

'What's happened to the people in the houses down there?' Meg asked a warden.

'If they weren't already taking shelter they'll have been evacuated. We've got an unexploded bomb. I'd make yourself scarce if I were you. It's dangerous round here.'

'But where have they been evacuated to?'

'I can't help you, I'm afraid. Stand back, now!' shouted the warden, herding people away from the barriers as the bomb disposal came roaring down the street. The drizzle had become steady rain. Dan put up his umbrella.

Meg turned to him. 'Whatever it was you were returning to my mother, you can give it to me, and I'll see it gets to her.' Her voice was shaking. Dan could tell that shock and anxiety had brought her close to tears. He looked into her face.

'Meg?'

'Please. I don't need you to stay with me.'

He took the jewellery roll from his pocket and handed it to her. 'Where do you intend to go?'

'Kensington. I'll stay with Diana.'

'I'll walk with you.'

'I don't need you to.'

'You'll get soaked otherwise.'

But the area to the north of the King's Road had been hit by the air raid, and everywhere streets were blocked off. The rain poured down relentlessly.

'This is no good,' said Dan. 'Come on.' When he took her arm she didn't resist, huddling with him under his umbrella.

'Where are we going?'

'South Eaton Place, my father's old house. You can shelter there tonight.'

Five minutes later they reached the house.

'Thank God to be out of that,' said Dan, shaking out the umbrella as they stepped inside.

Meg could see nothing in the darkness of the hallway, and the house had a cold, musty smell. Dan fished a torch from a drawer in the hall table and went ahead into the drawing room, the beam from the torch making a ghostly light. She watched in the doorway as he drew the blackout blinds, then switched on lamps.

'Come in.'

Meg stepped into the room, still in her coat. Dan pulled dustsheets from the furniture.

'Have a seat. Sorry it's chilly. I'm not here a lot.' A fire was laid in the grate. Dan found a box of matches and lit it. 'I'll find something else to warm us up.'

He disappeared and returned a few moments later with a bottle of wine and two glasses. He poured the wine and handed her a glass.

'Here's rot to Hitler's guts.' He stood by the fireplace and drank off a glass, then poured himself another.

Meg said nothing, watching the firelight play on his features. She drank some wine, feeling warmth kindle in her chilly limbs.

'Three years,' said Dan. He studied her face. It was closed, impassive. 'Have they really made that much of a difference between us? You've hardly said a word tonight.'

'We've nothing to say to one another.'

'No? So everything that happened between us was utterly meaningless?'

'No, not for me – but for you, evidently.'

'I don't understand.'

'You told Eve about us. According to her, I was simply – unfinished business. A conquest.'

Dan stared at her. 'What utter rot. When did she tell you this?'

'Does it matter?' The past swam into the present, then receded. Meg was suddenly aware of the intensity of connection between them, like an electrical current being switched on. 'It was two years ago, just before Diana's wedding. We met in town, and had lunch.'

'Well, she was lying.'

'I don't see how she could possibly have known about us otherwise.'

'She made a lucky guess. I never mentioned your name, but she knew there was someone I cared for. More than her.' Meg said nothing. 'Do you really think I would cheapen something so precious by talking about it – to Eve, of all people?'

Meg raised her eyes, scrutinising his face. 'It doesn't matter.'

'Yes, it does.' He put his glass on the mantelpiece and sat down next to her on the sofa. 'I think about you every day. You made your choice to stay with Paul, but it doesn't stop me loving you.'

Meg gazed at him, struggling to reconcile his words and the look in his eyes with the things she remembered Eve telling her. Then suddenly she saw very clearly that they must have been lies. Eve couldn't bear the thought of Dan caring for anyone else. 'And you still love me, too,' Dan went on. 'Don't you?' She shook her head, unable to speak. 'Don't you?'

She was filled with a sense of weariness and futility. 'Yes.' Her voice was no more than a whisper.

He took her in his arms and kissed her, and she gave in, as she had known she would. But after minutes of kissing him, of drowning in the pleasure of holding him, she pushed him away.

'Dan, please, we mustn't do this. Nothing's changed. My life is with Paul and Max.'

Dan let go of her and stood up. He went back to the fireplace and poured himself some more wine, then stared into the fire for a long moment. He thought about Paul's name on the list, about what it might mean for Meg, how disastrous it could be. He turned to look at her. 'Don't you understand, Meg? The rules don't apply any more.'

'What do you mean?'

'We're in a war. Things can change in a moment. You saw that tonight. I'm going away this weekend – I'm not even sure where yet – and there's no guarantee I'll come back. It isn't about right and wrong, or who you belong to. Those ideas don't matter. It's about you and me, and the fact that we love each other. That's all there is.' He held her gaze. 'This, here and now, may be all we ever have.'

It was enough. She rose and kissed him, and clung to him as though she would never let him go, overwhelmed by feelings she had been denying for three years. He led her upstairs to his bedroom. He was about to draw the blackout curtains, but Meg stopped him.

'Don't. The light is beautiful.'

Outside, the rain had stopped, and the moon was out. Clouds drifted across it intermittently, so that ghostly light came and went in the room. Dan cupped her face in his hands and kissed her, then began to undress her. She moved against him with an urgency which was so intoxicating that they made love before they even got between the sheets. The relief of having her was greater than he had thought possible.

'I was afraid this would never happen,' he told her. 'I have lain awake at night thinking about it, tormenting myself with the idea that I could get to the end of my life and never be able to love you again.'

'Hush.' She put a hand to his mouth, her fingers warm against his lips. 'Let's get into bed. I'm cold.'

The next morning Meg was woken by early light streaming through the window. She turned over. Dan was still sleeping. She propped her head on her hand and gazed at him. How one's life could change in the space of a few hours. It had happened once before, and she had never thought it would happen again. But here they were. The randomness of everything frightened her. What if she had got the bus, instead of walking... What if the air raid had been on another part of London... What if...

No, she decided – there was a destiny that meant they should be together. As she contemplated his features, she experienced an overpowering feeling of love, and her heart seemed to rise in her throat. Nothing would separate her from him again. But even as she vowed this, she knew how badly the odds were stacked. There was the war. There was Paul. There was the need for her to keep a stable home for Max. There was the mere practical difficulty of seeing one another in these fractured times. There would be so many moments of pain, and the first would come in just a few hours, when they had to part. She should not look ahead. She should simply exist for now, for this moment of being together. It so easily might not come again.

Dan opened his eyes sleepily, unaware of anything for an instant, like a child. Then he saw her and smiled.

She leaned down and kissed him. 'Good morning.'

'Morning.' Dan yawned, and pulled her down to nestle against his shoulder.

'Are you really going away this weekend?' asked Meg.

'Yes. I get my orders tomorrow.' The thought of Dan in combat filled her with dread. This was what love did to you, made you a hostage to fortune. 'But don't worry. I'll be back.' He spoke with casual confidence, reaching out to the bedside table for his cigarettes.

She laughed sadly. 'I don't know how you can sound so certain.'

'Because I am.' He snapped his lighter and lit a cigarette. 'I have something to live for now.'

'You have everything to live for, regardless of me.'

He pulled away from her a little so that he could look at her face, then smiled. 'The rest is just window dressing. You are what matters.'

She rolled away from him. 'Don't. It's going to be unbearable, not knowing where you are, or what's happening to you.'

'If I can write, I will. I'll send letters addressed to you here. Can you come here now and then? I'll give you a set of keys.'

Meg thought. 'I don't know. I haven't many excuses for coming to London. But I'll try.' If Diana came to live at Hazelhurst, that was an excuse gone. She would have to find others. Her mother, perhaps.

'I'll let you know every leave I get, if I can, and then we can be together, here.' He set his cigarette in the ashtray by the bed and drew her to him. 'And do this. Over and over.'

Later Meg walked to her mother's house. Attempts at clearing up the damage wrought by the bomb which had fallen on the Embankment had already begun. She gazed at the awful destruction. Neat houses which she had walked past all her life were reduced to smouldering ruin, fragments of the lives of their inhabitants – flowered wallpaper, a broken bed, charred books – pitifully exposed in the morning sunshine. She picked her way through the litter of dust and broken brick on the pavements and made her way to her mother's house. The cook-maid answered the door, an indication that some kind of normality prevailed. Meg expected to find her mother in a state of agitation, but in fact Helen was quite calm.

'Well, thank goodness you're alive,' she remarked, when she saw Meg. 'I've been rather worried, but I assumed you'd be staying at Diana's.'

'No, I was at the top of the road when the sirens went off. I finished up in the crypt of the church. You won't believe who I met there – Dan Ranscombe. He was on his way here to give this back to you.'

'Well, what a coincidence!' Helen took the jewellery roll. 'I'm certainly glad to have my rings back.'

'We ended up in Belgravia, his father's old house.'

Helen seemed to think nothing of this. 'I'm glad you found somewhere safe for the night. I was just relieved to find my house still standing when I came back this morning. It could have been much worse. Obviously not for some of the poor people around here, but I've been very lucky.'

'Where did you stay?'

'Oh, they evacuated us to the air-raid shelter at the school round the corner. Not the most comfortable of nights, but everyone was in remarkably good spirits. It was quite a heartening experience. What will you be doing today?'

'I'm having lunch with Diana, then getting the train back. I can stay on another night, if you'd like. We haven't had any time together.'

'Darling, not on my account, please. I'm sure Max is missing you. We can have a late breakfast together now, before I get off to my WVS salvage drive.'

*

Meg and Diana met for lunch. Diana was radiant; Roddy had telephoned last night, and she had told him about the baby. Meg listened as Diana talked happily. This is what it should be like, she thought. The way she and Dan could have been if only she'd known better, known more about the world and about herself. She passed a hand over her eyes at the thought of the deceit she and Dan were going to have to practise to have any happiness.

'Are you all right?' asked Diana.

'I'm fine. Just a bit tired.' She told Diana about the events of the air raid.

'What a stroke of luck running into Dan. Better than being crammed into some dreadful shelter with loads of people. I'm afraid I just hid under the table and hoped for the best,' said Diana. 'And while I was listening to the bombs going off, I decided to accept your invitation to come and live at Hazelhurst. Actually, Roddy had already decided for me. He said the bombing's only going to get worse, and that I'd be mad not to go.'

'That's marvellous. When do you want to come?'

'Well, I have a number of things to arrange, but perhaps next week, if I can get myself in order.'

'I'll tell Paul. I know he'll be delighted.'

On the train journey home, Meg reflected on what her future would now be. She remembered this feeling from four years ago, when she and Dan had first become lovers. What a false start that had been. This time would be different. It would involve lies, deceit, and any amount of guilt, but she didn't care. Dan was right. Each time they met might be the last. She had to take her happiness where she could find it. The best she could do for Paul was to maintain a semblance of affection, so that he should never suspect.

When she arrived home late that afternoon, she found Paul in his study, pipe in mouth, going through papers. Her manner as she kissed him was bright and cheerful, and felt entirely artificial.

'I've been hearing all about your air-raid adventures from Diana,' said Paul. 'Just as well you had somewhere to stay.'

'Yes, it was kind of Dan, wasn't it? It was all quite terrifying, though. At least Mother's house is still standing, to say nothing of Mother.' She pulled off her gloves. 'I'll just go and see Max.'

As she reached the door, Paul said, 'Good news about Diana's baby. And about her coming to live here.' He turned back to his work. 'Though I do think you might have asked me first.'

Meg was astonished. 'Why? Would you have said no?'

'Of course not. But it's the principle of the thing. A man likes to be consulted on who he's to have living in his home.'

'For God's sake, Paul, she's your sister. Don't be so pompous.' The pretence at affection collapsed instantly. They were back to the mood of mild animosity which had prevailed before her visit to London. She turned and went to the nursery before he could reply.

A few days later Meg made a pragmatic decision and went to see Dr Carr, and asked to be fitted for a diaphragm. It took some courage, but she felt she had no choice. Given her situation, she couldn't afford to get pregnant again.

Dr Carr raised his eyebrows at the request. Meg could sense his disapproval. 'If that's what you wish. Though I'd have thought you'd be thinking of extending your family, a healthy young woman like you. I take it you've discussed this with your husband?'

'I have.'

The doctor uncapped his pen and began to write. 'This is something for the nurse to attend to, not me. Take this through and she will arrange all that is necessary.'

6

THE DAY AFTER Meg left, Dan reported to an address in Baker Street for a pre-operation briefing. In a nondescript meeting room, he found himself together again with the men he had trained with in Scotland, all in a motley array of uniforms. Dan and Brendan greeted each other with wary cheerfulness, and a sense of being on the brink of something. Brigadier Gubbins, their commander from the Highland training, was there. He was a middle-aged man with a markedly erect bearing, piercing eyes beneath thick dark brows, and a neat moustache. His somewhat stern aspect was softened by the warmth of his occasional smile. Next to him stood a tall man with a lugubrious, unsmiling face, who now called the room to order.

'Please be seated, gentlemen.'

They took their places in rows of chairs, facing a long, polished table with three seats and a large map of Europe behind it. The atmosphere of grim anticipation was laced with a scarcely suppressed boyish enthusiasm.

'Gentlemen,' said the tall man, 'I am Admiral Sir Roger Keyes, Director of Combined Operations. Brigadier Gubbins is of course already well known to you. We are here today to set out the scope of the work that you will be undertaking over the next months, and for which your training has specially prepared you. Now, as you men know, Special Operations Executive has been established specifically to undermine German fighting capacity and morale, and to help tie down its forces in peripheral theatres away from the main battlefronts. You will be carrying out raids and acts of sabotage and subversion, undertaking *coup de main* operations, and will be involved in covert, so-called black propaganda. In occupied areas you will be preparing secret underground armies based on local resistance groups to be organised and preserved in readiness to support a landing by regular forces at a time determined by Britain and its allies.'

There was faint, eager stirring in the room.

Brigadier Gubbins, casting a keen eye along the rows of expectant faces, now spoke. 'We intend to harness the potential for resistance in the occupied countries and create secret armies that will support Allied landings as part of an eventual liberation of Europe. It is part of an attritional strategy to wear down Axis power. The objective is to harass the enemy and cause as much material damage as possible. In short, you will be a thorn in Hitler's side.'

The admiral rose and went to the map. 'The focus of SOE's missions in the coming months will be Norway. Since the surrender of Norway, as you can imagine, there are thousands of Norwegian servicemen in hiding who need only arms and communications to become an effective underground resistance movement. Indeed, such organisations already exist in a rudimentary form. SOE's task is to send agents to western and southern Norway to contact or form resistance groups, and at the same time undertake sabotage operations on vital infrastructure – harbours, bridges, pipelines.'

'Thank Christ they taught us to ski,' murmured Brendan.

'A base has been set up on the north-east coast of Shetland' – he rapped the map with his pointer – 'here. Shetland has become a place of strategic significance, not least because of its potential to be used as an alternative entry point for a German attack, and we are boosting its defences. At the same time, we shall be launching missions in Norway using fishing boats which have been transporting refugees from Norway.'

A long way from London, thought Dan. *A long way from Meg.*

'Which brings me,' said the admiral, 'to the details of your first mission.'

After the briefing Dan went back to Belgravia. Before leaving, he wrote two letters. The first was to Bill Shirer, asking if he remembered any rumours circulating in Berlin about an Englishman called Paul Latimer, or if the name meant anything to him. *Certain information has come my way which raises concerns about his reliability, and as he is engaged in what I believe is sensitive government work, it is important that I verify it one way or another. Most grateful for any light you can shed.* He marked it 'Strictly Private and Confidential', and addressed it care of the CBS office in New York. He had no idea whether Shirer still worked for CBS, but he hoped the letter would find its way to him. He doubted whether Shirer would know anything, but it was worth a try.

The second letter was to Meg, full of love and optimism, with a couple of jokes thrown in to make her laugh. He left the envelope on the hall table, propped up against a small silver vase. As he was about to leave he glanced back at the letter. The empty vase made it look forlorn. He dropped his bag, went back into the house and found the key to the communal gardens. There were plenty of shrub roses in bloom, but he wandered around until he found, tangled through a laurel bush, a rose which had run wild. He cut off a spray, took it back to the house, filled the little vase with water, and tucked the roses into it. Then he locked up and left.

Bombs continued to fall on London, and Helen reluctantly concluded that, for safety's sake, she should follow Diana's lead and move to the country. In Cheyne Walk the carpets were rolled up, the furniture covered in dustsheets, Helen's precious miniatures and Limoges enamels were removed to storage, and she took up residence at Hazelhurst. She had relished the WVS work she had been doing in London, and had no intention of letting her energy and talents go to waste in the countryside. Within a week she had joined the Alderworth Women's Institute, which was then in the throes of a drive to prevent the waste of surplus fruit in the district, and a few weeks later she was helping to organise a grand jam-making session at the village school.

On the final day she announced at dinner the amount of jam produced. 'Five hundred pounds, from five hundred and seventy-eight pounds of fruit. Quite splendid, don't you think? Hitler's not having it all his own way.'

'Marvellous,' agreed Meg.

Diana grinned, and whispered to Meg, 'Does your mother know that she and the other WI women are now known in the village as the jam tarts?'

Helen, oblivious, went on, 'I shall have to ring Sonia later and tell her.'

Ever since she had arrived at Hazelhurst Helen had been thinking of ways to rival Sonia's enterprises at Woodbourne House. Meg and Paul already kept chickens, and pig-keeping would look rather like copying, she decided – besides which, she didn't really relish the thought of looking after pigs and she didn't think Meg would, either – so she was pleased when she hit upon the idea of beekeeping.

'I met a most charming land army girl at the jam-making session,' she told Meg. 'She's leaving the area soon, and has two hives which she's offering for sale for seven pounds ten shillings. I think I shall buy them.'

'But you don't know the first thing about beekeeping,' protested Meg. 'And besides, you don't like insects. I've seen the way you behave when there's a wasp around.'

'I feel very differently about bees,' said Helen. 'There's no malevolence in a bee.'

'Well, there isn't in a wasp, either,' observed Diana.

'I've been speaking to Dixon. His father kept bees, and Dixon used to help him. He knows a great deal about it. I think between us we shall manage perfectly well.'

Privately Meg thought that the project would come to nothing once her mother realised what it entailed, and she was surprised and faintly dismayed when, the next day, Helen announced she had bought the hives from the land girl.

'Just make sure they're put well away from the house,' sighed Meg. 'I don't want Max getting stung. Honestly, Mother, I think you're mad.'

But Dixon, who badly needed projects to occupy him besides the Home Guard and his work at Hazelhurst, was full of enthusiasm. He saw to it that the hives were placed well away from the house, behind the now defunct racing car workshop, and made enquiries locally to obtain the necessary protective equipment, which Helen paid for. He even made his own honey extractor out of two cake stands, a couple of biscuit tins soldered together, and the gearing from a discarded butter churn from a nearby farm. He effectively took charge of the entire undertaking, with the providential result that Helen could take credit without having to go near the bees too often.

Everyone except Dixon was astonished by how much honey the hives yielded in the very month that Helen bought them.

'Sixty pounds,' she informed Sonia over the telephone. 'It's going to be quite a cottage industry. We're collecting jam jars, and we'll be selling what we don't need ourselves and donating the money to the war effort.'

'And to think,' said Meg to Diana, 'that I was worried she was going to be bored in the countryside.'

When Dan next came home on leave, he found his letter to Meg still propped against the silver vase. So she hadn't been here. He picked up the pile of mail from the doormat, and found among it a letter from Bill Shirer. He took it into the kitchen to read.

Dear Dan,
It was good to hear from you, and I hope you're well. By the time you get this you and your fellow countrymen will doubtless be heartily sick of the sight and sound of my compatriots in your peaceful shires, but I hope you Brits will forgive us Americans our idiosyncrasies and recognise us as friends and allies. We're in this wretched war together now, and if it brings about a quicker end to Hitler's crazed regime, I for one am glad of it.

To address your specific question: the name you mention in your letter did not spring immediately to mind, but I took the time to go through my notes and diaries (remind me, if we ever meet again, to tell you the story of how I got those out of Germany), and yes, I find his name crops up. Paul Latimer seems to have been regarded by Himmler – when I was working in Berlin, at least – as a useful friend to Hitler's regime, and acquainted with a number of Nazi sympathisers in Britain who might be in a position to provide intelligence to the German government.

Dan took a breath and looked up. He did not want to believe this. He almost wished he had never written to Shirer. How was it possible that the man whom he had known since their schooldays could be a traitor? It was, quite literally, incredible.

He carried on reading.

This, of course, was before the war, and whether or not Latimer has since then been garnering intelligence which might be useful to the Nazis, I'm not in a position to say. I do not know who his contacts in your country were or are. But if he is, as you say, operating at a sensitive level, then I would say it is certainly a matter that needs looking into urgently.

I hope this is of help. If ever you are over our way when the war ends – as it must at some time, and with God's help on the right side – I hope you will take the time to look me up.

With kindest regards,

Bill Shirer

Dan folded up the letter and put it in his jacket pocket, then lit a cigarette. So what was he supposed to do now? He had to speak to someone, and the only person he could think of was Brigadier Gubbins. He rang the number in Whitehall which had been given to SOE agents for their sole use, and was told the brigadier was in London. When Dan indicated that the matter was one of the utmost importance and could only be discussed directly with the brigadier, he was instructed to go immediately to Whitehall.

On the journey to Whitehall Dan wrestled with what he was about to do. Shirer's letter couldn't have been clearer. If Paul was a Nazi sympathiser then he could be doing untold damage, passing on information that came his way through his government job and from other contacts, possibly fatally undermining the war effort. What choice did he have but to tell someone? But when he thought of Paul he didn't picture a traitor. All he could see was Paul the seventeen-year-old schoolboy gloriously, single-handedly bowling out the Harrow opposition; Paul, who loved Meg and his son and, so Dan had thought, his country. He struggled to believe it of him. If the powers-that-be uncovered evidence of treachery, Paul would hang. Dan went cold at the thought, not just of Paul's death, but of what it would mean for Meg, and for Diana. Their lives would be ruined, the disgrace and misery would never leave them. Max would be burdened by his father's dishonour for the rest of his life.

No, he couldn't do it. He almost stopped the taxi. But then he realised that these were considerations that properly belonged to Paul – and Paul, if what Shirer wrote was true, must have weighed them up and decided that he was prepared to betray everyone and everything he knew and claimed to love. It had been his choice. *It is not mine*, thought Dan. *I have no choice.* As for Meg, if all of this was true, and disgrace and dishonour awaited Paul, then it would be better for her to break with him now, before the worst happened. Whether he could persuade her to do so was another matter.

Dan was shown into the brigadier's office. The brigadier returned his salute and invited Dan to sit down.

'I understand you have something of vital importance to discuss, Lance Corporal. Fire away.'

Dan told his story, how he had been a correspondent in Berlin before the war, and had met Bill Shirer and Alice Bauer. He then talked about his relationship with Paul, their time at school together, and then Cambridge. From there he moved on to the list, on which Paul's name appeared.

'You actually saw this list?' asked the brigadier.

'Yes, sir. I have a copy.' He reached into his pocket and produced the list, handing it to the brigadier.

The brigadier unfolded the document and scanned it with keen eyes. 'How long have you had this?'

'A couple of months. Perhaps I should have brought it to your attention sooner, but I wanted to find out more information as to the reason why Paul Latimer's name might have appeared on it. He's a friend, and I didn't want to create needless trouble for him. You see, he was – is – a keen racing driver, with a team car he used to race all over Europe before the war. He was in Germany a lot, and he had friends there. English friends who might, with hindsight, be seen as being sympathetic to the Nazi regime. I thought his name might be on that list for the wrong reasons – or innocuous ones, at any rate – and I wanted to be doubly sure before I spoke to anyone. So I wrote to Bill Shirer in the United States, thinking he might be able to shed some light, and this morning' – Dan dipped into his breast pocket and produced Shirer's letter – 'I received his reply.' He handed the letter to the brigadier, who unfolded and read it.

'You did the right thing in coming to me. One could wish you had done it sooner, but I think I understand your reasons.' The brigadier folded the letter up and returned it to Dan. Then he uncapped his pen and wrote a few notes. 'Latimer's name isn't familiar to me, but you say you think he's been engaged in government work since the beginning of the war?'

'That's my understanding, sir. Possibly before, for all I know. Naturally, he's said nothing to anyone about what he does, but he's away from his family for weeks at a time, and they assume that's what he's doing.'

The brigadier tapped his thumb with his pen thoughtfully. 'I'll get on to this straight away.' He stood up, and Dan rose, too. 'You may hear from me about this – and then again, you may hear nothing at all.' He flashed one of his quick smiles.

Dan saluted and left the brigadier's office. He went back to Belgravia. He could scarcely believe what he'd done. Perhaps he should have waited. Perhaps he should have put the accusation to Paul to see what he said. But that would have been ridiculously foolhardy, and might have led to more damage, possibly even lives being lost. No, he'd done what he had to. Now events must take their course.

It was late autumn before Meg managed to go to Belgravia. The silence in the house was profound. On the mat lay several letters. She leafed through them until she found one addressed to her, postmarked Scotland, from Dan. Then she noticed the envelope propped up next to the little vase, and went into the drawing room to read both. She read the most recent letter first. Dan gave no details of where he was and what he'd been doing, just that it had been 'bloody cold', but that thinking of her made it bearable, that he was well, and that he would have two weeks' leave over Christmas. He would be home on the eighteenth. Could she get away to be with him? She stared at his handwriting for a long time, as though its very shape and form could bring him closer. Then she put it away and read the first letter, which was charged with the passion and intimacy of their time together, still fresh in his heart at the time of writing. She read it through twice. She was about to put the letters in her handbag, but hesitated. She wanted to have them with her, so that she could reread them whenever she wanted, but she knew, too, that she mustn't allow the remotest possibility of anyone finding them. Reluctantly she opened the drawer of the hall table and slipped them inside.

As she was about to leave, she noticed the dried-up stem of the rose spray in the silver vase, and the dead petals lying on the polished wood, and guessed he must have left it there. She remembered the wild roses he had given her the first time he had kissed her, the idle, spur-of-the-moment way he had plucked them, and the sad end they had come to – crushed to dust and flung away. How little she had known of life, or love. She locked the house and went away.

When December arrived, Meg racked her brains for a pretext to go to London to see Dan when he came home on leave. If she suggested a Christmas shopping expedition, either Diana or Helen or both would want to go with her. Then in the second week of December, Paul announced that he had to go for London for a fortnight. Meg decided that, although the hypocrisy was foul, she would use him as her excuse.

A few days after he had left, and the day before Dan was due back, Meg remarked at breakfast, 'Do you know, I think I'll go up to town tomorrow to spend some time with Paul. It's a chance to go out together, see the town. We haven't done that in an age.' The lies were glib, easy.

'A romantic interlude. What a nice idea.' Helen, who had detected that things were not entirely right between her daughter and son-in-law, was pleased that Meg was making an effort.

'I might stay for a couple of days.' On inspiration Meg added, 'I can go to Hamleys and buy Max a Christmas present. In fact, if anyone wants me to pick anything up on the shopping front, just say.'

'I need some Coty face powder, as it happens,' said Helen. 'And I'm sure there are one or two other things. I'll go and make a list.'

Diana raised her eyebrows at Meg. 'Prepare to queue.'

Meg arrived at the house in Belgravia at lunchtime. She waited there all afternoon, afraid to go out in case Dan came. She had no idea when he might arrive. She had brought a haphazard bag of food from Hazelhurst so that they wouldn't have to go out. The house was cold. Meg kept her fur coat on and roamed the rooms in search of electric heaters. She found three in the bedrooms upstairs, and brought them down to the kitchen and plugged them in. The heat was feeble, but better than nothing, and if she kept the door closed the room would grow warm eventually. When dusk fell she drew the blackout blinds and switched on the light in the kitchen, all the time listening, praying for the sound of a key in the front door and Dan's footsteps in the hall. The hours slipped by. When it was almost nine o'clock she felt like crying. Something had happened. He couldn't possibly come now. As she sat in the kitchen, wishing she had so much as a wireless to pass the time, she suddenly realised she hadn't eaten since breakfast. Food had been the last thing on her mind. It would give her something to do to prepare a meal, whether Dan arrived to eat it or not. She contemplated all that she had brought from Hazelhurst, and set about boiling a few small potatoes, which she would slice and fry in the butter – an extravagant waste, but she didn't care – and whisking eggs to make omelettes. She cut and diced two slices of ham, then ransacked the cupboards and found salt and pepper. The idea that Dan would step through the door at any moment to eat the food she was making invigorated her, and she pushed to the back of her mind the likelihood that he would not come at this hour, that she might wake up tomorrow alone in his bed, with nothing ahead of her but the lonely journey home. She took off her coat, unbuttoned the cuffs of her blouse, and rolled up her sleeves.

She was slicing the cooked potatoes, keeping an eye on the butter foaming in the frying pan, when suddenly she heard the front door open. The sound shook her with dizzying relief. She swithered, not sure whether to rush out and meet him, or tend the butter which was about to burn. Then a happy calm descended on her. He was here, he would see the light and know she was here, and no one needed to hurry anywhere. Smiling without realising it, she put the potatoes into the frying pan. They began to spit and fry. The seconds passed. Had she imagined the sound of the door? She was halfway across the kitchen when he came in, and in another second she was in his arms. His lips were cold at first, then warm, and she clung to the rough stuff of his greatcoat. They spoke in loving murmurs that were hardly words at all, kissing over and over. Meg remembered the potatoes. 'I'm burning our supper!' She tugged free and hurried back to the cooker.

When she turned around again Dan had sunk into a chair in a posture of utter weariness, legs stretched out, head back, eyes closed. He hadn't shaved. He opened his eyes and looked at Meg, and a smile transformed his face. He beckoned her to him and she went to sit on his lap, burying her face in the lapel of his coat. They said nothing. After a moment she raised her face. 'I need to make the omelettes.'

'Omelettes?' said Dan. 'Now there's an unheard-of luxury. In the last few months I've had plenty of herring, but no omelettes.' He gave an exhausted laugh. 'Get off my knee, woman, and let me fetch some wine.'

*

'Did you say this is your mother's honey?' asked Dan the next morning at breakfast.

'She takes the glory, but I think the bees deserve most of the credit.'

'Damn good.' Dan took a sip of tea. 'What's that?'

'Helen's list. She wants face cream and powder, and some Vinolia soap that the village chemist doesn't stock.' She put the list down. 'I'm sorry to have to condemn you to shopping. But I was foolish enough to ask people if they wanted anything from town. And I'd like to go to Hamleys to get some things for Max for Christmas.'

A small fear touched her – Paul was somewhere in London. Was it really safe to go out with Dan? The chances of their being seen together were slim, but not impossible. No, even in that unlikely event, she told herself, she would have a perfectly good explanation – that she'd come up to town to do some Christmas shopping and bumped into Dan on leave. All entirely innocent. Then she thought of the story she had told her mother and Diana. She could see the lies all weaving into one another, tangling hopelessly, becoming her eventual undoing. But she could do nothing about any of it now.

'I don't mind in the least. I want to go to Trumper's for some shaving soap. It's the one luxury I allow myself in the blasted wastes of the Shetlands.'

She put her chin in her hand and gazed at him. 'Can't you tell me the tiniest thing about what you've been doing? I promise I'm not a Nazi agent.'

He shook his head. 'It's not terribly exciting, I promise you. You'd be hugely bored. Suffice to say that I've been blowing up a train, amongst other things.'

Her eyes widened. 'That's hardly boring.'

'It sounds more exciting than it was. I didn't even get to see it explode.' He screwed the lid on the honey jar. 'Come on. Let's go shopping.'

To her surprise, Meg managed to get all the things on her

mother's list without much difficulty at Fenwicks, but when she and Dan reached Regent Street, they were dismayed to see the damage wrought by recent bombing.

'I had no idea,' said Meg. 'I suppose Hamleys must be shut.'

But as they got nearer to the store they saw Hamleys' staff in tin hats outside the boarded-up shop, taking orders from people on the street, retrieving goods from inside the store, and carrying out the transactions on the pavements. There was quite a throng, and the mood was excited and cheerful.

'How wonderful!' laughed Meg.

'What are you after?' asked Dan.

'A teddy bear's the only thing I'd thought of. I was hoping I might get inspiration for something else in the shop.'

'Wait here.' Dan made his way into the crowd.

Meg waited. She pulled the collar of her coat tight, glancing around, and froze. That was Paul, surely. Standing on the other side of the road. The pavement was busy, and people were in the way. Or was it just another anonymous Londoner in a raincoat and trilby? She didn't want to look again, but she had to. The man had turned away and was walking down Regent Street. His height and the set of his shoulders were like Paul's but it wasn't him. She watched the man's retreating figure. Her imagination was playing tricks on her, a foretaste of all the guilt and anxiety she would experience from now on every time she and Dan were together.

Dan returned a few minutes later with a bear and wooden toy train. 'I had one of these when I was a kid, and it was my favourite thing,' he said. He refused her proffered money. 'We can settle up later. Let's go and find tea somewhere.'

Meg hesitated. 'Perhaps it's best if you don't take my arm, darling. It's absurd, but just knowing Paul might be here in London makes me jittery.'

'Paranoia of the worst kind. But as you wish.' He dropped her arm. 'Come on. It looks like it's going to rain.'

*

The next morning, after breakfast, while Meg was getting ready to leave, Dan heard the post arrive. He went to the hall and found a letter marked 'Private and Confidential', and bearing all the signs of officialdom, lying on the mat. He tore it open and read the brief contents. It was from Brigadier Gubbins' private secretary, asking him to contact the War Office as soon as possible. His throat tightened; he imagined he was about to find out the truth about Paul at last.

At that moment Meg came downstairs. 'You look rather grim.' She glanced at the letter in his hands. 'Bad news?'

Dan folded up the letter. 'No, just army stuff. Come on, I'll make you some breakfast.'

When they stood in the hall half an hour later, about to say goodbye, Meg felt as though there was a dead hollow where her heart should be.

'How will I know when you're next on leave?' she asked. 'You can't ring the house – it's taking too much of a chance. And I need to save my excuses for coming to town for when you're actually here.' She thought for a moment. 'I know – why don't you write to me care of the post office in Alderworth? Use some made-up name. Or my maiden name – that will do. I can go down every week and check for letters.'

'All right. I'll do that.' Dan kissed her. The thought of what lay ahead, what he might hear about Paul this very day, lay on his soul like a weight. He was almost tempted to tell Meg, to beg her to leave Paul before the worst happened. But he couldn't. He might be utterly wrong, after all. He forced a smile. 'I'll write and tell you when I'm going to be in London next. It might be months, though.'

'I don't care. I can wait.'

When Meg had gone, Dan rang the number given in the letter. He was put through to the brigadier's office, and was told that he would see him straight away.

The brigadier was on the telephone when Dan arrived in his office, and Dan waited until he had finished his call, then saluted smartly.

Brigadier Gubbins flicked a quick salute in return. 'Sit down, Lance Corporal.' He planted his elbows on the desk and folded his hands. It was a moment before he spoke. 'About your friend, Latimer. I'm afraid that national security prevents me from telling you what my enquiries have uncovered regarding his activities. The reason I called you here is to instruct you to forget everything you think you know, and all you have seen. You are to say nothing to anyone about your apprehensions, or about the list, and if you are approached by the person who showed you the list, you must avoid having any discussion about it. No matter what they say, or what further information they offer to provide, you must close the subject down – but not in such a way as to excite any suspicion or interest. Do you understand?'

'Yes, sir.' Dan hesitated. 'But...'

'Yes?'

'Sir, can I at least know—'

'There is nothing for you to know, Lance Corporal. I am sorry if it causes you difficulties, given that Latimer is your friend, but,' he flashed one of his rare smiles, 'as Aeschylus said, in war, truth is the first casualty.' He nodded in dismissal. 'That will be all.'

Dan snapped to attention, saluted, and left the room. To have been ordered to say nothing and forget everything meant that there was some truth somewhere – but he hadn't a clue what it could be. And unless and until Paul was arrested and imprisoned, it would remain a mystery.

When she got back to Hazelhurst, Meg distributed various parcels to Helen and Diana.

'You got everything? How wonderful,' said Helen.

'Did you and Paul have a lovely time?' asked Diana.

'Yes.' Meg hoped she wouldn't have to deal with too many questions.

'Which hotel did you stay at?'

'Oh, some little place not far from Paul's club. I forget the name. Now, I must go and hide Max's presents before he sees them.'

She hurried upstairs, hoping that when Paul got home, no one would think to mention her visit. That would be fatal. She was beginning to understand the hideously unstoppable way in which one lie spawned the necessity for another.

When Paul came home, however, no one mentioned her trip to London. But the day after, when Meg and Diana were going through dress patterns in the drawing room, Paul sauntered in with a smile.

'I've just come across a rather magnificent bear and a train set at the back of the cupboard in our room. I assume they're for Max's Christmas – unless of course they're meant for me. When did you pick them up?'

The telephone began to ring in the hallway. Meg heard someone pick it up, then Helen put her head round the door. 'Diana, dear, it's for you.'

Relief swept through Meg as Diana left the room. She answered quickly, 'I got them at Hamleys. I went on a shopping trip a week or so ago.'

'You should have told me you were in town. We could have had lunch.'

'Oh, it was rather a smash-and-grab affair. Helen wanted some cosmetics as well.' Meg bent her head over the pattern book.

'See any friends while you were up there?'

'No. As I said, it was just a spur-of-the-moment thing.' She prayed Diana wouldn't return before the conversation ended.

'Well, I'm sure Max will love them. Well done.'

Paul went out, leaving Meg shaken. If Diana had been there when that conversation had taken place, the entire edifice of lies would have come tumbling down. She was going to have to be more careful in future.

PART V

1942–5

1

IN MAY THE following year, Diana's baby girl was born, and was named Morven in honour of Roddy's maternal grandmother. Roddy had been given a six-month break from flying enemy missions to train cadets, and with Diana's anxieties temporarily soothed, and with the delight of a new baby in the household, Hazelhurst felt to its inhabitants like an island of tranquillity in the midst of the sea of war.

Meg's sense of isolation was somewhat different. She listened to the nightly news bulletins and the reports on the various theatres of war, wondering which one of them Dan was in, glad to know from his occasional letters that at least he was alive. Maintaining an affectionate relationship with Paul was a strain; his very presence at Hazelhurst, ostensibly engaged in his nameless government work but with nothing to show for it, while there were weekly reports of local men killed or missing in action, had blunted Meg's respect. When she wasn't taking him for granted, she felt irked by him. The feeling was possibly a product of her own guilt, but it was real enough, and she found it hard to reciprocate his attempts at affection. She hated herself for her behaviour, but seemed helpless to control it. She tried to be kind, but invariably she failed. Their sex life barely existed, simply because there was no real desire on the part of either of them, and the effort only underscored the problem. And so matters limped unhappily along.

Helen had long been aware that things were not right between Meg and Paul. Several times she thought of saying something to her daughter, but a fear of being thought interfering always stopped her. In the end, she made it her business to be placatory and to try to disguise any disharmony for the benefit of the rest of the household.

One morning at breakfast, Paul announced that he was going into Alderworth to buy some pipe tobacco.

'Rather a nice day for a stroll,' he observed, folding up *The Times* and glancing out of the window at the June sunshine. 'Anyone fancy joining me?'

'I'd love a jaunt,' said Diana, 'but Morven kept me up half the night and I'm completely fagged.'

'I'm afraid I'm too busy to come with you, Paul,' replied Helen, 'but I have some posters for the War Weapons Week that need dropping off at various places, if you wouldn't mind. I'm sure all the shops will take them.'

'Happy to oblige,' replied Paul. He turned to Meg. 'Care to come along, old girl?'

Meg's instinct told her it would be a good thing to say yes, but she couldn't bring herself to it. It wouldn't be hard; conversations with Paul were always easy and friendly, if she allowed them to be, but that in itself could feel like a betrayal of Dan. Having her heart tug her in the direction of Dan meant, inevitably, constantly pulling away from Paul. Her mother's glance hadn't escaped her, however, and she said, 'Darling, I'd love to, but the wind has brought some of the fruit canes down, and I need to see to them.'

Paul walked alone into the village and went round the various shops, dropping off the posters, his final stop the post office-cum-newsagent, where he handed the last poster to Mrs Bainbridge.

'Oh yes, I told Mrs Slater I'd put one in the window. Not that anyone really needs reminding.'

'And I'll take a tin of St Bruno Flake, please.'

'Certainly. Here you are. That'll be two shillings.' As she took the money, Mrs Bainbridge added, 'Two hundred thousand pounds, they hope to raise. I think it's wonderful how everyone's pitching in. Our Denise is in the dancing display, and Leonard's going in for the boxing tournament. Are you taking part, Mr Latimer?'

'In the cricket match, yes,' replied Paul. 'And Mrs Latimer has roped me into the whist drive.'

'Nice to have the time to get involved. Oh, by the way' – she moved over to the post office counter – 'there's a letter here, addressed to a Miss Slater, care of here. Mrs Latimer generally picks them up, but you can save her the bother.'

'Thanks.'

Paul took the letter without a word and put it in his pocket with the tin of tobacco. He walked until he reached the bus stop halfway between Alderworth and Hazelhurst House, then took the letter out and examined it. It was postmarked Scotland, and at first he couldn't place the handwriting, though it seemed vaguely familiar. Then he realised whose it was. He stood thinking for a long moment, but in the end he didn't open it. Instead he ripped it methodically into small pieces, dropped them into the litter bin, and carried on walking.

Because she didn't receive Dan's letter, it was by the merest chance that she found out that Dan would be visiting Woodbourne House on leave, when she called Sonia to see if she was in need of honey – Helen's hives having produced another bountiful supply.

'Yes, please,' said Sonia. 'We're always most grateful, especially now we have the evacuees back. Perhaps we can give you something in return. We had one of the pigs slaughtered and butchered a fortnight ago – of course we have to give half to the government, but the rest is ours.'

'What do you do with half a pig?'

'Oh, everything. We've cured it for bacon and ham, made sausages and black pudding, all that kind of thing. We've even made our own lard.'

'Goodness, you are clever! I must tell Mother. She'll be terribly jealous.'

'Well,' conceded Sonia, 'I can't pretend I've had terribly much to do with it. There are two Italian POWs from the camp at Wormley working on the local farm, and one of them is a butcher. He did the slaughtering, and the curing. We have a good deal of bacon, and a couple of very nice hams hanging up in the barn. You can help yourself to some of that.'

'Some lard would be good, too, if you can spare it. Butter goes nowhere these days.'

'Come and fetch it any time you like.'

'Well, it will have to be soon because they're stopping petrol coupons at the end of the month.'

'Oh, so they are. Well, that settles it. Come over this Friday and make a day of it. Colin and Sidney are back in residence, and Dan is spending a couple of days here on leave, so we shall be quite a gathering. It must be an age since you last saw Dan.'

'Yes. For ever.' Meg's mouth felt dry. 'We'll come over just before lunch – make a day of it, as you say.'

'Let's just hope the weather holds. Goodbye till then.'

'Goodbye.' Meg hung up. To think if she hadn't called – and she so very nearly hadn't – Dan would have come and gone and she would never have known. Why hadn't he written?

Paul came downstairs at that moment, on the way to his study, and barely gave her a glance.

'Sonia's invited us to Woodbourne on Friday.'

'I'm afraid I can't come,' said Paul. 'I have to go away tomorrow.'

'What a shame.' She paused. 'Dan Ranscombe's there on leave. I'm sure he would have enjoyed seeing you.' She didn't know why she said this. To taste the furtive pleasure of uttering her lover's name, perhaps – or simply because it was what she would have said anyway, had everything been entirely innocent.

Paul's gaze met Meg's, and he gave a half-smile. 'That is a pity. As a matter of fact, I'll be away for longer than usual. A couple of months at least.'

Something jarred in Meg's mind. In the past, before uttering those last words, he would have taken her hands in his, or pulled her towards him to bestow an affectionate, apologetic kiss, but his manner now was quite dismissive.

'Oh. That's a long time.'

'Yes. I'm sorry, but there it is. Can't be helped. I shall leave a telephone number through which you can contact me if you need to, as always.'

'No, well…' She made an effort. 'It will be a miserable old time without you.'

'I expect you'll get by. You women are so self-sufficient these days, you hardly need a man about the place.'

'That's not quite true.' She paused, caught in a moment of uncertainty. She took a step towards him, putting her arms around his neck for an awkward moment, and kissed his cheek. 'We'll all miss you.'

Paul scarcely responded, merely disengaged himself from her embrace and went into the study, closing the door.

'Isn't it going to be rather a squash?' asked Helen dubiously, as she prepared to get into the car.

'Not at all, Mother. You and Lotte will be fine in the back seat with Max, and Diana and the baby will sit in front. Max, sit nicely next to Grandmama, and don't kick.' She gave her mother a glance. 'You needn't come if you don't want to.'

'Oh, no – I wouldn't miss Sonia's bacon-curing triumphs for the world. Is the honey in the boot?'

'Six jars of it.'

'I'm looking forward to comparing notes on our war efforts. Sonia does very well on the self-sufficiency front, but I like to think my efforts benefit the wider community. I was particularly proud of my idea for the house-to-house collection. A great success, though I do say so myself. And the thirty-eight pairs of string gloves I've knitted for those poor men on minesweepers in the Arctic – I rather imagine Sonia couldn't begin to rival that.'

They could hear the throb of an engine as they came up the drive, and when they came in view of the house there was Lobb on the big lawn, operating a tractor-drawn cutter. Meg parked the car at the rear of the house, and everyone piled out.

'What a lovely lot of hay you're going to have,' observed Diana, as Sonia came out to greet them.

'Aren't we just? Lobb is like a man possessed. He's been dying to cut it for weeks, but we've only recently had a long enough dry spell. It's too long for the motor mower, so he had to borrow a tractor from the farm. Oh, how pretty Morven is growing!' Max came running up and she bent to give him a kiss. 'I mustn't forget my favourite boy, must I? If you go and see Mrs Goodall, I think you may find she has some sweets for you.' Max scampered off towards the kitchen, Rufus and Domino at his heels. 'Carrot fudge,' she said to Meg. 'One of Mrs Goodall's wartime inventions.'

They made their way to the house, and as they came into the kitchen Sonia remarked, 'I've decided that it will simply be mayhem if the children have lunch with us, as we are so many, so I propose that they have their lunch in the nursery – Effie is up there with Laura now – and we grown-ups shall have a civilised time of it in the kitchen.' She turned to Mrs Goodall. 'Where are Colin and Sidney?'

'Mr Ranscombe took them off to the woods to build a den. He's a proper boy scout, that one.'

Meg felt a shiver of relief. Dan was still here. She'd had visions of arriving and finding he'd left early, called away to his unit. But he was here, and she would see him. Tension she hadn't been aware of ebbed away.

'Well, lunch will be ready shortly, and we need to have everyone shipshape. Have they gone far?'

'Just to them trees beyond the tennis court.'

'I'll go and find them,' said Meg quickly. 'I'm sure Max would love an expedition to the woods.' She took the tin of carrot fudge from Max. 'And no more of that before lunch, my boy.'

She and Max set off. They found Dan and the boys working in a clearing next to a stand of coppiced birch, with Star snuffling among the leaves nearby. Colin and Sidney were busy gathering ferns and brushwood, and Dan, cigarette in mouth, was hacking stems of birchwood and laying them in a row on the ground. Meg stayed silent for a few moments, drinking in the sight of him, the sinews of his forearms below his rolled-up sleeves as he worked, the blondness of his hair that seemed to grow a little darker each time she saw him. Then he turned suddenly, as though aware of her gaze, grinned, took his cigarette from his mouth and laid down his knife and the freshly cut stake.

'Hello.'

She smiled. 'Hello.' Colin and Sidney looked up and briefly inspected the new arrivals, then carried on with their work. Max ran over and began to help the boys with their work heaping up branches and ferns.

'I had no idea you were here till the other day,' said Meg, as Dan stepped towards her. With the children nearby, they knew there was no possibility of so much as a kiss. 'It was the merest chance that I telephoned Sonia.'

'Really? I wrote to tell you.'

'I didn't get it. It must have gone astray.'

'Possibly just as well. I went a bit over the top. I was missing you like hell. It must have been so much confetti after the censor had finished with it. Anyway, you're here.'

'Yes.' She longed to hold him. She felt a shining happiness just being able to look at him. It was true, she thought – this was all they might ever have, here and now. She felt no guilt whatsoever.

'Mr Ranscombe, when are we going to start building the den?' Sidney's peremptory tones indicated that he wasn't best pleased at the interruption to their task.

'I've come to fetch you for lunch,' said Meg.

'Sounds like it's going to have to wait, boys.' Dan pinched out his cigarette and put what was left in his shirt pocket.

Colin and Sidney groaned.

'Come on,' said Meg, 'let's go in and have a wash.' She took Max's hand. 'How are you two?' she asked Colin and Sidney, as they walked through the woods. 'Happy to be back?'

'Kind of,' replied Colin. 'But it wasn't half exciting at home when the bombs come.'

Sidney danced along next to his elder brother, eager for attention. 'Want to hear me make the sound of a bomb comin' down?'

Colin gave an approving nod. ''E's good. You oughter hear him.'

Sidney screwed up his face till he was puce and let forth a thin and frighteningly realistic high-pitched sound which built to a screaming intensity.

'I say, that's a bit too much like the real thing,' said Meg, as the boys leapt around flinging leaves in the air to depict the explosion.

'It's good fun playin' in the bombed-out houses,' said Sidney, 'only the wardens are always chasin' us off.'

'I should think so, too,' said Dan. 'You're both better off down here out of harm's way.'

'Yeah, it's not bad here. And wait till we get our den built,' said Colin. The edge of the wood was in sight, and the three boys set off at a run, Star at their heels, Meg and Dan following.

After lunch Dan took all the children, including Max and Laura, back to the woods to finish building the den.

'It's terribly sweet of him to spend his leave playing with them,' said Sonia, as the women settled down on the terrace to talk and knit.

'He loves it,' said Diana. 'He's just a big kid at heart. Always has been.'

Sonia, taking out her knitting, glanced across at Diana. 'My dear, whatever are you doing?'

'I'm unravelling an old jumper. Then I'm going to use the wool to knit something new.'

'Goodness, how clever. I never thought of that. Effie discovered a bolt of pillow cotton at the bottom of the linen press the other day. It'll do to make dresses for the girls. I had hoped Avril's school would relax their uniform rule, but they refuse to, so that will take any number of coupons. And she grows out of things in no time.' She counted her stitches below her breath, then added, 'It's quite wonderful how resourceful we have all become. Lobb has suggested we should get a cider press and make our own cider. Don't you think that's a splendid idea?'

Helen darted a glance at her sister. 'Rather ambitious, wouldn't you say?'

'No more so than keeping bees. If anything, less so. I must compliment you on the quality of your honey, Helen.'

'Thank you. The ham at lunch was excellent.'

Sonia smiled at her sister. 'Kind of you to say so, though really the credit goes to Alfredo.'

'Alfredo?'

'One of the Italian prisoners of war working at Godley's farm. He did the butchering and the curing. So clever. And such a handsome young man. We've become quite the best of friends. Strictly speaking, the prisoners aren't allowed to have contact with locals, but Farmer Godley thought it would be a kindness to let him talk to me since I speak Italian. A little rustily, of course, but Alfredo was quite enchanted to meet someone who can speak his language. We had a lovely long talk about his home in Umbria, and he gave me a recipe for an Italian dish that Mrs Goodall is going to try out.'

'I think you should be careful, my dear – fraternising with the enemy, I mean,' said Helen, though it was evident from her expression that she envied Sonia her tame Italian POW.

After an hour or so Colin and Sidney came racing back to the house to inform everyone that the den had been completed, and that anyone who wanted to could come and see it.

'I think we must all definitely see this wondrous creation,' said Sonia, folding up her knitting.

'I'll pass,' said Diana. 'I'd better go to the nursery to see if Morven's woken up from her nap.'

The den was a very professional affair, consisting of two low, sloping roofs made out of birch poles, supported by uprights at either end, and thatched with brush and ferns and grass.

Sonia gazed at it admiringly. 'How splendid!'

Max and Laura were dancing around, their faces streaked with lines of black, pretending to be red Indians.

'We're going to store our treasure in it,' said Colin. 'Look.' He opened a canvas bag and produced a handful of bullet casings. 'We got lots of these. You can swap two of them at school for a cap badge. But this is the best.' With some difficulty he tugged out a fragment of rocket tail. 'We ain't swappin' that for nothin'.'

'Dear me, it's a rather grisly hoard, but it's doing no harm, I suppose,' murmured Sonia. 'Just as long as you don't have any unexploded bombs.'

'Can we sleep here tonight? Mr Ranscombe says when he builds one of these he sometimes has to sleep in it for days on end, an' build a fire every day an'—'

'No, young man,' said Sonia firmly, 'you most certainly cannot. It's fine to play in in the daytime, but you're not catching your death out here at night. Now, I think Mr Ranscombe needs a rest. You've worked him hard enough.'

People began to wander back to the house.

'Where's Max got to?' asked Meg.

Max and Laura had crept back inside the den to play, and Dan went in to fetch them, emerging with a giggling child under each arm. He set them down, and they ran off after the others. Meg was about to follow them when Dan held her back. 'Hey. Come here.'

Meg glanced warily in the direction of the house. 'I don't think we should.'

But Dan ignored this, taking her in his arms and kissing her. After a moment Meg broke away with a laugh. 'Stop. We have to catch them up. It will look odd otherwise.' They began to walk back through the woods, happy just to be together.

Diana was standing on the terrace with Morven, who was now awake, as the others returned. 'Well?'

'It's a quite magnificent structure,' said Sonia. 'You should go and see. Here, I'll take Morven.'

Diana walked down the side of the tennis courts and met Max and Laura as they came running out of the woods.

'Where's Mummy?' she asked Max.

He pointed behind him. 'She's at the den.'

Diana stepped into the shadows of the trees and walked a little way in. She stopped when she saw Meg and Dan coming towards her. They hadn't seen her, and were walking close together, talking. The intimacy was unmistakable. Since coming to live at Hazelhurst, Diana couldn't help noticing that Meg's behaviour towards Paul was an odd mixture of artificial affection and dismissive irritability. As she watched now, she was struck by how different her manner was with Dan. She was relaxed and happy, glowing. He said something, and she turned and looked up at him, laughing, resting her hand lightly, briefly on his arm. It was the way Meg should be with Paul, but was not.

She took a step forward to make herself heard, and Dan and Meg looked up, startled. Meg took her hand from Dan's arm.

'I thought I'd come and see this famous den,' said Diana.

'It's just back there, where the coppice is,' said Dan. 'Come on, I'll show you.'

'I'll leave you to it,' said Meg. 'I should get back and make sure Max has a wash before tea. He's filthy.' She carried on towards the house.

Diana and Dan turned and went back into the wood. They walked a few yards in silence, then Diana observed with a smile, 'It's clear you're still rather sweet on my sister-in-law.'

'What makes you say that?'

'Oh, Dan, darling, I've always been able to read you like a book. Do be careful. She and Paul are going through a bit of a rough time, and she's rather vulnerable.'

Dan turned and looked at her. 'What are you suggesting?'

Diana shrugged. 'Nothing. Nothing at all. I just don't want my brother to be made unhappy.' She turned and met his gaze. 'Now, show me this remarkable den.'

On the journey back to Hazelhurst after tea, Helen and Lotte dozed in the back seat, while Max slept with his head in his grandmother's lap.

'Dan's looking wonderfully well, don't you think?' remarked Diana. 'Active service seems to suit him.'

'You could say the same for Roddy. I think certain men actually thrive on the excitement of war. Well, some of them, anyway.'

They drove in silence for a while, then Diana remarked, 'You know, I think Dan still has something of a crush on you.'

Meg's face was imperturbable. Months of being deceitful had changed her, and a remark which would once have provoked fluster and embarrassment produced not the slightest ripple. 'Do you think?' she replied idly. 'I suppose I should be flattered. But I'm afraid it's simply that he's an incorrigible flirt. Europe is probably littered with hearts he's broken. Or no doubt he'd like to think it is.' She changed gear as they crested a hill. 'He is very charming, though. That never changes.'

Meg knew better than to look at her sister-in-law to see the effect of her words, but she hoped they were enough to allay the suspicions she detected. She had no idea how long Diana had been standing in the woods this afternoon, or what she'd seen. Nothing damning, Meg assumed, otherwise her manner would have been quite different. But she clearly was fishing for something.

2

A FEW WEEKS LATER, Diana was going through the morning mail at breakfast. 'One for you, Meg.'

Meg took the letter, and recognised Constance Davenport's handwriting. She opened it and scanned its contents as she finished her toast. 'Constance is being sent overseas.'

'I suppose they need all the doctors they can get,' observed Diana, dabbing Morven's mouth with her bib. 'Can't say I envy her.'

'She sounds quite excited about it. She suggests I pop up and see her before she's shipped out.'

'I'm surprised how chummy you two have become,' remarked Diana. 'You never used to be, as kids.'

'I always liked her more than you did. She's very interesting, when you get to know her.'

Meg was mildly disgusted by her own hypocrisy. She didn't care particularly for Constance – she had simply been a convenient excuse to go up to town when necessary. Where Dan was concerned, nothing else mattered – she would use anyone, or anything, to be with him. She returned the letter to its envelope, thinking that she would have to go to the village post office to see if there was anything from him. Constance had said in her letter she wasn't going till the end of the month, so if by chance Dan was going to be in London on leave between now and then, she could make use of her for one last time.

'Anybody need anything from the village?' Meg asked the

others. 'I have to pop down and get some linctus for Max's throat.'

'Could you fetch me two reels of white cotton?' said Helen. 'We're nearly out.'

Meg walked down to the village. She went into the chemist's for Max's linctus, then to the haberdasher's, and lastly to the post office, where a letter from Dan was waiting.

She took the letter and pocketed it, and waited till she was outside the village before ripping it open. Dan was going overseas on some extended operation, and might be away for months, but he would be in London in a fortnight's time on a week's leave. Just in time for her to make one last visit to Constance.

There was no excuse for Meg to stay more than one night, so she and Dan would have to make the most of their time together. She arrived at Belgravia to find him busy unshrouding all the furniture in the drawing room.

'I'm tired of camping here,' he said. 'This is going to be our home in the long run, so let's start living in it properly.' He folded up a dustsheet and added it to the pile on the carpet.

The truth of this had never occurred to Meg, and her heart gave a little jump at the thought that at some point she might leave Paul and come and live here with Dan. She tried to picture life in peacetime, Max having a bedroom here, the three of them being a family, but somehow it didn't work. Belgravia was fixed in her mind as a house of clandestine shadows, of secret meetings.

Meg kissed him, and ran a hand over his unshaven chin. 'I'm not seeing Constance till three, and then she's got to be back at the hospital for her evening shift. We have two hours now, then the whole evening to ourselves.'

'It's lunchtime. Aren't you hungry?'

She smiled. 'It's not food I want.'

He kissed her. 'You are utterly shameless.'

*

Later they sat in the kitchen, eating a lunch of bread and cheese.

'Sorry I didn't have time to pick up anything more inventive,' said Dan.

'This is fine. We can have a meal this evening. Why don't we splash out and go to a hotel? We could see a film, too.' Meg relished the intimacy of being alone in the house in Belgravia with Dan, but she equally enjoyed the opportunity to pretend, if just for a few hours, that they were a normal couple doing normal things.

'If you like. What time shall we meet?' asked Dan.

'Constance wants to spend the afternoon shopping – she has to get a few things before she goes abroad. Why don't I meet you outside the cinema in Kensington High Street around five? There's bound to be a decent film on.'

'No point in going to Oxford Street,' said Constance, when Meg met her outside her lodgings. 'The bombs have made rather a mess of John Lewis and Selfridges. But Kensington should be fine.'

Meg was struck by the ability of the city and its inhabitants to cope with and work around the carnage wrought by the German bombers. Everywhere there were yawning gaps where buildings had been obliterated, but shops which otherwise looked abandoned had the words BUSINESS AS USUAL painted on the boards replacing their blown-out windows, and their entrances shored up with sandbags. After a couple of hours of shopping, they went for tea in a Lyon's Corner House.

'You've been a brick to come and visit me so often,' said Constance. 'It's been pretty lonely this past year. I haven't made any friends among the nurses. They seem to resent the fact that I'm a doctor, and the male doctors – well, they're men, aren't they, and in their eyes I'm rather an oddball. Perhaps it's my own fault. Mother says I'm too intense.'

'Nonsense,' said Meg. 'How is your mother?'

'Full of beans with her WVS work, rushing about organising everyone and everything, as I'm sure your aunt's told you. She positively relishes the war. I'm going home to see her the weekend after next, on embarkation leave.'

'Then the great adventure begins.'

'Mmm.' Constance glanced at the clock. 'I say, it's nearly five o'clock. What time's your train?'

'Oh, I decided to go back tomorrow. It's a bit of a fag, making the trip here and back in one day, especially as one doesn't always get a seat on the train. I'm staying at a hotel in Piccadilly.'

'Well, how splendid! We can go out somewhere this evening.'

Meg felt a stab of dismay. 'But what about your evening shift? You said in your letter you'd have to be back on duty at six.'

'They cancelled it. They keep changing the rotas round. It'll be nice to have some company. Evenings off are usually rather dull. I know – why don't we go to the pictures? They're showing *The Little Foxes* at the Majestic round the corner, and I know you love Bette Davis.'

Meg realised she was stuck. She could think of no reason or excuse why she and Constance shouldn't spend the evening together. She did her best to smile. 'What a good idea.' She would just have to deal with Dan as best she could.

As they approached the cinema, Meg could see Dan waiting on the pavement, smoking a cigarette. She hoped he would play his part.

'Why, it's Dan Ranscombe!' exclaimed Constance. 'What a lovely coincidence. How are you?'

'I'm very well, thanks. Good to see you. And you, Meg.' He shot Meg a quizzical look. 'As you say, quite a coincidence.'

'You *look* very well,' said Constance rather too enthusiastically, gazing admiringly at Dan's uniform. 'Are you on leave?'

'Yes, just a few days.'

'Are you waiting for someone? Meg and I are going to see the Bette Davis film.'

'No. That is, I'm just sort of… killing time, as it were.'

'Well, why don't you join us? Three old friends together – what could be nicer?'

Dan caught Meg's almost imperceptible nod, and hint of a smile. 'Yes, why don't I? Absolutely. Very jolly.'

They joined the queue, and Dan paid for three balcony seats. Constance was seated between Meg and Dan, and Meg was amused by how much attention Constance paid to Dan, whispering little remarks during the Pathé newsreel, touching his arm when she laughed at the cartoon. She didn't speak to Meg once.

They emerged an hour and a half later. 'Wasn't that splendid?' said Constance. 'She's so intense, Bette Davis. And infectious. I go around feeling like her for hours when I've seen one of her films. And doesn't Herbert Marshall remind you of Paul, Meg? So dependable and good.'

'I know what you mean,' murmured Meg. It had seared her soul to watch the scene where Bette Davis's character had poured her scorn on her poor, pathetic husband, to hear words uttered which might have been the echo of her own thoughts; '*You were so kind and understanding, and I didn't want you near me.*' Even a silly Hollywood film had the ability to wring her with guilt.

'So, where now?' said Constance. 'I'm famished. I vote we all have dinner somewhere. Meg, are you hungry?'

'I suppose so.'

'Dan?'

Dan caught Meg's eye briefly. 'I can't think of anything better. Where would you like to go? A hotel? The Royal Garden's not far from here.'

'I'm afraid that's rather too expensive for me,' said Constance.

'My treat,' said Dan gallantly.

Meg had never seen Constance as talkative as she was that evening, and put it down to a combination of wine and her evident infatuation with Dan. She had certainly changed a good deal from the awkward girl of four years ago. In fact, Meg thought, she was becoming very much like her mother. Maybe

Daphne Davenport had been shy and retiring once, though Meg couldn't imagine it. She was remembering Constance as she was the year of the house party, when Constance suddenly said, 'Do you remember that picnic we all went on in the summer of... what was it? Nineteen thirty-six?'

'Funny, I was just thinking about that,' said Meg.

Dan nodded. 'I remember the weather. Ominously hot and still. Diana brought gin. Warm gin and cream cakes. And I recall there was a most terrific thunderstorm later.'

'I'm trying to remember who came on the picnic. You two, and Paul and Diana, my mother and the Haddons, some old people whose names I forget...'

'The Cunliffes,' murmured Meg.

'That's right. And there was that serious young man – Charles someone.'

'Charles Asher,' said Dan. 'I met him a year later out in Spain, a few months before he died.'

'Oh, how sad.' Constance gave a sigh. 'What a different time it was, before the war. And what different people we all were.' She put her head on one side and smiled at Meg. 'I think you were rather sweet on Paul even then. Did you have the faintest inkling that you might marry him?'

Meg considered this. 'Yes, I suppose I did.' She looked up and met Dan's gaze. 'I always thought I might, even when I was a little girl.' The frankness of her admission, and the folly it entailed, pained Dan.

'That's so romantic. Don't you think so, Dan?'

'Very.'

'And still to be in love. Quite perfect.'

'I say, shall we get the bill?' said Meg. 'It's been a long day, and I feel quite exhausted.'

As they were leaving the restaurant, they were hailed from a nearby table by Guy Hitchens. He was in naval uniform, and was with his wife, Amy. For the first time that evening, Meg was grateful for the presence of Constance. Had she and Dan been alone together, she would have had sleepless nights in case word got back to Paul.

'Do you know Constance Davenport?' said Meg, by way of introduction.

'I think we met at Diana's wedding,' said Amy, shaking her hand.

'How lovely to see you again. The most marvellous coincidence – Meg and I were shopping, and we met Dan on the pavement, and so we whisked him off to the cinema and dinner.'

'Lucky man,' said Guy. 'Won't you join us for a drink?'

Fearful that Constance might be about to accept, Meg said hastily, 'Thanks, but we can't stay. I have an early train. Awfully nice, meeting you like this.'

They chatted for another moment, then left the hotel. Dan whistled up a cab and after a little negotiation and lying it was agreed they would drop Constance off first.

'I have never,' said Meg ten minutes later, as she waved to Constance from the taxi, 'been so glad to see the back of anyone.' She slumped against the seat. 'Which is a wretched thing to say, because she's a cleverer, nicer person than I'll ever be, and she's going to serve overseas. I feel horribly ashamed of myself. When I think of how I've used her over the past few months.'

Dan put his arm around her. 'Don't think about it. Think about me. Think about us.' He kissed her all the way back to Belgravia, and when they got inside the darkened house he carried her up to the bedroom and laid her on the bed. He closed the blackout and switched on a lamp, then sat down next to her on the bed and began slowly to undress her. He kissed her breasts, then her stomach, and she arched her back and let out a sigh of pleasure. Dan kicked off his shoes, unbuttoned his shirt, unbuckled his belt, and pulled off the rest of his clothes, then lay down next to her. 'Delayed gratification. That's one thing we can thank Constance for.'

*

A week later Paul returned from London. That evening after dinner he remarked, 'I met Guy Hitchens while I was in town.'

'What a coincidence. So did I,' replied Meg, pleased by her presence of mind.

'Yes, he mentioned that.' Paul took out his tobacco pouch and began to fill his pipe.

'Oh, Paul, your pipe smoke is quite beastly,' said Diana. 'For heaven's sake have one of my cigarettes instead.'

Paul put his pipe away and took a cigarette. 'He said he met you dining with Dan Ranscombe.'

'And Constance Davenport.'

'Really? He didn't mention her.'

Meg, aware of Diana's curious glance, replied swiftly, 'Ask Amy, if you don't believe me. She was there.' As soon as she had uttered the words she realised how defensive they sounded. 'Constance and I met Dan when we were out shopping. He was at a loose end so we all went to the cinema and had dinner together.'

'It's nearly nine o'clock,' said Helen with a yawn. 'I'd like to listen to the news on the wireless, if no one minds. Then there's Tommy Handley.'

'Yes, let's decamp to the drawing room,' said Diana, getting to her feet and ending the discussion.

But Meg was troubled by the exchange, and by the fact that Guy had made no mention of Constance, thereby undermining an alibi which she had regarded as secure. When she and Paul went to bed that night she said, 'Why did you make such a point this evening about my having had dinner with Dan and Constance?'

'I didn't know Constance was there.'

'Are you saying that if she hadn't been, it would somehow have mattered?' Paul said nothing. 'Dan's a friend.'

'It's perfectly fine.'

Meg got into bed. Paul laid a hand on her shoulder, trying to pull her gently towards him.

She shrugged away. 'I just don't like what you're implying.'

'I'm not implying anything.'

After a moment's silence, in which he stroked her shoulder in a way she found maddening, she turned over to face him. 'I shouldn't have got cross.'

He kissed her, and she tried not to shrink. She suddenly thought of the film, the desperate pathos of the scorned husband and heartless wife, all now seeming too close to home. She disengaged herself gently from his embrace, and said wearily, 'Let's get some sleep.' Before he could say or do anything more, she turned over, drawing the covers around her shoulders, inching away from him. When he turned out the light a moment later, she breathed a sigh of relief into the pillow, and gave her mind over to her lover.

3

THE FABRIC OF the year that followed was, for Meg, woven of two realities – the cheerful homespun of keeping a household of seven people running amid the difficulties and privations of war, and, like small, silken threads glinting through this coarse weave, the times when she and Dan could be together. The latter were few and far between. With Constance overseas, Meg had lost a useful excuse, but she managed to make excursions on her own to coincide with Dan's spells of leave – occasional shopping trips, and once to fetch her mother some clothes from the Chelsea house – but she could never stay overnight, and the hours spent together were frustratingly short.

Paul was away so much that she scarcely gave him a thought. Their relationship had become perfunctory, and so preoccupied was Meg with her secret love affair that she neither noticed nor cared whether or not he was affectionate towards her. Their mutual love of Max was enough of a bond to maintain their marriage for as long as was necessary. For Meg now felt as though she was merely marking time until the day came when she could be with Dan for good. She did not dwell on the practicalities of how that was to be brought about. She simply saw it as the purpose of her life, one which would make all that she was living through worthwhile. *When the war ends*, she kept thinking. Then everything would be different. She just needed to keep going until then. There was a strange contentment in this suspended existence, with the constantly demanding preoccupations of the present and dreams of the future. She never stopped to think that the only thing that anchored her, that gave her a solid, day-to-day sense of purpose, was Hazelhurst and the reality of the life lived by its inhabitants within its walls. Even when she imagined a life with Dan, she never thought beyond it.

On an airless August night in 1943, while the rest of the household slept, and Paul was away, Meg was sitting in the kitchen on fire-watching duty. She had raised the blackout blinds from the windows to let in air, preferring to sit in the darkness, thinking, than try to read with them down, which would inevitably make her fall asleep. That would be the worst possible thing. On her fire-watching nights, which came every three weeks, she was always filled with an invincible sense of patriotism, and the idea of failing to guard the sleeping acres of wheat and barley around Hazelhurst seemed almost sacrilegious. The moon was almost full that night, so the kitchen wasn't entirely dark. Ghostly light painted familiar objects, and beyond the window she could make out the silhouettes of trees at the edge of the garden. She thought of Dan, wondering where he was tonight. There had been no letter at the post office in weeks, which wasn't like him. She had gleaned that the work he did was out of the ordinary run of soldiering, and the knowledge of the dangers he must face on whatever operations he was on had bred in her a constant, quiet dread, which only his letters could alleviate. But she would not let herself believe that he was anything but safe and sound. She felt she would know instinctively if it were otherwise, so closely bound to him was she in her head and heart.

The open windows didn't help to make the room much cooler. The air was as warm inside as out. She picked up a copy of *Lilliput* magazine and fanned her face for a moment. Then she dropped it on the table with a sigh, and let her hands fall back in her lap. The memory of a night just like this one came to her. A hot, still August night seven years ago, when she was just a girl, and Dan had come to her room. He had been not much more than a boy himself. She had known nothing then. Nothing. Would that she had been wiser. Without even realising it, she closed her eyes.

Moments later she came out of her doze with a jerk. She got up and put the kettle on the gas to make a cup of coffee, which she took into the garden. She sat on the stone bench by the mulberry tree, tasting the fragrance of the night air, listening for a nightingale. She glanced up at the sleeping house as she sipped her coffee. Being the only one awake, on watch, filled her with a sense of protectiveness. She thought back to the first time she had come to Hazelhurst. It seemed a lifetime ago. She had been content – or so she thought – and utterly without self-awareness. She had surrendered herself to Paul, entirely believing in his ability to make her happy and keep her safe. She knew, now, that one had to make one's own life, not leave it in the hands of another. The marriage had failed – and she had helped it to fail by her betrayal – but at least she was prepared to face that fact and start afresh. She wasn't sure that Paul even recognised that things had gone wrong. And when the time came to end it, all this, the house she had grown to love, would be part of her past and her home no longer. She ran her hand over the lichened stone, chilled by the thought.

She yawned and rubbed her eyes, and took another gulp of her coffee. An owl hooted somewhere in the woods. Then suddenly there rose on the air the lifting whine of the sirens from the camp beyond the village. She put her cup and saucer down and hurried inside to fetch her torch and whistle. Above her the household was stirring. She went into the hall and called up. Helen appeared on the landing in her dressing gown and slippers.

'It is *such* a bore having to go to the shelter every time,' she grumbled as she came downstairs. 'I don't know why we bother. A bomb hasn't landed in these parts since I came here.'

'There's a first time for everything. Come on, I have to be off. Where is Lotte?'

Lotte appeared, hand in hand with a sleepy-eyed Max, then Diana came down with Morven. They trooped out to the shelter at the end of the garden, padding across the moonlit grass. As she set off at a brisk walk down the driveway, Meg could hear Max behind her shouting excitedly about planes.

Sure enough, a swarm of bombers came thundering low across the sky, and swept onwards. Meg walked for five minutes until she reached the first house in the village, then turned around and started to walk back. She would keep on doing this until the all-clear sounded. On the horizon to the east a dull red glow was growing. London taking another pounding. She wondered fleetingly if Paul was there, if he was safe. He could be anywhere in the country, for all she knew, or even out of it. That fact, not knowing where he was or what he did, was a further estrangement. Around her the wheatfields lay silent. A momentary breeze rippled them into shivering loveliness. The heat was dropping. She came round the bend in the road. The gates of Hazelhurst stood etched in moonlight. Then Meg heard the sound of a lone plane bursting across the sky in a fury, more terrifying in its singularity than any fleet of bombers. In a matter of seconds the bombs fell. She didn't know how many, but as she threw herself face-down on the grass she could feel several enormous explosions shake the ground. Something pattered on her like hard rain, and she realised it was small clumps of grass and earth. She got to her feet and began running towards the gates of the house. Please God, let the shelter not have been hit. She ran, stumbling up the driveway, the stench of high explosives mixing in her nostrils with the smell of ripped earth. She shouted out, but the bombs had temporarily deafened her, and her own voice came to her as though from far under water.

Hazelhurst had taken a hit. Through the smoke she could see that one side of the house had collapsed entirely, and the roof pitched at an angle over the gaping brickwork of the exposed rooms, lit by the blaze of the burning ground floor. She stood staring, her mind numb, feeling the heat of the fire, then staggered across the grass towards the shelter. It seemed intact. She hurried towards it and banged frantically on the corrugated iron roof. After a moment Helen emerged, her face scared and white. Meg realised her mistake, and shouted, 'No, go back in! Stay there!' She thought that was what she shouted, but her voice came from far away. She looked round, and saw a party of wardens from the village hauling the stirrup pump up the drive at a run. One of them still had his pyjamas on. She saw Dixon, who had his lodging above the workshop, in vest and underpants, dragging a hose around the side of the house.

Meg sank to the grass on her knees. Across the air, behind the crackle of the burning house and the shouts of the men as they directed their pitiful jets of water at the flames, she could hear the faint ghost of the steady all-clear. Burning debris had somehow landed in the mulberry tree and had set the branches alight. Below it, on the stone bench where she had been sitting a short while ago, by the light of the flames she could see her coffee cup sitting there where she had left it, intact, presumably with the warm dregs of her coffee still in it. How absurd, she thought. How utterly absurd.

The next morning, when Meg awoke, she found herself gazing at a large gilt mirror hanging above an ornate fireplace. For a moment she had absolutely no idea where she was. Her eyes roamed the room, taking in the swirling pattern of birds and flowers on silk chinoiserie wallpaper, and then she remembered. She was at Anna's. Max lay next to her in the big bed in a tangle of sheet and blanket, dark hair stuck damply to his forehead, his thumb in his mouth, fast asleep. She sat up. Lotte lay asleep on a camp bed a few feet away. Meg fell back on the pillow and let the events of last night play out in her mind. They had an unreal quality, like scenes from a film. She turned her head to gaze at the shafts of sunlight slanting in at the sides of the curtains. *I will get up*, she thought, *and go to the window, and look out, and there will be Hazelhurst, whole and intact. It didn't happen. If I think hard enough, it needn't be real.* What was it that someone had said when they heard George Gershwin had died? *I don't have to believe it if I don't want to.*

But as she got out of bed and pulled aside the heavy brocade curtain, she knew in the depths of her heart that it was all too real. Her ears were still ringing from the force of the exploding bombs. Her body retained the memory of the crumps and crashes shuddering through it as she lay by the roadside. She stared out of the mullioned window. Beyond the grounds of Alderworth Hall, beyond the trees, she could see the jagged outline where half the house had been taken out, the dark smudge of smashed garden. Little drifts of smoke still rose from the ruin. She could see where another bomb had fallen in the field behind the house, another further away on the outskirts of the village, close to All Souls. She let the curtain drop back and sat down on the edge of the bed. She was wearing only her slip, and glanced around for the frock she'd had on last night. She found it over the back of a chair, and put it on. It smelt of smoke, and as she fastened the buttons she saw that the front was grazed with dirt where she had flung herself down. She put on her shoes and went downstairs to find Anna.

'I must get in touch with Paul,' said Meg, as she and Anna sat drinking tea together at the breakfast table. 'I need to go back to the house.' She thought for a moment. 'The kitchen side of the house is still standing, the morning room and the drawing room.' She rubbed her forehead. 'I can't remember if I left my handbag there or in the bedroom. That's where I put his telephone number.'

'I'll walk over with you,' said Anna.

At that moment Helen appeared in the dining room. Clad only in the dressing gown and slippers she'd had on last night, she looked frail, like an invalid.

'Come and have some tea and breakfast,' said Anna, and drew out a chair.

Helen sat down. 'Diana will be down in a moment. She's with your nanny, seeing to Morven.' She smiled at Anna as she handed her a cup of tea. 'Thank you.'

'Everyone will feel better after some breakfast. What an awful night you've all been through.'

'I'm going over to the house with Anna,' Meg told her mother. 'There are things I need to find. Paul's telephone number, for one. And I need to see what's salvageable. The whole house hasn't gone. We may be able to find clothes.'

Helen shook her head. 'I think I could see last night that the front bedrooms are gone, and the nursery. You'll be able to get a better idea by daylight.'

It was another hot day. The countryside lay in its summer loveliness, indifferent to the awful events of the night before. Meg and Anna took the bridle path and walked through the woods until they reached the road leading to Hazelhurst. They talked about Anna's husband, who had been a prisoner of war for two years.

'He's been moved to some place called Colditz. It's where they put prisoners who keep trying to escape.' Anna gave a rueful smile. 'Indefatigable James. He hates being bored. Taking risks is a way of life for him. I wish he'd just spare a thought for us. He's likely to be shot if he keeps on doing it.'

'You must miss him.'

Anna nodded. 'Dreadfully. But raising money for the POWs helps me feel I'm doing something to help. And of course, I write and tell him all our news. ' Both women paused, shading their eyes to watch a fleet of Hurricanes sweep through the skies and disappear towards the coast. 'One thing I haven't been able to bring myself to tell him,' continued Anna, as they walked on, 'is that the Hall is being requisitioned. I got a letter saying they need it to house overseas troops. I had hoped we might escape, but there's nothing we can do about it. The children and I shall have to squeeze ourselves into a few rooms and give the rest over. What's ironic is that James suggested at the start of the war that we should offer the house to the government – you know, to be used as a school, or something of the kind, when all the evacuations were going on. But I wasn't keen. I wish we had now. Schoolchildren might have been a sight more civilised than a load of soldiers.'

They came in sight of the gates of Hazelhurst, and Anna laid a hand on Meg's arm. 'Are you all right?'

Meg nodded. 'I'm prepared for the worst. Maybe it won't be as bad as I remember.'

But it was worse. Seeing the stricken house by daylight was agonising. More than half the building had been obliterated, the rooms on the left side no more than heaps of rubble and smoking beams and cinders. Meg spotted the shattered remnants of familiar furniture – pieces of a walnut escritoire which had stood in Helen's bedroom, the singed door of a large wardrobe flung on to the lawn among bricks and ash, and worst of all, spars of the white cot in which Morven had slept poking through a charred lump of mattress.

The right-hand side of the house was largely intact, but the floors of the upper rooms pitched perilously downwards. The kitchen, dining-room and drawing-room windows were all shattered, but the rooms themselves had not been destroyed. Treading through the mess of glass and rubble, Meg walked round the back to the kitchen door. It stood open, just as she had left it when she had come outside with her coffee last night. She stepped tentatively inside. The force of the bomb had pitched the dresser forward and it lay heavily askew, its fall broken by the kitchen table, and its contents smashed and heaped on the tiled floor. Pots, pans, tins, jugs and plates had been flung from every shelf and surface in the room. There on a chair, filmed with dust, sat Meg's handbag, with Paul's telephone number in it. She picked it up, then went to the doorway and looked down the passageway that led to the hall. Daylight gaped beyond it where the other side of the house had disappeared. She wondered if she might venture further in, to see if anything could be salvaged from Paul's study or the drawing room, but thought better of it. The entire structure of the house was surely weakened to a point where the rest of it could collapse at any moment. Anna echoed her thoughts.

'I don't think you should go any further,' she said.

'No.' Meg came back and went through the door to the laundry room. Two baskets of washing stood on the table near the mangle. She sifted through them. Enough clothes for Max and Morven to be going on with, some crumpled frocks and trousers, a number of blouses which just needed the attentions of a flat iron, and a useful assortment of underwear. She unhooked a large hemp bag which was hanging behind the door and bundled as many of the clothes into it as she could. Then she went back through to the kitchen.

'I don't think there's anything else I can retrieve at the moment,' she said to Anna. She looked around again, then a sudden wave of grief overwhelmed her and she leaned against her friend's shoulder and wept.

'I know,' murmured Anna, although she couldn't imagine what it must be like to lose one's entire home overnight. 'Don't worry. You have a home with us for the time being. Though I believe the troops will start arriving next week.'

Meg fished a handkerchief from the pocket of her dress and dried her eyes. 'You've been more than kind. We'll make some kind of arrangement.' She picked up the basket. 'Come on. I can't bear to stay here a moment longer.'

As they went outside, Meg glanced across the paddock and saw Dixon coming out of the stables. 'Oh! The horses! How could I forget them?' She dropped the basket and ran across the garden and field, calling to Dixon.

'Dixon, how are they? They must have been terribly frightened by the bombing.'

'Morning, Mrs Latimer.' Dixon touched his cap. 'They've been all a-tremble, right enough, but they're settling. Good job the stables are on this side of the house and far enough away. I'm keeping an eye on them.'

'Thank you for staying here.'

He smiled uncertainly. 'Here's my home. Not rightly sure where else I'd be.'

'I can hardly call it home any more,' said Meg sadly. They both glanced at the devastated house.

Dixon took off his cap and scratched his head. 'I'll stay on here for the time being, if I may, look after the horses, and that.'

'Of course, Dixon. We'll keep paying your wages, don't worry.' Meg glanced up at the flat above the workshop. 'Is your place all right? Any damage?'

'None to speak of. Bits and pieces on the floor, a few things broke, but nothing that can't be put right.'

'Well, that's good news. I'll be back to tell you what arrangements we're making, when we've worked something out. We have to find somewhere to live.'

'Right enough.' He hesitated. 'I'm sorry for your loss, Mrs Latimer. It were a lovely house.'

'Maybe we can rebuild it. I don't know. I've never been bombed before.'

She bade Dixon goodbye, retrieved her bag of clothes, and set off back to Alderworth Hall with Anna. There she rang the number Paul had left, and after what seemed like endless delay she was put through and was able to tell him what had happened. She had become so convinced over the last year that she no longer loved him that she hardly expected the familiar sound of his voice to reduce her to tears. But it did.

He listened, asked questions, and did his best to soothe her distress. 'The important thing is you're all safe and well. I'm sad about the house, but let's see what can be done. I'll be on the first train up this afternoon.'

As Meg put the phone down, Helen came downstairs, still in

her bedroom slippers, but in one of the dresses salvaged by Meg, freshly ironed.

'I called Sonia while you were out and told her what happened. She asked if you would telephone back as soon as you could.' She gave a little shiver. 'My nerves are still in pieces.'

Meg telephoned Woodbourne House.

'My dear, I cannot tell you how sorry I am,' said Sonia. 'You poor thing. I'm just glad that none of you was hurt. How are you? Helen said you've been up to the house.'

'Yes, I had to see how bad the damage was by daylight. It couldn't be worse. Half the house has gone, and the rest looks as if it could fall down any minute. I managed to salvage some clothes. Paul's in town, but he's getting the train up this afternoon. Anna has been wonderful, looking after all of us. When I think of people who get bombed out and have simply nowhere to go, I suppose we've been lucky.'

'Well, I have a proposal to put to you. Unless you have some other plan, I suggest that all of you come and live here for the time being. Sidney and Colin are going back to London when school starts, and we have plenty of space. You'd all be most welcome. Will you think about it?'

'I certainly shall. But are you sure? You have enough going on without a toddler and a baby and four more grown-ups.'

'Nonsense. I love nothing better than having the house full of people. You know that. Besides, a few more pairs of hands will be most welcome, as will the extra coupons. It will be just like having paying guests – only you won't pay a thing.'

'We certainly shall, Aunt Sonia – I refuse to come otherwise. Although the government have told Anna they're requisitioning Alderworth Hall, and a load of American soldiers will be billeted here soon so she can't possibly have us for more than a couple of days.'

'Then that's settled. We shall organise a removals van, and you can be here by the weekend.'

Meg gave a sad laugh. 'I hardly think a van will be necessary.

We've nothing except the clothes we stand up in. I should think I could just about put all we own in the dog cart and bring it over myself. Anyway, let me talk it over with Paul when he comes, and I'll let you know later. And thank you for being so kind.'

Paul arrived three hours later. Meg caught sight of him from the nursery window coming up the gravel driveway. His strong, familiar figure was so reassuring that she felt a pang of affectionate longing, and a sense of remorse. She hurried out to meet him. He accepted her hug, but she could detect reserve in his manner. In her fragile emotional state she needed his affection, and that it wasn't forthcoming made her feel frightened.

His first thought, once he had greeted Anna and thanked her, was for Max. He spent a good fifteen minutes in the nursery with the little boy, listening to his excited account of the air raid first, then talking to him gently about the house, and what would happen now.

Meg, not liking to intrude, hung about just outside the door, listening.

'As long as you have Mummy and me, you have a home. Houses are just places, you know, and we'll find another one just as nice. Or maybe we can rebuild the old one.'

'It's all in pieces, Daddy.'

'I know, old fellow, but it was just a load of bricks before they built it. It can be done again. I'm going up to take a look at it in a moment, to see what can be done.'

'Can I come with you? I need to look for Henry Rabbit. I left him behind when the siren went and we all had to run to the shelter.'

'Not today. Maybe another time. Now, you need to look after Mummy. She's had a dreadful shock. We men have to be strong, don't we?'

Meg, peeping through the doorway, saw her five-year-old son nod uncertainly. Paul straightened up, and Meg moved away from the door and went downstairs.

Paul came down a moment later. 'I'm going to take a walk up.'

'Would you like me to come with you?'

'No, I'd rather go alone. Besides, you've been once today. I shouldn't think you'd want to see it again.'

'As you like.' His words suggested he was sparing her, but she sensed she was being rebuffed. 'Dixon's up there. He's staying on to tend the horses. His flat wasn't damaged. Neither was the workshop. So your car's safe.'

'I don't care about the car,' said Paul shortly. 'I'll be back later.'

Meg walked to the door with him in silence, and watched as he strode off down the driveway, following his figure as far as the road, until he disappeared from sight. She went through to the empty morning room and sat on the window seat. Something was very wrong. Perhaps the shock of the house being bombed had affected him. But she sensed it was more than that. There was a complete estrangement. Well, of course there was – she'd brought it about herself, carrying on with another man, thinking she could keep the protective shell of her marriage intact for as long as it suited her. She had created a gulf between them, and she shouldn't be surprised that he felt and reacted to it. He had always responded gratefully to her affection in the past. Not today. Yet she knew that, whatever he felt, he would look after her. That was the kind of man he was. That was the kind of man she was in the process of destroying.

Paul returned an hour later, when everyone was in the drawing room having tea. The French windows stood open to the summer air, and the maid came and went in her neat uniform with plates of sandwiches and cakes.

'Come and have a cup of tea,' Anna said. 'You look as though you could do with one.'

'Thanks.' Paul sat down, his face grim. 'Well, they've certainly made a mess of it.'

'It's only half the house,' ventured Meg. 'The left-hand side—'

'The whole lot will have to come down. There's no question of rebuilding.'

There was a brief silence, broken only by the tinkle of Helen's spoon as she stirred her tea, then Meg said, 'Sonia has invited us to go and live with her for the time being.'

Paul sighed. 'That might be for the best. I can't think how else we'll manage.' He drained his tea and took his pipe from his pocket. 'Excuse me, everyone. I'm going outside for a smoke. I don't feel like eating anything right now.'

'Poor Paul,' said Anna, when he had left. 'Your lovely home. You both worked so hard to make it what it was. He's obviously wretched about it.'

Meg rose. 'I'm going to go and talk to him. He bottles things up. It isn't good for him.'

She stepped through the French windows and saw Paul pacing the lawn next to the driveway. She walked over and sat down on a nearby stone balustrade.

'Paul, darling, what's wrong?' She was conscious that she hadn't used the endearment much lately. 'It's more than the house. I can tell.'

Paul sat down next to her. 'As if the house wasn't enough.' He paused. 'Everything we worked for has gone, hasn't it? At least it wasn't something that had been in the family for centuries, like this place. Imagine a whole heritage being destroyed. I hope to God Alderworth Hall will still be standing when James comes back.'

'I suppose every house is precious to its owners.'

He nodded. 'That's very true. Hazelhurst was precious to us for a while, wasn't it?'

'What do you mean – for a while?'

'Until it was bombed.'

But Meg didn't believe that was what he meant at all. 'Paul, what else is the matter?'

'Oh, any number of things, really. Can't put them all into words.' His gaze roamed the gardens for a moment, and she felt fear in the pit of her stomach as she waited for what he might say. 'The fact is, Meg, I've had enough.'

'Enough?' Her mouth felt dry.

'Enough of what I'm doing. It's a vitally important job – I wouldn't be doing it otherwise – but there are men risking their lives every day to defend this country, men like Roddy, and the sons and husbands of everyone we know, and I should be part of that.' Meg felt a tightness in her chest loosening. 'I've put in for an RAF commission. I can fly a plane, which is more than most chaps who sign up, so I don't think it'll be long before I'm in uniform.' He gave a short laugh. 'In fact, given the turnover rate, it should be any day now.'

'Are you sure about this, Paul?'

'As sure as I've ever been about anything.'

'Well, of course, I'll support you whatever you decide to do.'

'I have to deal with what's left of our home first. I'll be making arrangements to have the car put into storage. And we'll have to sell the horses. I told Dixon, and he recognises the situation. He says it won't be hard to find other work, given the shortage of labour hereabouts. I offered to pay him a month's wages.' He sighed. 'It'll all work out. You and Max will be at Woodbourne House, and I'll come down whenever I'm on leave. And when the war's over, maybe we can start again.' His eyes searched her face, but she looked away.

'Yes.' She stood up. 'I'd better go and tell the others about moving to Sonia's.'

'Fine. I'll stay out here for a bit, and have a smoke.'

'I suppose it's the logical thing to do,' said Diana. 'I don't think Morven and I would manage very well on our own in Kensington. It's awfully good of Sonia to volunteer to have us all.'

'Oh, she'll simply adore it,' said Helen. 'She'll be like a mother hen. Though it's a pity we can't stay on here.' She glanced appreciatively around Anna's drawing room. It had been a refreshing change to have tea served properly by a maid in cap, cuffs and apron, instead of higgledy-piggledy at Meg's kitchen table. 'One forgets what it's like to have servants. The Kentleighs are lucky to have kept so many staff. I suppose it will be every man for himself at Woodbourne House.'

'I'm sure we'll get by very well,' said Meg. 'In the meantime, we have to think about practicalities. You all need shoes, including the children. I'll go down to the clothing depot in the village and see what I can find. There's no point in buying new things until we get to Woodbourne.'

'How are we to get there?' asked Diana.

'Bus, I suppose, since we can't drive.' Meg thought for a moment. 'I was joking when I told Sonia I would jog over in the dog cart, but I don't see why some of us can't. Sonia might find the dog cart useful, and it would mean not having to sell Grisette.'

'I refuse to go all the way to Woodbourne House in a horse and cart,' said Helen firmly.

'I don't mind,' said Diana. 'If you think the weather will hold.'

'Good. I'll go and tell Anna we'll be out of her hair by tomorrow.'

4

DAN WOKE WITH a start, his heart racing, convinced for a moment that he was back at the top of the glacier with Black and Tenby and the other commandoes. He'd been having a terrifying dream in which he was swinging across a fathomless chasm, downwards, ever downwards, in stomach-lifting loops, with dark walls of water – which he knew would carry him to certain death – cascading on either side of him.

His body was damp with sweat. He drew his hand across his face and lay waiting for the thudding of his heart to slacken, gradually taking in the realisation that he wasn't in a sleeping bag in the biting chill of the Arctic morning, but in his bedroom in Belgravia – albeit fully clad and still with his boots on.

He wasn't sure which were worse – the nightmares or the flashbacks. At least the flashbacks were real memories – Captain Tenby knocking the ashes from his pipe as they prepared to begin the ascent of the glacier; the clatter of Reinertsen's pistol falling into a ravine when he almost lost his footing; that moment when he had frozen with fear halfway, convinced he could go neither backward nor forward, until Tenby's calm voice had willed him on; the terror of inching his way beneath the massive water pipes of the hydroelectric dam to strap on the explosives; the explosion itself rocking the valley. Those he could cope with, though they came without warning, knocking him momentarily for six.

The nightmares, on the other hand, were ghastly distortions of reality. In one of them he was wedged beneath the pipes, unable to escape, horribly aware as the seconds ticked by that he was about to be blown to smithereens in a torrent of water and metal and rubble, only to wake sweating and shouting. In another he and Brendan were within sight of the Swedish border, when the grassy meadow through which they were tramping dissolved into sticky mud, and they were struggling in vain to move their legs as behind them the German patrols roared closer and closer.

The nightmares might be bad, but at least he woke from those. The flashbacks were relentless, inescapable.

As the details of the hellish dream receded from his brain like a tide from a rock, he became conscious that he was hung-over. As badly hung-over as he'd ever been. He retraced the events of the previous day – the train journey down from Scotland, the debriefing at the War Office, that chap Mountbatten congratulating them on the success of the mission, and giving them a month's leave and offering them the use of his staff car to take them wherever they were going. They had gone instead to the pub. His last clear memory was of pulling Brendan out of a Soho bar, where he had been trying to start a fight with two fusiliers.

Brendan. What had happened to him? Dan got gingerly out of bed and made his way along the landing. To his relief he found him, also still in uniform, sprawled untidily on the bed in a spare room, fast asleep. Dan went to the bathroom and splashed his face with cold water, then went downstairs. In the cellar he tipped the last of the anthracite into the boiler and lit it. He would have to remember to order some more. The luxury of twenty-eight days in which to attend to such minor domestic chores stretched ahead of him. Above all, he would, with luck, be able to see Meg.

After a bath, Dan took his duty ration book to the shops and bought what food he could for breakfast. When he got back Brendan was up and about, albeit in a fragile condition.

'That was a night, that was,' said Brendan. 'How are you feeling?'

'Fragile.' Dan badly wanted to know whether Brendan was suffering the same mental repercussions from the mission as he was, but during the past ten days, from the morning they had crawled over the fence to the Swedish border until the afternoon when they had left the British Embassy in Stockholm for the flight home, he had never talked about it. Now was not the time to begin. He slipped four rashers of bacon into the frying pan. 'Good news,' he told Brendan. 'We have an egg apiece.'

'How are you going to spend your month's leave?' asked Dan, when breakfast was finished.

'I'm going to my sister in Balham for a couple of days, see my nephews, then head for Liverpool and get the Dublin ferry, see my folks. You?'

'I don't honestly know. Take it easy, I suppose.' He could think of no therapy which would heal his shattered nerves, beyond a few quiet days at Woodbourne House.

After Brendan had left, Dan washed up the dishes and then sat down to go through the mail that had accumulated during his weeks of absence. There was a letter from Harry, now a private stationed in Huddersfield, grumbling with witty invective about the tedium of army life and the constant cleaning of kit, and a letter from Sonia dated three weeks earlier.

Great changes here – poor Meg and Paul lost their house, hit by a bomb in August. No one was hurt, which is a mercy. Everyone who was at Hazelhurst is now living here at Woodbourne, so we are a motley crew. Laura is very glad to have Max as a playmate.

Dan digested this news. Hazelhurst had symbolised everything Meg had hoped for from her marriage. Perhaps now it was gone, it would be easier to persuade her to leave Paul. With this unworthy thought, he carried on reading through the rest of Sonia's letter, which concluded:

> *I hope this finds you safe and well, and that if you have some leave soon you will pay us a visit. You know how I love to see you, and a bed is always waiting.*

Dan folded up the letter. After the horrors of the past weeks a visit to Surrey would be a balm to his soul, particularly since Meg was there. He would go down this weekend.

As Dan made his way up the path towards Woodbourne House, past the barn and through the orchard, the tawny, pleasantly decaying scent of autumn was just beginning to creep into the air. The apple trees were laden with a late crop of apples, and against the brick wall of the kitchen garden the quinces and medlars were ripe and ready to be picked. The kitchen garden itself was almost twice the size it had been before the war, a patchwork of beds of autumn vegetables. Laura was playing by the fountain with Star, holding up a length of dead raspberry cane at which the little dog kept leaping.

'Hi, there,' said Dan.

She looked up. 'Hello, Mr Ranscombe.' With Haddon's dark, intelligent eyes and well-defined brows, and her mother's blond delicacy, she was turning into a remarkably pretty girl. 'I'm trying to teach Star to be a circus dog, but he's too silly. We saw a dog at the circus that could walk with a ball on his nose and jump through hoops, and sit up and beg, and everything. He looked a bit like Star, but I suppose he must have been a lot cleverer.'

'Where are Colin and Sidney? I thought you three were thick as thieves.'

'They've gone back to London.' Laura's expression was forlorn. 'What's thick as thieves?'

Dan was just searching for a reply when Sonia emerged from

the house in dungarees and gumboots, carrying a hopsack. Her eyes widened in surprise and delight when she saw Dan.

'Dan! How lovely! Why didn't you telephone to say you were coming?' She embraced him.

'I thought I'd give you a surprise. I only got back a couple of days ago.'

'Goodness, you look...' She hesitated.

'Rough? I certainly feel it. I've had rather a hairy time of it. Glad to be back in one piece, but still feeling a bit shaky.' It was true. His nerves still felt like taut wires.

'Well, I'd like to promise you plenty of peace and quiet, but we're a rather hectic household. How long can you stay?'

'As long as you'll have me.'

'Splendid. I shall tell Effie to make up a bed. Now, go inside and say hello to everyone. I'm off to feed my chickens, and then we can sit down together and I can hear all your news.'

Sonia departed in the direction of the chicken coops. At that moment Meg came out of the house, calling to Laura. She stopped in her tracks when she saw Dan.

She turned to Laura. 'Run inside, darling. Lotte wants you to tidy your toys away before tea.' She sat down weakly on the edge of the fountain and gazed at Dan, then said in a low voice shaky with emotion, 'I'm so glad to see you. I've been out of my mind with worry these past two months. Where have you been? You look all-in.'

Dan sat down next to her. He smiled, but it was an effort. 'Can't tell you, I'm afraid.' He picked some moss from between the stones and scattered it on the water. The goldfish rose expectantly, then nosed away, disappointed, into the dim depths. 'But yes – I've been through the mill a bit. Badly in need of some rest and quiet.' He paused, then said, 'Sonia wrote and told me about Hazelhurst. I'm truly sorry. I know how you loved that place.'

'Yes. Rather a rotten show.' Tears sprang to her eyes, and she wiped them quickly away, adding, 'But maybe it's for the best.'

'Don't say that.'

'For us, I mean. It will make it easier to end everything with Paul, when it happens.' She looked away. 'Oh, just listen to me. I never used to be this kind of person. So callous. So selfish.'

'We can't help what's happened.'

Diana was passing the landing window. She paused when she saw Dan and Meg by the fountain. She couldn't hear what was being said or see Dan's face, but from Meg's expression she could tell the conversation was intimate and intense.

'That's not true. We could have, if we'd been better people. Paul doesn't deserve what I've done to him. He's far too good for me. You know he's in the RAF now? He gave up his desk job. He's with bomber command. Couldn't stand not fighting for his country.'

'I see.' This didn't sound like someone who was trying to undermine the war effort. If Paul really was working for the Germans, surely Whitehall was a better place to be than in the cockpit of a Lancaster, facing Heinkels and Messerschmitts.

She made an effort at brightness, and got to her feet. 'Anyhow, come inside. Everyone will be thrilled to see you.'

Diana moved away from the landing window, and came downstairs to the kitchen moment later.

'Dan, darling, what a nice surprise!' she exclaimed. 'You look like a member of the foreign legion. All sunburnt and gaunt. How long are you on leave?'

'Twenty-eight days.'

'Goodness, you must have done something rather special to deserve that.'

'Nothing to speak of.'

'I'm sure you're being modest. What will you do with all that time?'

'I don't know. I hadn't really made any plans, but now that I find Woodbourne House full of scintillating women, I might just stay here for a while.'

*

If Dan had thought he would be happy at Woodbourne House, the closest thing he had to a proper home, with Meg there, he quickly discovered he was wrong. Being with Meg in circumstances where he had to behave with artificial restraint was trying enough, but when he heard at the end of his first week there that Paul was coming home on weekend leave, he knew he couldn't face the prospect of the three of them being under the same roof. Added to which, he was still sleeping badly, and was afraid the fractious state of his nerves and his short temper might be disturbing the harmony of the household. He decided he would cut his visit short.

He told Sonia so after lunch on Friday.

'I wish you could stay longer,' said Sonia. 'Perhaps we'll see you at Christmas?'

'I can't honestly say, but I'll try.' If there was a likelihood of Paul being at Woodbourne House for Christmas, Dan had no intention of coming back.

'I need to talk to you before you go,' murmured Meg, as she took the plates from the table.

When lunch had been cleared away, Dan volunteered to take the pigs' pails to the sty.

Laura clapped her hands. 'Can I come, please?'

'And me!' cried Max.

'Come on, then,' said Meg. 'Let's add the lunch leftovers to the pail. There's a bucket of beer dregs that Lobb got from the pub. We can put those in, too.'

Meg and Dan walked across the jagged, hay-cut turf that had once been Woodbourne House's spectacular lawn, carrying the pails of swill, the children running ahead.

'Why on earth are you leaving so suddenly?' asked Meg.

'I can't possibly be here when Paul comes back. It's hard enough being around you and not being able to so much as kiss you or touch you, or talk to you properly. I can't act normally. Everything I do or say seems to strike a false note. And Diana's watching us like a hawk.'

'I'm sure you're mistaken.'

'I don't think so. Anyway, I'll be in London till the end of my leave. Can you find a way to get up to town?'

'I'll try to think of one. It was hard enough when I was at Hazelhurst, but now...' She sighed. 'Oh Dan, I'm so tired of doing everything in secret, scraping around for excuses, snatching days and nights with you here and there. And the guilt, the deceit. I feel so worn down by everything.'

'Then leave him. I know you think it's too soon, but frankly, it seems to me the only honest way. Why wait till the end of the war?'

'Come ON, Mummy!' shouted Max. 'The pigs are getting hungry.'

Dan emptied the slop pails over the wall of the sty, and the children watched excitedly as the pigs jostled and grunted, nosing among the scraps. Dan and Meg leaned on the fence a little further off, so that they could talk.

'The longer we go on deceiving him,' went on Dan, 'the worse it's going to be when he finds out. I don't understand why you don't just end it now.'

'Dan, it's impossible. If I were to break with Paul while he's flying these dangerous missions, I don't think my mother or my aunt would ever forgive me. Or Diana. It simply isn't the right time. I still haven't got over losing Hazelhurst. It's as though everything is in limbo, out of kilter and unreal.' She fought for words to explain to him how the bombing of her home had fractured her world, how it was all she could do these days to hold together some sense of normal life for Paul and Max.

'So you and I – we're just some wartime romance? And when everything is back to normal you'll find another lovely house and carry on being Paul's wife.'

'Don't be ridiculous. That won't happen. I want us to be together. And we shall be. But it can't be now.'

Max came running up. The novelty of pig-feeding had evidently worn off. 'Mummy, can we go back now?'

'You and Laura run along. We'll be back in a minute.'

The children scampered across the grass towards the house. Meg turned to Dan.

'You don't realise what losing my home has done to me, Dan. It's changed my perspective on a lot of things. You see...' She struggled for a way to say all that she had been thinking. 'I've decided that when I leave Paul, it's going to be in a certain way. You and I, we have to come later. I don't want people judging me – thinking, my God, all the time her brave husband was fighting for his country, she was having an affair. I don't want them to know about this. Any of them. Not Paul, not Sonia, or my mother—'

'You want to be blameless?'

'Yes, since you put it like that.'

'But you're not, are you? Neither of us is.'

'That's not the point. I don't want Max to grow up thinking less of me. Knowing I was unfaithful to his father.'

'So you won't leave Paul now because you don't want your son and other people to think badly of you?'

'You make me sound like a coward.'

'You've been afraid all along. You should have left him in the beginning.'

'I know.' She grew tearful. 'I know, I'm weak and pathetic. But we can wait, can't we? If we love one another, we can wait till the time is right. When the war is over I can leave Paul, and after a while you and I can be together. And he won't be hurt so badly—'

'What? Meg, stop this. You have to take responsibility. We both do. You can't have it all ways. To care so much about what people think of you – it's positively feeble.'

'You don't understand. I can't take the risk of people finding out. It would mean losing everyone I hold dear. They wouldn't love me any more. How could they?'

Dan's fragile nerves collapsed into anger. 'You mean this, don't you? You're afraid, so you want to end us—'

'No, we just have to be patient—'

'I'm past all that. If you're not brave enough to love me, and admit it to the world, there's no real point. It's over.'

'Don't say it like that, Dan. Please. We'll be together when it's possible—'

'Meg, whatever you feel for me, it isn't enough. You love yourself and the people around you more, including Paul. You've made the choice. Don't ask me to wait until you feel brave enough, or until it's easy or convenient enough. I won't.'

'But if you love me—'

'Oh, stop! What do you mean – "if I love you"? Meg, if you loved me, you wouldn't care about them.'

'It's not that easy—'

'Yes, it is. If we don't have a present, then we don't have a future. It's finished, Meg, just as you want it to be. Stay with the people who matter to you.' He picked up the empty pails. 'I need to go and pack.'

'Dan, wait...'

But he carried on walking.

Diana was in the kitchen garden, picking raspberries, when Max and Laura came running back.

'Where have you two been?' she asked.

'Feeding the pigs.'

'On your own?'

'No, with Mummy and Dan. They're still up there talking,' said Max. 'They're always talking. It's so boring. Come on, Laura, let's go and find Star.'

A few moments later Diana looked up to see Dan striding across the grass with the pails. His expression was angrier than she'd ever seen it. She watched wordlessly as he flung the pails down and went into the house, not even looking at her. It was obvious that he and Meg had been arguing. Suspicion settled on her soul like a frost. Only lovers argued in such a way. The idea that Meg and Dan were having an affair seemed at once absurd, and yet at the same time wholly believable. Events and incidents began to crystallise. The time that Meg had gone up to town to see Constance before she left to go overseas. She'd stayed the night then, when it had hardly been necessary. The visit to London at Christmas – surely Paul wouldn't have asked about the presents she'd bought, if he'd been there, too? The time she had seen Meg and Dan coming through the woods together, deep in intimate discussion. Dan and Meg by the fountain just last week, the intensity of their conversation evident in the fact they had thought themselves unobserved.

She took the bowl of raspberries back to the house, gathering her thoughts, working out how best to handle this.

Dan packed, said a hasty goodbye to Sonia, and returned by train to London. Unable to face the solitude of the Belgravia house, he took a taxi to Bellamy's. He went to the bar and ordered a large Scotch, still brooding over everything. His nerves were so wrecked that he could hardly rationalise his angry thoughts. He might have ended it, but it was she, through her weakness and fear, who had destroyed everything. Her love for him was too thin a thing. It was evident she had no intention of leaving Paul. Why stay with him if she didn't think the relationship still had some meaning? Perhaps she was hedging her bets. The war could claim both him and Paul; perhaps she knew that if she made the wrong choice, she could be left unprotected and alone. But the relationship couldn't survive being put in abeyance until the war ended, to salvage her reputation and conscience. Who knew how long the bloody war would last?

In this cynical frame of mind, he ordered another double. He glanced at his watch. Almost half past eight, and he was hungry and in need of distraction. He felt ragged, restless. He was a free man now, and could do as he liked. He took out his address book and flipped through the pages until he found Eve's number.

He couldn't remember the last time he'd spoken to her. She might have moved again. She might have left the *Herald*, taken up war work. He doubted if she would want anything to do with him now, but he had nothing to lose. He went to one of the club's private booths and called her. The phone rang for a long time at the other end, and just as he was about to give up, she answered.

'Welbeck 878.'

'Eve? It's Dan.'

The silence at the other end told him everything. Before she could hang up, he went on, 'Look, I know it's been a long time, and all that, but I'm on leave in London, and I wondered if you'd like to meet for dinner?'

He closed his eyes against the anticipated reproach, and when it came it was gentler, sadder than he expected.

'My God, all this time without a word. Not a phone call, or even a letter. It was only thanks to friends that I knew you weren't dead. And now you ring up out of the blue and suggest dinner, as though...' She stopped, seemingly lost for words.

'Can't a girl make some allowance for a chap being on active service?'

'Are you telling me you couldn't have picked up the telephone in all that time? Or put pen to paper?'

'I have been busy, honestly. Look, let me make it up to you. How about Claridge's? Can you be there by nine?' She said nothing. 'I tell you what – I'll leave you to think about it. If you can bring yourself to forgive me for being a heartless ass, that will be wonderful. If you decide you can't – well, I'll just have to dine miserably on my own. And serve me jolly well right. But I hope you'll be there.'

Dan put the receiver in its cradle. In his present mood the attempt at charm and lightness of touch had probably failed. He wondered whether he should even have bothered. Still, the invitation had been extended, and he would have to go, just in case she showed up. He wasn't sure now whether he wanted her to or not.

*

After the argument with Dan, Meg went back to the house and straight to her room. She felt numb, hardly able to comprehend what had happened. All she had wanted to do was to persuade Dan to wait. How could he just end everything like that? Perhaps he was as tired as she was – not just of the lying and deceit, but of her, of the whole thing. He must be, to have done it so easily, with just a few words, without a backward glance. She stayed in her room on the pretext of having a bad headache until it was time for dinner. Then she bathed her tear-stained eyes, put on a little powder, and went downstairs. She didn't want anyone in the household connecting Dan's departure with any apparent distress on her part, so she did her best to be composed and cheerful.

Diana was watchful, but she couldn't detect anything untoward in Meg's manner. In fact, it was Meg who remarked what a pity it was that Dan had to go back to London so soon.

'He seemed very much out of sorts when he left,' said Sonia. 'I expect that mission he was on has taken it out of him. He didn't look well when he arrived. I hope he'll be all right.'

Despite Meg's calm demeanour, Diana suspicions remained. She was seething with defensive instincts, not just on behalf of Paul but the entire Latimer family. After dinner she volunteered herself and Meg for washing-up duties, so that she and Meg were left alone in the kitchen. While Meg finished drying the dishes, Diana sat down at the kitchen table and lit a cigarette, screwing up her courage.

'Meg, I need to speak to you about something.'

Meg, putting away the last of the plates, turned to Diana. Something in her sister-in-law's tone made her wary. 'What?'

'I know that you and Dan quarrelled this afternoon. Was that why he left?'

Though caught off-guard, Meg managed to shrug and reply casually, 'It was nothing. You know how he's been these past few days. He'll fly off the handle about absolutely anything. He'd already decided to leave, so I don't think I was the cause. At least I hope not.' She smiled. 'I'd hate to think something so trivial as an argument over pig-feeding would send him packing.'

Diana was unmoved. 'I saw his face. You'd been arguing about more than that.'

Meg closed the cupboard and stood with her back against the sink. Her heart had begun to beat hard. 'What on earth are you implying, Di?'

Diana hesitated. In her experience it was easy to tell if Meg felt guilty or uncomfortable, but at this moment she appeared to be neither. Still, there was no going back now.

'That something's going on between you and Dan.'

'What?' Meg gave a disbelieving laugh. 'Are you serious? Dan?'

'You deny it, then?'

'Of course I deny it! What possible grounds could you have for thinking such a thing? Simply because he and I had a disagreement?'

'I've seen the way you are with him.' Even as Diana said this, she knew it sounded weak. Trying to articulate her suspicions made her realise how lacking in substance they were. 'Don't pretend you don't know what I'm talking about.'

'I don't have to pretend. Dan is my friend. I've always been fond of him. Yes, I'll admit I was rather keen on him once upon a time. We all were, as I recall, you included.' Meg regarded her sister-in-law with a frank expression, intent on maintaining a confident exterior. 'But to accuse me of having an affair with him is laughable. Honestly, Di.'

There was a long silence. At last Diana said, 'If I ever find out that you have wronged Paul and betrayed our family, you will be very sorry, Meg.' She stubbed out her cigarette in the ashtray and left the kitchen.

Meg stood by the sink for a long time, hugging herself as though cold, waiting for her racing pulse to slow. It had been an effort to lie her way out of that conversation as convincingly as she had. At least, she hoped it had been convincing. She'd had no idea that Diana had real suspicions. Things must have been closer to the surface than she'd realised. Her heart felt hollow. She had lost Dan, and now she was fighting to protect the only security left to her.

5

AFTER A WASH and brush-up, Dan walked to Claridge's, where he managed to secure a table. He knew he'd had more than enough to drink, but he ordered more whisky all the same. Just after nine fifteen, to his surprise, Eve arrived. He stood up as the waiter showed her to the table. She looked as stylish as ever, in a grey dress of some soft material, with a gently gathered skirt and white collar. Her dark hair was fashionably rolled on top, and hung in glossy waves to her shoulders, and she looked extremely pretty. He felt a momentary exhilaration. This was the freedom he needed. Dining in the sociable bustle of a fashionable restaurant with a lovely and sophisticated woman, instead of conducting a claustrophobic love affair in snatched, secret hours in Belgravia. But even as he kissed Eve's cheek, he thought of Meg, and the silent rooms haunted with their passion and laughter, and was filled with a wrenching despair and longing. This was a terrible mistake, but it was too late now to do anything about it.

The fact that Eve had come indicated that he was to be forgiven, but it was clear from the cool condescension of her manner that she was determined not to do so too readily. He resigned himself to playing the necessary game, and did his best to be charming and convivial. By the time dinner had been ordered, and he had finished his Scotch and Eve her cocktail, he knew he had earned his pardon – and he scarcely cared. He felt mildly drunk and strangely desperate.

'Do you know,' said Eve, glancing around the restaurant, 'that at the beginning of the war they rounded up all the Italian waiters working here and put them in prison? I suppose you can't blame them, though – you never know who might be the enemy. The paranoia of wartime.' She took a drag of her cigarette. 'That reminds me – the last time I saw you was when I gave you Alice Bauer's famous list. Whatever happened about that?'

Dan remembered the brigadier's instructions. But since Eve was the one who had given it to him, she was entitled to some kind of answer. 'I gave it to the authorities, after I'd made my own investigations. It was as I thought. Someone had made false connections, based on all his trips to Germany before the war, and the people he knew there.' It could be a lie, or it could be the truth. The more time went by, the less Dan felt he understood about Paul's situation.

'Oh. Well, I'm glad that's all it was.'

'Yes. As you say, the paranoia of war. People get fearful. Their imaginations are heightened to the point where they'll take the tiniest suspicion and turn it into reality. Or what they think is a reality.'

'I suppose you're right.'

'Perhaps being in a war drives everyone a little mad. Maybe they do and say things they never would otherwise, if life were normal.' It was only because of the war that Meg had allowed herself to become his lover. It wasn't real to her, just another escapade, one she had grown tired of. 'It makes people dishonest.'

'Why do you sound so angry?'

'Do I? I'm sorry. Let's order some wine.' Dan scanned the wine list and ordered a bottle of claret. 'So, tell me how you are, how work's going.'

'Going, soon to be gone.' She stubbed out her cigarette. 'I've been called up. I'm joining the WAAF. My training starts in two weeks, at some deathly place in Gloucestershire. Can you see me in uniform and wool stockings?'

'I'm sure you'll look very fetching in uniform, and your legs will always be delectable whatever you put on them,' said Dan with a smile. He felt he was buckling under the strain of being charming.

The waiter brought and poured the wine, and the food arrived. Over the meal they talked about mutual friends, about the paper, and about the war, but Dan was conscious of the effort he was having to make. The occasional silences hung heavily.

At the end of the meal, Eve rested her hand lightly on his. He stared absently at her slender, white fingers.

'Is there something you need to talk about?' she asked gently. 'It feels like you're hardly here at all.'

He drank the remains of his wine – he had drunk most of the bottle, since Eve had had only one glass – and wondered how she would react if he unburdened himself about Meg. He toyed with her hand, stroking the soft spaces between her fingers, hoping to feel some kindling of desire. Sleeping with Eve would be a way of cauterising the wound, marking the change. It was definitely what he should do. He no longer belonged to anybody. If Meg wouldn't separate from Paul, then it was over. He looked up at Eve.

'It's been a rough time. Though no harder for me than for every other soldier, I expect. I think I'm just exhausted – body and soul.'

'You're also rather drunk, aren't you?'

'Yes, I'm afraid I am. And I wish I were drunker.'

'That's not very flattering.'

Dan suddenly felt very tired. He couldn't maintain the façade much longer. 'It's not about you. It's about all the things I don't want to think about.'

She was silent for a moment. 'Why don't we go back to your house in Belgravia for coffee? I still haven't seen it, you know.'

'No.' It came out sharply, and he tried to soften his tone, adding, 'It hasn't been lived in very much. Rather cold and bleak.'

'Well, then, let's go to mine instead.'

His eyes searched hers, and he wondered what it was that allowed her, after the months, years of silence, to accept him so readily, to be prepared to take him to her bed without question or argument. Love, he supposed. He knew, in an abstract way, that he should feel bad about this, but his sense of guilt, never the keenest among his small stock of moral susceptibilities, seemed to have been utterly blunted. He continued to stroke her hand, then her wrist, waiting for the familiar tingle of desire. It didn't come. Perhaps the alcohol was to blame. It would be better when they were at her place. He suddenly felt the most extraordinary sensation in his skull, as though his mind had turned to glass, and was shivering into tiny fragments. A shudder passed through him.

He was conscious of Eve taking her hand away, and her voice saying, 'Oh – Dan, would you give me a moment? There's a friend of mine over there that I haven't seen in an age. I'll be back in a minute.'

Eve left the table. Dan sat staring at the tablecloth, waiting for the cold, shattering sensation in his brain to settle. He signalled to the waiter and ordered a large brandy.

Eve returned a few minutes later and sat down, glancing at the brandy. 'Don't you think you've had enough?'

The glow of anger that burned through Dan seemed to rise volcanically from the depths of the last two years, fusing the bleak terror of the last undercover mission with the suppressed sense that everything he knew and loved had shown itself to be false and fragile; he was drunk, teetering on the civilised edge of normality, only just able to contain himself. His fingers tightened and relaxed on the stem of the brandy glass as the washing sense of despair subsided like a tide at the back of his brain.

'Yes, I've had more than enough of just about everything.'

He drained the brandy, and as he set the glass down his hand was shaking visibly. Eve stared at him in alarm. 'Let's get the bill.'

'First, I have to tell you a few things.' He rested his forearms on the table, leaned forward, and began to talk in a low voice. He took her through each day of the last operation in Norway, from the rank claustrophobia of the submarine, through the nerve-paralysing terror of the glacier climb, the hours spent lying, sodden and frozen to the bone, waiting for night to fall, the bowel-clenching fear of the operation itself, to the days spent walking, exhausted and starved, in search of refuge and in constant fear of German patrols. Eve tried to soothe him, to stop the flow of words, but he had to talk until it was all told. Then at the end, his voice trembling, he said, 'And the worst of it is, I don't see the point. I don't see the point in any of it.' He flattened his hands on the tablecloth. At least they'd stopped shaking.

'You're emotionally exhausted. In fact, I'd say you're not entirely well, Dan.'

His eyes had been fixed on his empty brandy glass as he talked. Now he looked at her with tired, dead eyes. 'I shouldn't have told you any of that. But I had to explain to someone. I don't understand why I'm here, now, sitting in this restaurant, while most of the others are in some concentration camp – or maybe worse. I survived without rhyme or reason, just to go back and do it all over again. With any luck, I won't survive the next time. I think I'd rather not.'

'Don't say that.'

He passed a hand over his face. 'I'm drunk and full of self-pity. I'm sorry. But I'm utterly washed up. I can't see any future. I feel empty. And terrified. I shouldn't have invited you here tonight. Do you want to know why I did?'

'I'm not sure I do.' She signalled to a passing waiter for the bill.

'Very wise. I won't tell you. You wouldn't like it.'

'You're drunk. I'm going to ignore everything you say.'

There was silence until the bill arrived. Dan fumbled for notes in his wallet, and paid.

Outside, the doorman hailed them a taxi.

'I should go home,' said Dan. 'I shouldn't do this to you. All this. So bloody unfair, the way I treat you.'

'Yes, it is. But I don't mind. Go on, get in.'

They got into the cab and Eve gave the driver her address in Marylebone. Dan closed his eyes as the taxi rolled slowly through the darkness.

They reached her flat and went in. Eve clicked on the lights in her sitting room. The flat was on the ground floor, small, but furnished with Eve's characteristic good taste. Dan stood in the middle of the room in his overcoat. He felt exhausted.

'Would you like some coffee?' asked Eve.

'I don't think so, thanks.'

She went close to him and put her hands gently on either side of his head. He looked into her eyes.

'You're so beautiful,' he murmured. 'Why isn't there some other man in your life?'

'There could be. Maybe there has been. But they don't matter. I love you. And you know how it is when you love someone. You'll put up with – anything.' She kissed his mouth lightly. 'It's not very clever of me to tell you that.' She kissed him again more deeply, and he tried to respond, but there was only emptiness. 'Come to bed,' she whispered.

Her bedroom was chic and feminine, softly lit, and smelt delicious. *I love the way women live*, though Dan hazily. The double bed looked so enticing that he found himself wishing wearily that Eve wasn't there, so that he could just fall into its softness and sleep away his unhappiness. But she was busy loosening his tie and unfastening his shirt buttons. *I will do this and it will mend everything*, thought Dan. Those wretched days within touching distance of Meg had been enough to drive him mad with frustration. She didn't want him, but here was a woman who did. He began to undress Eve in turn, pausing to kiss her, hoping that if he could inject some urgency and enthusiasm into everything, he might begin to feel desire. It was presently eluding him. As they lay together naked, Dan marvelled at how the skin and smell of one woman could intoxicate and excite, and the skin and smell of another, every bit as soft and fresh, have no effect whatsoever. He could not respond to even the cleverest of her caresses, and eventually he rolled away from her, his eyes shut, resting his knuckles on his forehead.

Eve kissed the skin of his stomach. 'You mustn't blame yourself,' she murmured.

'I shouldn't have come here tonight. I should never have called you. It was entirely wrong.'

'Dan, you're tired and not very well. You just need some rest. You'll be better in the morning.'

There was no point in explaining further. She would find out in due course. Another blow, another needless piece of cruelty on his part. What a mess he was making of everything.

She snuggled close to him, drawing up the covers, and kissed him softly. 'Get some sleep.'

He closed his eyes gratefully, and was unconscious within minutes.

He woke a few hours later, his heart thudding, his mouth dry, and his brain on fire. He lay for a while, going over the events of the last twenty-four hours. What on earth was he doing here? He turned his head. Eve lay sleeping soundly next to him. He needed to get out of bed as quietly as possible, gather his things, get dressed, and leave. He couldn't face the alternative, which was to wait till morning and tell her it had all been a mistake, that she wouldn't be seeing him again, ever. He might be brave about some things – and even that was in doubt – but not this.

Gently he pushed back the covers, sat giddily for a moment, then got out of bed. He went down on all fours, feeling around for his clothes, unable for the life of him to remember where various items had been discarded. He found his trousers, his socks, his underpants and one shoe. Where the hell was the other? And had he taken off his jacket in here, or in the living room? What about his overcoat? In the darkness he pressed his forehead to the carpet and let out a groan of misery. He heard a rustle from the bed, and staggered to his feet, clutching his clothes. Eve sat up and switched on the bedside light. For the first time in the past seven hours, as he looked at her he felt a rush of desire. Her hair was tousled in a dark, soft cloud, and her full, pale breasts grazed the top of the sheet as she stared at him. He sat down on the end of the bed.

'Were you trying to leave?' she asked.

'I'm afraid so.' He caught sight of his shirt and tie and bent down to pick them up. There was silence in the room for a moment, then Dan said, 'I'm not in a good way. I meant it when I said I shouldn't have rung you.' He put on his shirt and began to button it.

Eve leaned across and laid a hand on his arm. 'I don't understand why you have to leave. Stay and get some more sleep, and we can talk about it over breakfast.'

Dan took a deep breath. 'You might as well hear it now.' He sat threading his tie through his fingers. 'The fact is, Meg and I met again just a few days after I last saw you. We've been having an affair for the past two years. Yesterday we had a row about her leaving her husband, which she refuses to do. I looked you up because I thought... I wanted to see if I could get over her. And I find I can't.' It was several seconds before he could look at Eve. Her eyes seemed enormously large and dark, brimming with misery in the pinched whiteness of her face. 'You see? I treat you like a cad, and you let me. It's no good.'

'I *let* you? So I'm to blame?'

'I didn't say that. I just wish you didn't love me. I wish you'd hung up when I called you last night.'

'So do I. But for rather different reasons. You only want to be spared embarrassment and... and squalid explanations. You don't care about my feelings.'

'I do. I bitterly regret causing you pain.'

'No, you don't. You didn't think twice about lying to me and using me.' She flung aside the sheets and blankets and got up, snatching a dressing gown from a nearby chair. 'All that stuff last night about your desperately dangerous mission – no doubt that was just to make me feel sorry for you so that I'd let you sleep with me.'

'That was your idea, if you recall. Not mine. And it didn't turn out too marvellously, did it?' Dan stood up and put on his tie. He still felt drunk. 'And if we're on the subject of lies, why the hell did you tell Meg that I told you about her? Spite and jealousy, I assume.'

'God, you're detestable. Get your things on and get out.'

Dan finished dressing and put on his shoes. He went to the bathroom briefly, then to the living room, where he found his jacket and overcoat. Eve appeared in the doorway.

'Look,' said Dan, 'you don't know how much I regret all this—'

'Please. I think I've heard enough about your regrets.' Her eyes were black with anger. 'When you dropped me last time, I felt rejected, used. And such a fool. I hated you. Then it began to wear off, the way feelings do. Last night, I'd forgotten I hated you. That was the mistake. I won't forget this time.'

There was nothing more to say. Dan didn't want it to end on this note, but perhaps it was inevitable. He felt vile, mentally and physically. He picked up his overcoat and left quickly.

Eve heard the sound of the front door closing. She stood in the kitchen doorway, her arms folded, her face expressionless, for several moments. Then she crossed the room, dropped on her knees by the sofa, and buried her head in the cushions and wept.

6

AT THE END of an autumn afternoon spent in the kitchen garden with Lobb, Sonia came in to the kitchen and sat down wearily.

'We have an outbreak of soft rot in the potatoes, Mrs Goodall. Such a dreadful waste, after all the hard work we've put in. It's been a thankless year, what with caterpillars eating the celery, leaf spot on the runner beans – and look what happened to the marrows. Now this.'

'We'll just have to buy in,' observed Mrs Goodall phlegmatically.

'Lobb says we need to rotate things more. It's the potatoes I regret most. Cabbages I can live without. But the potatoes should have lasted us through to next year.' Sonia took off her muddy boots and stretched out her legs, leaning back and closing her eyes.

Mrs Goodall, who was busy stewing apples, gave her a glance. Who would have imagined elegant Mrs Haddon, as she was four years ago, with her fancy tea gowns and fine jewellery and lovely kid shoes, sitting now in the kitchen in her stocking feet and a pair of old dungarees, mud under her nails, and her hair any-old-how. Funny how the war had changed everything. Mr G always said it was about time the well-offs saw how the other half lived, but then he was a socialist. She didn't mind everyone muddling in together while the war was on, but she couldn't help thinking there'd been something comforting about the old order. Mrs Haddon upstairs writing her letters and having her guests to stay and being driven about in the Bentley, with a maid attending to her clothes, housemaids seeing to the rooms, Lobb and his men looking after the garden and the grounds, while she herself had been queen of her own domain, with a kitchen maid to boss about, and no one to interfere or come in scavenging for biscuits and making cups of tea. There had been a rightness to it all. Now almost all the old rituals and formalities had disappeared, which was a pity, in a way.

As though in response to Mrs Goodall's thoughts, Sonia opened her eyes and said, 'Do you know, Mrs Goodall, I'm tired of going about like a land girl. I shall go upstairs and have a bath, and put on something nice, and have tea in my sitting room. It's been an age since I did that. Would you bring a tray in about half an hour, please?'

Sonia put her boots in the scullery to dry and went upstairs to the chilly bathroom. She sighed as she ran her permitted few inches of water. Oh, for a hot, deep, foaming bath into which one could sink properly, instead of shivering in a miserable puddle with horrid cheap soap that barely produced a lather. As she watched the water trickle into the enamelled bath, she was dimly aware of a sense of anxiety, and as she sought its source, a rebellious urge suddenly overtook her. Turning the tap on full, she let the hot water gush into the bath, and went to her bedroom and fetched from a cupboard a bottle of rose and cucumber bath milk which she had bought from Harris the chemist in St James's Street before the war. She had been saving it, succumbing to the wartime instinct for eschewing all luxuries. She went back to the bathroom and purposefully poured in a liberal amount, watching it melt into foam as the steaming water crept upwards. She was above her allotted inches, but now had enough for a decent soak. The war would surely not be lost because she, Sonia Haddon, had an extra six inches of water in her bathtub. She'd read somewhere that the Queen had a line painted inside her bath to ensure her maid didn't run too much. Well, bully for the Queen still having a maid to run her bath.

Sonia undressed and got into the bath, sinking with pleasure into the hot, scented water, feeling the grime of the chicken coop and the ungratefully mouldering kitchen garden soaking away. She closed her eyes and searched for the source of the disquiet which had assailed her a few moments earlier. For a couple of weeks now she had been aware of a coolness between Meg and Diana, which she had put down to some minor disagreement or other, assuming it would right itself in time. With so many women living together under one roof, little quarrels were bound to happen – there were days when she and Helen were scarcely civil to one another – particularly with both Diana and Meg under the strain of having their husbands in constant danger. But matters did not seem to have put themselves right. Meg in particular seemed utterly dejected, and she had noticed that the two young women, such close friends for so long, no longer walked down to the village together with the children, or sat sewing and gossiping by the wireless. Something was amiss, and she needed to find out what, and remedy it if she could, for the sake of her peace of mind and for the good of the household.

'Don't bother with any for me,' said Diana, as dinner was being served that evening. 'I had tea with the children in the nursery. I'll get myself some supper later.'

'That's the third time this week she hasn't sat down with us,' observed Helen, after Diana had gone. 'And the amount of time she spends at the piano going over and over that Chopin piece. We don't have much of her company at all these days.'

'It's dreadfully hard for her,' said Sonia. 'I know her nerves are perpetually on edge over Roddy. She goes white whenever the doorbell rings.'

'Half the women in the country are in the same boat,' went on Helen, helping herself to vegetables. 'Look at Meg. It's just as hard for her with Paul, but she doesn't constantly shut herself away in the music room.'

'Oh, well – Diana clearly needs time to herself. I think we should leave her be.'

'I rather think it's she who is leaving *us* be,' replied Helen. 'She'll need to buck up. I'll be needing helpers for my rummage sale soon.'

After dinner Helen went into the village on some WI errand, and Sonia invited Meg to listen to the radio with her in her sitting room. A cosy fire was burning in the grate, and Rufus and Domino lay snoozing on the hearthrug.

Meg and Sonia settled in armchairs, Meg with her knitting, Sonia her sewing.

'*The Brains Trust* will be on in a minute,' said Sonia. She paused, then added, 'By the way, I've noticed you and Diana don't seem to be getting on as well as you used to. I'm sure it's none of my business, but it worries me when there's tension in the house. Have you had a quarrel?'

Meg sighed. She had hoped Sonia wouldn't broach the subject. 'Yes. A few weeks ago. I'd rather not say what it was about.'

'Well, don't you think it's time you two made it up? No one likes an atmosphere.'

Meg nodded. 'I suppose so. I'll talk to her, I promise.'

Sonia resumed her sewing. Rufus wheezed and rolled on to his side, blinked at the fire, then fell back into his doze. After a moment Sonia said, 'Are you sure that's all that's the matter, Meg? Quarrels are upsetting, I know, but I wondered if there wasn't something else amiss. You seem terribly listless lately. One would almost think you were unhappy.'

Meg gazed fixedly at her knitting. Unhappy was hardly a big enough word to describe her state of being. Since the argument with Dan she had been wretched, unable to sleep properly, her appetite gone, and her concentration shattered. Behaving normally on Paul's last leave had been the hardest thing of all – mercifully he'd only been back for twelve hours. She had no idea whether he'd noticed. In the past weeks Paul had become less distant towards her, treating her with his old affection, as though trying to heal things between them.

'I suppose I'm still unhappy about Hazelhurst.'

'That was dreadful, but you and Paul will make a fresh start when the war is over.'

Meg nodded, bending her head over her work again, pretending to count the stitches. How ironic. The fresh start was to have been with Dan, and that would never happen now. She would simply have to pick up the pieces with Paul and carry on. There was no one and nowhere else to go to. Her fingers faltered as she counted. She suddenly saw herself for the coward she was. She had put her fear of being friendless and alone above her love for Dan, and had told him so. No wonder he had ended it.

Sonia reached to the wireless and switched it on. As they waited for it to warm up, she added, 'Grieving for a home you loved must be as hard as grieving for someone who has died. But there are always other houses, and after the war you and Paul can make another home every bit as wonderful as Hazelhurst. At least for the present you're safe with those who love you.'

'Yes,' murmured Meg. 'I don't think anyone could have been kinder than you've been, Aunt Sonia.' *Stay with the people who matter to you.* That was the last thing Dan had said.

The announcer's voice drifted into the room, and the programme began, putting further conversation at an end.

When it finished half an hour later, Sonia looked up from her sewing and remarked, 'I always enjoy listening to Professor Joad. He sounds like the kind of person one would like to have to dinner. Will you stay and listen to the news?'

'I think I'll go and talk to Diana, if you don't mind, Aunt Sonia. No time like the present.' Meg rolled up her knitting and went out, closing the door. She paused and listened. Sure enough, she could hear the distant ripple of piano notes. She went down the hall to the music room and opened the door. Diana didn't hear her come in. Her fair head was bent over the keys as she repeated a phrase over and over, trying to get it right. Only when she looked up to frown at the music did she become aware of Meg's presence. Abruptly she stopped playing.

'It's chilly in here,' said Meg, rubbing her arms and pulling her cardigan further round her.

'I don't really notice.'

Meg walked around the piano. 'Your knuckles are blue.' There was a silence, then she added, 'Please carry on. You play so well. I never really got past "Three Blind Mice".'

Diana shook her head. She looked candidly at Meg. 'You didn't come here to listen to me play.'

'No. I've been with Sonia. She's noticed things aren't right between us, and it's upsetting her. I told her I would speak to you.'

Diana shrugged. 'Not much to say.'

Meg drew up a chair and sat down. 'I think there is. I'm prepared to forget what you said, if you are.' Her conscience pricked her, but there was no other way to deal with this.

Diana stared down at her hands, then rubbed them together to warm them. Ever since she had accused Meg of having an affair with Dan, the idea had seemed more and more outlandish. What had Meg been doing for the past two years? Running her home in wartime, looking after Paul and Max and Helen, then coping with the loss of her house, accommodating herself to the new surroundings of Woodbourne House. How would anyone find time for a love affair?

'I don't know why I said it, or thought it. Something. Nothing.' She sighed. 'I don't know.'

'Why don't we just forget it ever happened?'

Diana looked up, her eyes searching Meg's, and something in her gaze made Meg's soul shrink. She was effectively asking Diana to admit she'd been in the wrong. But Dan was gone from her life, so there was some small justification for what she was doing.

'Very well.' Diana closed her eyes, and suddenly her shoulders began to shake, and she was weeping. 'I don't know what's wrong with me. I feel as though I'm... as though I'm deranged, somehow. I've been like this for weeks now. Every morning I wake up convinced that this will be Roddy's last day. I tell myself he can't possibly survive. It's just a question of when the telegram will come. Will it be this morning, or in the afternoon? Will he be blown to smithereens, or burnt alive?' It was the opportunity Meg needed. She pulled her chair forward and put her arms round Diana as she wept.

'Don't. I know how dreadful it is. But you have to tell yourself he's survived this far because he's good at what he does, because he's experienced and clever.'

Diana pulled a handkerchief from her pocket and wiped her eyes. 'No. Only because he's lucky. And no one's luck can last for ever. Do you know, ten of Roddy's squadron were killed last week? He said not one of them was over twenty-one.'

'But what good will it do to work yourself up into such a state all the time?'

'None. I know that. But I can't help it. Every time he leaves I think, why didn't I tell you how much I love you? Because we don't, you know. It's not our style. We just rag each other all the time, and say silly, offhand things.'

'I think he knows how much you love him. Men always know, without you having to say a thing.' She pushed the thought of Paul from her mind.

Diana was silent for a while, fiddling with her handkerchief. 'It's been even worse not having you to talk to. You're right. Let's forget what I said. It was ridiculous, and I'm ashamed of myself.'

Meg winced inwardly. The deception was never-ending. She took Diana's hands in hers. 'Darling, you're positively icy. I vote we go and join Sonia in her room. She's got the nicest fire, and I'm sure we can prevail upon her to break out the sherry. I think it's just what we both need.'

Diana smiled. 'Let's. I can't stand much more of this Chopin, anyway.'

'I don't think any of us can.'

'Cheek!' Diana wiped away the last of her tears and stood up. 'I feel so much better. I'm glad you came to talk. It must have been difficult, after the awful things I implied.'

'Let's never mention it again. Ever.'

Max sat forlornly on a footstool and cast a sad glance at the Christmas tree. Lobb had gone to great pains to get hold of a decent one, and had erected it in a red-painted bucket at the far end of the drawing room. Meg and Diana had decorated it with Sonia's rather cumbersome old Christmas ornaments, and the children had added festoons of coloured paper chains, which they had spent happy hours gumming together in the nursery. Underneath were such presents as people had been able to buy, or make, wrapped in paper which Sonia had been carefully harvesting and reusing for two years now.

'But *why* isn't Daddy coming home? It's Christmas Eve. He should be here.'

'Because he's got operations tonight. It can't be helped, darling. I'm afraid the war doesn't stop for Christmas.' Meg stroked Max's cheek. Poor darling. He worshipped Paul, and had been looking forward for weeks to his father's Christmas leave. For her own part, Meg was relieved. It had been hard enough putting on a cheerful, normal face for Paul when he did come back now and then, but she thought she would have found Christmas particularly difficult.

'Perhaps he'll get here for Boxing Day,' she added reassuringly.

'That's not the same.'

'You know, I don't think Daddy would want you to be miserable like this. If he were here he'd say "chin up, old boy", wouldn't he?'

Max nodded glumly.

'Come on. Let's get you to bed. Father Christmas will be here in a few hours. That's one chap the Germans can't stop getting through.'

Roused by this interesting thought, and speculating on whether Father Christmas might possibly have a rear gunner on his sleigh, Max went upstairs with Meg to the nursery to hang up his stocking.

On Boxing Day Paul came back to Woodbourne House on leave. Meg was shocked by how grim and weary he looked. He managed the Boxing Day meal cheerfully enough, but fell into an exhausted sleep on the sofa afterwards. Max, on orders from his mother, waited patiently for two hours before gently shaking his father awake and dragging him off to the nursery to show him his new toys. At teatime Paul and Roddy had a couple of sandwiches and a slice of Mrs Goodall's Christmas cake, and then took themselves off to the living room for an hour, where they sat by the fire with glasses of whisky, smoking and talking. It wasn't until later in the evening that Meg was able to talk to him alone. Before that she sat with him as Max lay tucked up in his bed, subjecting his father to a cross-examination on the progress of the war, particularly Paul's part in it.

'Mummy said you couldn't be here because you were on operations.'

'That's right. I'm sorry I missed Christmas, old man. It couldn't be helped.'

'Were you on a night run?'

'Yes. Most of our ops are at night, you know.'

'Did you see Father Christmas? I mean, might you have seen his sleigh, do you think?'

Paul laughed and ruffled Max's hair. 'Do you know, I think maybe I did? One can never be sure, though, with so much going on.'

'What was your target?'

'Some enemy transport.'

'Were there enemy planes on your tail? Did you have to corkscrew?'

'No, no corkscrews last night. But I had to do a bit of rolling, and it was quite hairy.'

'Did you hit the target with your bombs?'

'It was hard to tell. When it's dark, and you don't know if you've identified the right thing, and with the plane wobbling about and being shunted with flak, it's quite tricky, because it only needs the plane to swing a little and you'll miss your target by a mile. There were shells exploding everywhere, and a lot of black smoke, so I was flying blind.'

Meg noticed Paul clenching and unclenching the fingers of his left hand, which was out of Max's sight, as he spoke.

'That's really dangerous, isn't it?'

'It most certainly is. I think it's the most frightening thing I know. Except for flying low. We have to do that a lot, as I've told you.'

'You get a better aim if you fly low, don't you?'

'That's right. But it's risky. Luckily, Scotty's a very good navigator, and when he shouts "up!" I don't argue. I just pull the stick and up we go.'

Max wriggled further down the covers. 'I bet you didn't miss. I bet you smashed the Jerries to smithereens.'

'Well, who knows? Now, that's enough war talk. Do you want Mummy to read you a story and hear your prayers?'

'Can't we talk some more?'

'Maybe tomorrow. Come on, snuggle down. This is a late bedtime for you.'

Max grinned. 'I know.'

Paul leaned across and kissed Max's forehead. 'Night night, old fellow.'

'Night, Daddy.'

Meg read to Max for a short while, listened to him say his

prayers, then switched off his light and went through to the bedroom where Paul was sitting on the edge of the bed, buttoning up his pyjama jacket.

'Honestly, Paul,' she said mildly, 'must you go into grisly detail? I'm sure it will give him bad dreams. He's only five.' She sat down on the edge of the bed.

'I doubt it. He's a boy. He finds it exciting.'

Suddenly she remembered a piece of news. 'Oh, I haven't told you – Lotte's going to go and live with her brother in New York. She's managed to get a passage on a ship in the New Year.'

'I'm pleased for her. Though no doubt you'll be sorry to see her go.'

'There's been less for her to do since Max started at the village school. He was upset at first, but he's come round. I think he likes the idea of having my full-time attention. There's no question of getting another nanny. I don't really think I need one, despite what my mother says.'

Paul laced his fingers through hers, and her stomach tightened. Did he want to make love? Lately when he was on leave he did, not with Dan's mad, lovely overwhelming desire, but as though it was a form of consolidation, a way of anchoring himself to his marriage. Mostly, though, he was too exhausted. She waited.

At last he said, 'Do you like it here?'

She looked at him in surprise. 'Yes, of course I do. I'm so grateful to Sonia for giving us a home – when you think how grim the alternative might have been. Finding good houses is well nigh impossible these days. Why do you ask?'

'Well, I'm grateful, too, for being given food and a bed when I come here on leave, but I always feel like a guest. I suppose it's because that's what we are. Guests. Besides, lovely as Woodbourne House is, it's a hell of a slog from Mildenhall. I'd much rather you and Max were closer at hand, in a home of our own. I know wartime isn't the best time to be trying to find a new place to live, but even if it's just something temporary, I think we should.'

Meg's heart fell. The last thing she wanted was to be in some wretched house in deepest Suffolk, just the three of them. She looked down at his hand clasping hers, his thumb stroking the palm of her hand. She longed to pull away. She felt utterly no warmth or connection.

'Paul, we've only just got used to living here. Max is happy at the village school. Everything's working so well. Couldn't we wait just a few months?'

There was silence for a moment, then Paul said gently, 'Meg, don't you want a home with me?'

She looked up, startled. 'What do you mean?'

'Things haven't been entirely happy between us for a while. We both know that. Whatever the problems are, I think we can put them right. But I need to know you want to be with me. If you don't want to be, now's the time to tell me.'

This could have been the moment, she realised, when she might have told him everything, been brave, taken her chance, and left to be with Dan. But there was no Dan to go to.

'Yes,' she said at last, in a low voice. 'I want to be with you.'

He squeezed her hand. 'I'll start looking for a place. Perhaps you should tell Sonia sooner rather than later that we'll be leaving in the New Year.'

When Paul returned to his base the next day, Meg told Sonia of their decision over dinner.

'We've have been so grateful, Aunt Sonia, and we've loved being here with you, but we've decided we should find a place of our own. We can't live off you for ever. And the journey to get here isn't the easiest for Paul when he's on leave.'

'I do understand,' said Sonia, who was disconcerted nonetheless. 'Of course this was always going to be a temporary solution. I shall miss you and Max terribly. And Paul, of course.'

'Perhaps I should say this now,' said Diana, 'since we're talking about it. Roddy and I have been having the same discussion. Morven and I will be moving to Norfolk, just as soon as we can find somewhere near Roddy's base. It's been wonderful living here, Sonia. But like Meg and Paul, we feel we have to move on.'

'Oh dear, it really is all change, isn't it?' said Sonia, with a little attempt at a laugh. 'What a quiet place it's going to be, without all of you.' She glanced at her sister. 'Don't tell me you're thinking of going back to London, too?'

Helen had in fact been giving thought to how long she would stay. She was grateful to be in the country and under her sister's protection, rather than in London, but it was something of a mixed blessing. Woodbourne House was Sonia's domain, and she had no say in its management. And she missed her home. She thought often of her precious belongings, her china and her pictures all wrapped up carefully in baize, her lovely furniture lying shrouded in dustsheets. Decay would already have begun, the silver slowly tarnishing, infinitesimal spores of damp seeping into the fabric of the sofas and chairs and filming the wood of cabinets and escritoires. She dreamt of returning to Cheyne Walk, throwing back the shutters, lighting fires to warm every room, unpacking her belongings and settling back into her old life, defying the bombs to fall. But Meg's account of how the area had suffered, and a feeling that she might find London rather bleak and lonely, told her that it made sense to stay put for the time being. Besides, she had her WI work to occupy her, to say nothing of the beehives.

'I'm very happy to stay here for as long as you need me, Sonia.'

'Well,' said Sonia, mildly irked by the suggestion that Helen's continued residence at Woodbourne House constituted something of a favour, 'I'm sure I'm grateful for that, my dear.'

That night in bed, Sonia lay mulling over everything. She had no right to feel upset that Meg and Diana were leaving. The young people had to make their own lives and run their own homes. It was just that she enjoyed having a household teeming with people. Life was so full. Planting all those vegetables, keeping hens and pigs, what would be the point of it for so few people? Even fewer, when Helen eventually went back to London, as she would in time. Well, she had to face the fact that nothing stayed the same for ever.

She switched off her bedside light and lay in the dark, thinking of the days ahead. Relief at the thought that Avril would shortly be going back to boarding school filled her with guilt. Avril had been so difficult over the Christmas holidays – surly to everyone, mean to Laura. It was hard to find any connection with her, as though Avril was intent on shutting her mother out. She wondered if it was her own fault. There had been those problems after Avril's birth, of course. Avril, though she seemed to crave love and attention, never properly returned one's affection. Not like Laura, who had such a loving disposition. Was it wrong to love someone else's child as much as one's own daughter? She thrust away the thought that she might love Laura more. No, no. It was just that Laura was such a sweetly demonstrative little thing. It dismayed her that the bond she had expected to develop between the two girls had so far not materialised. In the beginning, despite Helen's warnings, she had been convinced that Avril and Laura would become like sisters, sharing toys and secrets and laughter. That hadn't happened so far, but perhaps it wasn't surprising. After all, a six-year-old wasn't much of a companion for a twelve-year-old. Maybe the age difference would smooth itself out as they got older.

She shut her eyes tight, telling herself she had done the right thing, that Laura could not have a better home and that all would come right with Avril. She prayed for sleep to come.

7

MEG AND MAX left Woodbourne House in early January. The house that Paul had found for them stood in the countryside on the outskirts of Bury St Edmunds, and was set back from the road and surrounded by an acre of garden. It was decent enough in size, with four bedrooms, a drawing room and dining room, and a cosy living room next to the kitchen, but it was a far cry from the glories of Hazelhurst. The kitchen was north-facing and somewhat gloomy, and the old-fashioned, darkly solid furniture wasn't to Meg's taste. The village in which the house stood was more of a hamlet, and had no shops worth speaking of, so Meg had to take the bus into Bury St Edmunds to do her shopping, where she had to forge new relationships with the grocer and butcher and fishmonger to wheedle those scarce little extras – the odd onion, a couple of oranges, a cod tail, a piece of liver – which made all the difference to the weekly rations.

As she began to get to grips with her new existence, Meg realised how easily she had taken for granted the bounty of Sonia's kitchen garden, and the extra bacon and lard from her pig-keeping, to say nothing of the jars of Helen's honey which had obscured the meagreness of the sugar ration and cheered up the daily slice of toast. Hard fruit, such as apples and pears, had been abundant at Woodbourne House, lasting all winter thanks to Lobb's careful storage, but in the depths of winter both were hard to come by. All Paul's money couldn't buy them more than their ration books would allow. Faced with the prospect of just one egg a week for each of them, she thought of building a hen coop in the garden, but discovered that the wire netting which she needed was impossible to obtain. She considered taking a trip to Hazelhurst to see if she could salvage some from there, but she couldn't face seeing the wreck of her former home, or envisage the possibility of carrying such a thing home on a train heaving with soldiers and dispirited civilians. So, like all other British housewives, she abandoned the idea and made do with sachets of powdered egg.

When spring came she thought that at least turning over part of the garden to growing vegetables would require no more than a bit of spadework, but when she first tried she found the ground still too cold and hard for her to manage. There was no Lobb or Dixon to come to her assistance. She would have to wait for milder weather or for Paul to come home on leave, assuming he had enough energy.

For the first time in her life Meg was without servants, except for a woman from the village who came in once a week to scrub floors and do the dusting. At Woodbourne House there had been Mrs Goodall to shop and cook, Effie to do most of the basic cleaning, and the rest of the general housework had been shared by everyone, so that the odd spell at the mangle, changing beds, or airing blankets, hadn't seemed like much of a chore. When one had to do all the shopping, cooking, cleaning, washing and ironing oneself, it was sheer drudgery.

As 1944 unfolded, it seemed to Meg the hardest year of her life. Never had she felt so hopeless and loveless. Had it not been for Max, she might have fallen apart utterly. It was difficult to sustain affection in her relationship with Paul, though she did her best because Paul himself was unfailingly cheerful and kind. He seemed to have rekindled his faith in their marriage. Even when he came back exhausted from his operations, he always had time for both of them, playing with Max and answering his endless questions, fixing shelves, helping in the vegetable garden, sitting with her in the evenings by the wireless, smoking his pipe and trying to soothe her evident sadness with bright conversation. She knew she was being petulant and selfish, but the confusion of her feelings, the knowledge that she had destroyed her relationship with Dan, and committed herself to a marriage to which she could offer almost nothing, left her without moral strength. The only events which relieved the monotony of her existence were trips now and then to London to visit her mother, who had decided that spring to move back to Cheyne Walk, and the occasional visit from Diana.

In December Sonia wrote to say that Dan had been badly wounded.

> *He says his right shoulder and left leg are rather badly smashed, but that he hopes to be right as rain in a few months, though he fears he may have something of a limp at the end of it. I am just glad he is alive, and capable of writing at all. It could have been much worse. He is in a hospital in Perthshire, where he says there are lots of pretty nurses (typical Dan!) and that he has plenty of time to refine his chess skills. Reading between the lines, I suspect he is lonely and in a great deal of pain, so I propose to make a visit in the New Year.*
>
> *I am the closest thing the poor boy has to family, so am more than happy to brave the trains, and I have a cousin I can stay with in Inverness.*
>
> *If you care to write to him, I am sure he would be delighted to hear from you. The address is at the foot of this letter.*
>
> *With love,*
>
> *Sonia*

Meg's first impulse was to pick up a pen and write, and tell Dan how much she still loved him, to try and keep something alive for the future. The hope rose and faded in almost the same instant. She knew in her soul that too much harm had been done. Their love was like a plant which had struggled to survive in the harshest circumstances, and was now so badly blighted and damaged that it could never grow green and vital again.

The wee, small hours, as Sister McInnes called them, were the worst for Dan. It wasn't so much the pain of his wounds, which throbbed infernally no matter what the hour, as the thoughts that beset him. At two o'clock in the morning a man might feel he was the only person awake in the whole sleeping world. It was a lonely feeling. The loneliest. Dan would lie listening to the mutterings and groans brought on by the pains and dark dreams of his injured fellows, and think about Meg. Sometimes he would relive the times they had had together in the house in South Eaton Place, sometimes he would summon up the memory of the first time he had kissed her, then all the times after that, before she finally became his, or remember how she looked in some particular dress, or at some special moment. But these thoughts, while they helped to ease the deadliness of the early hours, only ended in the wretched knowledge that she was further from him than she had ever been. He had gone over and over that last argument, and he no longer knew who or what was to blame for the way it had ended. Maybe it was simply that people and events had conspired to defeat them, so that carrying on with their affair had become too difficult. Or perhaps it lay in Meg's ultimate weakness, her need not to estrange those whose good opinion seemed to count for more than his love. Thus he would torment himself, thoughts going round and round in his tired mind, until eventually sleep would descend for a few blessed hours before the nurses began their six o'clock rounds, and the journey of another day would begin.

He had received his injuries during a raid on the Norwegian coast in mid-December, a combination of a bullet wound to his shoulder, and severe damage to his left thigh from a grenade which had killed two of his comrades. The military hospital to which he had been sent to recover, Moray House, was a former grand country house on the outskirts of Inverness, and he had been there for several weeks. The bullet to his shoulder had smashed his collarbone, and the wound was taking a long time to heal. The damage to his left thigh was considerably worse; his thigh bone had been broken in three places, and he had lost a lot of muscle tissue. On the day that Sonia was due to visit, he had only been hobbling around with the help of a crutch for a few days, but he was glad that at least he would be able to greet her on his feet.

That morning Nurse Blain helped him to shave. The stiffness in his shoulder still made such tasks tricky.

'Another couple of weeks or so and you'll be able to do this all by yourself,' she said, rinsing the suds from the safety razor in a tin bowl of water next to the bed. She had a soft Ayrshire accent which Dan particularly liked.

He dabbed the remnants of soap from his chin. 'That's a shame. I like being shaved by you. You have a delightful touch.'

Nurse Blain raised an eyebrow. She was small, with a neat figure, mischievous eyes and soft, curly brown hair, and was far and away Dan's favourite. She and Dan had developed a flirtatious relationship laced with jokes, and her manner with him held a mild suggestiveness which made Dan wish he were better placed to explore its possibilities. Dan, who had never quite lost the vanity of his younger years, knew he was something of a heart-throb among the nurses, and doled out his charm in what he thought was an admirably even-handed manner, but he kept a special reserve of it for Nurse Blain.

'You can help me get dressed, too, if you like,' added Dan.

'Away with you. You can get dressed fine by yourself,' she retorted with a smile, bundling together the towel and shaving kit, and picking up the basin.

'Such unkindness,' sighed Dan. He reached for his crutch and rose stiffly, then limped away to put on his fatigues.

*

Sonia's journey from London to Inverness in January 1945 was every bit as bad as she had anticipated. After sharing a sleeper compartment on the train north with a fat woman who snored thunderously for the entire night, she arrived in Edinburgh in a state of exhaustion. The canteen at Waverley Station had run out of food the previous evening, forcing her to go hungry while she waited two hours for her next train. There was then a heart-stopping moment on the way to Perth when the train halted on the Forth Rail Bridge while a fleet of German bombers flew overhead, but their target apparently lay elsewhere, and she reached Perth intact, though in a famished and somewhat nervous condition. Fortified by a lunch of a cheese sandwich and a cup of tea, she then endured a long and very chilly bus journey to the house of her cousin in Inverness. After a sound night's sleep in a comfortable bed, however, she was refreshed and in good spirits, and looking forward to seeing her godson.

Dan was waiting for her in the recreation room, formerly one of the Moray House drawing rooms, where the patients met to play cards or board games, or to read and write letters. It was a handsome room with large windows leading to a terrace overlooking the sloping gardens, the snow-covered peaks of the Cairngorms visible in the distance. Sonia was relieved to see that despite his wounds Dan looked well. She kissed him warmly.

'Oh, it's so good to see you. We've all been so terribly worried about you. Come, sit down again. I'm sure you shouldn't be on your feet.'

'You're a brick to come all this way to see me, Sonia. How was your journey?'

'The less said about that the better.' She smiled. 'But I'm here now.' She glanced around at the handful of men scattered round the room, some playing cards, others chatting. 'I must say, this is a very nice room. Lovely and warm. And such a view.' She turned her attention back to Dan. 'Now, tell me how you are.'

'Better than I was this time last month. The doctors seem happy with the way I'm coming along now. I've had the best possible care. The staff here are pretty marvellous.' Nurse Blain appeared at that moment bearing a tray, with two cups of tea and a plate of biscuits. 'And here's the most marvellous of them all. This is Nurse Blain. Nurse Blain, my godmother, Mrs Haddon.'

'How d'you do,' said Nurse Blain with a smile. She set down the tray. 'Your godson is quite the charmer, Mrs Haddon. We're all very fond of him.'

'I hope he's a good patient.'

'Good as gold. Now, enjoy the shortbread. It's from a tin my mother sent. The hospital's a wee bit short on biscuit rations at the moment.'

'How kind of you,' said Sonia. 'Thank you.' She watched as Nurse Blain left the room. 'What a pretty girl.'

'Isn't she? I'll miss her when I leave.'

'When will that be?' Sonia stirred her tea and took a sip.

'The doctors say it'll be at least another two months until everything heals. Then there's talk of sending me south to some convalescent place in England so that I can recover my strength properly. I'll be glad of that. Much as I like Scotland, I miss home.'

'Well, now, I should like to invite you to Woodbourne House to recuperate. Would the powers-that-be allow that?'

'I suppose I can pretty much convalesce where I like, so yes, thank you.'

'I'll be glad of your company. It's very quiet now. Helen has gone back to London. She is convinced the tide of the war is turning our way, and I'm sure I hope she's right, but according to her last letter the bombing goes on just as hard as ever.' Sonia nibbled a piece of shortbread, then went on, 'Still, we do seem to be making progress. Wonderful that the Russians have taken Warsaw. Do you remember the poor Mayor of Warsaw making that brave, despairing broadcast back in nineteen thirty-nine? I suppose he's long dead.'

They talked for another hour or so, until Dan had to go and have his dressings changed, and Sonia went back to Inverness.

Sonia came to visit Dan every day that week. The late-January weather was bitterly cold, but clear, and each day they would take a walk around the hospital grounds, Dan in his greatcoat and boots and a woollen cap, leaning on his crutch, Sonia in her fur coat and hat. They would go as far as the fishpond, then walk slowly back. After that they would have tea, and chat and play draughts or dominoes. They talked about everything – the war, politics, art, the keeping of pigs, the future of the world.

On the final day of Sonia's visit they took their customary walk and had tea in the recreation room.

'I'd best be going,' said Sonia at last. 'My train is in an hour and I have to collect my things.'

Dan rose and helped her into her coat. 'Thank you for coming all this way to see me. You don't know what this week has meant. The chaps here are a decent bunch, but it's been pretty lonely.'

'Well, I look forward to seeing you in a few weeks. Just write and tell me when you expect to be travelling and I shall have everything ready.'

A few weeks after Sonia's visit, the doctors pronounced Dan well enough to leave hospital.

On his final morning at Moray House he washed and shaved and breakfasted, and finished the little packing he had to do, then took his customary walk. Ever since Sonia's visit, when he had taken his first tentative steps to the fishpond and back, he had been extending the distance of his daily exercise, and for the past two weeks he had been able to make the three quarters of a mile to the shores of Loch Ness without difficulty. The majestic sweep of the grey waters, the hazy spring tints of the heather on the surrounding hillsides, and the utter silence were a balm to his soul.

He sat for a while on an outcrop at the shoreside, mulling over his thoughts, then walked to the water's edge and picked up a few flat stones, sending them skimming across the glinting loch. He had been exercising his right shoulder in this way for the past fortnight. His first efforts had been achingly feeble, but he had persisted, and now his muscles were stronger, and the stones scudded over the loch with a satisfying smoothness. He sent the last stone flying, and counted ten bounces before it sank into the grey water. Not bad. He turned and began the journey back to the hospital for the last time.

His taxi was due at half past two, and after lunch he went in search of Nurse Blain, who had been on leave all weekend, to say goodbye. He found her in the laundry room, paper and pencil in hand, counting sheets and pillowcases. She looked up, vexed at having her calculations disturbed, but smiled when she saw who it was.

'Hello, there.'

'Nurse Blain, the goddess of hospital linen. I've been wondering all morning where you were.'

'I only came on my shift an hour ago.' Realisation dawned. 'It's never today that you're leaving, is it?'

'How could you possibly forget?'

'Conceit. You're not exactly number one on my list of priorities, Lance Corporal Ranscombe.'

'Aren't you the least bit sorry to see me go?'

She sighed. 'I cannot possibly keep count with you havering on. Yes, of course, you silly man. I miss all the patients when they leave. Well, the nice ones.'

She turned her attention back to her list, but he saw that her cheeks were lightly flushed. He moved forward a little on his crutch until he was within touching distance of her, then reached out and stroked the curling wisps of hair escaping from beneath her cap.

'A whole four months, and you still don't call me Dan, and I don't call you Catriona.'

'I hardly think that would go down well with Sister McInnes, do you?'

Her look was inviting, expectant, and he leaned forward and kissed her parted lips. Then he put his free arm round her, drew her towards him and kissed her again, this time with great thoroughness. The sense of mutual desire was so strong and sudden that it left them both breathless. Dan looked down at the keys dangling from her belt and murmured, 'Does one of those lock this door?'

She nodded, unhooked the keys from her belt, and went swiftly through them. 'This one.' He took the keys from her, pushed the door to, leaned his crutch against a shelf, and turned the key. A minute later she was in his arms, backed up against a snowy bale of towels, her starched skirt and apron around her waist, and Dan was tugging her serviceable knickers down over her black stockings. Between kisses she fumbled with his belt buckle, pulling his trousers open. He held back momentarily, looking down at her. 'Gently, Nurse Blain, gently. I'm a recovering invalid, remember.'

It went on for longer than he could have thought possible, after all the months of abstinence. When it was over, she let out a long, shuddering sigh, her eyes closed.

'I think I'm well on the road to recovery, don't you?' said Dan, kissing her neck.

'You are that,' she murmured, then opened her eyes. 'We must be mad,' she whispered. 'What if Matron was to find us here?'

She straightened her cap and pulled up her knickers, then smoothed down her skirts. 'Where are the keys? Oh, crivvens, I never thought I'd do a thing like this. Never.' She found the keys and swiftly unlocked the door, then opened it and peered round. The corridor was empty.

'You'd better go before someone comes along,' she said. She had resumed her brisk tone, and in spite of what had just happened – or perhaps because of it – could not meet his eye.

He put a finger beneath her chin, turned her face up to his, and kissed her. 'It's been a pleasure knowing you, Nurse Blain. In a different world and time, I should like to have known you better.'

'I think we know one another quite well enough now, Lance Corporal Ranscombe,' replied Nurse Blain, and whisked away down the corridor.

On a damp day in early March, Paul was home on weekend leave working in the vegetable plot, with the assistance of Max. Meg had decided to embark on the cathartic business of washing sheets and pillowcases. At the end of the afternoon, when Paul came in from the garden, she was busy arranging them on the long kitchen pulley.

'Here, let me attend to that,' he said, and hauled on the cord to raise the pulley to the ceiling so that the linen could dry high in the warmth of the kitchen.

'Thanks,' said Meg, unpinning her overall. She was bedraggled from washing, scrubbing and mangling, and when Paul put his arms around her and gave her a hug, it irked her, because it reminded her how unattractive and unkempt she felt these days. Still, she returned his embrace, and dwelt for a moment in its safety and comfort. It made her sad to think how thrilled she had once been to feel his big, masculine body against her own, and how naïvely she had confused that feeling with love.

'Poor old girl. I hate to see you working away like this. Why don't you try to get yourself a maid to help with all this? And maybe a cook?'

She gave a short laugh. 'Is that a comment on my cooking abilities?' She left his arms and turned to the sink, running water to peel the vegetables for the evening meal. 'You know very well that every girl and woman in the country is doing war work. There are hardly any maids to be had. And cooks are an impossibility.' She knew what she was about to say next was pointless, but frustration compelled her. 'You can't imagine how often I wish I was back at Woodbourne House. At least there I had company, and everyone worked together. And we had decent food.' She scraped savagely at the carrots. 'I'm afraid I can do no better than pilchards and boiled vegetables for supper, and the two apples I've baked won't go very far. They're all I could get at the greengrocer's. I wonder you don't go back to the mess early and get something decent to eat.'

'I'm not going back to the base this evening,' said Paul mildly. 'I've been called to London for a meeting tomorrow. Being Wing Commander involves new responsibilities.' He sat down at the kitchen table and stared at his earth-stained hands. 'I know it's hard for you here. I hoped having our own home again, seeing a bit more of one another, might make up for it. Having you closer has certainly helped me. When I go out on operations I feel... well, I just like to feel that I have you and Max, my family, to come back to.' Meg laid down her knife, listening. He went on, 'But I see how difficult it is for you. And how lonely. What I hoped would happen between us hasn't, has it? I was probably a fool to think it would. So if you want to take Max and go back to Woodbourne House, I would understand.'

There was silence in the kitchen. Meg gazed out at the back garden, where Max was still playing. This was her life. What she and Dan had had was over. It had receded like some distant dream. With every passing day and month he had grown further and further from her.

She turned to him. 'No. I shouldn't have said such a selfish thing, and I only said it because I hate not being able to make the kind of home for you that I want to. The kind we used to have.' It was true. If they'd still had Hazelhurst, how much better everything would be. 'And if it's hard for me, then it's just as hard for everyone else. We have to carry on, and see what happens when things get better. When the war ends.'

He stood up, crossed the kitchen and took her hands. 'I need to believe you think things will get better. I need to believe you think we are worthwhile, because without that, I don't think I could fly these missions, or care about any of it.'

Tears filled her eyes, and she leaned against him. She could find no more words. She was filled with a sense of utter unworthiness. He was such a good man, for all his problems, and she… well, she had failed him in every possible way.

Max came through the back door. 'Mummy, is tea nearly ready? I'm starving.'

Meg wiped her eyes hastily and moved away from Paul. 'Yes, darling. We're having an early evening meal, because Daddy's got to go to London. It should be ready in fifteen minutes or so.'

'Will there be time for me to listen to *Children's Hour* afterwards?'

'I should think so. Now, run upstairs and give your hands a thorough wash. Take your shoes off first, there's a good boy.'

After the meal the three of them sat around the living-room fire, Paul with his newspaper, Meg with her sewing, while Max listened to *Children's Hour.* An episode of an Arthur Ransome serial was followed by music from *Peter and the Wolf*, and then members of a boys' club talked about their garden plots. Six-year-old Max listened with interest.

'They're going to grow potatoes and cabbages, just like me. And marrows. Will we be growing marrows, too?'

'Not if I have my way,' said Meg. 'I don't like the taste at all. Besides, they take up too much room. Now, quiet while we listen to the news.'

When the bulletin was over, Paul knocked out his pipe and switched off the wireless.

'The Russians may have let us down last time around, but they've jolly well come back with a vengeance.'

'Hitler must be throwing fits in a back room somewhere,' said Meg, biting off a piece of thread.

Max rolled his toy fire engine across the rug. 'Does that mean we're winning the war?'

'Not quite, old fellow,' replied his father. 'General de Gaulle is right when he says the Germans aren't beaten yet. But if the Allies can cross the Rhine and get to Berlin – well, then we'd be making real headway.'

'Now,' said Meg, folding up her sewing, 'Daddy has to go

soon. Go and put your shoes and coat on, and we can walk him to the bus stop.'

Paul caught the train to London, arriving at Liverpool Street just after eight. He had intended to catch a taxi and go straight to his club for the night, but on his way out of the station he ran into a fellow pilot with whom he'd trained at RAF Halton, Alec Hammond. He was a thin man in his early thirties, with a spruce moustache and a bright, eager manner.

'What brings you to town, old man?' he asked, shaking Paul's hand. 'I'm on leave. What about you?'

'I've been summoned by the brass for some sort of meeting at the War Office tomorrow morning. I'm Wingco now.'

'I say, that's capital. Have you plans for the evening, or can I tempt you to a drink?'

'No plans. A drink sounds like a splendid idea. Where had you in mind?'

'I'd rather steer clear of pubs, if it's all the same to you. They're all stuffed with Yanks these days – nothing against our American brethren, you understand, it's just that a chap likes to drink his beer in relative peace. There's a rather jolly service club I know near Shepherd's Market. How about trying that?'

'Fine,' said Paul. 'Let's see if we can find a taxi.'

They took a taxi to Berkeley Square and made their way to the club, which was packed with servicemen and -women.

'So much for what I was saying about noisy GIs,' said Alec. 'Look, there's a table over there with some chaps just leaving. You try to bag it, while I get the drinks.'

Paul successfully claimed the table, and Alec returned a moment later with two pints of beer.

'That was a stroke of luck,' he said, setting down the glasses. He took off his coat and cap and hung them next to Paul's, and sat down.

The two men sat supping their beer and exchanging accounts of their various operations, and the fortunes of those they had trained with. Paul talked fondly about Meg and Max. After a while Alec glanced towards the bar, where a few RAF men and two WAAFs in uniform were drinking, talking and laughing loudly.

'They're a rowdy lot.'

'Comes with the job,' said Paul. 'They need to let off a bit of steam. Can't say I blame them.' He studied the group. 'Actually, I know the dark-haired girl. She's a friend of my sister's. Haven't seen her in an age.'

'She's quite a stunner,' said Alec, stroking his moustache. 'Wouldn't mind being introduced.'

'Well, I will, if she comes over.'

Glancing in the direction of the two officers, Eve recognised Paul and raised her glass with a smile. She'd been waiting for an opportunity such as this for a long time. She left her friends and came across to their table. Any sense of rank couldn't displace Alec and Paul's lifelong habits of courtesy, and they got to their feet. Eve offered Paul a cheeky salute.

'Paul. It's been an age. I don't think I've seen you since Diana's wedding. All those stripes. Are you someone terribly important now?'

'Wing Commander.' He shook her hand. 'Nice to see you, Eve – and in uniform, too. May I introduce Squadron Leader Hammond? Alec, this is Miss Meyerson.'

'Oh, please – call me Eve.' Alec shook her hand and she added, 'Help – I should probably be calling you both "sir", shouldn't I?' The way she laughed made both men realise she was a little drunk.

'I'm sure we can dispense with formalities when we're all off-duty. I'd much rather you called me Alec than Squadron Leader,' said Alec. He pulled out a chair. 'Won't you join us? We were just about to order more drinks.'

'Thanks, I will.'

'What will you have?' asked Paul.

'Gin and it, please.'

Paul went to the bar and returned with their drinks.

'I was just telling Alec what fun we all had at the shooting party a few years ago,' said Eve as he sat down. 'Though as I recall, some of us were frightfully badly behaved.' She gave Alec a smiling glance. 'There was some bed-hopping going on, if you catch my drift. Paul caught his sister in flagrante with a very dashing racing driver. But he married her, I'm happy to say. Though you didn't approve much at the time, did you, Paul?' Paul smiled stiffly. 'At least it had a respectably happy ending.' She drank some of her gin. 'Not like us, though.'

'I'm sorry?' said Paul.

'Well, our mutual friend Dan. He rather did the dirty on us both, didn't he? It seems to be his forte, making a fool of people.'

Alec gave Paul an uneasy glance. He didn't properly understand what Eve was saying, but he earnestly wished she would stop.

'After all,' Eve went on, 'I trusted Dan, you trusted your wife. And we both turned out to be fools.' Paul stared at her, his face white. 'Don't tell me you didn't suspect something was going on. It probably still is. Perhaps it was tactless of me to bring it up, but I think it's always good to know where one really stands with one's friends and family, don't you?'

Alec got to his feet. 'I think perhaps you should return to your friends, Corporal Meyerson.'

Eve tossed back the remains of her drink and stood up. 'I think so, too. Nice to have seen you, Paul. Thanks for the drink. Give my best to Meg, won't you?'

Alec sat down and looked intently at Paul, who was staring at his beer.

'Perhaps you should pay no attention to what she said. She was obviously a bit tipsy. Probably talking a load of old bunk.'

Paul gave a twisted smile. He got to his feet. 'You know, I think I'll call it a night, if you don't mind, old man. Got a bit of a long day tomorrow.' He took his coat and cap from the peg and put them on. 'You'll forgive me, won't you?'

'Of course,' murmured Alec. But Paul was already gone.

8

IN EARLY APRIL Meg received a letter from Sonia giving news of Mrs Goodall's death. She had just made herself a cup of tea, the Forces programme was on the wireless, and Max was sitting at the living-room table, sticking pictures of aircraft into his scrap book.

'Oh, dear,' murmured Meg, as she read the letter.

'What's wrong, Mummy?' asked Max.

'Some upsetting news,' said Meg. 'Don't worry – it isn't Daddy. Aunt Sonia's cook, Mrs Goodall, has died. Most unexpected.'

Max stopped his crayoning. 'That's sad. I liked Mrs Goodall. And she was very clever. She could make sweets out of carrots.'

'She was very fond of you.' Meg pondered. The funeral was the day after tomorrow. She felt she should go. Perhaps Max could stay for tea with one of his schoolfriends. The funeral was at noon. If she left at half past eight she could be back by teatime.

She went to ring Sonia.

'Only come if you feel you want to,' said Sonia. 'It's a long way, with the trains as bad as they are. Your mother doesn't feel up to coming.'

'No, I'd like to. I was so fond of Mrs Goodall. Did anyone know she had a bad heart?'

'She never said anything. I am quite at a loss without her – not just as a cook, but as a friend. I am feeling quite wretched. Though having Dan here helps, of course.'

'Dan?'

'He's staying here for a few weeks while he convalesces.'

Meg's heart seemed to rise in her chest. So Dan would be there. She would be able to see him, and be in his company for a while, and that was something.

Later, after Max had gone to bed, it occurred to her that at least Mrs Goodall's untimely death would be something to talk about to Paul when he came home on leave tomorrow, something to leaven the dead atmosphere that currently existed between them. Over the past month their relationship seemed to have deteriorated again, inexplicably. On the rare occasions when he was home, he didn't seem to be trying any more. Meg, who scarcely ever tried herself but had become used to Paul's attempts to keep things cheerful, was perplexed by this change, and even a little alarmed. She was concerned that Max might sense something was not right, and grow unhappy, so in an attempt to right the balance she had recently been making efforts of her own to keep things harmonious. It hadn't entirely worked. How appalling to find herself relying on dismal news to provide an artificial means of bridging the emotional gulf that yawned between them.

But when Paul came home the next morning and heard the news, he said only, 'Oh, the cook.' He hung up his cap and took off his jacket. 'Where's Max?'

'He's playing in his room.' She followed him to the foot of the stairs. 'Is that all you have to say?'

'What would you have me say?'

'Paul, I simply don't understand...' She stopped.

'What?'

'Why you're so unfeeling. So cold – about everything. And to me especially.'

'Don't you? Really?' His eyes met hers for a moment, then he turned and carried on upstairs to see Max.

She stood uncertainly in the hallway. He must be talking about the stress he was under. It probably made dealing with ordinary feelings so much more difficult. She had to remember that.

For the rest of the day, and over the evening meal, and while Max was around, they conversed on a nominal level about domestic matters, and items on the news. In bed, there was silence. Meg was weary of making further effort.

After Paul had switched off his light, she said, 'I intend to go to the funeral tomorrow. Mrs Lewis has said she will have Max until I get back.'

'I can't come, obviously.'

'No. Though you wouldn't, even if you could – would you?'

'That's right,' he said after a moment. 'I wouldn't.'

Meg switched off her own light and lay in the darkness, and wondered how it had come to this. Then she let herself slip into the sad little fantasy she so often indulged in these days, even though she knew it would leave her heartsore, full of regret and longing. She pretended she was nineteen again, lying asleep in her bedroom at Woodbourne House, and that any moment now Dan would rap lightly on her door. Then the rest would unfold exactly as it had that summer's night. She closed her eyes.

The next day Meg's journey to Surrey was fraught with delays and frustrations, and she arrived late. When she reached the church the service had already taken place and people were at the graveside. Quietly Meg joined the handful of mourners in time to hear the vicar's words of committal.

'We have entrusted our sister Dorothy to God's mercy, and we now commit her body to the ground...' Dan was standing a few feet away, on the other side of Sonia. Meg felt her heart tighten at the sight of him. '... through our Lord Jesus Christ, who will transform our frail bodies...' Dan turned and met her gaze, then looked away. Meg was dazed by the emptiness of the moment. '... was buried, and rose again for us. To him be glory for ever.'

As people filed from the graveside, Sonia turned and saw Meg.

'Oh, my dear, I was worried you might not be coming.'

Meg exchanged kisses with Sonia. 'I'm sorry I was too late for the service.'

'Not to worry. You're here now. I've arranged for a little gathering up at the house. I think Mr Goodall is very glad of that. Poor man, he's not really up to providing luncheon for all.'

'I'll just go and say hello to Dan,' said Meg. 'It's been a while since I've seen him.'

Dan was standing reading the headstones, leaning on a stick, and glanced up as Meg approached. They smiled awkwardly at one another, then Dan said, 'This is a bit of a sad occasion, isn't it?'

'Yes. Dear old Mrs Goodall.' There was a silence in which Meg fought for something meaningful to say. 'How are you?' she said at last. 'I heard you were wounded.'

'Just a bit of a scratch. Sonia insisted I come here to recuperate. I'm pretty much mended now.' He wagged his stick. 'Don't really need this thing, but Sonia insists I should use it.'

'Paul says the war might be over soon. Maybe you won't have to fight again.'

Dan squinted into the spring sunshine. 'Maybe. Things seem to be moving that way. But who knows?'

There was a silence. She looked into his eyes, hoping to find some eloquence there, but was disappointed. 'Dan,' she said with difficulty, 'I wanted...' She stopped, having no idea what words she wanted to utter, except that she loved him. And to say that would be trite, senseless.

Dan poked at a piece of moss with his stick, and said, 'There's a biblical saying – something about perfect love casting out fear. Seems to me that it's more a case of perfect fear casting out love, wouldn't you say? Your fear, Meg. Not mine.'

Meg had nothing to say to this. Dan moved away to join the others, who began to make their way out of the churchyard.

Effie had done her best with lunch, but her talents could stretch no further than a few sandwiches and salad from the kitchen garden. Even so, Mrs Goodall's family lingered for some time. By the time everyone had left it was almost three, and Sonia suggested to Dan and Meg that they should go to the drawing room and have coffee.

Meg glanced at the clock. 'I'm afraid I'm going to have to go, Aunt Sonia.'

'In that case,' said Sonia, 'I'll walk down to the village with you. I need to speak to Mrs Tremlett about our whist drive. Dan can stay here and rest.'

Meg's spirits plummeted. She'd been desperately hoping Dan would walk down with her. She couldn't bear to leave so much unsaid. She glanced at him to see if her feelings were reflected, but his face told her nothing.

She put out her hand to Dan and he took it, letting it rest in his for as long as was decently possible.

'Goodbye,' he said.

She met his gaze, hardly able to bear the strength of all she felt. In a few weeks, unless it ended, he would be back in the war, and she might never see him again. She should have been brave, and taken a chance on their happiness. How she had failed them both.

'Goodbye,' said Meg.

He let her hand slip from his, and at the last touch of her fingertips his mind seemed to turn to ice. He couldn't bear to see her go. But he could do nothing except watch from the window as she walked away down the driveway towards the gates, her arm linked in Sonia's. *Turn around*, he thought. *Look at me*. But she didn't turn round.

That evening, before Paul went back to his base, Max insisted on the usual lengthy bedtime chat with his father. Meg, putting away sheets in the linen cupboard, overheard the tail end of it. She always liked listening in on their conversations. They showed a side of Paul which she didn't often glimpse these days, and which gave her reassurance.

'Mummy says if you get a nice long leave we might go to the seaside this summer.'

'That sounds a topping idea. You haven't been to the seaside much, have you?'

'We went to a place one day the summer before last, when we were all living at Aunt Sonia's. I don't remember its name. There were donkey rides, and I dropped my ice cream.'

'When I was a boy we used to go to a splendid place down in Devon called Ilfracombe. There's a beach you can only get to through a tunnel, and wonderful rock pools.'

'Can we go there?'

'I don't see why not. Now, enough chat for one night. Snuggle down.'

'Daddy?'

'Yes, old fellow?'

'One of my friends told me that his daddy won't be coming home any more. He's very sad about it.' Meg paused, a bale of pillowcases in hand. That would be the Ashcroft boy. They'd heard just the other day that his father had been killed in Burma. 'When you go away I get frightened you might not come back.' Meg could tell from Max's voice that he was a little tearful.

'Well now, don't you worry about that. Come on, dry your eyes. I always do come back, don't I?'

'Yes.'

'Well, then. Now, off you go to sleep. I'll see you next time, old man.'

In bed that night, Meg played her usual part, talking in a way that allowed them both to pretend that things were fine.

'I overheard you talking to Max about us all going to Ilfracombe this summer. That sounds like a nice idea. Do you think you'll get enough leave?'

'I don't know. I hope so.'

'Max loves having things to look forward to.'

Paul laid his book on the bedside table. He lay looking at Meg, then after a moment he put out a hand and stroked her hair.

'Can I kiss you?' he asked.

How sad, she thought, that he had to ask. She turned to him and let him kiss her, feeling nothing, knowing she should feel glad, after the deadness of the past months, that he even wanted to touch her. He moved closer, slipping his hand beneath her nightgown, attempting to caress her in a way she had shown him in the past, in the days when she was hopeful that things might be made to work between them. She pushed his hand away gently, trying not to show her distaste and impatience.

'Paul, I'm sorry. I'm simply not feeling that way tonight.' Suddenly despair overwhelmed her, and she began to weep. She buried her face in her hands and sobbed.

Paul lay gazing at her. After a few moments she grew calmer, and her tears subsided. She wiped her eyes and shook back her hair. 'I'm sorry. I'm just tired. So terribly tired.'

'I understand,' said Paul. Then he switched off the bedside light and rolled over, away from her.

A week later, on a mild April morning, Dan was planting seed potatoes in the kitchen garden, while Sonia was sowing broad beans.

She glanced at Dan as he worked. 'Do be careful of your leg. You shouldn't put too much strain on it.'

'It feels fine. Exercise is good for it. By the way,' Dan laid down the garden fork, 'I got a letter this morning. I have to go up to London for a medical tomorrow. If they give me the all-clear, I go back to my unit.'

'Oh.' Sonia pushed a stray wisp of hair from her eyes. 'It seems absurd, getting you fit and well so that you can go off to be cannon fodder again.'

Dan laughed. 'That's a nice expression. Not many cannon about these days. The thing is, I could get my orders in a matter of days. So it makes sense for me to stay on in London, rather than come back here. I hope you don't mind.'

'Of course not. Though I had hoped I might have you for a little longer. It's going to be another quiet summer. To think that just the year before last the house was full of people, almost as busy as when Henry was alive, though in a different way. And now...' She straightened up, wiping her hands on her overalls, and sighed. 'Perhaps I should take Avril and Laura on holiday somewhere. A change of air might be good for everyone—' She broke off as Effie came hurrying from the house. 'Oh dear, what new drama?'

'It's Miss Meg on the telephone, ma'am.'

Sonia trudged in the direction of the house. A few moments later she returned, walking slowly, her hands pressed together. When she spoke, her voice shook.

'Paul has been killed.'

Dan put his arms round Sonia and she wept on his shoulder. His mind blazed with shock. He was already despising himself for the first thought that had entered his mind.

'When did she hear the news?' asked Dan, as they sat at the kitchen table drinking the tea which Effie had tearfully brewed.

'First thing this morning. It happened overnight. Meg wasn't in any state to go into details, but I gather Paul had been on a bombing raid over Germany. His plane was attacked, and though he completed the mission and made it back, he died of his wounds.' Sonia shook her head. 'Helen is already on her way from London. The funeral is tomorrow. We must go, of course. Effie can look after Laura.'

'I hate to say it, but I don't think I can come to the funeral,' said Dan. He was the last person Meg would want to see at a time like this. Her grief would no doubt be compounded by the most terrible guilt. Any meeting must come later. 'My medical is at noon. There isn't time to postpone it, and I can't duck it.'

'I suppose not,' said Sonia doubtfully. She sighed. 'Meg won't want to stay on in Bury St Edmunds on her own. I'll speak to Helen, of course, but I think it might be an idea for her and Max to come here until they decide what to do, rather than go to

Chelsea. Max knows Woodbourne House, and it may help him to be somewhere familiar. Poor little boy. Poor Meg.'

Dan hadn't been to the house in South Eaton Place for nearly six months. It had a dead, stale air about it. Crockery washed up after the last meal still sat in the rack on the kitchen sink. Ashes lay unraked in the drawing-room grate. He sat down in the drawing room, gazing around, remembering all the times that he and Meg had spent here, ruthlessly, carelessly deceiving Paul.

He still hadn't properly taken in the fact of Paul's death. He had been a solid, constant presence in Dan's life for so long that it was hard to believe he was gone. To all outward appearances he had been the most straightforward of men, reliable, frank, kindly, occasionally pompous, courteous to a fault, and with an apparently abiding love of his country and the influences and institutions which had shaped him. The truth could well be stranger and far more complex, and might never now be known. The business of Alice Bauer's list, Shirer's letter, and the brigadier's orders would probably remain a mystery, now that he was dead, as would his relationship with Arthur Bettany.

Best not to dwell on all that, Dan decided, and instead remember Paul as he had known him. Best, too, not to dwell on all the wrongs he had done his friend. At least Paul had died knowing nothing of them, loving Meg and his son to the end. God, no – perhaps that made it worse.

Dan glanced at his watch. It was almost half eleven. He might as well set off for the hospital.

The doctor who examined Dan's shoulder and leg seemed satisfied with his progress.

'The bones have knitted well, and the muscle in your leg seems pretty much restored. It says here in your notes that your particular service requires exceptionally high levels of fitness.' He glanced at Dan. 'I suspect you may have to undergo a fair bit of retraining to get you back to where you were, but your leg and shoulder should be up to it. How's the appetite? Bowels all in working order? Good. I'll pass on my report.' He scribbled a few comments, then closed Dan's notes and smiled. 'Though who knows, the way things are going, maybe you won't have to worry about going back on active service.'

'Let's hope so,' replied Dan. For the war to be over, and to have a new beginning with Meg. It seemed too much to hope for.

'Good luck, and keep up the physio regime they gave you in Inverness.'

Dan left the hospital and went back to the house. Everything was in limbo now. He had no idea how long it would be till he got his orders, or whether he would have the chance to see Meg before he went. All he could do was wait.

The day of Paul's funeral and the ones that followed gave Meg little time for reflection, filled as they were with the presence of people, the arranging of affairs, and the business of maintaining a routine for Max and keeping him occupied, as a distraction from his bewilderment and misery. That first night, after Meg had told him the news, had been dreadful. He had insisted on spending the night in her bed and had sobbed himself to sleep. The day after the funeral he had begun to pester Meg for details of the circumstances of his father's death. At first Meg had tried to deflect his questions, until she realised that it might provide some consolation for him to know everything that had happened. Meg knew the outlines, but not the details, so she spoke to colleagues from his squadron and to his group captain, and pieced together the story, which she recounted to Max that night by the fire, as he sat on her knee.

'I found out everything that happened to Daddy,' she said gently. 'Do you want to hear it?'

Max, his head resting against his mother's chest, stared into the fire and nodded.

'Well, he was on a raid to Bremen in Germany—'

'In his Lancaster?'

'Yes. There were a lot of planes. Six hundred altogether. And when they were flying over Holland—'

Max lifted his head. 'What was their target?'

'A factory, I believe.' Meg paused. How mundane. But the workings of war were all, in the end, mundane. 'Anyway, over Holland they were attacked by some German planes.'

'Were they Messerschmitts?'

'I don't know, darling. Maybe.'

'I bet they were. They're the best German fighter planes.' Max's tone was reflective.

'And their plane was hit. Daddy had a head wound, and the plane was damaged, but he kept flying.' She had decided that Max must know how brave his father had been, wounds and all. 'Then, not long after that, another plane attacked them. Daddy was wounded again, and some of his crew were, too.' Meg knew that Paul had often talked to Max about his navigator, Scotty Harrison; it would do Max no good to know that at this point Scotty had been killed, and the wireless operator fatally wounded. 'The plane's compass was destroyed, but Daddy kept on flying towards the target.'

'How did he know the way? You need your compass, you know, to find your way.' Six-year-old Max was now entirely bound up in the story.

'I wondered that, too, but it seems Daddy had memorised the route to Bremen. Your father was very clever that way.' Meg's eyes filled with tears. She had to pause for a moment before she could carry on. 'And they got to the factory.'

'Did they hit it?'

'Well, I was told Daddy released the bombs exactly over the target, so I imagine so.'

'I'll bet he blew that old factory to bits.'

'On the way back he had to navigate by the moon and the pole star.' She stared into the fire, imagining Paul with his eyes fixed on the guiding points of light in the fathomless night sky. An unbearable memory came back to her, of Paul saying *I need to believe you think we are worthwhile, because without that, I don't think I could fly these missions, or care about any of it.*

Max's voice broke into her thoughts. 'Mummy, go on. What happened after that?' He lifted a hand and wiped her cheek clumsily, gently. 'Don't cry.'

'I'm sorry, darling.' Meg took her handkerchief from her pocket and wiped her eyes. 'Well, when they were over the Channel all the engines failed, because with everything that was going on they had forgotten to change the fuel tanks. But the flight engineer managed to change them over in the nick of time, and Daddy got the engines restarted.'

'That was lucky,' said Max, head on his mother's breast, utterly absorbed.

'Yes, wasn't it?' Again Meg had to pause, to keep her voice steady. 'But Daddy wasn't able to get the plane back to its base, so he headed for an American air base on the coast. It was very misty, but he brought the plane down safely and a lot of the crew survived, even though Daddy didn't.' No need to tell Max that Paul had made it back despite being half-blinded, the blood from his head wound frozen by icy air streaming through the shattered cockpit screen, or how, as he was being pulled from the plane, he had bled to death from the stomach wound sustained in the second attack. All he needed to know was that his father had been heroic, and had died doing his duty.

'Daddy was very brave.'

'Yes, he was.'

'They'll give him a medal.'

'They might.' This hadn't occurred to Meg. How futile it all seemed, Paul dying now, with Germany on the brink of defeat and the end in sight.

They sat together for a while in silence, each with their own thoughts. Then Max said, 'I don't want to go to the seaside this summer. Not without Daddy.'

9

DAN HAD STILL received no orders from his unit. It had been weeks since any bombs had fallen on London, and the imminent lifting of the blackout filled everyone with a sense of elation. He could no longer imagine himself in civilian life. He could no longer remember himself as he had been before the war.

He wondered whether Meg was at Woodbourne House yet, and whether he should telephone or write. It felt unfitting so soon after Paul's death, and he wasn't sure what he would say, in any event. He had no way of knowing how Paul's death had affected her. She might not have been in love with Paul, but he had been her husband. They had shared things together which he would never know about. They had a son. Had it not been for him, they might have made a successful life together, whatever the problems. Perhaps Meg was thinking all these things, too.

Then on the second day, an unexpected letter arrived in the morning post. It was from Arthur Bettany, and was short and to the point.

Dear Ranscombe,
As I understand you are in town at present, and as there is a matter I wish to discuss with you, I wonder if we might meet. I shall be in the French House in Dean Street around five this afternoon, if that is convenient.

Yours very sincerely,

Arthur Bettany

Dan folded the letter up, speculating on how Bettany had got his address. Any number of sources, probably. He was intrigued as to what he might want to talk about. Well, he would find out at five o'clock.

When he arrived at the French House, there was a small crowd of early-evening drinkers at the bar, but no sign of Arthur. Dan bought himself a pint of beer and sipped it, glancing around the bar. Then he saw Arthur sitting on his own at a corner table, smoking and staring at what looked like a glass of gin. Odd that he'd never been in uniform. He couldn't think of any ailment which might excuse Arthur, an excellent athlete at school and university, from active service. He went over. Arthur looked up, like a man coming out of a reverie, and Dan sat down.

'How are you?' asked Dan.

Arthur's handsome face looked tired, and there were dark patches under his eyes. 'So-so. I'm having a few days in town, away from…' He shrugged, shook his head, and raised his glass to his lips. Then he said, 'By the way, I still owe you an apology about the rooms, skipping off like that. I was called away suddenly, and the landlady was out.'

'Not to worry. I squared her. It was ages ago, anyway.' There was a pause. 'You said in your note that you had something to discuss.'

Arthur sat back, regarding Dan thoughtfully. After a moment he asked, 'Did you hear the Eric Linklater play, *Cornerstones*, that was on the wireless recently?'

'No,' replied Dan, rather bemused. 'I can't say I did.'

'That's a pity. You might have found it interesting. It was set in the Elysian Fields, and it took the form of a conversation – well, more a sort of philosophical dialogue – between Lincoln, Lenin, Confucius and a British airman. The war came into it, obviously. Much of it was sanctimonious rot, though some of the dialogue was rather witty. The airman was very clear-sighted and honourable, with an utter belief in all things British, that Britain is the natural guardian of decency, and that our nobility and courage will prevail in this fight. He reminded me very strongly of Paul Latimer.' He took another pull of his gin. 'You heard he died, I suppose.'

So now they came down to it. It was Paul he wanted to discuss. 'Yes,' replied Dan. 'Desperately sad.'

Arthur nodded. 'He was a good man.' He pushed his cigarettes across the table to Dan, and Dan took one.

'You think you know things about Paul Latimer that no one else knows, don't you?' said Arthur.

Dan's mind ranged over the possibilities, and fixed on the gossip of Harry's friends, and what he himself had suspected about Paul's homosexuality. Presumably that was what Arthur was referring to.

'I'm not sure quite what you mean. I have certain speculations about Paul, but I don't think any of them are worth airing, now he's dead.'

Arthur shook his head. 'It won't do, you know. To sweep conjecture away, to paint the truth' – he waved a hand lightly – 'a different colour. "The evil that men do lives after them", and so forth.'

'If he had a private life, relationships he wanted to keep secret, then I think that's best left alone. He had a wife and child. None of it matters now.'

Arthur's dark, girlish eyes widened in surprise. 'I'm not talking about that kind of thing. My dear Dan, that was not an aspect of himself he ever explored. He had courage in regard to all kinds of things, but never that. Sadly.' He paused, gazing at his cigarette. 'No, I'm talking about something else entirely.' He took another sip of his gin. 'The list.' Dan stared at him. 'The one with Paul's name on, that you spoke to the authorities about.'

Dan leaned forward. 'How on earth do you know about that?' He kept his voice low, glad that the table was out of earshot of other drinkers.

'In my line of work I find out about all manner of things. The thing is, though, you of all people really do need to know the truth. In point of fact, the whole world should, though the whole world is never likely to.'

Dear God, thought Dan, if there was any substance to this business about Paul and the list, Arthur might be implicated, too. He shouldn't even be having this conversation.

Arthur smiled. 'I know what you're thinking. No, I'm not a fifth-columnist. Neither was Paul Latimer. In fact, the whole point of what he did, and the reason his name was on that list, was to divert information to the wrong channels.'

'I don't understand. What do you mean?'

'There are quite a few Nazi sympathisers in Britain. Anti-Semites, fanatical followers of Mosley. Distasteful, I know, but there it is. Paul was recruited in the years running up to the war to keep tabs on them, and then, when the war started, to infiltrate them, convince them that he was working for the Gestapo. They gave him information – names of other sympathisers, plans, details of secret research and weapons development. Quite sickening, the ways in which certain people were prepared to betray their country. Some of them went to great lengths to assist the Germans. They believed that Paul was the Gestapo's man in England, channelling all this information on to his masters in Germany, when in fact he was passing it back to our chaps, and saving hundreds, possibly thousands of lives in the process. He built up a convincing identity for himself in Germany over a number of visits, and through various contacts, with his racing car business as a cover, and while it lasted it was invaluable work. But it couldn't last. These things never do. Somehow his cover was compromised. So he had to pack it in and turn his hand to active service. He never gave up working for his country.'

'But... how do you know all of this?'

'As I said, in my line of work, one hears and sees a great deal.'

'Your line of work?'

Arthur reflected for a moment. 'Intelligence. Paul and I didn't operate together, but we each knew what the other was doing.

In some ways, what he did was more straightforward than my work. Though what I do sounds simple. Numbers. You know, zero to nine.' He took another sip of his drink. 'If we win this war – and it looks pretty much like Hitler's show is over – then we'll have that little handful of numbers to thank for it.'

'You shouldn't be telling me any of this,' said Dan.

'Of course I shouldn't.' Arthur leaned across the table, his expression intent. 'I'm only telling you because he's dead, because he was a friend to both of us, and because if his reputation is in doubt in the mind of anyone who knew him, then that, to me, is an injustice.' His eyes brightened with a hint of tears. 'I loved him, you see.'

Dan sat back. 'I'm sorry.'

'And he loved me – once. But – *vincit qui se vincit*. That was what he believed. He conquers, who conquers himself. I was fifteen when he first said it to me. I didn't understand what he meant then, but I came to, eventually. He didn't hold with certain things. You know the kind of thing I'm referring to. You and I were among the more attractive boys at school.' Arthur drained the remnants of his gin and stared into the glass. 'But it was his inescapable nature to love other men. It might have been better for him if he hadn't tried so hard to be the kind of person he thought he should be, instead of the one he was.'

'Better for us, for his country, that he did, in some ways.'

'Indeed. A good point.' Arthur set down his glass. 'It's all classified, of course. No one will ever know – not even his family. But it makes no odds now that he's dead. You were his friend for a long time. The list must have sowed all kinds of doubts and suspicions in your mind, and it seemed important to me that you should know the truth. So that whatever memory of him you carry in your heart, it's not... tainted in any way.'

'I'm grateful,' said Dan. He could hardly tell Arthur how he himself had sullied that memory, or all the wrongs he had done Paul.

Arthur glanced at his watch and rose to his feet. 'Well, I have to be somewhere. Cheerio, Ranscombe. Let's hope it's all over soon, eh?'

They shook hands, and then Arthur was gone, the pub door closing behind him.

10

MEG AGREED WITH her mother and aunt that it would be best if she and Max returned to Woodbourne House for the time being, to give Max some sense of security. Three days after the funeral Meg packed what she and Max needed and made the journey to Surrey. She would deal with the Bury St Edmunds house, and matters such as the lease, and what to do with Paul's belongings, in due course. At this moment she needed to be in familiar surroundings and to take stock. The suddenness of Paul's death had left her dazed. She had grown so accustomed to the notion that she didn't love him that the emptiness she felt was beyond anything she could have anticipated. She was utterly bereft. She saw now how much she had taken for granted. His dependability, his kindness, his enduring good humour – qualities which eclipsed every one of his faults. Those didn't matter, in the face of what was lost. He had simply always been there. And now he was not.

On the afternoon of their arrival at Woodbourne House, while Max was renewing his acquaintance with Laura and the nursery toys, and Meg and Sonia were having tea, her aunt broached the subject of Paul's will.

'I hadn't given it any thought,' said Meg. 'I suppose I should go and see the solicitor. I only met him a couple of times, when we were purchasing Hazelhurst and when we made our wills.' She sipped her tea. 'Perhaps I should telephone the office and see if I can make an appointment for tomorrow.'

'I think that's a good idea,' said Sonia. 'You need to know how you stand financially.'

'Oh, there are no concerns on that front. Paul's fortune was very considerable. His will left everything to me, and mine to him, so Max and I should be secure. I just never imagined...' Meg felt tears spring to her eyes. It kept happening all the time, the sudden sense of loss, compounded with overwhelming guilt.

Sonia laid a sympathetic hand on her arm. 'I know it's hard having to face these dismal practicalities. Would you like me to come with you?'

'That's kind, Aunt Sonia, but I think I have to do this on my own. I'll go and find the details and telephone now.'

The next day Meg went to the solicitor's offices in Chancery Lane. She was shown into the dark-panelled room she recalled from previous visits, when she and Paul were starting out, full of happiness and hope.

The solicitor, Mr Bradshaw, was a small, stout, bespectacled man in his sixties, seated behind a large mahogany desk whose effect was diminishing, rather than aggrandising. After they had exchanged courtesies, and Mr Bradshaw had expressed his condolences, there was a brief silence. Meg became aware that the lawyer was not entirely at his ease. She waited for him to begin.

'Well, now, Mrs Latimer, I believe the last time you and I met was in nineteen thirty-seven, when I drew up wills for you and Mr Latimer.'

'That's right.'

He gave a little cough and nodded several times, staring at the documents before him. 'Were you aware, Mrs Latimer, that your late husband recently made another will?'

Meg was taken aback. 'No, I had no idea.'

Mr Bradshaw nodded again. 'I should explain that where a testator makes a subsequent will, it has the effect of revoking the contents of the previous will. So you must appreciate that the only will which has any testamentary effect is your late husband's most recent one.'

Meg nodded. She felt a faint chill. Paul had changed his will without telling her. Why would he have done that? 'What does the new will say? I take it it's different from the old one?'

'Quite different. Would you like to read it yourself, or would you like me to explain its contents?'

'I'd rather you told me.'

'Well, whereas the previous will bequeathed all your late husband's real and personal property to you in your sole capacity, under the new one your late husband's entire estate is left in trust for your son, Maximilian. The trustees and executors of the will are myself and Mr Latimer's sister, Mrs Diana MacLennan. The trust will provide funds for Maximilian's maintenance and education – I should add here that your late husband also left directions that he would like Maximilian to attend, when he is old enough, the same school that he attended – and when he is twenty-five Maximilian will come into the entire property. Mr Latimer also bequeathed a legacy of thirty thousand pounds to Mrs MacLennan.'

Meg was stunned. 'Does it... does the will make any kind of provision – for me, I mean?' It was an invidious question to have to ask.

Mr Bradshaw shifted in his chair. 'Yes. You are to receive an income of one thousand pounds a year, until such time as you remarry.'

Meg was at a loss for words. A thousand pounds a year was barely enough to live on. Certainly not enough to buy a house, or rent a decent one. 'I see,' she murmured.

'Please – I think you should take this copy of the will and read it for yourself. And' – he picked up a long, white envelope and handed it to her – 'your late husband asked me to give you this, in the event of his death.'

'What is it?'

'He didn't inform me of the contents.'

Meg sat for a moment, both documents in her lap. Then she opened her handbag, put them in and closed it. Shocked as she was, she fought to retain her composure. 'I suppose there really is nothing left to discuss, is there?'

Mr Bradshaw's expression was almost apologetic. He rose from behind his desk.

'I shall attend to the grant of probate, of course, and to the execution of the will. I will be in touch shortly with Mrs MacLennan. As Maximilian's mother, you will be kept fully informed of the administration of the trust, as and when necessary.'

'Thank you.'

Meg got to her feet. She left the office in a daze. Outside she hesitated, not sure what to do next. She turned and walked up the street, and kept walking, her thoughts in confusion, until she found herself in Lincoln's Inn. She sat down on a bench beneath a tree. It was late morning, and a watery April sun shone on the peaceful gardens. A few barristers and clerks were coming and going along the pathways. Meg opened her handbag and took out the copy of the will that Mr Bradshaw had given her, and read it through. It was as he had said. Paul had left her enough to keep body and soul together, but no more. She folded it up and put it back in her bag, and took out the envelope. She sat for some moments before she could bring herself to open it. She unfolded the pages.

Dear Meg,

Even as I write, I pray that there may yet be a chance for us to put right everything that has gone wrong between us, and that this letter can be destroyed without you ever seeing it. But if you are reading these words, it is because I am gone, and so that chance is gone, too.

I know now that you and Dan Ranscombe are lovers – or have been. There were signs along the way which I could have read, but I never wanted to doubt you. The evidence is inescapable now. You are so beautiful and vital, and so in need of being loved in a way that I, unworldly as I am, cannot manage, that perhaps I should not be surprised. When I had my doubts and anxieties, I convinced myself that if there was an affair, it might end, and you would come back to me, thinking our marriage still worthwhile, and we could try again. In fact, when we moved to Suffolk, I had the feeling that it had ended, and that there might be hope for us. I realise now that is impossible.

I do not blame you entirely. I have long been a puzzle to myself. Certain feelings I have had for close friends have confused and even disgusted me, and I have always tried to conquer them. I thought that loving you – easy as you are to love – would help me in that regard. Perhaps it was inevitable that you should look elsewhere, and seek love from someone not bedevilled by such weaknesses.

In the end, however, I have to acknowledge the fact of your unfaithfulness. I wish I could say that you would never do anything intentionally to hurt me, but I know now that isn't true. I have therefore taken steps to protect Max's future, and to ensure that the Latimer fortune stays with him and cannot be diverted, through you, to someone who has also betrayed my trust and friendship. I do not ask you to forgive me, because we both know it is you who should seek my forgiveness. And I give that freely, and ask only that you think well of me, and always speak well of me to our son. Whatever your feelings for me, I know we both share the same love for him.

Paul

She folded the letter up, her eyes swimming with tears. He had only ever tried to love her, and do his level best to make their marriage work. The idea of the pain she had caused him, the misery and uncertainty he had had to endure, racked her very soul. The knowledge of her affair with Dan might even have hastened his death. And she had no way of atoning for it. The guilt was a burden she would have to bear for ever. He had punished her, and she deserved it. His letter showed her as she really was. Someone who was prepared to betray her marriage, yet who had still expected, if the worst happened, to receive everything that belonged to him. There was nothing she could do now to restore herself in his eyes. He must have died despising her.

She leaned forward on the bench, her head in her hands, and let her misery and self-loathing spend itself in tears. Afterwards she sat for a long time, her mind a blank. What to do now? Go back to Woodbourne House and wait for people to find out what Paul had done, as they eventually would. There would be consternation and puzzlement – and suspicion, perhaps. But before she faced all that, she had to see Dan, if she could. She knew he had left Woodbourne House to await his next orders, but she had no idea whether he was still in London. Perhaps he had already left. She opened her handbag and thrust the letter into it, then rose from the bench and walked down to the Strand.

When she reached Belgravia she let herself into the silent house. A few letters lay on the doormat. She went to the drawing room and then the kitchen, looking for signs that Dan was still here, but apart from an unemptied ashtray, there were no clues. She went upstairs to his bedroom. The bed was neatly made. She walked to the window, remembering the last night they had spent here, the last time they had made love. The ache of longing and regret was raw and painful. Then, as she turned from the window, she saw his suitcase and kitbag standing next to the wardrobe. Thank God, he hadn't gone yet. She went back downstairs to the drawing room, prepared to wait all day and all night if she had to.

An hour later she heard the front door open and close, and the sound of keys being thrown on the hall table. Then there was silence. After a moment she rose and went out. Dan was standing in the hall, reading one of the letters he had picked up from the mat. He turned and saw her. For a moment neither said anything, then he chucked the letter on the table and put his hands in his pockets. 'It is trite and inadequate, after all that's happened, but I'm sorry about Paul.'

'I had to come to see you,' said Meg. 'I've just come from the solicitor. Paul knew about us.'

Dan passed a hand over his eyes. 'Christ.' After a moment he muttered, 'I need a drink.'

They went into the drawing room. Meg sat down and Dan poured them both whiskies.

As she took the glass from him, Meg said, 'He left a letter with the lawyer. I think you should read it.' She opened her handbag and handed the letter to Dan.

He sat down in an armchair opposite and read it. Then he looked up. 'What did he mean about taking steps to protect Max?'

'He changed his will. Presumably when he found out about us. Everything is left in trust to Max. I get next to nothing.' She sipped her whisky and let out a long breath. 'I'm glad of it. I see now I couldn't have touched his money, anyway, after what I did to him.' She gazed at Dan. 'It's worse than I could ever have thought possible. I can never forgive myself.'

Dan folded the letter up and gave it back to her. 'He would have found out, anyway, in the long run. It was never going to work the way you wanted it to, Meg, even if he'd lived. When people do what we did, there is no escaping blame, or responsibility.' He put his head in his hands, thinking of what Arthur Bettany had told him, of the selfless individual Paul had been, and of the brave way he had died. He had cheated a lifelong friend, betrayed the trust of someone who was, he now saw, a far better man than he could ever hope to be. Now he and Meg would have to live with the consequences. At last he lifted his head and looked at her. 'Do you still love me?'

Something seemed to give way within Meg's heart. 'Of course I do. I never stopped loving you. I never shall. But it's all dirty and tainted now. We can never—'

'Stop.' He came over, knelt by her chair, took her face in his hands and kissed her. 'We will live with this for ever, but we still go on living. I want you to come here – now. Bring Max, make a home here, and we can be together when the war's over.'

Meg shook her head. 'I can't. Everyone would know. They would hate me. And what would Max make of it, being brought suddenly to live in some other man's house? He's a little boy. His father was everything to him. It's impossible.'

Dan stood up. He gazed at her in anger and despair. 'Meg, we did what we did, and we must live with the consequences. Otherwise everything is useless. Our love. Paul's death. Everything. Sooner or later you have to accept that.'

She said nothing for a moment, then rose from her chair. She felt utterly drained, unable to think properly.

'Then it will have to be later. I can't face up to it now, Dan. I can't do it. But you have to believe I love you. I always did, and if I could go back nine years and do things differently, I would.'

'Only then you wouldn't have Max. And he is what matters most, isn't he?'

'Not more than you. It's different.'

'It's your choice, Meg. It always has been. I'm here if you want me.'

'I know. I just feel so utterly dead inside. You need to give me time.'

She gathered her things and he kissed her goodbye, knowing it might be the last time he ever did, because if she wasn't prepared, even now, to come to him, then there was no hope.

Over the next few days Meg could resolve nothing. She made no mention of the contents of the will to her aunt, unable to face the inevitable questions. She let Woodbourne House close its arms around her, soothing her, taking her back to a time of innocence, and looked neither back nor ahead. She worked with Sonia in the kitchen garden, and helped with mindless household chores, pegging out sheets to flap in the spring wind, their blankness reflecting her own state of mind. She played with Max and Laura, and took them for walks in the woods. In one of these they came across the den Dan had built for the children. The winters had taken their toll, felling one of the supports, and making holes in the brushwood roof. Meg gazed at it while the children ran in and out. He might be going back to war any day, to face fresh terror and danger, while she stayed here, irresolute and fearful.

On Friday she received a telephone call from Diana, who had been contacted by Mr Bradshaw regarding Paul's will.

'Darling, I don't understand any of it. Why didn't you tell me? I have no idea why Paul made me an executor, and this trust business is beyond me.'

'It was rather a surprise,' said Meg weakly.

'We need to discuss it all, but not on the telephone. I shall be coming down to Woodbourne tomorrow. Tell Sonia I'll be there in time for lunch.'

When Diana arrived, it was an unexpectedly warm and sunny spring day. Sonia had managed to engage a new cook, whose abilities were still rather raw, but who had prepared a tolerable meal of early salad from the kitchen garden and some cold salmon.

'Poached. Literally. By dear Alfredo,' Sonia murmured to Meg. 'Diana, why don't you sit here? It's just the three of us – the children have already had their lunch, but we thought we would wait ours till you got here.'

'Thanks.' Diana sat down, glancing sadly out of the window at the garden beyond. Her face was drawn with misery. 'Isn't nature heartless, the way it lets the sun shine and the birds sing, and everything look so lovely, when things are as they are? It's hard to believe Paul won't ever be here to see all this again.'

Sonia turned to Diana. 'Did you know he's to be awarded a posthumous Victoria Cross?'

'No! When did you hear?'

'The letter came this morning,' said Meg. 'I'll go and fetch it.' She left the table and returned with the letter and handed it to Diana.

'Oh, my word...' Tears filled Diana's eyes as she read aloud. '"Wounded in two attacks, without oxygen, suffering severely from cold, his navigator dead, his wireless operator fatally wounded, his aircraft crippled and defenceless, Wing Commander Latimer showed superb courage and leadership in penetrating a further 200 miles into enemy territory to attack one of the most strongly defended targets in Germany, every additional mile increasing the hazards of the long and perilous journey home. His tenacity and devotion to duty were beyond praise."'

Sonia took her handkerchief from her pocket and wiped her eyes. 'He was a very fine man.'

After lunch Effie brought out coffee.

'Meg and I have a bit of business to discuss,' said Diana. 'We'll take ours to the summerhouse, if you don't mind.'

'Of course,' said Sonia. 'I'll see you both later.'

Diana and Meg went to the summerhouse and settled themselves in the cane chairs with their coffee cups. The doors were wide open to the warm air.

'I love this view,' said Diana, gazing over the gardens and across the Surrey Downs. 'Paul did, too.' Her voice shook a little. She took a cigarette from a small shagreen case and lit it, and at the sight of the cigarette case Meg had a sudden memory of the two of them sitting here together years before, the day that Paul and Diana had arrived for Sonia's last house party. The summer she had met Dan.

In a steadier voice Diana went on, 'I hope you weren't too put out about the will. You know Paul's views on the fairer sex. Doesn't trust us to count a row of beans.' She paused, sipping her coffee. 'Didn't. He probably thought it would be less of a headache for you for everything to be put in trust. Though why he made me a trustee is a mystery. He always thought I was utterly hare-brained.' Her eyes filled with tears. 'My bossy big brother.' There was silence for a moment, then Diana, brushing away her tears, went on, 'As for the wretched sum he left you, I don't know what that solicitor was thinking, allowing him to draw up a will in that way. I almost told him so. That's the reason I came here today. I've had a talk to Roddy, and we both agree that I'll make over to you the sum that Paul left me. I don't know why he left me anything, after my marriage settlement. Probably to make up for how beastly he was to me when we were kids. But I'd rather you had it.'

Meg had been gazing out at the view across the Downs as she listened. Her glance fell on the tangle of briar rose outside the summerhouse door, newly in bud. She remembered the roses Dan had plucked for her that summer years ago, how they had dried to dust between the pages of a book. The roses, too, that he had left for her in the vase on the hall table in South Eaton Place. They had been brown and shrivelled by the time she found them. Had Dan died, they would have been the last token of his love. But he had come back, and their love had gone on. Suddenly everything suddenly seemed very clear and simple.

She turned to Diana. 'That's very fair of you. Far fairer than I have ever been to you. But I can't accept.' She set down her cup. 'Paul wrote that will to punish me – no, perhaps that's too harsh. To rectify matters. He was right to do so. I don't deserve anything that belonged to him.'

'What do you mean?'

'It's far too late for the truth to do anyone any good, but you should know it anyhow. Dan was my lover. We had an affair for four years. Paul found out about it. Hence the will.'

Diana set down her cup and stared at her, appalled. 'So it was true. And yet you denied it. I put it to you, and you denied it! I even asked you to pardon me for thinking such a thing.' Her eyes darkened with angry tears. 'That means my brother went to his death knowing… Oh God, how could you? How could you do that, Meg?'

'I didn't mean for Paul to suffer. I didn't mean to hurt him.'

'How can you say that? You betrayed your marriage, and you didn't intend that he should suffer? It's the most selfish, cowardly—'

'Yes, all of that. I know all of that. And I have reproached myself a thousand times for everything. But the fact is, I should never have married Paul. I think even you knew that at the time – that he wasn't really cut out to love any woman.'

There was silence for a moment, then Diana said, 'Poor Paul.'

Meg wondered whether she was thinking of Paul the betrayed husband, or Paul the man who had fought against his own sexual instincts and won, to his cost.

'Please don't think I'm trying to escape blame. I know what I did. I deceived him, I deceived you, and everyone else – Sonia, my mother, so many people – because I was in love with Dan, and he with me, and nothing and no one else mattered.'

'I don't understand why Paul didn't just throw you out when he discovered what the two of you were doing,' said Diana bitterly.

'I don't either. Perhaps because he loved Max, and he didn't want Max to be without his mother.'

Diana regarded her with hate-filled, tearful eyes. 'What did you think would happen? If he hadn't found out, were you just going to go on deceiving him for ever?'

'I don't know. I was too afraid to face the truth of what I was doing, and accept the consequences. Dan told me I should be honest with Paul and end the marriage, but I didn't want anyone to find out I'd been having an affair. Not you. Nor my mother, or Aunt Sonia. Not Max. Especially not Max. I thought if I left Paul when the war was over, and waited a while, then Dan and I could be together without anyone knowing what I'd done.' She sighed. 'But one can never escape the truth.' She stood up. 'I think that's all there is to say.'

'Where are you going?'

Meg paused at the door of the summerhouse. 'To do what I should have done long ago.'

She walked to the house, where she packed her own and Max's few belongings in a suitcase. She found Max on his own in the nursery, playing with his model aeroplanes.

'Max, we have to take a trip up to town.'

'Why?'

'We're going to visit Mr Ranscombe.'

'Why?'

'Because he's offered to let us stay in his house for a while.' *And because very soon he may be the only friend I have in the world.*

Max accepted this explanation with equanimity, and scrambled to his feet. 'Can I bring my planes?'

'Of course. We'll put them in the case. Come on.'

She left Max and their luggage in the hallway and went in search of Sonia. She found her in the kitchen garden.

'You have your hat on, Meg. Are you going somewhere?'

'Max and I have to go up to London. I'll let Diana explain.'

'Oh, I see.' Sonia gazed down at the beds. 'The asparagus is looking rather spindly this year. I must ask Lobb to give it a good soaking.' She sighed. 'I do like the asparagus season. Such a lovely harbinger of summer.' She smiled wistfully. 'When the peace comes, perhaps we shall be able to have summer house parties again, like the ones we used to have before the war. They were such good times – the house full of people, lovely weather, tennis, picnics. Do you remember the one we had the year Henry died?'

'Yes,' replied Meg. 'I remember it very well.' She gave Sonia a gentle kiss.

'Hurry back, my dear.'

Meg went out to the hall, where she found Max and Laura chasing Star and a tennis ball up and down the hallway.

'Oh, children, not in here – something's bound to get knocked over. Laura, take Star outside. But before you do...' She bent down, enfolded Laura in a hug, then kissed her. 'Max, come and say goodbye to Laura.'

'Bye, Laura. We're going up to London.'

'Bye.' Laura picked up the tennis ball, made a little coaxing noise to Star, and the pair of them raced off through the back of the house.

Meg picked up her handbag and the suitcase, and she and Max set off down the driveway. When they were almost at the bottom they caught sight of the bus heading out of the village.

'Look, Mummy,' said Max, 'there's our bus. Let's run.' And they began to run.